Tamara Walks on Water

Tamara Walks on Water

Shifra Horn

W F HOWES LTD

AUTHOR NOTE

The story and its plot were inspired by the period –
from the beginning of the twentieth century to the eve
of the establishment of the State of Israel – and any
connection between the book's plot and characters to
real people is purely coincidental.

This large print edition published in 2004 by
W F Howes Ltd
Units 6/7, Victoria Mills, Fowke Street
Rothley, Leicester LE7 7PJ

1 3 5 7 9 10 8 6 4 2

First published in the United Kingdom in 2003
by Piatkus Books Ltd

English translation by Anthony Berris

A CIP catalogue record for this book is available
from the British Library

ISBN 1 84505 726 0

Typeset by Palimpsest Book Production Limited,
Polmont, Stirlingshire
Printed and bound in Great Britain
by Antony Rowe Ltd, Chippenham, Wilts.

To my son, Gilad
and Peter Bolot – my beloved best friend

PROLOGUE

Like a hermit crab trapped in the cast-off shell it has chosen for its temporary home, I carry with me the city of Jerusalem.

Guilefully, Jerusalem managed to impose its gloom upon me and I, who live in it in exile, seek cracks and escape routes in its walls and like a traitorous refugee return to Jaffa, the city of my childhood and youth that haunts me with memories and pervades my dreams.

In Jaffa, my treasured city, the houses were once palaces, the markets were thronged with people and cattle, gardens of oranges and pomegranates dotted it in shades of green, replacing the salty sea air with a sweet fragrance.

Today the city resembles a woman whose beauty has faded. In days gone by she drove men mad and now she peers into the mirror and looks aghast at her tattered dresses, her cracked face and her hands with their mildewed spots.

And I photograph this city of mine in its shame and poverty. Like one obsessed I perpetuate on film the desolation of a place bare of make-up and festive attire, with its withered citrus groves, houses that have collapsed into the sea, balconies that have crumbled and miserable people who hold onto the ruins because they have nowhere else to go.

And in my chilly nights in Jerusalem I lie in ambush, waiting for the pictures swashing about in the developer, and they are revealed so slowly, almost spitefully, under the red bulb. And as if from within an old magic lantern that casts one picture after another onto the screen with no rhyme or reason, the ghosts of my past return to me like the main characters in a play come back on stage at the curtain to exact more and more love for themselves. Then I look carefully for the image of Christodolos, my beloved monk-archaeologist, hoping that perhaps this time he has found his way onto the film and I will find him hiding in one of the photographs between the ancient walls and roofless buildings.

I decided to put my fragile memories down on paper, as they are reflected in the pictures stored in my head that I gathered into albums and showed at my photographic exhibition, 'Memories of Jaffa'.

'To understand the end you have to look for the beginning,' Christodolos once told me, when in his digs he revealed the first strata of the end before he reached the last ones, which were the beginning.

And I'm trying to follow in his footsteps and discover the end of my story from within the beginning.

CHAPTER 1

That night, right after he was circumcised and given a name, my grandmother Simcha's baby was buried. The infant's body, enshrouded in a diaper and his tiny penis bandaged, was hastily cast into the small pit that had been dug deep in the ground for fear of the scavenging hyenas. My grandmother did not go to the cemetery, perhaps because she was too weak to stand or maybe because she didn't remember she had given birth to a live infant and handed him over dead. But the rabbi who performed the circumcision, and who helped dig the grave, consoled the small congregation that gathered with the words, 'This tiny soul is now a complete Jew and will return to us with the resurrection of the dead that will come speedily in our days, Amen.'

And in that sandy, desolate patch of the new cemetery on the outskirts of Jaffa, where his mother had been hastily married under a 'black canopy' – the symbolic wedding canopy erected in a cemetery, under which orphans of the town's poor were married to ward off plague and pestilence – they put up a small headstone of porous limestone purchased from public funds, and carved on it: 'Here lies the infant Yisrael, son of Simcha and Fishke Mendel. Born and died on 2 Tishri, 5660 (1900)'.

They said of this baby who died, that when he was born he looked chubby and healthy and his head was capped by bright golden hair so long that it reached the nape of his neck.

'He even cried as a baby should when emerging from the womb, a sure sign of well-developed lungs,' said Widow Ziso, who had helped with the delivery. My grandmother Simcha was seventeen when she became a mother, exactly seven months after that short night she spent with Fishke her groom in the ritual purification room at the new cemetery which, due to the epidemic, had been converted into a private room where the marriage could be consummated. From there, so the story goes, she fled from her bridegroom, scratched by the thorns of the prickly pear bushes and lemon trees, her feet tangling in the undone hem of the splendid wedding dress she had borrowed from Rashella Abulafia.

Seven months from that day, when they placed the naked baby in my grandmother's arms, she gazed at his face with anguished eyes and with a trembling hand stroked the long hair he had grown in her darkness and ran it over his body, still wet with birth fluid and blood. When she handed him back to the midwife a few minutes later she vainly

4

tried to support his dangling head that lolled from side to side on its broken neck.

'They gave her a living child and she gave us back a dead one,' said Widow Ziso to anyone willing to listen. Immediately afterwards, amid all the confusion, she had more contractions, her features contorted and her insides turned over until she voided her belly, and as the midwife extended trembling hands to clean away the afterbirth, a tiny infant smoothly slid out, her face as wrinkled as a monkey's and her skin transparent, and lay there silent at her mother's side, not making a sound even when her skinny bottom was smacked. They took this baby, who was to become my mother, from her, lest it, too, was harmed.

For three days both mother and daughter were disgruntled by their separation. The one whimpered with hunger and spat out the teat of the feeding bottle they stuck into her mouth, while the other complained about the milk filling her bound breasts that threatened to burst. Only at the end of the third day they gave her back the baby and explained, again and again, how to hold it and checked that its head was protected and fully supported in its mother's arms. And when the baby cried too much Widow Ziso anxiously hurried to Simcha's room, tore the infant from her arms and examined the tiny, screaming body, feeling it, scrutinising the diaper and, when no damning evidence was found, returned it to its mother.

'I'm scared I'll kill her,' confessed Simcha to Widow Ziso, and Avigdor Ben-Ari, who was a tenant in the house, translated what she said from Russian. 'What if she cries and I pick her up and she suddenly falls and dies?' Nobody knew if these words were evidence that she remembered the first baby she had brought into the world and who had ended his life with a broken neck.

Ever since those terrible events, opinions in Jaffa were divided. The more sympathetic souls felt that it had been an accident and that the unfortunate baby had slipped from Simcha's untrained hands accidentally. The more stringent voices claimed that she dropped it intentionally because its face reminded her of its father whom she wanted to forget. How can you even suspect Simcha of such a thing, asked her defenders, after all, she's almost blind and can barely distinguish people's features and certainly not the still-indistinct, wrinkled features of a new-born baby. But the accusers contended that all she had to do was feel his face to recognise the features of the man who had possessed her.

There was no point in interrogating Simcha about what had happened. Even a doctor, accompanied by a Turkish policeman, who had come into the room to examine her, the dead baby and the live one, was unable to extract any details of the event from her. She lay there exhausted in the dense air of the room whose windows had been closed to keep out the soot from the chimney of the adjacent bathhouse, gaping vacantly with sun-scorched eyes, not understanding what they were saying or what all the row was about.

They said that immediately after the tragedy her memory took pity on her and vanished, and in return she was given the gift of forgetting. In any event, many days later when Widow Ziso tried talking to her gently about the son who was born and died soon after, she made out she was deaf. Then she claimed she didn't know, that there hadn't been a son, and she clasped her remaining baby to her breast so strongly that its tiny face turned blue and Widow Ziso had to warn her lest she accidentally kill this one too. They said in the town about this baby, whose name was Nechama, that because her mother had conceived her in fear and her birth was linked to death, misfortune had claimed her from the moment she was planted in the womb until she emerged from it, and would plague her until her dying day.

The infant Yisrael's grave and memory were no longer visited and were relegated to a dark corner, and as the years went by they became dimmer until both sank into blessed oblivion.

Had the baby boy born to my grandmother Simcha lived, so I was told by Widow Ziso, he would have been my uncle, and she went on to teach me that 'babies born in pairs are called twins'.

I first visited my grandmother's dead baby about a month after her own death. Swinging on my chest was the camera I had gotten from Christodolos, my lost lover. I found the headstone, eroded by wind, sand and rain, after wandering in the plot set aside for the city's founding fathers. Back then, so I was told by Widow Ziso, when they buried him, his grave stood alone and desolate in the middle of the cemetery's sandy ground. But when I visited him thirty-six years after his birth, my baby uncle was mingling with a great many of Jaffa's and Tel Aviv's citizens, men, women and children who had gone to meet their Maker. I photographed the tiny stone that was sheltered by the splendid monuments of the famous and wealthy community leaders who had built the first Jewish city, and thus immortalised on film the weathered grey stone that was covered with moss and lichens in a smeared tracery of death. I pulled out the weeds that had taken over the grave, scraped the headstone with a smooth pebble to remove the moss that had taken a stubborn hold and was eroding it, and tried to visualise this baby who had been born to die.

He bore no similarity at all to his twin sister, my mother. They emerged from two eggs fertilised by two seeds, said Widow Ziso, quoting the midwife's words after my grandmother's death. And just as he was big and strong, she was tiny and fragile and translucent, so much so that you could see her heart beating with effort beneath her skin and the blood flowing in the tiny veins. When she cried, her whole body wept with her and the tiny heart pulsed faster, giving her the strength to cry incessantly.

'And when she cried,' said Widow Ziso, 'your Grandma Simcha would always turn her head aside and purse her lips.'

'Your grandmother didn't love your mother.' Thus Widow Ziso would put an end to the many talks I had with her in my childhood and youth in an effort to dredge up further details and elucidate for me the complex relationship between my grandmother and mother.

'But why?' I asked again and again.

'She'll tell you if she wants to,' she said without further explanation.

And then I would invent my mother in my imagination.

Some weeks before her death my grandmother told me her secret. She had made a recovery from the amnesia that had plagued her and with total clarity suddenly remembered things forgotten, all those terrible events which, had she not repressed them in secret places all those years, would have driven her out of her mind. And when she recalled them, she was unable to contain the sights and sounds that engulfed her and she told me, her granddaughter, at great length and mercilessly, what had taken place on that terrible night, and mixed her narrative with other stories from the past, all in the greatest detail as if it was all happening to her now. Her feeble, hoarse and aged voice was transformed into the voice of a little, hurting girl, and from her eyes, that had stayed dry all those years, flowed tears that glimmered like salt pearls, and her crown of white hair shone around her head like the halo of a saint in a Christian icon.

And I wept with her, while in my heart I said over and over, 'God in heaven, Grandma, what have they done to you.'

Much later, when I asked a wise man, whose name I've forgotten, the meaning of this sudden appearance of forgotten events that pop up into one's mind and surprise us in our final days, he told me that 'Nobody collects something for which he has no need, but before your grandmother returned her soul to the Creator, she apparently needed to tell you the story.'

In retrospect, if you ask me whether she did wrong by telling me the things that drive sleep from my eyes to this day, so many years after I heard them, I wouldn't know what to say. Should a person take the dark secrets he has concealed all his life to his grave, thus sparing those close to him from their horror, or would it be better to reveal them before his death and free himself of them?

In any event, I decided to preserve my grandmother's secrets that are inseparable from my own memories of Jaffa, and put them down on paper.

Some might say that my nostalgia for Jaffa impelled me to do so.

I first heard the word 'nostalgia' from Christodolos

who described with yearning his village of Rodia in Crete for me. I was lying in his arms sated with loving and he explained that it is made up of the two Greek words, *nostos* and *algos*, the first meaning 'a return home' and the second 'pain'.

And today, once a week, on Sundays, when I get away from Jerusalem and visit the city of my childhood, I fulfil the *nostos* while I experience the *algos* every day as I look at the photographs that emerged from the developing fluid and were later published in Israel and abroad and displayed in my exhibition, 'Memories of Jaffa', that travels the world bringing me distinction and pain.

But this story was not written out of a desire to dwell on the past, or nostalgia, but rather because I imagined that through writing which brings me closer to the dead than the living, I would succeed in conjuring up the ghosts of my life and bring peace and order to the chaos of my childhood. After all, wiser heads than mine have said that stories of the past can explain and settle events of the present, and can even be used to predict the events of the future, as it is written: 'What has been is what will be', and 'Like mother, like daughter', as I was told – in the masculine – by a huge banner hanging in my school's cafeteria.

And my family's history has proved this again and again.

CHAPTER 2

'Every family story, especially if it tells of calamity and has many characters, becomes a legend for future generations,' explained Avigdor Ben-Ari, who lodged at Widow Ziso's house where we lived. Avigdor Ben-Ari was the most knowledgeable person I knew in my childhood and whatever he said I diligently wrote down in a notebook that contained words of wisdom. 'The passing years,' he said, 'shroud the truth in the mist of oblivion, the heroes become blurred, leaving behind them ghosts, shadows. Anyone hearing their story years later must understand that it is told from the storyteller's point of view, who even if he actually underwent some of the events, wove the plot in his own way and according to his own disposition, and painted it in his own colours. And the listener, who takes the story onward, also stamps his fingerprints on it and we must understand that his listeners will also expropriate it from his possession to theirs and repeat it in a different version, and so on, by word of mouth, from generation to generation, until . . .'

'Until the story becomes a legend.'

And indeed, as the years went by the story of my grandmother Simcha's wedding became a legend that was even inscribed in the annals of the city of Tel Aviv-Jaffa.

I first heard it from Widow Ziso and as she had not taken sides in the age-old conflict between my two grandmothers – my grandmother Simcha and Grandma Abulafia – in my view she was a most reliable witness. But I was still forced to complete it with the help and supplements of Rashella Abulafia, my paternal grandmother, between whom and my maternal grandmother Simcha there was a long-lasting enmity. In this story, pieced together as it was from different versions, I added my own fingerprints and completed and invented sentences that perhaps were not spoken, and deeds and scenes that were not described.

It was Widow Ziso's idea to marry off my grandmother Simcha a short time after her arrival in Eretz Israel from Russia, when she was only sixteen years old. Three days after she met her at Jaffa Port, she realised that the orphan girl she had chosen to adopt as her daughter would remain blind and lame and that she had struck a bad bargain.

At first, on doctor's orders, Simcha lay for two whole days in a darkened room so that the darkness would banish the excessive light that had destroyed her sight. Pads soaked in a lukewarm infusion of camomile were laid on her afflicted eyes and her burnt leg was wrapped in an oiled dressing. And Widow Ziso, who came to bring her meals and change the pads, looked at her compassionately, her doubts increasing as to the wisdom of the adoption. She quickly realised that the best thing to do was to find a way of rectifying her hasty decision; from that moment she wasted no more time and three weeks later Simcha was standing under the wedding canopy. Some say that my grandmother Simcha also married in haste because of the death that was abroad in Jaffa, gaily cutting down its inhabitants in an epidemic of incurable cholera, and Simcha, the young girl, was chosen to save the city.

For the fateful talk with Simcha, Widow Ziso asked the gentile Natasha, a pilgrim who had decided to stay on in Palestine, to serve as her interpreter.

'*K'to?*' The word echoed around the room when Natasha informed the bride-to-be about the wedding.

'Who?' Natasha translated for Widow Ziso.

'Fishke Mendel,' replied Widow Ziso.

'Fishke Mendel,' translated Natasha for Simcha.

'Fishke?' asked Simcha.

'Fishke,' repeated Widow Ziso more confidently on seeing that the girl was not being rebellious.

'Fishke,' Natasha translated once more.

'Fishke? *Bozhe moy*,' my God, sighed Simcha resignedly and turned her face back to the wall.

There was a great resemblance between Simcha

and her husband-to-be Fishke, whom she had met on the ship that brought them to Palestine. She limped and so did he, she on her right leg and he on his left, but her lameness was caused in the pogroms while he had been crippled almost from birth. It was said of him that at his delivery his feet had emerged before his head. The confused midwife had pulled his left leg so hard that she had dislocated it, and when it turned black they had been forced to amputate it. From the time that Fishke learned to walk he had hobbled about on a peg leg with a leather-covered brass ball on the bottom, and as he walked the ball's drumming could be heard as it dragged behind. On particularly cold and damp days he rubbed his stump because of the strong phantom pain that drove him crazy, and cursed the day he was born.

She was an orphan and so was he. Their parents had been killed in the pogroms. He had been saved only because he had hidden in the cellar of their house, among churns of butter and piles of green-eyed potatoes stored there for the winter, into which, for some reason, the mob had not come.

It was said of Fishke's and Simcha's faces that they were alike as two peas in a pod, as if they had been moulded in the same womb. They both had light hair, blue eyes with a playful slant, a nose that turned up to the sky, white skin so transparent that you could see the blood flowing in the arteries and veins, and thin lips that on the rare

15

occasions they broke into a smile, shyly revealed a gap between the two front teeth, the same gap between his and hers.

So it was no wonder that Fishke desired only Simcha, who because of the resemblance she bore him he viewed as having been taken from his own rib, and whoever falls in love with someone like himself, then in retrospect he loves himself.

But one difference between the two is worthy of note: while he was short and stocky, she was tall and slim.

He first saw her as she limped up the ship's gangway, her head high above those of the other, younger orphans. She looked around her proudly and haughtily, as if she were there only by chance and had nothing to do with this wretched rabble of uncombed children dressed in threadbare clothes who crowded and shoved one another like a flock of sheep frightened by a beast of prey. Fishke, who followed her defiant progress and upright carriage, stood facing her and looked into her eyes that were so like his own. At first she lowered her eyes, but immediately raised them and stared at him in rebuff. And he, unlearned in the ways of love, saw this as encouragement and an invitation and from that moment and until her last day, he never left her alone but stuck to her and the smell of burning that emanated from her, a smell that was like a sweet perfume to him. On deck he limped after her on his left leg, she limping on

16

her right one, and even then the wags said they were a match made in heaven, that if they wed, their portion from heaven would be one pair of healthy legs.

For three days the ship rolled in a stormy sea and Simcha stood on deck and vomited her very guts into the waves. Not once did she go down to the dining room during that time, and Fishke looked at her from the side, pretending he was interested in the fish darting after the bile swallowed up in the ship's foaming wake, and standing guard over her lest she fall, heaven forbid, into the turbulent water. When the storm abated and Simcha finally went below to eat something, Fishke grabbed a place next to her and they sat side by side, embarrassed and silent. Until she dropped a slice of bread and Fishke bent to pick it up his head met hers under the table, and his hand encountered her groping one. Their hands intertwined, sticky fingers tangled with sticky fingers until the loss was recovered. Blushing and with dishevelled hair the two heads came up and her eyes were imprisoned in his that so incredibly resembled her own. After the meal they went up on deck, leaned on the rail, their faces to the darkening sea, and had the longest conversation that they were to have in the course of their lives. Immediately after it, after they had bared their souls to one another, the two sealed their lips and went back to wallowing in their silence. And what had they revealed to one another? As if from a monotonous, remote inventory she enumerated, one by one, her family members who had been killed, and he recounted his family's dead while doing his best to impress her with their greater number. To this end he included the names of two younger brothers he never had. Later, when she asked him to, he showed her what he would never have shown others, even when they entreated him: hesitantly, he rolled up his left trouser leg, laid bare his wooden leg, snapped his finger over it to banish the evil eye, and released the leather straps that bound it to the stump. Red-faced, as if he had been forced to stand naked before her, he revealed the ugly scar that adorned the striated skin and flesh like a bas-relief. Captivated, Simcha gazed at his deformity, lowered her face, and with soft lips kissed the scar, drawing his pain into her warm mouth. Fishke shivered, holding back his tears and knowing that he would love this girl for as long as he lived.

'Simchi', he called her affectionately, and she did not forbid it.

When they reached Jaffa, Fishke was the first to see disaster about to befall her and led her across the sand step by step, shielding her eyes from the sun's rays with his stretched-out hand. When they finally stood on terra firma and she was wracked with nausea and vomited, he held her forehead, ignoring the sour stench of the depths within her, did not let go until she had completely voided her stomach and then wiped her face with his shirt tail. It was then that she was spotted by the childless Widow Ziso who had come to the port to find a child for herself among the orphans.

She liked Simcha's height and beauty and went over to her, tenderly put her arms around her shoulders, whispered some comforting words in a language she didn't understand, and led the dazzled girl to a cart harnessed to an emaciated mule. Right away Fishke detached himself from the band of orphans waiting on the jetty for distant relatives or kindhearted people who might want to adopt them, and hurried to follow the cart as it rolled through the alleys bustling with people and cattle. They came to a large house, almost a palace, painted pink and surrounded by a garden, where the cart came to a halt. The widow helped Simcha down and led her up an outside staircase to the second floor.

Fishke looked in amazement through the slits of the richly wrought-iron gate into the locked garden that was surrounded by a brick wall. Then, like someone examining a piece of property and deliberating whether or not to buy it, he slowly walked around the wall whose clay bricks were laid like a piece of lace work. He did a complete circuit until his feet led him back to the gate. Now it was open wide and Fishke went into the garden captured between the walls of what seemed like a roofless prison, and walked along the path that led to the entrance. There his hands stroked the pair of Corinthian columns standing at the front, with a carved acanthus-leaf wreath on their capitals that supported the weight of a broad balcony. His eyes wandered upward to the wrought-iron balcony rail, and at the sight of the intertwined Stars of David, the work of a master ironsmith, his lips parted in a smile. He pressed his face to the slats of the wooden window blinds and after despairing of seeing anything through them, went to look at the names of the house's residents that were engraved in Hebrew and Arabic lettering on the doorpost. He managed to decipher them with great difficulty: *Ziso, Avigdor Ben-Ari* and *Zerach Levin*, etched them on his memory, limped to the market and went into the first carpenter's shop he came across at the city entrance.

There, at Mr Rachmanov's workshop, the fine-fingered Fishke found work as an apprentice. At night he swept the sawdust and wood shavings into a corner of the workshop, spread out an old sheet on the pile and fell onto it, enjoying the fresh smell of the shavings, their brittleness and the crackling sound they made as the weight of his body lay on them. In the morning, before Mr Rachmanov arrived, he shook the yellow wood curls from his hair and clothes, folded his sheet and swept the wood shavings that had been pressed under his body all night out of the workshop. There he burned them in the open field, placed a blackened kettle on the fire, and when Mr Rachmanov arrived, he had a brimming tin mug of cardamom-spiced coffee waiting for him.

Fishke rapidly acquired a reputation as an unparalleled woodworker and Mr Rachmanov gave him the wood relief work, the carving and turning of the wardrobes, sideboards and chests of drawers his customers ordered. Piece after piece Fishke embellished with palm leaves, doves, hands spread in the gesture of the blessing of the priests and Stars of David, so that everyone would know the carving had been done by the hands of a Jew. In his spare time he carved himself a new leg with a kneecap, a shin and a wide foot that he designed using the pattern of his right foot. He even added toes and toenails, and it was said that he also etched, with great precision, the lines that furrowed the sole in a perfect mirror image of the existing foot. He then went to a cobbler and had fitted to both feet, the real one and the wooden one, a pair of fine leather shoes, and he finally felt like any other man in the street.

On the day that Fishke was informed of the impending wedding, he began carving their marital bed. He put all his love into the wood, planing, polishing, moulding and sculpting, and the wood was like putty in his hands, submissive and soft as dough. He carved a huge Star of David on the headboard, embellishing it all around with palm leaves and doves that seemed to be alive and cooing as if they were about to spread their wings and fly. The bed was so beautiful that people made a habit of stopping at the door of Mr Rachmanov's carpentry shop to peep in, and some even ventured in to pass their hands over the polished wood that was as smooth as marble. That bed brought numerous orders to Mr Rachmanov's carpentry shop, but Fishke never again managed to fashion a masterpiece the like of this one.

Everybody was preparing for the hasty marriage that was to save the city from the epidemic. And so, when Simcha awoke on the morning of her wedding day, she found in her room a beautiful wedding dress that belonged to Rashella Abulafia from Neveh Zedek, of whom it was said that she could work wonders with her sewing and embroidering of clothes that even the angels would not be reluctant to wear. In honour of her own marriage to Avraham, a senior bank official, Rashella Abulafia embroidered a dress, the beauty of which had not been seen since, neither in her own neighbourhood nor in the entire city of Jaffa. The dress was to blame for her three-year-long engagement, because until she had finished making it she would not consent to set a date for the wedding. For three years she sewed and embroidered, day in, day out, except for Sabbaths and festivals, and decorated the silk material with flowers whose petals were pearls and whose tiny leaves were embroidered with silver thread. She sewed and embroidered and unstitched, unstitched and embroidered and sewed until she was satisfied with the dress, and then it astounded everyone who saw it. A long time later, when Rashella Abulafia heard about the poor, orphaned, blind bride at a meeting in the synagogue's women's section, she was happy to be able to fulfil the precept of collecting a dowry for a poor bride and from the depths of her hope chest took out the famous dress that had brought her so much happiness, and willingly offered it to Simcha.

Embarrassed, Simcha ran her hand over the cool silk, feeling with her fingertips the pearls inset into the flowers, listening with pounding heart to the rustle of the fabric between her hands and smelling the faint perfume of jasmine and rose-water that had been absorbed into the armpits and décolletage. But despite straining her eyes, which furrowed her brow, she could not see the dress, not even by the light of a lamp brought to her in the middle of the day. She then put on the dress hastily, ashamed of being seen naked by the watching women, and the dress swallowed her up, making her disappear inside it, flowing from her shoulders in a waterfall of flounces, and soft waves of material flooded at her feet as if seeking to trip her up.

'Thin and dry and good for nothing,' someone whispered behind her.

'As thin as a twig,' answered another whisper.

'I didn't know that the dress was so big. What, were you so fat at your wedding?' Widow Ziso chided Rashella Abulafia. 'And I, in all innocence, thought you'd put on weight from happiness only after the ceremony.'

Rashella Abulafia held her peace at the insult,

perhaps because her mouth was filled with pins and her lips pursed around them as though in a kiss. Pin after pin was angrily jabbed into the rustling material and came out the other side, pinning layer to layer in an effort to fit the dress closely to Simcha's thin body. Then Rashella Abulafia knelt heavily and stuck pins into the bottom of the dress too, adding a hem to the existing one so that Simcha, who despite her height was shorter than Rashella, would not tread on it and soil it, heaven forbid.

'Don't you move at your wedding,' Rashella Abulafia tried to explain to her using sign language with sweeping movements of her arms and the tiny pricks of a pin, 'because if you do the pins will come out and you're liable to be pricked.'

Then Rashella Abulafia shoved into Simcha's hands a pair of white silk shoes with a pointed toe and a chain of red glass beads, that she had also embroidered for her own wedding and had never worn since, not even once. Simcha's hands felt the beads and she smiled in embarrassment, but when she tried to get her feet into them her smile faded because only after folding her big toes was she able, with great difficulty, to push her feet into the shoes.

At a snail's pace she limped down the steps of Widow Ziso's house to the carriage that had come to take her to the cemetery where the ceremony was to be held. The shoes were an instrument of torture on her feet, especially the burned one, and the tight dress was burdensome, shortening her breath and hampering her movement.

On feet cramped and aching from the ill-fitting shoes, her body fettered and tortured by the shrouds of the white dress, my grandmother Simcha stood at Fishke Mendel's side under the black wedding canopy as prescribed for male and female orphans marrying in haste in a cemetery to remove the curse of an epidemic from the community. Throughout the ceremony she was frightened of breathing freely lest a pin work itself free and stab her in the heart, and she was totally unable to concentrate on the rabbi's words, despite Avigdor Ben-Ari's efforts at translating them into Russian for her.

Three thousand men and women had already succumbed to the epidemic that came out of Gaza and had been brought to Jaffa in the folds of sailors' clothing. The cholera did as it pleased in the city, sowing illness and reaping death. The trains stopped running, the schools closed down, the children were sent home and the city put in isolation until the danger was past.

As the Jaffa Jewish Cemetery was completely full, so much so that not even the tiny body of an aborted foetus could be buried there, Mr Rokach, the leader of the Jewish community and its neighbourhoods, now had good grounds to request a new plot of land for burial of the epidemic's victims. In the second week of the epidemic, he put on his white, gold-bordered *galabiyyah*, put a *kafiyyeh* on his head and went up the steps of the town hall. In his soft voice he told the *kaimakam* that if the Jews were not given a new plot of land outside the city, their dead would be buried one on top of the other inside Jaffa, thus endangering the living and healthy.

The *kaimakam* hastily convened his advisers, spread before them a map of uninhabited Eretz Israel and looked for a *matrukha*, an uncultivated piece of public land that would be the Jews' new cemetery. For a long time the advisers discussed the matter but did not reach agreement, until the *kaimakam* lost his patience with their useless argument and he silenced them, jabbed his thumb, with its broad gold ring inset with a ruby, into the map and asked his aide to draw a circle around it. And so, with the jab of a thumb into the desolate dunes, far from any habitation, the site of the new Jewish cemetery was settled.

And then, on a hot summer's day, Mr Rokach and the *kaimakam*'s assistant trudged over the high dunes and, sinking up to their ankles in the burning sand, climbed and descended, descended and climbed for three hours until they found the place marked by the thumb. And with the words of the Patriarch Abraham to Ephron the Hittite at the Cave of Machpelah ringing in his ears, Mr Rokach took from his pocket ten gold napoleons, and as if he were standing on a theatre stage facing a huge audience, handed them over with a noble flourish and signed the deed.

The new cemetery was registered in perpetuity at the *tabu*, the Land Registry Office, in the name of the Committee of the Jews of Jaffa.

Immediately afterwards Mr Rokach asked his people to find two orphans, male and female, preferably handicapped and poor, and have them married in the cemetery at the community's expense.

'You will bring down God's mercy and the epidemic will stop,' explained Mr Rokach's emissaries to Simcha and Fishke separately, and placed on their shoulders the responsibility for terminating the horrors.

That is how my grandmother's wedding festivities were turned into the consecration of a cemetery, and death and life were bound together into a mockery of fate that would later harm me as well.

A fiddler, drummer and flautist played and danced through the alleys of Jaffa before the couple, and a host of people, their faces white with terror of the disease and their eyes weeping for the dead and sick, danced and sang with them. And the Christian and Moslem people of Jaffa, who hid from the epidemic in their shuttered houses, opened the slats a crack and peeped out at the crazy Jews trying to gladden the hearts of a bride and groom in such evil times. Simcha and Fishke rode to the cemetery in a carriage that drove along the beach, and when the wheels sank into the sand the congregation was asked to lend a hand to pull them out. The carriage drove along for about an hour in the moonlight until the light of the lanterns lit by the night watchman was seen as they flashed and flickered on the dark sea and guided the celebrants to the venue of the ceremony.

Two graves had already been dug there in two corners of the plot, separated and far apart from one another to demarcate the limits of the cemetery. One, the grave of an unknown labourer who had come from Lydda carrying the disease and who died in a hostel in Jaffa and on his grave was inscribed 'unknown', and the other that of Anushka, daughter of Reb Gabriel Brumberg, who had also perished in the epidemic and was buried five hours before Simcha and Fishke stood under the wedding canopy accompanied by the bitter weeping of Anushka's betrothed, whom she had not had time to marry.

To the mocking laughter of the hyenas and the crying howls of the jackals, the two orphans entered into the sacred covenant of wedlock. And when Fishke smashed the glass commemorating the destruction of the Temple under his good foot, the weeping of the congregation welled up, begging God's mercy. While the musicians did their best to disperse the cloud of gloom hanging over the congregation, the couple were led to the ritual purification room that this evening was to serve as a private room for their seclusion.

Nobody knows what happened in that room.

Rachmanov, the owner of the carpentry shop who volunteered to stand guard at the door to ensure that no one except the couple went inside, said that Simcha stormed out after a few minutes, her face burning, hair dishevelled, her dry, flat eyes trying to cry and her hands clutching the material of the dress at the neckline as if she was trying to hide something. She escaped limping through the cemetery's iron gate and felt her way directly to the fence of prickly *sabras* that surrounded the adjacent lemon grove. The pins that held the dress to her body came loose and pierced her flesh and the heavy material came loose and slid from her shoulders. When she reached the *sabras*, they caressed her bare shoulders with their broad, flat hands, clasped her in a painful embrace and shed a fine, stinging fluff of tiny spines onto her. After managing to extricate herself, she was caught up among the spiny arms of the lemon trees that dropped a veil of fragrant flowers over her that withered and became like the residue of thwarted dreams.

Simcha paid no heed to the pain and continued her blind flight until her feet became entangled in the hem of the dress and she was thrown to the ground. In a fit of anger she tore off the silk shoes that restricted her steps, and tried to get up. But as she managed to stand on her bare feet, Fishke, who had pursued her, reached her and grasped her, and the loosened pins pricked the pads of his fingers and tiny bloodstains spread over the dress, adorning it with the buds of red flowers.

Simcha fought him with all her might, flailing her arms, kicking and screaming in terror. And when he finally managed to get hold of her, she bit his hand, imprinting in the flesh two rows of bleeding crescent moons. But Fishke did not give up. He clasped her to him forcefully, her back to him as the pins in the dress pricked both of them. Like a father trying to pacify a fractious baby, he whispered in her ear, 'Simchi, *sha, sha, sha*.' Even when she became nauseous and vomited over the dress and his new shoes, he did not let her go. With a starched handkerchief he took from his jacket pocket he wiped her face, sat her down on a rock and ran back to the cemetery to bring her a glass of water. When he got back he saw Widow Ziso supporting her elbow, leading her away from there weeping and catching her feet in the hem of the stained dress. Sheepishly, Fishke shakily followed his absconding bride and his handicap intensified and spread to his good leg, too. After them trailed the congregation, clicking their tongues and nodding their heads about this wedding, and declaring that they knew in advance that a marriage that begins in this way, under a canopy in a graveyard and in the privacy of a ritual purification room, is bound to end badly.

When they reached Widow Ziso's house, the widow signalled to Fishke with a short, angry gesture that he should not come upstairs with them but should go on his way. For a long time Fishke stood in the street, facing the house and looking at the light of the lamp burning in his bride's room. When it was finally extinguished, he slowly wended his way to the carpentry shop. Once there, he angrily removed his wooden leg with its new shoe and without taking off the bridegroom's clothes he had been given by the Committee of the Jewish Community of Jaffa, and that now gave off a sour smell of sweat, he lay down on the pile of sawdust and shavings that had once more become his single bed.

In her room, Simcha tore off the dress that had become prematurely tattered, and laid her stabbed body and swollen feet on the bed and did not get out of it for three days.

That night the skies darkened. Heavy, unseasonal rain pelted down on the city, permeated the fresh graves of the epidemic's victims, flooded and cleaned the markets, washed the streets of dust and cleansed the city of the filth of the epidemic.

Next day it was announced that the cholera had left Jaffa and the closure of the city was lifted.

Torn and holed, its hem black, the material decorated with the yellow stains of gastric juices from an empty stomach and tiny spots of blood, the dress that had not brought luck to the orphan bride was returned to Rashella Abulafia. The beaded shoes she had ripped off as she fled were never found. Even a search party sent out by the shoes' generous owner returned empty-handed.

The shifting dunes that surrounded the cemetery,

she was told by the search party, had sprouted feet and overnight had moved from where they had once been. And they had taken with them, like someone who moves house and takes his chattels with him, everything that was in and on them: vegetation, small animals, and also the embroidered silk shoes.

So it is entirely possible that to this day they are buried under one of the buildings of Tel Aviv that has meanwhile sprung up from the sands.

About a month after the wedding, Fishke went into Simcha's room with Avrum, the Kurd porter, whose arms, back and head were loaded with the parts of a disassembled bed. With mouths filled with nails the two silently put the parts of the bed together until it stood whole and magnificent on the stone floor of the room.

Fishke threw a last look at the work of art he had fashioned with great love, stroked its carvings in farewell, enclosed the relief of the doves in his hand, caressed the Star of David, and left the room.

Another month passed and when Simcha's belly began to swell, the men of the neighbourhood slapped Fishke on the back. 'You were alone for five minutes and already your bride's pregnant,' they said in sincere admiration and male comradeship. But when they tried to get out of him just how he had managed it so quickly, he shrugged modestly as if he had nothing to do with it. At the carpentry shop he filled his mouth with nails, grasping them with wrinkling lips, and kept silent.

The inquisitive women pleaded with Simcha, too, and tried to persuade her with honeyed words to tell them what exactly had transpired between her and Fishke during their few moments alone. But Simcha puffed up her cheeks and she too tightened her lips lest the secret be blurted out against her will, fly up and away into the neighbourhood, gain independence and become public property.

In this matter, despite being separated, Fishke and Simcha were united and concealed what had happened in those few moments. But people would not let the affair rest and discussed and rediscussed it, especially on the birthday of my mother Nechama, the daughter born to Simcha immediately after her twin brother who had died under strange circumstances. All kinds of presumptions were presumed and guesses guessed until the dates and even the names became mixed up, and the story became a legend. But in the annals of the city of Tel Aviv-Jaffa the wondrous story was written as something that actually took place during the great cholera epidemic that beset the residents of Jaffa at the turn of the century, when two orphans were married under a black wedding canopy at public expense in the new cemetery, and the following day the epidemic had run its course. Oral testament has it that the bride fled from the groom immediately after the ceremony because the spirits of the dead had entered her, and seven months later she gave birth to twins, a boy and a girl. And because the mother had defied death, the soul of the boy had been taken immediately after his birth and only the girl survived.

From the day of the wedding Simcha refused to be alone again with her husband, and she asked Widow Ziso to allow her to carry on living in the room she had given her when she arrived. And Widow Ziso, whose conscience was tormenting her because of the hasty marriage, agreed and even bequeathed her the room for life, for her, her daughter, and her daughter's sons and daughters, if there were any.

It was at that time that Simcha discovered the art of cookery and began cooking, baking, roasting and concocting confections for the widow and her lodgers, Avigdor Ben-Ari and Zerach Levin. And when the neighbours smelt the aromas they, too, ordered dishes from her, and she agreed on condition that the money be paid to her benefactress.

Fishke couldn't accept Simcha's decision to live without him. Many nights he stood under her window calling, 'Simchi, Simchi,' in the softest voice he could muster, and he even sang her love songs in Russian. In the evening, when she went out to take the cool air on the beach, he would accompany her from a distance, guarding her lest she be harmed, heaven forfend, by man or beast.

But she refused to live with him as man and wife, and in order for there to be no attempts to marry her off to another, she did not ask for a divorce. She told Widow Ziso – and Avigdor Ben-Ari translated her words from Russian into Hebrew – that she wanted to remain on her own, 'Because there is no man in the world of whom I can be worthy.'

After seven months elapsed she gave birth to twins, the boy that died and the girl that lived, and who later had me.

With all the excitement of a new father Fishke heard the news at Mr Rachmanov's carpentry shop. He immediately washed his body, brushed the wood curls from his head, put on his bridegroom's clothes, strapped his new leg to his stump and went off to Widow Ziso's house. With an assured step he went into Simcha's room, closing the door behind him. Muttered sounds came from the room and the widow related that after a short time Fishke came out in tears, and passers-by said that he wept all the way back to the carpentry shop. There he washed his face, put on his work clothes, stuck some nails into his mouth and remained silent for many days, only speaking when he had something important to say.

Three days later, when they gave Simcha's baby back to her, he reappeared in her room carrying a beautiful walnut cradle with two hands outspread in the blessing of the priests carved into the head-board, to protect the baby from malefactors. From that day onward, Fishke made it a habit to visit the mother and baby every Sabbath eve. As baby Nechama started to grow she looked forward to his visits impatiently, because he always brought her a gift he had made: a rattle filled with tiny clinking stones, a wooden doll with long arms and legs and moveable joints, a whistle carved in the shape of a bird, a sanded soup bowl, and a splendid set of tiny chairs and a table, that all befitted a royal palace nursery. Simcha's small room was rapidly filled with dozens of wooden objects, all for Baby Nechama.

On those evenings Fishke silently ate the Sabbath meal with them, and after Simcha had cleared the table, she would ask him to read to her in Russian from a book of selected Chekhov stories and plays that the widow had bought for her from a pilgrim who needed the money for food. My grandmother Simcha particularly liked *Rothschild's Fiddle* and *Three Sisters*, and even after hearing all the stories and plays numerous times, she was never bored and begged him to read them again: another one, just one, until he got tired and asked permission to leave.

When Fishke concluded his Friday evening visit, he limped down to Lower Jaffa, the city of sin, Sodom and Gomorrah, and stopped in front of a house painted in shocking purple. The house's windows had coloured panes of stained glass and a grey bed of couch-grass stood by the entrance and flourished, thanks to the washing water thrown onto it from the balcony. On purple velvet sofas, wearing short silk dresses that revealed their curves, sat the women in Madame Louisa's lounge waiting to welcome him in the age-old act of seduction, with fluttering eyes and black-shadowed lashes. Happy, forced smiles shone in welcome from red-painted lips and hoarse, lewd voices solicited him in many tongues. With his rough carpenter's fingers Fishke stroked their cheeks, hefted their breasts as if weighing them, felt their bellies as round as a pillow, fingered their shining hair sticky with oil of lavender, and then chose one of them to share his bed that night. He always chose Latifa, clasping his hands as though apologising to her friends, and then limping with her to her room.

They said of Latifa in that house that she had been thirteen years old when she married her forty-year-old cousin, becoming his fourth wife. And when he found no evidence of a maidenhead on the first night he mounted her – perhaps because he took her from behind, so thought Madame Louisa – he beat her mercilessly, and next morning intoned the divorce incantation, '*Talaq, talaq, talaq,*' and threw her out of his house, much to the joy of his three other wives who feared a threat to their status. He kept her gold bracelet, rebuffing her pleas and not agreeing to return it to her. Had she returned to her village, said the women at Madame Louisa's house, who later found her wandering barefoot and hungry in the Jaffa market, her father

37

and elder brother would have slaughtered her for besmirching the family honour. The women took pity on her and brought her to the house, fed her and gave her something to drink, bathed her and combed her hair, massaged her dry flesh with sesame oil, picked the lice from her hair, darkened her eyes with kohl, dressed her in new clothes, and pinched her pale cheeks to redden them.

After she slept with the first man who wanted her, they found virginal blood on the sheet. That day the people of the neighbourhood saw Madame Louisa running after the man, stumbling in her high-heeled shoes, shouting after his retreating back and claiming a double fee for Latifa's virginity.

Latifa was as black and shrivelled as a grape forgotten on the vine until it turned into a raisin. Short and skinny, her breasts like flattened figs, her belly sunken and her legs as thin as twigs. From the moment Latifa offered him her heart, all the intoxicating juices promised by the others who were plumper than her, the taste of honey and nectar and olive oil, were no longer a consideration for him. Because she had a big, expansive and generous heart and she brought it to their bed where she twined her legs around his back, clasping him to her, and as if by magic her core trapped his member, wrapped itself around it and suckled on it, and he was sucked into its depths and her glowing ember eyes were fixed on his. She knew how to work miracles on him, so much so that the pleasure that spread through his body did not skip his phantom leg, conducting currents of pleasure to it as well. Then he closed his eyes and felt Simcha's lips kissing and tickling the scar on his stump and he shouted, 'Simchi!' and spilled his semen into Latifa's body. For a long time he moved inside her until Latifa released her hold on him and whispered that she had to answer a call of nature, and one of her friends came to take her place in bed. And when she too was tired out, she was replaced by yet another. Towards morning, before the first light came in through the window, all the participants in the night's festivities gathered in the room, emptied Fishke's pockets and shook his trousers lest the odd coin had escaped them. They piled the spoils on the floor, and as he slept, snoring lightly, they divided the money as if dealing cards: a coin for this one and a coin for that one, but they invariably took pity on him and left him some money for a cigarette or a bowl of soup or a handful of dry chickpeas. They sometimes discovered a wooden toy in his pockets and fought over it, pinching, hair-pulling and taunting one another. And when a spirit of foolishness took over, they pulled off the sheet covering his nakedness, giggling salaciously at his still-erect member whose touch reminded them of the fire between their legs. One tried encircling it with finger and thumb, as though seeking to estimate its thickness, another measured its length by a hand span, while a third tickled its crown as if hinting that it should be lengthened a little. And their friends, for whom there was no room in the bedroom, stood at the door watching the show, holding their chests and bellies and crowing with stifled laughter. That's how it was every Saturday when Fishke awoke from his sleep and found himself naked among the many women. And as though ashamed of his actions the night before, he did not meet their eyes, but silently strapped his wooden leg to the stump, put on his empty-pocketed clothes, and limped down the stairs. By the bed of couch-grass he again opened his trousers, peed in a long arc, looked with interest at the splashing puddle he made, sniffed with pleasure the steam that rose from it, and made his way limping to the carpentry shop.

From the windows the women and girls poked their heads, dishevelled from the long and stormy night, accompanying him with loud shouts of encouragement in time with his unequal strides, and asking him to come back again.

Until he disappeared from sight around a bend in the alley.

CHAPTER 3

My grandmother Simcha kept many secrets from me. One led to another and there were secrets within secrets like the links of a long and complex chain of events that together formed a totality.

The first, the most terrible of all, my grandmother told me on my third birthday.

On that day my memory took root and it engraved on my heart pictures, scenes and fragments of sentences which hurt me so much that to this day, even as I write these lines, I have not managed to overcome the pain.

In that accursed fall of 1916 event followed event and my life was rocked until it changed beyond recognition. That year, immediately after the secret was revealed to me, I fell ill with acute rheumatic fever and my heart became irreversibly defective. To mollify me I was given Ben-Zion as a gift and every morning I went to the kindergarten with him until he was cruelly slaughtered. Then the war reached the gates of Eretz Israel and my grandmother, whose livelihood was affected, started to work for the Turks and when they deported all the city's inhabitants in the great expulsion, baby Yousuf, Latifa's and Fishke's own son, came to us. But that's another story.

Anyway, within one year my life, that on the face of it had been stable until then, was shaken to its very foundations and so it is small wonder that those days, and the ones that followed, became etched on my memory despite my being a small child.

As I said, all this began when my grandmother, who had no choice, revealed the first of the chain of secrets that was the most awful of all.

This she did when she was forced to register me for the School for Infants. She decided to confess to me for fear I hear the facts from the kindergarten children, who had probably heard the story from their parents, and in a way that would be crueller tenfold.

A week later I fell ill. My temperature rose, my head ached and my arm and leg joints swelled up and reddened until I was unable to get out of bed, and so for a whole month I lay on my back, peeping out at the world through the gaps in the wooden shutter. 'Rheumatic fever,' said Dr Aberbuch, who was urgently called to see me as my temperature climbed yet another degree. Hallucinating, I saw my grandmother's worried face through the mist of the fever, and at dusk, when my temperature shot up until it quickly evaporated the dampness of the cold pads she placed on my forehead, I called her 'Mother' and she didn't correct me.

42

Throughout my illness she limited her excursions from the house and Khaled the greengrocer delivered everything she needed. Towards evening Fishke locked up the carpentry shop earlier than usual, loaded her wooden cart with the food she had cooked, and went out to Jaffa's citrus groves to sell her dishes to the Russian pilgrims who impatiently awaited their arrival. On the days when my pain abated, he lined the cart with soft cushions for me and, despite the oppressive end-of-summer heat, wrapped me up in a thick blanket and laid me down in the cart that smelt of garlic, onions, fish, confectionery and spices. With a gay rumble of wooden wheels he took me for a walk along the beach to 'breathe some air and see the sun', and along the way he sang songs in Russian in his deep voice.

About a month later when I got up, swaying, from my bed, Dr Aberbuch found that my heart had been permanently damaged and was murmuring like a piece of paper crumpled in a clenched fist. It was doubtful whether I would be able to marry, conceive and bear children, he informed my grandmother, because my worn-out heart would be unable to bear the load of a foetus and carry the burden of pumping blood for two. I didn't hear about this from my grandmother and I first heard about my defective heart from Widow Ziso when one day I went up the steps two at a time, and suddenly felt I couldn't breathe. In her quiet voice Widow Ziso ordered me to accompany her into her room, gave me a glass of water sweetened with sugar, waited until my breathing returned to normal, told me about my heart murmur and demanded that I modulate my movements.

When I grew up and talked to her about my ill health, she opined that my illness was the result of the shock caused to me by the revelation of the secret; the shock had convulsed my soul and opened a crack for the illness to penetrate my body and damage it.

'Tamara's a carrot-head,' 'Tamara-another-one,' 'Your ma's your grandma,' the children chanted after me tirelessly with mocking tunes when I joined the pupils of the School for Infants, weak and pale from my illness. I was particularly hurt by the phrase, 'Your ma's your grandma.'

'Your ma's your grandma'; over and over I repeated the hateful words so I wouldn't forget them, God forbid, and so I wouldn't ever call my grandmother 'mother' again.

The way she told me was erased from my memory by the blessed power of forgetting that protects us from memories too painful. I have never been able to reconstruct the exact words she chose to reveal the truth to me, and I can't even now. I can only remember scenes. My grandmother sitting at the table in a festive white blouse, her back to the window, and between us a cake she had baked for my third birthday. Rays of light burst out and came in through the shutter slats, flowing over her fair hair, sprinkling it with sparkling motes and encircling her body and head with a brilliant halo of light. Her movements, too, are imprinted on my memory: her fingers tearing out the inside of a loaf, kneading and rolling it, and the small, dark, elongated balls she stood before her like little dough soldiers. I can't remember the timbre of her voice or the words or what I said and thought at that moment. But I have no doubt that orphanhood then took control of my body, dug into my flesh, resided in my bones and heart and established a life of its own in my belly, that to this day sometimes suffers attacks of nervous pains, spasms that incense oblivion.

More than anything I was angry that she had misled me in my early years and had not corrected me when I called her 'Mama', but revelled like a real mother worthy of that name. I was so angry that I was engulfed by the thought and feeling that it had been my grandmother who killed my mother. But I couldn't adapt to the new name, 'Grandma', either. It was a strange woman who was suddenly standing before me and I insisted on calling her by her forename, Simcha. That moment, which decided my fate, aged her in my eyes and turned her into a real old woman, despite the fact that she was only in her thirties. Since that revelation I carry within me the knowledge of the lack in my life like a final, absolute sentence and with it the sense of misery that I was different from all the other girls. A flaw had been imposed on me from birth and annexed me to the community of the different, the exceptions, to the human detritus of those born unlucky.

When I grew up I talked to Avigdor Ben-Ari about it, and he tried to explain to me what loss is. I took care to write down his words in my red notebook in which I collected a treasury of the sayings and commentaries of the wise people who tried to solve life's riddles for me.

'Loss is disappearance,' I wrote what he said, word for word. 'The disappearance of a person, an animal, even an object of sentimental value, of something that is irreplaceable, is unique.'

'And if loss is disappearance, then everything that disappears is dead.' I tried to understand.

'But if you've lost a doll and another girl finds it,' replied Avigdor, 'for you, the doll has disappeared or died, but the other girl can play with it.'

'So what is dying?' I wanted to know. Avigdor scratched behind his ear, which for me is a sign of embarrassment, hesitated for a few moments and then searched through one of his boxes, took out a leather-bound book with Russian lettering embossed in gold on it, and beneath it the portrait of an old man with a splendid beard and white curls covering his head.

'Socrates,' he introduced him to me proudly, as if he were one of his relatives. 'Socrates, one of the fathers of Greek philosophy and the most important of them.' I asked what philosophy is and he explained that the word is made up of two words, *philo* and *sophia*, which means the love of wisdom. But if I wanted to know what Socrates had said about loss and death, I must listen and not interrupt him with questions. Then he blew on the curls and beard of Socrates, who to me looked like God, raising from them clouds of dust that made me sneeze, leafed through the book, found what he was looking for. Many years later I found the quotation from the philosopher that had been translated from Greek to Russian in my notebook, and Avigdor Ben-Ari translated it from Russian to Hebrew: '"People fear death as if it is the greatest of calamities,"' he dictated. '"To fear death, my friends, is only to think ourselves wise, without being wise: for it is to think that we know what we do not know. For anything that man can tell, death may be the greatest good that can happen to them." And apart from that,' Avigdor added his own special interpretation for me, 'you certainly have nothing to fear from death, because thanks to it you will come to the place where your mother Nechama has gone, and perhaps you'll meet her there. Meanwhile, remember her through the stories about her.'

And I tried to elicit the stories from those who had known her.

As if she had waited all her life for the moment of my birth, my grandmother Simcha used me as an amendment, an amendment of her own childhood and the mother who had not wanted her, and an amendment of her adulthood and her help-lessness towards her own daughter, who had been my mother.

When my grandmother Simcha came home from the hospital with me in her arms, she put me down into the cradle that Fishke had carved for my mother the baby, and two outspread hands protected me in the blessing of the priests. With repugnance she refused Widow Ziso's suggestion that she bring in a wet nurse. For a whole month she avoided going to the citrus groves of Jaffa and for a whole month the pilgrims who disembarked from the ships in Jaffa port went hungry. All that time she did not leave her room; she boiled goat's milk, strained it through fine gauze, filled bottles with the white liquid and cooled it on the windowsill, recruiting the help of the cool wind blowing from the west. She held me in her arms for hours, clicking her tongue and coaxing me to eat, said Widow Ziso, who was the most reliable witness of my infancy.

When I got a bit bigger she made me soft cheese from milk that she strained through a cloth, and patiently pushed it into my mouth, spoonful after spoonful. When I cut my first tooth she made me her royal *borscht* and fed me the first meatball of my life, which she broke up into bits and dipped into the soup. From that time forward, our lives revolved around food. A good meal, so my grand-mother believed wholeheartedly, heals both body and soul. Chicken soup will cool a forehead burning up with fever, puréed garlic will banish a toothache, *borscht* will cure an infected throat, *kreplach*, dough pockets stuffed with meat, will bring consolation to a doleful soul, and bone marrow will strengthen brittle bones. I particularly enjoyed my grandmother's concern for my stomach. Whenever I complained of stomach ache, either genuine or fake, she hurried to take her rye bread from the *tabun*, the charcoal oven, and while it was still steaming she wrapped it into a piece of sheet with her heat-resistant hands, stuck it onto my stomach beneath my nightgown, and laid both of us down in bed. The merciful and consoling aroma that rose from the bread and its heat, that spread throughout my body, sent me to sleep.

I awoke in the morning with a cold loaf in my arms, hard and partially nibbled. Then I gave the broken loaf back to my grandmother and she nodded her head and put the blame on the mouse that had again gnawed at the bread during the night. And I, enjoying the only game she would play with me, whispered, 'Simcha, it was me, it wasn't the mouse.' And she quickly picked up the rolling pin and chased after me, limping and shouting at the top of her lungs, '*Mish, mish, mish!*' – 'mouse' in Russian. And I fled, screaming in mock terror, until we both fell onto the bed in each other's arms, me gurgling with laughter and she with her one and only smile that was broken and threadbare, despite the fact that she didn't use it often.

For the first three years of my life there were only two people, Widow Ziso and Fishke, whom she allowed anywhere near me, and always under her supervision. She would never agree to leave me with strangers, and even when she was busy in her kitchen and was forced to hand me over, like a pledge, to Widow Ziso, her ears were pricked to listen to her conversations with me. A mélange of baby syllables and sounds that Widow Ziso compiled for the babies she had not had could be heard coming from her room, and my grandmother listened with great concentration to ensure that no undesirable words would reach my ears. And when Fishke looked after me, she listened to the thunderous silences he shared with me. So it is surprising that my first word was 'Mama'. Some time later, Rashella Abulafia, my paternal grandmother, gave Simcha, my maternal grandmother, away, and heatedly said of her that she repeatedly spoke this word, morning and night, and asked me to repeat it after her. 'Doesn't a parrot to which you repeat the same word finally succeed in croaking it from its beak?' she said mockingly, bringing Widow Ziso as her witness who had heard her telling this with her own ears, and even accompanied her words with sighs of pity. When I grew up and asked my grandmother Simcha if the story was true, she shrugged and hissed, 'Don't believe her. That one's a liar.'

And once again I found myself torn between my two grandmothers.

Today I believe that 'Mama' was nothing more than a random combination of the first syllables that came out of my mouth as I became pleasantly addicted to the experiments I made with my vocal cords, and like any other baby I expelled into the air random sounds and combinations of phonemes.

'But you,' insisted Grandmother Abulafia, 'said "Mama", and Simcha didn't try to correct you.'

As excited as any mother whose daughter has just spoken her first word, said Widow Ziso, completing the story, my grandmother Simcha ran to her with me in her arms, and coaxed me into repeating the word for her. Then she knocked on the doors of Avigdor Ben-Ari and Zerach Levin, awakening them from the sleep of a hot Sabbath day, and pleadingly tempted me to repeat the miraculous word for them as well. And later, because her face glowed every time I mumbled that word, it took root in my mouth and I repeated it over and over again, and once I matured somewhat, I too believed in what I was saying, I believed with all my heart that Simcha was my mother, and that's what I called her in front of others until I reached the age of three and she was compelled to send me to the Infants' School.

It was then that I first heard the name Nechama, my mother's name.

After I recovered from my illness, my grandmother was beset by a heavy sense of guilt and delved into the wooden box that Fishke had made, where she kept a few photographs of my mother. With the help of Widow Ziso, who was her eyes, she found the one she was looking for, gave it to Aliza, the artist from Neveh Zedek, and asked her to copy it in colour. After much pleading, and in exchange for a fistful of coins, Aliza agreed and painted, in rough lines and vivid colours, a reproduction of my mother as a girl as she appeared in that photograph taken on the beach by an itinerant photographer. As he had photographed my mother with a friend, their arms around each other's shoulders, Aliza surgically removed the friend from my mother's body and filled in the empty space with rough contours from which the brushstrokes deviated. My mother's slim legs faded into the yellow sand painted in the background, and the arm that embraced her friend remained bent and detached in the air, like an arm that had withered. The artist reddened her cheeks like a pair of overripe apples, she coloured her lips in shocking purple, and her hair in phosphorescent yellow. Her upturned nose was downturned and most of my mother's freckles were forgotten as if Aliza's hands had tired in the middle of dotting them. Aliza also failed with her depiction of the eyes, painting them dark green (despite my grandmother's request to paint them sea blue), encircling them with a dark frame of kohl and fixing in them the look of a street whore weary of life. The features that gazed out of the portrait were like the grey visage of a corpse wearing warm, gay make-up so that the dear departed would be seen at his best in the coffin. And so, as embalmed and dry as a mummy, my mother has looked out on us from the wall, present and absent, with her titivated face and coloured clothes, the work of Aliza the artist.

Today, years later, when I look at the portrait whose colours have meanwhile faded, I believe that Aliza was simply slovenly in her work. And despite her reputation at the time, perhaps she wasn't a good artist but a mediocre, even a bad one. In any event, every time the subject of the portrait came up, my grandmother Simcha sadly recalled the large sum of money she offered Aliza the artist until she relented and agreed to paint the dead woman from the photograph.

Much later, I discovered the photograph that had served the artist as a model in a wooden box. Its background was shining bright due to the strong light bared to the lens, which searingly whitened the sand, and my mother is standing there with her arm around her friend forever and her face is in fact happy, because those were the days of her great love for my father. But then I could have forgiven the artist for removing the laugh from her face, putting weariness and sadness into her eyes and freezing her lips in an expression of suffering, because I believed then that this was appropriate for the features of a person who is no longer among the living.

Yet in my childhood I believed that if I looked straight into the eyes in the portrait and did not lower my eyes for a long time, I would manage to bring her back to life. So during the many hours that my grandmother was out of the house on her various errands, I sat facing the portrait, focused my eyes on it, scrutinised each detail, and hoped that just as I was seeing her, she was seeing me. I prayed for a movement, the slightest movement, that would tell me she had decided to emerge from her repose and from the canvas on which she had been painted, and quickly peel herself off the painting, skip over the obstacle presented by the frame, come down and sit next to me on the carpet. For hours we feverishly gazed into each other's eyes until I got tired, and two, sometimes three mothers floated before my eyes inside transparent balloons that hovered in the air. I sometimes played 'Who looks like Mother?' with her, searching for myself in her features and build. I used to dissect her body, patiently separating part from part, and compare them with my own. Her eyes, sad and slightly slanted, resembled my own, her fleshy lips resembled mine, I could have stuck her hands onto mine, and only her hair that adorned her face like a golden fleece was dissimilar to mine that framed my face in flames of fire. Her gaze regarded me with sorrow, like someone from the past peeping into the future in which she will have no part.

For years my mother was with me in this way, hanging on the wall, silently following the changes taking place in my body, caressing my face with her eyes that were so like my own, running her fingers through my hair and secretly giving me advice in a whisper so that it would not reach my grandmother Simcha's pricked-up ears. And in those moments of closeness between mother and daughter, I knew that nobody would love me like my mother who was no more. At those moments I was dominated by sombre thoughts of longing and loss. A longing for the love of a lost mother, the only one who could have been mine alone, a flowing, self-evident love, and abundant, unlike the love I was given, that I viewed as the too-small portions of food in an inadequate meal. And then I gazed at the ceiling, to God who I thought was there, despite my grandmother not believing in His existence at all, and I would insolently tell Him that He had four mothers while I had only one, and she had been taken from me before I even got to know her.

A great fear sometimes stole into my heart and again I asked her if, in addition to her eyes and hands, she had also bequeathed me her wounds and especially her fate. And she continued gazing at me sadly, in her silence that made me shudder. I thought that the hatred of a mother for her daughter is an inherited attribute in the women of our family, like the colour of their eyes and the size of their hands, and that being so, perhaps God had been good to me when He took her to Him, because it stands to reason that she would have despised me just as my grandmother – and this I was told by Widow Ziso – hated my mother. And then, when my grandmother Simcha came home to her room in the evening after a long day in the markets and her kitchen and the citrus groves of Jaffa, I would look deep into her extinguished eyes and wonder if she had really suckled the hatred from a mother who had not loved her, and that's how it would be with us until the end of time.

Some said of my grandmother that she was a beautiful and captivating woman, and despite life treating her harshly from the day she was born, its trials had neither left their scars on her beauty nor managed to damage it. Her beauty, so they said, was a cold beauty and whoever reached out to touch it would have their fingers frozen. As her eyes, as blue as the sky on a day the hot, dry *hamsin* was blowing, could no longer fulfil their task, one could look at her for hours without her knowing it, like into a portrait on canvas, a portrait of a beautiful woman whose eyes gazed into the distance beyond the field of vision of sighted people. Her hair framed her face in light silken waves, soft and unruly, her nose was upturned at just the right angle, her lips, that were sometimes clenched, seemed as if they had been painted on by the thinnest of an artist's brushes, and her skin, that was only rarely exposed to the sun, was transparent. Her body was narrow, tall and supple, and at dusk, when she went to the citrus groves, she walked like a princess among her massed admirers, her head held high on the stem of her neck and her blank eyes staring forward without moving left or right, as if she feared meeting the looks of the ordinary people lest evil thoughts come into their minds.

'Your grandmother was such a beautiful woman that she could have won the Queen Esther Prize at Mr Agadati's Purim party every year,' said Widow Ziso as she repeatedly praised my grandmother's beauty. But in my childhood I only saw her shabby clothes, I was revolted by the smell of burning that she emitted, I was ashamed of her slight limp and was sorry for her hands that were always scarred with cuts and burns because she was careless in the kitchen. But it was her blindness that bothered me more than anything else, and the Hebrew nickname 'Simcha Full-of-Light' – a euphemism for blindness – she was given in the neighbourhood because of it. When I asked Avigdor Ben-Ari what it meant, he explained that this Hebrew expression existed in my grandmother in full, for its meaning is 'great light' and is a euphemism for blindness. Then he told me that my grandmother had taken so much light that even had it been given to her bit by bit, it would have lasted her all her life. He backed this up with a story about Abu Ali al-Hassan Ibn al-Hashem, better known as Alhazan, who lived in Iraq a thousand years ago. This Alhazan empirically proved Aristotle's claim that a beam of light travels from the sun to the eye and not, as many thought, the other way round. To prove his claim, he wickedly suggested a simple and 'enlightening' experiment to the sceptics: dozens of his antagonists gathered at noon in the cities, turned their eyes to the sun, and gazed at it for a long time. Their world was plunged into darkness and the poor wretches began feeling their way around in the dark by the light of the burning sun.

Simcha didn't like the sun and did her best to avoid it and hide from it. She left the house before sunrise and under cover of the shadows made her way to the market and the port, and did not go out again to the citrus groves until the sun was close to sinking into the sea. When she was in her room, she closed the wooden shutters and shut herself off in the dimness. I sometimes asked her to angle the shutter slats to let a little light in, but she refused, saying that to see the light she needed darkness because it was impossible for her to see light without it. And as I grew up I could no longer stand the gloominess of the room and was attracted by the brightness outside so I'd go out into the street. In the transition from dark to the great light, the brightness hit my eyes too and blinded them mercilessly at first, bringing darkness down on me in the middle of the day. Then I would become frightened and was also filled with pity for my grandmother Simcha for whom this darkness was a constant companion. But a few minutes later the light would be victorious, driving the darkness away, and the houses gleamed at me in their whiteness, the sea sparkled for me blue and deep and I would confidently make my way through the city's alleys and forget my grandmother's blindness.

On numerous occasions I wondered what a blind person could see and I questioned her about this. She pacified me, saying that she sometimes could see light and shadows and the outline of objects in her way. Sometimes, she told me, and I wanted to believe her, the dark-coloured curtain that obscured her world would move and she was able to see the extreme edge of a picture. A leaf, a lock of my red hair, the beard of a beetroot, the surface of the soup bubbling over the flame, and the cruci-fixes gleaming against the back robes of the pilgrims who surrounded her every evening holding bowls of food.

But Avigdor Ben-Ari told me he did not believe that she could actually see all this with her dead eyes. She might possibly see, he explained, the lock of my red hair and the green leaf in her imagi-nation, while she remembered all the other scenes from her past, from the time she was still able to see, and now they intermittently come back to her from the darkness and present her with illusory visions.

And indeed, this explanation of Avigdor's was reinforced by my grandmother Simcha when she sometimes agreed to relate childhood memories to me, and she always told them in colour.

She painted the thick forest that stood at the edge

of the village in gloomy colours, so gloomy and dark it was that whoever went into its denseness was liable to be swallowed up inside it forever. She spread out the fields in strips of green, she painted the sunset in red, and red were the raspberries they picked at the edge of the forest, white was the milk that jetted into the milking pails, and white, too, was the snow that covered the universe with cold, woolly carpets. And when, in a voice choked with emotion, she coloured her father's beard and the sunflower kerchief on her mother's head yellow, I realised that I mustn't ask questions about them because some things are better left unasked.

CHAPTER 4

One Friday evening, a few months before my third birthday, after Fishke finished his dinner with us and went off to Madame Louisa's house at his usual time, he didn't find his beloved.

'*Mush mawjouda*, no Latifa, Latifa gone,' he was answered gaily by the prostitutes in Arabic and Hebrew, who refused to tell him where she was. When he insisted on looking for her in the rooms lest she be engaged there with another man, he was pursued from room to room by Sarita the Jewess who mimicked his heavy gait and accompanied him with shrieks of laughter. When he didn't find her, Sarita offered him her own fleshly delights as a substitute. On the salver of her cupped hands she offered him the oblation of her heavy breasts that she took out from her dress, and with a wink and licking of lips she tried to solicit him. When he remained indifferent to her charms, she called to her friends for help and they stood facing him and lifted their dresses, giggling and revealing their pudenda that twinkled at him in dark seduction, and reached out to touch his privates that despite their efforts remained placid and inert. Even as he left the house they did not give up and leaned on the windowsills, their breasts tilted downward and their nipples aimed at him with their brown, pink and golden eyeballs, and they called after him, asking him to come back.

Disappointed, insulted and tired, Fishke limped to the carpentry shop and there, on his sawdust bed, consoled his member, imagining the faces of Simchi and Latifa, until he reached his climax that brought in its wake the sleep that alleviates sorrow. Next morning he washed his sticky hands, stuck some nails into his mouth, clenched his lips around them, and, as was his wont, kept silent.

Since Latifa's disappearance, Fishke avoided Madame Louisa's house, until a few months later his lust overcame him and once again he made his way there. Almost casually he chose the first woman he was offered, black Natalia who could sing drinking songs in Russian and curse heartily during the act of coition, and went upstairs with her to her room, and some minutes later came down, gave Madame Louisa her douceur, and returned to the carpentry shop.

Six months had gone by since Latifa left, and Fishke thought that she would never return. And then one evening he saw her peering at him through the open door of the workshop. He got up and excitedly hurried over to her, hopping on his good leg because that day he had not yet strapped his artificial leg onto his stump, and stood rocking before her and looking suspiciously at the bundle she cradled in her arms. Latifa proudly drew back the blanket from the face of a sleeping baby; Fishke scrutinised the faces of mother and child by the light of the lamp that burned in the carpentry shop, and his feet, the good one and the one that had been truncated a long time ago, were riveted to the ground. With a shy smile Latifa tickled the baby's feet and Fishke looked amazed at a pair of blue eyes that opened before him, a precise miniature model of his own. When he told Simcha the story later, he told her that when he saw how much the baby resembled him, he felt as if he was looking at a photograph from his own infancy.

'*Shu ismo?*' he asked in Arabic, his voice shaking.

'Yousuf,' she replied.

'You-su-f.' Fishke sucked on the syllables as though rolling a sweet candy in his mouth.

'You-su-f,' he joyfully declared, 'Yousuf, Yosef!' taking the diapered bundle into his hands clumsily and embarrassed, lightly tapping the baby's back and again calling excitedly, 'Yousuf, Yousuf, Yosef, Yosef.' The frightened infant opened its toothless mouth and wailed at the top of its voice.

The following evening Fishke went to Madame Louisa's house carrying a rocking cradle he had laboured over all day, filing and sanding it lest a splinter stick into the baby's tender skin, God forbid. He had a broad smile on his face and in

63

his heart rang the lullaby his mother had sung to him when he was a baby that now out of nowhere surfaced into his mind.

Like a weary sultan receiving his subjects, Yousuf reclined on the embroidered velvet cushions that upholstered the bed with its untidy sheets which emitted the scent of the lovemaking of all the men and women who had spent time on it before him. He lay there wide-eyed, observing the noisy, colourful women who gathered around the bed, clucking in admiration, pleasurably sniffing his tiny body, stroking his black forelock and closely examining the marvel of his blue eyes. Yousuf's mouth opened in a smile and transparent saliva drooled from it to his chin and thence to his lap.

Fishke, like an embarrassed passer-by who had come to a party uninvited, stood in the doorway and looked at the convocation of women around the baby. And when they fell upon him, they showered him with their chirping laughter, enveloped him in the warmth of their hugs, pecked his cheeks with kisses, and flew away like a flock of plump pigeons with shouts of *mazal tov, mabruk*, and *pozdravliaiu s rozhdenyiem syna*. Only then Fishke went over to the baby, brought his face close to him and again was amazed at the sight of his own eyes peering at him in miniature from the face of the baby, but then the lines of Yousuf's mouth drooped and wailing burst from it.

Fishke set the cradle down in the centre of the room, padded it with a big cushion he took from the bed, laid the yowling Yousuf in it, and stood there rocking him. The baby fell silent, stuck a thumb into his mouth with a wondering expression and not many minutes passed before he calmed down and fell asleep.

Next day, Fishke came to our room holding a baby in his arms. My grandmother, who had not become at all infected by Fishke's excitement, as though he brought her a new baby every day, laid Yousuf down on her wide bed, placed cushions all around him so he would not fall, and closeted herself with Fishke on the balcony. I strained to hear what was being said but Fishke and Simcha were speaking in the secret language, Russian, and only the name Yousuf–Yosef that rang out again and again revealed the subject of their long discussion.

Fearful of my standing in Fishke's heart, I went to examine the new rival that had popped up into my life. I tugged his coal-black forelock and brought my thumb threateningly close to his eyes that sparkled like jewels. The baby rewarded me with gurgles of laughter and I rewarded him by sinking my teeth into his tiny biceps. Yousuf screeched, bringing his benefactors, Fishke and Simcha, rushing to his side.

Simcha took him in her arms, pacified him, and then took the time to explain to me that I now had a new little brother whose name in Arabic was Yousuf, and in Hebrew we'll call him Yosef, and Yousuf–Yosef would be living with us sometimes. I must love him and look after him and not bully him, heaven forfend.

Two weeks later Yousuf was circumcised at a modest celebration.

'If, according to their religion, Yosef is a Jew,' insisted Fishke, 'then it would be better to have him circumcised according to our religious laws and not theirs.'

A terrible row then broke out between Fishke and my grandmother Simcha, who didn't believe in God and was particularly revolted by symbols cut into living flesh. And as she would not agree to cooperate with him and did not offer her room and cooking for this ancient, primitive ceremony, as she put it, Fishke asked the *mohel*, the circumciser, to come to Madame Louisa's house. Madame Louisa, only too eager to please him, agreed to get rid of her clients for a short while and cover up the lewd pictures, and demanded from the girls that they cover themselves with large shawls to hide their licentiousness, still their tongues during the ceremony and not say anything that might be inappropriate for the ears of a rabbi.

To make up the required prayer quorum Fishke invited Avigdor Ben-Ari, Zerach Levin and the Jewish workers from the carpentry shop, and also Widow Ziso who insisted on participating in the happy occasion.

Fishke brought the *mohel* in a splendid carriage and, so that he would turn a blind eye to the Arab mother, he lined both his pockets and soul with a great deal of money, and then stood supervising him so that he would do the job in hand well and not, heaven forbid, cut off more than necessary. As the baby bleated with pain in his arms and the Arab whores surrounded the white-as-a-sheet Latifa, curled their tongues and clicked them against their palates and lips in ululations of joy, he repeated his son's name over and over as if he feared he might forget it.

Widow Ziso told me years later that a few weeks after the circumcision Fishke went to visit mother and son at Madame Louisa's house and found Yousuf sprawled on his back between the women who had volunteered to look after him when they had no clients. He heard them teaching him bad words, repeating them to him and trying to get him to repeat them. Gurgling joyfully, Yousuf parroted the sounds made by the women as best he could, while they rewarded him with sticky kisses on his cheeks and belly, leaving the marks of open red lips and black lines from eye make-up on his velvety skin. It was on that day that Fishke took Yousuf away from there, brought him to us, and after lengthy and exhausting negotiations with Madame Louisa redeemed Latifa for a princely sum and housed her in a small room in the Old City, where a sea view spread outside the only window in its walls. From then on Latifa was his alone. And when he, she and the baby came to us for Sabbath evening dinner, it seemed that Latifa was holding her breath, as if frightened of breathing the air she had already breathed close to Fishke, silently circling her beloved, brushing imaginary sawdust and wood shavings from his head and clothing with caressing movements of her hands, and serving him his food with soft, lazy and loving gestures.

'Of course she was afraid to breathe near him,' said Avigdor Ben-Ari in answer to my question some years after her disappearance, with a hint of unfamiliar malice in his voice. 'Latifa was inferior to him, after all she was an Arab whore and he was a Jewish man.'

It was only many years later, after the disaster befell him, that I fully understood.

It was at that time that my grandmother Simcha adopted Latifa and established a new routine at home. Every morning, after my grandmother returned from the market, Latifa came into our room, laid Yousuf-Yosef down on my bed and helped her in the kitchen. The moment the baby cried, she rushed to the room and pulled out a breast that smelt of onions fried in butter. And I looked with envy at Yousuf-Yosef who clung to her with his hungry lips, sucking noisily and then falling asleep with a satisfied smile. Once, when I asked to taste her milk, Latifa bared her other breast, stuck a big, dry nipple into my mouth, and the taste of the lukewarm milk, sweet and disgusting, spurted into my throat and killed off my craving.

When the two of them finished their work in the

kitchen and my grandmother loaded the dishes onto her creaky cart to sell them in the Jaffa orange groves, Latifa wrapped Yousuf-Yosef up in a wide kerchief, binding him to her body, and together they walked in silence with the squeaking cart loaded with food preceding them. When they came to a certain alley in the Old City, Latifa would disappear and Simcha continued on her way to the orange groves until she was swallowed up between the citrus trees.

On those days Fishke's features softened, his back straightened, the smile never leaving his face, and as if he had spat all the nails from his mouth once and for all he suddenly became someone you could talk to. He divided his free time equally between Simcha's room and Latifa's room and always found the time to amuse Yousuf-Yosef and me with the wooden toys he carved for us.

CHAPTER 5

I have already mentioned that eternal enmity existed between my grandmother Simcha and Grandma Abulafia, and at the time I didn't know when and why it sprang up.

At first I thought that it all began with their acrimonious disagreement over the food they shoved into my mouth: each of them used her culinary talents as weapons to win my heart, but to everyone's surprise I remained a thin-bodied and spindly-legged little girl. And I deliberated between buckwheat and *hamin*, rye bread and sesame cookies, and from a very early age I knew that I mustn't praise one's dishes to the other, 'lest all hell come down from heaven', as Avigdor Ben-Ari put it when he sought to caution about great danger.

Every Friday, with a groan, Grandma Abulafia took down the heavy *hamin* pot she had inherited from her mother-in-law, and on whose lid was engraved the name 'Abulafia', filled it with onions, garlic cloves, haricot beans, chickpeas, chunks of meat, potatoes and eggs, and onto all this poured oil and water, sprinkled spices, added the onion

70

skins and a heaped spoonful of honey and a handful of seedless dates for deepening the dish's brown colour, and then sealed the lid to the pot with a paste made of flour and water. When I grew up, she asked me in honeyed tones to take the pot to the '*fourneau*', Moushon's neighbourhood oven where all the neighbours put their *hamin* pots to simmer slowly over the whispering coals. On Saturday morning, when she was busy in the kitchen, I'd steal out of my grandmother Simcha's room with Yousuf-Yosef and we'd go to Moushon's bakery, take the pot and wrap it in a baby's blanket to keep the heat in and protect our hands, and carry it together to Grandma Abulafia's house. There we placed it on the table and shooed away the pair of cats who insisted on sitting on the lid to enjoy its warmth. With a knife Grandma Abulafia broke the dough seal that had risen and had been baked until it became a thick, hard crust of bread, and ladled out the steaming *hamin* we loved so much. We both hastily finished off our bowls, kissed Grandma Abulafia on her plump cheek, went back to the house in Jaffa, stole up to our room, and lay in bed feigning sleep. And with stomachs bloated with the slowly digesting *hamin*, we sat down at my grandmother Simcha's table that was heavily laden with all kinds of tasty dishes.

But not only in their cooking were the two as far apart 'as East from West' as Widow Ziso had it, but also in their tea-drinking habits. Grandma Abulafia used to put a few droopy leaves into her tea that emitted a fresh, green smell, sweeten it well and drink it lukewarm. My grandmother Simcha, on the other hand, drank hers black and steaming, with a sugar cube clenched between her teeth through which she strained the boiling liquid into her mouth, where it would filter through the sugar, dissolve it very slowly and melt into sweetness in her mouth.

Unlike those of Grandma Abulafia, my grandmother Simcha's dishes were not primarily intended to fill my belly. It wasn't for me that every morning she shut herself off in the kitchen to chop, roll, concoct, bake, stir, taste, stuff, salt, make rise, pepper and fry, until by the afternoon the clay floor was piled high with dented copper pots covered with bulky lids and filled with steaming dishes that made their thin sides red-hot. When the sun painted the sea orange and gold and the cool westerly wind extinguished the fire of the day and cooled hot faces, dried the sweat and drove out the heat compressed into the houses, my grandmother loaded all her pots, pitchers, baskets and the potbellied samovar onto the two-wheeled wooden cart that Fishke had made her, whose handles he had sanded and bound with leather strips he had obtained from Menashke the harness-maker, lest splinters injure her hands, harness herself to it and set out on her way with her dishes and a gay rattle of wheels and pots, leaving in her wake a mouth-watering aroma of fresh cooking.

Her destination was the citrus groves surrounding Jaffa that welcomed her with the familiar shade of their trees, pillars of smoke from the pruned branches that slowly burned on bonfires, and the stench of unwashed bodies. Most of all she loved the blossom season for then the fragrance of citrus enveloped her in a sweet, alluring gossamer that dissipated the smoke of the bonfires, subdued the stink of sweat and even overcame the smell of cooking that came from the cart. She stood at the edge of the camp, placid and silent, waiting for them to come to her. And they, the moment the aromas reached their nostrils, aromas that mingled with the smell of burning that came from her, hurried over and surrounded her in their black robes, felt boots, the copper crucifixes shining on their breasts, with their thick, lice-infested beards and infected eyes.

Then my grandmother Simcha placed a board on the cart and on it arranged the still-warm pots, removed the lids revealing lightly browned *piroshki* stuffed with finely minced meat fried with slivers of onion, boiled buckwheat, potatoes roasted in their jackets, round *pilimeni*, pale and oily, bursting with the meat stuffed into them, *golubtzi* rolled in cabbage leaves, and a big pot of steaming *borscht* with globules of fat floating on its surface. Next to all these she piled the heavy, round loaves of sour rye bread, the secret of whose baking she alone knew, and clay pots overflowing with orange-coloured butter.

73

With hands trembling with hunger and passion, they swooped down on her, and with hoarse throats emitting the sour smell of an empty stomach, they shouted their orders to her as people do when speaking to a blind person. But she, confident of her control of them, first demanded payment, pandering to their longings and cruelly charging extortionate prices for the dishes, from which the aromas of home and childhood were drawn into their lungs, sweetly kissed their lips and aroused in them yearnings for Mama's cooking. Only when her fists were filled with coins that she fingered fastidiously with the suspicion of the blind would she accede to the hands outstretched in supplication and give them the requested dish. And when all the solid food had gone, she ladled the *borscht* into scarred tin cups that clashed, ringing, with the ladle in her hand.

Almost invariably Fishke stole after her. Ready to give his life for her, he waited, suspiciously watching the tumult her cooking aroused, his body tense and ready to assault anyone daring to harm her, with either a touch, a word, or to rob her of her money. But Simcha had no need of his services and he was never given the opportunity of sacrificing himself for her in a heroic battle. And despite her knowing that he was spying on her, because her sharp hearing picked up the sound of his footsteps and the rustle of the dry leaves under his wooden leg, she paid him no heed and was generally so busy that she even forgot his very existence.

She wouldn't sell to anybody, said Fishke to Widow Ziso, who herself had taken Simcha to task for her dealings with them. Using broad gestures to save words, Fishke described how Simcha stood there among them, pricking her ears to hear their shouts and wishes, and then selected a victim, sold to everyone else but not him, and not only did she not heed his pleadings, but even announced in a loud, provocative voice that tonight the poor wretch would go to sleep on an empty stomach. Sometimes the man sentenced to hunger would argue with her and in hangdog tones ask her to explain why she was selling to everybody except him. There were also those who tried cursing and even threatened to smash her cart and destroy its cargo if she wouldn't sell to them. But Simcha just calmly stared at them with her eyes that had been extinguished by the sun, and hissed at them in Russian, '*Poproboi, posmotrim na tyebya*,' just try, come on, let's see you.

'Then Fishke's body would tense,' the story was later completed by Shimon the citrus grove watchman, who amusedly watched this drama unfold each day. 'He would tense, breathe rapidly, and clench his fists.' And Shimon added with a wink for the benefit of his male audience that, at moments like those, he even saw an admirable swelling in the crotch of Fishke's trousers. And Simcha spat in disgust and informed them firmly that as she had cooked the food with her own hands, she had the right to decide who could eat it and who couldn't, and once she had made up her mind and kept her reasons to herself, she would not budge. And the day's victim, hungry and ashamed, would invariably submit, turn his back on the cart and beg his comrades for their leftovers.

Exhausted from their fatiguing sea voyage, the heat and the humidity that played havoc with their bodies that were used to the chill of Russia, the rest of the pilgrims hugged their food, moving away from her with the staggering gait of sailors not yet accustomed to being on land, and on the way to their resting place hungrily swallowed the fresh food, tearing the stuffed cabbage, stuffing their mouths with pieces of dark bread, *piroshki* and boiled buckwheat, gulping down the thick soup, and strengthening their bodies for the long journey on foot to Jerusalem.

Once all the pots had been emptied, Simcha uncovered the heavy copper samovar she had wrapped in an old cotton-wool quilt to keep it warm, and they would all come back and stand before her in a long, obedient line, armed with kettles or tin cups whose sides were stained purple with the remains of the soup that also left a murky residue on the bottom. And one by one they put a couple of coins into her hand and she poured some of the dark liquid into their vessel and gave them sugar cubes to sweeten the drink through their teeth.

Once they had eaten and drunk, she stayed behind there for a long time, mainly listening to the conversations between the women crowded at the edge of the camp. Now and again she would hear women speaking in the dialect of her home district and then she hesitantly moved closer and asked where they were from, excitedly rummaging in her apron pocket and pulling out an envelope spattered with transparent oil stains, on which Avigdor Ben-Ari had written in his cursive and tempestuous hand the names of her married sisters: Leah'leh, Batya'leh, Sarah'leh, and Sheindaleh, who had stayed there and promised to follow her. But because she did not know their addresses, only the name of the town, she begged them that when they returned home they take the trouble to look for the addresses at the town hall and post the letter for her. The women looked at her compassionately, took the envelope from her and promised to carry out her wishes in return for the generous fee she gave them in hope. She persevered with this for a number of years, even when Avigdor Ben-Ari, who had written a few dozen letters for her, started to lose his patience and told her that there was no further point in writing, because she would never find her family. But she tempted him with a plaited *challah* garnished with raisins that smelled of memories of Mama's home, and he gritted his teeth, sharpened his quill, dipped it into green ink and wrote a letter, and another letter, to the lost Leah'leh, Batya'leh, Sarah'leh, and Sheindaleh.

She returned home in the evening, she and the cart before her and Fishke limping behind her, with the coins clinking in the pockets of her dress. Sometimes Widow Ziso would be waiting for her on the landing outside her room, and ask her the same questions, rebuke her with the same words, although she knew better than to expect a reply.

'How can you feed them after they harmed you like this?' she sermonised. 'And perhaps it was one of them who killed your parents and did what he did?' she scolded her, shaking her head. When there was no answer, she spat to the sides, one 'tfu' here and one there, and declared with hatred in her voice, 'Poison you should put in their soup, only poison, and may all the Jew-haters die.' And Simcha shrugged, went into her room, put the coins into a cloth bag and hid it under the mattress. At night I would awaken to her nightmares accompanied by pleading cries in Russian, and Widow Ziso would rush into the room, shake her awake, pass a damp cloth over her face, give her sugar-sweetened water, hold her in her arms and whisper, '*Sha, sha, sha,*' like a mother pacifying her frightened child.

Once a year, when the main streets of Jaffa were hung with green branches and the houses adorned with fir trees, and golden chains and red lamps were hung along the length of the alleys, my grandmother Simcha would go into a deep depression that had nothing at all to do with the winter season. At night she cried out more than usual and in the daytime Widow Ziso and Fishke prevented her from going to the citrus groves. She would pace the room restlessly, her eyes glazed with fear, and every sound she heard – a door slamming or the cries of the street traders – made her body contort and her face awaken.

Once, when I dared to ask her about the terrible things she dreamed about at night that made her shout like that, she pursed her lips, looked at me with her empty eyes, and did not answer.

And I decided to leave her alone and turned to questioning those around her and me.

During the years when my grandmother Simcha cooked for the pilgrims, she got up early, left the house while long shadows still fell from it in a last refusal to flee the pink light pouring onto them from the east, and harnessed herself to her cart. At the port the fishermen awaited her, standing in a line on the jetty with their pails filled with their catch that flopped around in salt water standing in front of them. The stink of fish that had already rotted, the smell of fresh fish cooking over coals, and the saltiness of the sweat of bodies burned by the merciless sun mingled in the damp air and seared her nostrils. She was deafened by the voices of the porters, the shouts of the fishermen selling their catch, the screech of tightening anchor chains, and the groaning of the planks of the ramshackle boats, gently rocking on the wavelets that batted them back and forth. When she reached them, the fishermen gathered around

79

her, one hand holding a pail full of small sardines and the other grasping a hook on which bigger fish hung and flopped around. They whispered words of enticement in her ear about particularly fat sardines and wonderful fish for stuffing and making soup.

'Si la mar era de leche,
Yo eriya pishcador,
Pishceria mis dolores,
Con palbriques de amor'

sang Simone the fisherman in Ladino, and bowed to Simcha's request that he sing it in Hebrew as well:

'If only the sea was milk,
I would become a fisherman,
I would catch all my pain,
In words of love.'

And Simcha's lovely face would blush, as if he had written the words especially for her. But as if hiding her embarrassment, she immediately bent down to his pail and with her hand energetically stirred the water reddening from wounded gills, pulled out a fish and another one, squeezed its eyes staring at her in terror, testing its freshness, bending it from left to right and right to left. And to hide her pleasure from the song that he sang her so sweetly, she haggled loudly with him over

80

the price, taking a few coins from her apron pocket and pushing them into the outstretched hands that were deeply scarred from fishing lines, sharp hooks and over-taut net ropes. Then, pushing her cart with its fish splashing around in a bowl full of turbid water, she made her way to the vegetable market.

She was the only woman in the market, striding like a queen among the men crowded around the stalls, because it was improper for the women of Jaffa to make their market purchases in public and so they sent their husbands. The greengrocers tried to persuade her to buy, pushing fragrant fruit under her nose or a vegetable still damp from the morning dew into her hand. But she was not tempted and always bought her produce from Khaled who lived in her neighbourhood, not far from Widow Ziso's house. Khaled knew what she wanted without her having to tell him and selected the best and freshest vegetables for her. Beets, carrots, onions and garlic with the damp soil still stuck onto them as if they had just been pulled from the ground, and cucumbers, squash, peas in their pods and peppers whose surface was still sprinkled with glistening dewdrops. After he weighed them he added a couple of cucumbers or a big squash. 'Perhaps my scales are cheating you,' he told her, 'and it's better I'm a righteous man and you gain a little.' After she finished with him he arranged the produce in her cart. He put the firm vegetables on the bottom, as far as possible from the bowl of fish, and on them he very carefully placed the soft ones, as if they were eggs, wished her all the best and politely asked her to come back tomorrow, despite his knowing that she would because she only bought from him.

From there she pushed her cart to the al-Faraj market, her thin nostrils flaring with excitement and guiding her along the right way, and those nostrils pleasurably inhaled the aromas of foreign fragrances and spices that had come from distant lands. There she haggled with the traders over the price of a pinch of powder, firmly refusing 'to pay much gold' for a few seeds that had no weight at all. But in the end she always gave in, pushing her hands into her apron pockets and pulling out the coins she needed, less one. The traders, their hands yellow from handling their spices, took the coins, carefully wrapped her purchases in newspaper, and Simcha hastily hid the fragrant and expensive twist of paper between her breasts. From there she limped, her body replete with pleasure and her head spinning, down the alley leading to the butchers' market where skinned sheep hung by their tails from metal hooks at the front of the shops, and bloody-handed butchers cleaved and dismembered animals of every kind on tolerant wooden blocks. Her butcher, the Russian Seriozha, sliced the fattest pieces for her and as a gift added thick bones full of quivering marrow for the *borscht*.

And then, before the sun illumined the day with

its full light and dazzled her, she made her way home, pushing her cart loaded with vegetables, fish, spices and meat.

Once a week, every Sunday, right up to her dying day, my grandmother Simcha made two pots of soup, either from necessity or not, out of habit. In the big pot she made the farmers' *borscht* and, in the small one, the royal *borscht* of which she said that soup like this only graced the table of the czars, and added that because of it the Revolution had probably broken out. When I once asked her why, she replied briefly that the farmers were forbidden to even taste the royal *borscht*, and so they made a revolution after which bowls of royal *borscht* were given to anyone who wanted it.

And I hated that soup of hers.

Every lunchtime my grandmother Simcha laid a table loaded with her dishes for Yousuf-Yosef and me: steaming *piroshki*, slices of thickly buttered black bread, boiled buckwheat, and in the middle of the table she placed the small pot filled with steaming liquid: her royal *borscht*. Each lunchtime she assured me that she had made it especially for us, in a separate pot, and that this *borscht* bore no relationship at all to the soup she made 'for them'. But ever since the day I saw her spit into the huge pot of *borscht* she made for 'them', I refused to eat even a spoonful. I was about four when I caught her in the act. Her face was contorted with hatred, her empty eyes concentrated on the pot, her nose sharpened and seemed to become longer, locks of her light hair fell over her forehead and twisted like slippery snakes over her eyes, and her hands angrily stirred the liquid she had diluted with her poison. At that moment my grandmother looked like Baba Yaga, the fairytale witch who eats children, about whom she had told me in a moment of grace, unable to resist adding that Baba Yaga had teeth of nails and liked to eat 'naughty little girls' in particular. Since then I had stolen looks at her again and again as she cooked, waiting to catch her red-handed. She did the deed in the blink of an eye, just as the liquid in the pot reached boiling point. As the soup began bubbling on the Primus stove, she cleared her throat, gathered the saliva in her mouth and expectorated into the boiling liquid in the big pot. She continued doing this, strictly observing the ceremonial, even after the pilgrims had disappeared from the Jaffa citrus groves. She sometimes even accompanied the expectoration with a long, juicy Russian curse that I didn't understand, but whose words I repeated to myself at night lest I forgot them. And once, when I repeated them to Fishke and asked him what they meant, all I got for my trouble was a slap with his cracked palm.

'You mustn't talk like that,' he rebuked me. 'Never, never, or I'll tell Simchi,' he threatened.

'But it's something she said,' I wailed, surprised and insulted, because Fishke had never raised his hand to me.

'She's allowed to,' he whispered in barely concealed anger, 'she's allowed to and you're not.'

Why is she allowed to and I'm not? I wanted to ask but didn't, both because I feared that his heavy hand would again land on my cheek, and because he had always stubbornly refused to tell me about my grandmother and her life before I was born.

In the afternoons, when my grandmother went off and about her business, I'd slide down the iron banister carrying a deep plate covered with a flat one and go to Leah my school friend's house. There we shut ourselves away in her room and I'd swap my grandmother Simcha's dishes for those of Leah's family. They cooked something different every day of the week. Sunday was *sofrito*, Monday *majadra*, Tuesday bean soup, and I especially loved Wednesday, that was washday. On Wednesdays at Leah's house they ate *lintajes* soup made of red lentils seasoned with lemon. I'd pile my plate with bits of yesterday's bread, pour the hot soup over them, chew the soup-softened bread with pleasure and inhale the scent of soap and cleanliness that floated in the air.

On those Wednesdays, the *lintajes* soup days, the Arab washerwomen from Jaffa in their black dresses with their floral-embroidered bodices came drumming down the alleys, straight and tall with a washtub on their heads. 'Ghasaleh-fataha,' they called, washerwoman and fortuneteller, a combination that the housewives of the time found hard to resist. They invited them in and they sat down on a low stool, hiked up their heavy dresses, revealing their knees and stretching out their swollen legs in front of them. And the girls of the house, fearful of their luck, went in to them one after another, held out their hands and listened tensely to what the coming week would bring. When the washerwomen finished foreseeing the future, they came back to the present. In a noisy, impressive ceremony they boiled water on a Primus stove, and with their faces dripping sweat and with hands whose skin gradually reddened, they scrubbed the clothes that had soaked in the washtub gripped between their spread legs for hours, with green laundry soap.

It was on one of those Wednesdays that I asked the two washerwomen who had come to Leah's house to read my palm too.

'*Bint d'ba'a! Bint d'ba'a!*', daughter of a hyena, they whispered to one another fearfully, as they looked at my left palm.

I had already heard this insulting name from Zerach Levin and the gypsies of Jaffa on the occasions I passed them in the street. I ignored the insult and remained standing facing the washerwomen with my palm outstretched. But they covered their eyes with their sleeves, refused to tell my fortune, and my hand froze in midair.

The following Wednesday I came equipped with a large number of coins I filched from under my grandmother's mattress. I brought them in a small cloth bag that I intentionally clinked as the two washerwomen bent over their washtubs. Rahima, the older of the two, got up and gestured to me to come with her into a corner of the room that was the best lit, and asked me to hold out my hand. With great concentration she peered at the lines on my palm.

'In your life there is one, a brother who was not born, and two men,' she announced festively, as though she was the bringer of joyful tidings. 'One walks in water and one walks in fire. One of theirs, one of ours, and none of yours. One from Sunday and one from Friday but he thinks that he is from Saturday. One son to two men. No luck from birth to birth,' she said vaguely and would not explain further.

And when I placed the bag of coins in her hand she returned it, refusing to accept a fee for her prophesies. At home I hurried to write down her words in my notebook of wise sayings so I wouldn't forget them, under the heading: 'What the future holds for me – as told to me by Rahima.'

Many years later, when I looked at the prophecy again, I was shocked to see just how right she had been.

On Thursday, chicken day at Leah's house, I didn't go there and with a sour expression I would chew the buckwheat and with great difficulty swallow the soup. That's because I can't touch chicken, not since that morning in the Jaffa market. I was three and it happened right after I got up from my sickbed. It was then I saw it for the first time. A yellow chick crushed between dozens of its brothers in a wooden tea chest that had once contained black Ceylon tea. I refused to budge, fearing that the magic would dissipate, and the Arab boy, the chick seller, looked into my wide-open eyes, took a chick from the cheeping mass, raised it to his cheek and slid the golden down over it. I looked at the boy and the chick captivated, losing interest in the gypsy boy with his monkey dressed in a jacket and red tarbush that jumped onto his shoulder, and the bear shackled by a ring in its nose that danced before me as though burned by a heap of glowing embers, first lifting one leg and then the other. My eyes were focused on the yellow ball and I wanted to feel the softness of its cottony down and its tiny, warm body against my own cheek. I asked my grandmother to buy it for me, and when she refused I threatened to throw myself to the ground and cry, so she ground her teeth and relented.

'What will we do with it when it becomes a big rooster?' she asked despairingly. 'Where will it sleep? In your bed?' And I drew it across my face as the Arab boy had done, and felt its pleasant warmth melting the sorrow in my body.

'It's small, small, it will die tomorrow,' she mumbled, consoling herself for her illogical act as she pushed the coin into the boy's filthy hand, after haggling with him for a long time.

I named the chick Ben-Zion, after consulting Avigdor Ben-Ari, while he, despite having given him his Hebrew name, called him Feigeleh. Ben-Zion slept in my bed and from my hand ate boiled buckwheat and the fried dough of *piroshki* that I crumbled for him, and he strutted after me wherever I went. When I took him for a walk in the yard he wobbled after me like a drunk, and when he decided to stop he informed me of his intentions by cheeping, lest I go on without him. Then he would turn around on the spot, hoe the soil with his claws, pull out a worm with his beak, swallow in rhythmic gulps, and then hurry after me like an untiring suitor.

'The first time Feigeleh opened his eyes, he saw you,' explained Avigdor Ben-Ari when the chick insisted on accompanying me to kindergarten, climbing with a happy cheep onto a chair and curling up on my lap. 'So, he sees you as his mother, and wherever you go – he will go, and wherever you dwell – he will dwell.'

Proud of my little offspring, I didn't leave him alone either. With the devotion of a caring mother I shooed away hungry cats, cut bitter weeds for him in the neighbourhood's fields, dug into the soil and pulled out juicy rain worms; I chased beetles for him and with his beak he gaily cracked their brittle carapaces with a small explosive sound, as if he were cracking sunflower seeds.

At Pentecost, when all the children carried baskets of fruit and vegetables as an offering for the redemption of The Land and a contribution to the Jewish National Fund, I put Ben-Zion – who in the meantime had grown into a young rooster – into a padded reed basket that my grandmother Simcha decorated with withered flowers that hung piteously from its sides like the wrinkled skins of mouldy vegetables. I heroically ignored the evil giggling that came from all sides and carried my basket proudly, placing it on the pile of first fruits that had already begun fermenting in the burning sun. At first, Ben-Zion crowed weakly but acceded to my request that he stay in the basket a little longer and not jump out. But in no time at all he was unable to resist the temptation of the aromas that surrounded him, and with clumsy movements lifted himself in the basket, pushed himself out with the help of his colourful wings, and flew heavily over the pile of first fruits, crowing excitedly and with his black beady eyes inspecting the abundance of food that had been laid out below, just for him. His low flight ended with a calamitous cry as he made a hard landing on his rump right on top of a pile of polished aubergines. Ben-Zion, with an embarrassed movement I knew well, shook his wings that had been slightly buffeted and, hopping joyfully, went off to spy out the fragrant hill, moving from aubergine to cucumber and from cucumber to tomato, stealing a beet stalk here and a lettuce leaf there, greedily pecking at the abundance that was now his. The giggling quickly turned into roars of laughter. 'Tamara Rooster, Tamara Rooster,' crowed the kindergarten children loudly, interrupting the ceremony and the oration of the high priest in his blue robe who was blessing the pilgrims to Jerusalem, and his laughter shook the cotton-wool beard stuck to his chin and made

90

his paunch quiver. I was insulted, but the bird, from which I had not taken my eyes, did not allow his mockers to dampen his high spirits. At the end of the ceremony I demanded his return, because I had never intended to offer him as a sacrifice, but just to show him.

For all this Ben-Zion repaid me with the love of a devoted son. With wings spread wide and excited crowing he chased off children who bullied me in the playground, and when my grandmother shouted at me he pecked the big toe of her right foot, the one with the burn scars, and her shouts drove both of us outside. First thing in the morning, before sunrise, he emerged from under the blanket that warmed his body and mine, and, excited by the prospect of a new day, loosed the traditional morning cockcrow of his species. When he grew and showed the signs of a fully fledged cock – his comb swelled and reddened, his wattles lengthened, his spurs sharpened and deep copper-coloured tones began spotting his wings and the soft down of his breast – my grandmother decided that he should be put into a cage. It was then that Fishke brought a narrow cell: a skeleton of unworked wood sown with thorns, with wire netting all around it. At the front of the cage there was an opening with a round door at its side to completely cover it. This time my protests and tears were of no avail. Fishke pushed Ben-Zion, who was clucking in fear and crowing for help, into his prison, and his black pupils bored into mine through the netting with the bitter look of one betrayed.

To make amends for the detention meted out to him, I fattened him up generously and when my grandmother harnessed herself to her cart and went about her business, I let him out, played with him in the garden and threatened anybody who saw us with durance vile if they breathed a word to my grandmother. And so Ben-Zion grew fat, his wings lengthened and soon the cage was too small to hold him. His bright red comb pressed against the roof, his claws peeped through the holes in the netting, and his wings, that were of no use, hung sadly at his side. One day, when I tried to free him, I found to my horror that his fat body could not longer squeeze out of the opening and that in order to take him out I would have to cut the netting. Like a convict serving a life sentence, Ben-Zion now stood crouched in his cell, his colours fading and his fat body lax from lack of movement. Only in the early morning did he remember his proud lineage as he extended his bent throat, stuck his head through a hole I had secretly widened in the netting with a soup spoon, loudly crow his morning call, and excitedly shed a few colourful feathers and some white excrement.

Towards evening, when my grandmother went out on her business, I took the heavy cage with the fat Ben-Zion inside it and with great difficulty walked backwards and forwards with it near the house so that he could absorb with his wings a little of the late afternoon sunlight and warmth. I walked with my head held high, stopping my ears from hearing the compassionate cluckings of the neighbours, closing my eyes to the heads nodding after me and the curious glances of strangers we met on our way. And the children, Jews and Arabs, who came together for this purpose, chased after us shouting, 'Tamara's a rooster, Tamara's a rooster,' and 'What does Ben-Zion do?' They also called me mad, but I faced up to all these trials and tribulations until that Saturday morning.

That morning I was not awakened by Ben-Zion's traditional cockcrow and so I went on sleeping until I was aroused by the smell of cooking. The cage wasn't in the room and I assumed that my grandmother had taken it to the lavatory to wash Ben-Zion and his prison as she did every Saturday morning, to get rid of the bad smell that came from it. I sat on the bed rubbing the sleep from my eyes while my grandmother hurried to put two deep soup plates on the table, filled with yellow, oily liquid.

I got up and sat down at the table, brought my plate closer, and a chicken neck bent familiarly protruded from it. Horrified, I looked at her and then at her plate and the fat chicken legs in it.

'Where's Ben-Zion?' I whispered hoarsely.

My grandmother lowered her head to her plate. A single bead of sweat appeared on her forehead, slid down the side of her nose, slowly wound its way down the wrinkle of bitterness at the side of her mouth, and from there dropped right into the plate.

'Murderer!' I screamed, getting up and knocking over the chair, and ran to Widow Ziso's room, far from the smell of the cooked Ben-Zion. But the fatty smell followed me, not even leaving me when I hid in Widow Ziso's wardrobe that was filled with the smell of mothballs. All that day I mourned Ben-Zion who had been made into soup, and that night my grandmother's sleep was troubled by pangs of conscience. She only fell asleep with the pink sky of the new day and slept deeply until noon. My grandmother Simcha didn't go to Jaffa port and the market that day.

After that event my grandmother's heart softened and she didn't cook chickens again.

Some months later, on a Saturday, we were awakened, alarmed, before dawn by a loud knocking. Before we even managed to open the door, a barefoot Turkish soldier was standing in the doorway of our room. He was bowlegged like a cavalryman and his face bore an abject expression of apology. He looked at us in embarrassment, rocked a little, raised one foot and with the long black nail of his big toe eagerly scratched the shin of his other leg that was covered in dry mud and sown with the infected sores of flea bites. I jumped from the bed and for a long moment we silently scrutinised one another until my grandmother's voice was heard from the depths of her dark room: 'Who's there? Who's there, Tamara?'

The soldier pushed me aside and stood stiffly by my grandmother's bed, while she sniffed the air and enquired firmly, in Turkish, '*Neh istiyursun?*' that is, what do you want?

'You have a mobilisation order from the commander of the Jaffa district, Hassan Bey,' he replied with the shyness of a reprimanded schoolboy.

'And what does Hassan Bey want from a blind woman?' she asked derisively.

'He commands you to cook for an important guest, it's an order and you're going to him this morning,' he declaimed, turned on his heel and left.

My grandmother didn't go to the market that day and once more the pilgrims were left hungry and thirsty. Fearfully, she put on her best dress, and feeling her way at the height of the day, walked to the palace, went up the steps and stood in a long line of officials and citizens standing with bowed heads.

'You're blind,' he said when she stood before him.

'I see a little,' she replied, trembling at the sound of his voice because she was unable to forget the stories she had heard about him and the harm he caused those who did not satisfy him.

'They say you're a good cook and I want you to assist my own stupid cooks,' he informed her. A Bavarian duke was due to visit him, he added, and a banquet must be prepared in his honour that would include a dish of young turkey's testicles, a favourite of the duke's according to the telegram received from his retinue.

My grandmother, who had never cooked for governors and dukes, joined Hassan Bey's kitchen staff and worked on the banquet with them. Twenty turkeys, their legs bound, angry and screeching, were brought to the kitchen, their featherless necks turning alternately red and blue, their wings flapping and their tails spread out in a fan. Bundle after bundle they were thrown into a wretched heap of feathers, combs, spurs and toes on the filthy floor of the kitchen, evacuating their white excrement in their terror. Twenty screeching turkeys greeted Mustafa, the palace slaughterer who had been hastily summoned, with a rusty butcher's knife in his hand. There, in that kitchen, my grandmother found absolution for the slaughter of Ben-Zion. She stood there between the flapping turkeys and the slaughterer with his knife, and confidently declared that there was no need to slaughter a whole, big turkey just for its small testicles.

'And what, in your opinion, should we do?' asked Mustafa mockingly.

'Cut out their balls,' she answered firmly.

And as the bound turkeys screeched in terror, the two argued for a long time and the Turkish cooks first took her side and then his, until my grandmother Simcha and Mustafa the slaughterer went to Hassan Bey's deputy to ask him to make the decision. Hassan Bey's deputy looked into my grandmother's clear eyes and decided that she was right. That is how my grandmother saved the turkeys' lives, the Bavarian duke enjoyed a remarkable dish of testicles seasoned with Oriental spices, and my grandmother Simcha, despite her Russian citizenship, received from Hassan Bey, whose very name aroused fear among the Jews of Jaffa and Tel Aviv, status and a certificate attesting to the Sultan's patronage.

My grandmother and her twenty bound eunuchs waited until the banquet was over, and once the guests had left and she had been praised to the skies and given a few silver coins, she loaded the tortured turkeys onto her wooden cart, moved away from the palace, the market and the houses, and released nineteen turkeys in a field at the edge of Jaffa.

Like fear-inspiring highwaymen casting terror into the hearts of travellers, nineteen fat, angry, vengeful and bloodthirsty turkeys roamed the outskirts of Jaffa from that day. And many years later, after they died without leaving progeny behind them, horror stories were rife in Jaffa about that band of turkeys with their eyes of fire and their steel claws. Avigdor Ben-Ari said that he heard from Shimon, the citrus grove watchman, that one day the turkeys surrounded Mustafa the testicle-snipping slaughterer on his way home, ripped his clothing and tore his flesh with their claws and beaks, and tried to gouge out his eyes. Tattered and torn, bleeding profusely, pale and exhausted, he fled with the turkeys in pursuit until he found a lemon tree and climbed up it, and the tree's branches and thorns, with no noise and tumult, nonchalantly finished off the turkeys' job. The squawking, agitated birds circled the tree for a long time until Shimon the watchman heard their screams and Mustafa's, and he came and hit them with a stout stave, driving them off and saving the slaughterer.

'I should have slaughtered every last one of them, I shouldn't have listened to that blind woman,' wept Mustafa as his saviour led him to his house, bruised, limping and blind in one eye.

When my grandmother later heard the story of the turkeys' revenge from Avigdor Ben-Ari, who had heard it from Shimon the watchman, she burst into one of her rare laughs and pressed a hot loaf of rye bread into Avigdor's hands.

The twentieth turkey that had the most beautiful feathers, according to my grandmother, she brought me as a gift in compensation for the massacred Ben-Zion. He loved me at first sight and I was disgusted by him at first sight: by his knobby bare neck, his noisy behaviour, his perverse habit of spreading his wings and blowing up his crop as his gullet rose and fell. I particularly despised his stupid insistence on courting me and his contemptible attempts to mate with me, perhaps in memory of the pleasures he had known before he was castrated.

My grandmother, too, ground her teeth every

time she stepped into the slippery excrement he generously spread in soft piles all over the room. And when he spread his wings or scratched himself with his spurs, downy feathers were shed from his breast, floated in the air, and found their way into the noses and mouths of the people of the house, or sank into the food. But Simcha bore all this bravely. Even when he adopted the despicable and wicked habit of pecking at her feet as she passed him and frightened him as he rested, even then she didn't banish him from the house. And even during the days of the great food shortage towards the end of the war, when food supplies were almost completely stopped, she didn't so much as think of placing the butcher's blade against his knobby neck and serving us his meat. He lived with us for many years and I didn't dare tell her that I didn't like Ben-Zion the Second at all, because there was no similarity between him, big and coarse as he was, and his predecessor, Ben-Zion the First, my beloved rooster. So all those years I was forced to suffer the lordly presence of this Ben-Zion in our room, and his hopping walk that followed me wherever I went, that reminded me daily of the real Ben-Zion, whose bent neck I had found in my soup plate one Saturday morning, and for whom there would never be a substitute.

CHAPTER 6

Perhaps it was my grandmother Simcha's finely honed senses that always stood her in good stead, because she always knew when I disobeyed her and went to see her bitter rival, Grandma Abulafia. At the time I thought she was assisted by her wondrous sense of smell that had sharpened in compensation for her impaired sight, and before I went into the room I could sniff my body for traces of the sweet aromas of Grandma Abulafia's cooking, the fragrance of jasmine perfume or the sour smell of her sweat. I sometimes thought that the tone of my voice, which my pangs of conscience might have changed, had given me away, or perhaps the sound of my footsteps that also changed when I was about to lie to her. In the evening, when she came back to the room before me, she greeted me stern-faced and interrogated me for a long time about what I had been up to. And I, so as not to grieve her, made up stories. Yes, I had been walking not far from her house, I told her, but I didn't go in. And Simcha looked through me with her extinguished eyes and then she would pour out her sorrows to Widow Ziso, who served as a deep receptacle for her pain. I could hear her speaking ill of Grandma Abulafia, telling Widow Ziso that, 'That one in Neveh Zedek, no good woman, all day corset on belly and do nothing because lot of money.' I was particularly alarmed when she whispered to Widow Ziso that, 'That one in Neveh Zedek buys girl because of money.'

Grandma Abulafia indeed liked to show off the wealth with which she had been endowed. She was especially proud of the big, sun-soaked parlour in her spacious house, whose ceiling was decorated with murals painted by Sasha, a Russian church artist of Jewish origins who had fled during the Revolution. Grandma Abulafia found him in a tent on the Tel Aviv seashore, his skin red and peeling and his artist's hands eaten by lime and full of wood splinters that had stuck in his flesh when he had worked as an unskilled labourer on the scaffolding of the houses of the new city. It was Grisha, the labourer who re-inforced her roof tiles before the onset of the rainy season, who told her about him. In a loud conversation between them, he shouting from the roof and she from the ground, he mentioned an artist who was looking for churches whose ceilings he could paint in the Italian Renaissance style. And my grandmother, who since her youth had dreamed of living beneath a painted ceiling like the one she had seen in a book of photographs of Italian *palazzi*, wasted no time in looking for and finding Sasha on the beach, brought him to her house, gave him food and drink until he was sated, and didn't say a word when he covered the furniture with sheets and erected scaffolding in the middle of her parlour. She gave him a free hand, asking only one thing: that the paintings be chaste so they shouldn't upset her son Yudaleh, God forbid. For a whole month Sasha lay on his back beneath the ceiling, and when he completed his work and removed the scaffolding, Rashella Abulafia stood beneath a canopy of blue skies sown with cottony flowers of white, woolly clouds, and upon them, in every humanly imaginable posture, lay naked angels, with pink, fat, flaccid bodies. During my secret visits I loved to lie on the soft carpet spread out on the floor and concentrate on the lower part of the angels' bodies, but despite all my efforts I never managed to discover what I sought there: Sasha had satisfied his client's wishes and concealed the private parts beautifully. Sometimes with a round, pink thigh raised with all the charm of a babe, sometimes with a golden sash draped between the legs, and sometimes with a white marble column twined around with green ivy. In contrast with the organs he hid, the artist armed each angel with a prominent musical instrument: a golden lyre, a silver horn, copper bells and tiny wooden viols. And so that blessings would never leave the house, heaven forbid, in the corners of the ceiling he planted cornucopias of plaited reeds that rained golden oranges, blushing apples, rubicund grapes and split pomegranates smiling with a thousand purple teeth.

Beneath the celestial world of the angels, everyday life went on. Twelve chairs stood around a mahogany table despite the number of diners never exceeding three, and when I came to visit I was given my meals by the kitchen pantry. In the four corners of the room crouched heavy armchairs standing on big cats' claws and covered in purple velvet, and behind them four huge mirrors with porcelain urns standing at both sides, their surfaces decorated with hunting scenes from faraway places, and peacock feathers, the longest I had ever seen, planted in them.

But Grandma Abulafia's holy of holies – black and shiny with a golden, winged sphinx dozing upon it as it stood on a smooth, specially made reddish table standing in a corner by the window – was a sewing machine. Not just any old sewing machine, but a Singer.

'Abulafia bought his wife a Singer sewing machine and paid cash for it,' said the envious neighbourhood gossips. Grandma Abulafia loved sewing. Not that she needed the money, God forbid. For herself she made white Egyptian cotton dresses, for me she made shirts, blouses, vests and underclothes I never wore, and for needy brides she made bridal gowns so beautiful that they aroused the envy of the wealthy women of Jaffa, who came asking her to make them dresses, too, but she would announce that she only sewed for charity and sent them away empty-handed. And when the pampered ladies of Ahuzat Bayit heard about her, they tried to work a fast one by coming to see her dressed in threadbare clothes and stood before her with lowered eyes, like the poorest of the poor. But she could always distinguish between the needy and the impostors. 'By their underclothes, and by the pride in their eyes,' she told me, adding that she sent the wealthy women to Alla, 'Who knows how to sew, because she learnt in Beirut, but not the tiny stitches and floral decorations that only I know how to do.'

Grandma Abulafia was the mistress of her sewing machine, as if it were part of her body. First she threaded the needle with thread that matched the colour of the fabric, placed her little feet on the wide treadle and under them trampled the legend 'Singer' made out on it in high relief, and worked the treadle rapidly, one hand turning the shiny metal wheel and the other guiding the material this way and that. And the needle, as though possessed, rose and fell, trembling like quicksilver, marrying material to material with ever-increasing speed, until it vanished and was replaced before my very eyes by tiny bolts of silvered lightning. Grandma Abulafia's pair of cats also followed the whizzing movements, shaking their heads left and right, up and down, as if trying to catch up with the speed of the sewing. And when her feet stopped working the treadle and she took her hand from the wheel, she would magically pull out a new garment, still joined to the needle by the last thread like a newborn baby joined to its mother by the umbilical cord. Then she lowered her head to the eye of the needle and bit off the thread, freeing the garment to a life of its own. And as Grandma Abulafia's feet worked the treadle, the needle flying, and her head bent to the material and her very being given over to the sewing, a hollow expression spread over her face like a woman totally concentrating on an arcane ritual, then I would ask her all kinds of questions that troubled me, and she answered me absent-mindedly, unintentionally revealing secrets and past events that my grandmother Simcha would not tell me.

At that time I was troubled by the question of why Grandma Abulafia had conceded me to my grandmother Simcha, for had I grown up with Grandma Abulafia my life would have been completely different. She answered this question once, directly and unhesitatingly, her head buried deep in the material of a gown for a needy bride: 'She kidnapped you, your grandmother. The moment you came out she snatched you and didn't ask anybody if it was permitted or not.'

'But why didn't you claim me from her?' I asked, hurt.

'It was impossible to stop her. There was a look in her eyes so terrible that I was afraid she'd kill me if I even touched you.'

'And my father, what did my father say? Why did he agree?'

'Your father,' Grandma Abulafia snorted derisively, her feet working the treadle and her hands busy, 'your father loved your mother so much that he fainted and didn't even know what had been born to him.'

When she finished her sewing she'd remember that she'd told me forbidden things and would try to divert my attention and hers to other matters. She would stand by the table that was already covered with a heat-scorched sheet, the coal-heated iron in her hand, and sigh sorrowfully for me and herself, angry at the whole world and especially at herself. The hot, steaming iron moved heavily over the material like a locomotive straining to climb a mountain, subduing and smoothing the new dress as it set sharp creases in the right places. Then my grandmother, with beads of sweat springing out on her upper lip, folded the still-warm dress and wrapped it in tissue paper. When I was old enough, she would ask me to hold out my arms, place a package in them, tell me the address and ask me to go 'to the one whose dress it is'. The houses she sent me to were poor and wretched, and, like her, I too refused to accept payment for my errand. But when Yosef began joining me, he demanded payment for the delivery services on behalf of both of us. Then we started hoarding the pennies we were given in a wooden savings box that Fishke made us, and when we had enough money we went to see a film at the Eden Cinema, whose roof was open to the skies and where alley cats roamed between our legs, begging us to leave them a bit of the ice cream or *pitta* we nibbled at.

Sometimes, before she went out into the street, Grandma Abulafia would ask me to tighten the laces of her pink corset, but despite the fact that its whalebone stays in their facings were flexible, they still almost snapped under the burden of her breasts.

'Tighter, tighter, tighter, tighter,' she begged in a voice that gradually weakened as the corset submitted to my tugging, reducing the fat, imprisoning her belly, crushing her lungs and slowly squeezing the life out of her. Thus trussed, her voice came from her throat strangled and weak and she spoke only little. In the house she loosened the corset's laces, allowing her oppressed lungs to expand and breathe deeply. As she walked the loops of the laces trailed behind her majestic buttocks, and at those times of grace the cats were convinced that this was solely for their amusement. They lay in wait on the velvet cushions of their paws for the laces that twisted like snakes to the floor, and leapt at them, their claws extended to capture their prey. She tried to shoo them away with a loud '*kishta!*' which they ignored, hanging onto the laces with their extended claws and with the weight of their bodies tightening her body armour. They were sometimes joined by Ben-Zion the Second, who came with me, crowing

107

loudly and trying to catch the laces in his beak, perhaps because he thought they were worms.

I once saw her when she took off the corset. Pink waves of flesh released from their captivity rose and flowed over her belly like an apron. Without the corset she was particularly patient, loving and kind, and so I tried to plan my behaviour with her according to the corset. When her figure told me that it had been forcefully tightened, I walked on eggshells, taking care not to annoy her, ready to immediately meet any request. When it had been loosened, and especially when she wasn't wearing it at all, I curled up in her lap, sprawled on the soft folds of her fat that enfolded me into her, and loved her more than ever. On one occasion when I was asked to tighten the corset and I put my knee into the small of her back, and with this purchase tightened the laces against her perspiring back with such force that the thick material could be heard creaking as it shrank and squeezed her, I asked her why she didn't give up this rigid armour, and Grandma Abulafia answered, in that feeble voice I hated, 'When you grow up, you'll wear one too.' And I didn't like her reply, either. When I told my grandmother Simcha, who was thin, about the corset, she ridiculed it. I once heard her hiss, 'How much that one is willing to suffer for a man,' and I didn't understand. Was it Grandpa Avraham, who died when I was a child and whom I didn't remember at all, who had decided to imprison his wife's flesh inside that constricting cage, and if not, who was the man for whom she suffered so much?

Grandma Abulafia lived in the last house that stood close to the sea on the edge of the Neveh Zedek neighbourhood, on the route taken by funerals. On the rare occasions that my grandmother Simcha submitted to my pleadings and allowed me to sleep there, I'd hide the pair of cats under my blanket, sometimes peeking at their eyes shining like little lamps, and wait expectantly for a funeral procession from Jaffa to pass beneath the room's huge window on its way to the new cemetery. A distant, winding line of fireflies reflected in the window heralded the procession's arrival, and then I'd jump out of bed, go to the window, and look for a long time at the mourners carrying candles to light their way. Avigdor Ben-Ari explained to me that in Jaffa they had adopted the Jerusalem custom of not keeping the body overnight, so they sometimes buried people in the middle of the night and that was the reason for the nocturnal burial processions I saw from Grandma Abulafia's house.

On the way home from her house in the late morning, I walked barefoot on the burning sand that was spotted with shards of mica and, when the heat became unbearable, I skipped along the strip of wet sand at the water's edge and for relief stood on the cold bottom that was festooned with lots of striped shells and the delicate white lacework of the spume that had dried in wavy lines.

109

But I especially loved to go back home in the afternoon, because then I'd wait patiently until the sun immersed its body in the sea, hesitantly and slowly, like a bather afraid of the cool salt water. And when it disappeared and the edges of the pink clouds around it were embroidered with gold, the cold wind heightened and sprayed me with dry sand. With nostrils seared by the salt and ears ringing from the breaking waves, I'd bend down in the posture of the washerwomen, dig a pit in the aerated sand, uncover seashells and frighten tiny crabs on their way, in a winding run, to nowhere. Then I'd wait for a wave to turn the pit I'd dug into a magic well from which I could dredge up handfuls of dripping sand to build a castle fortified with shells. And when the castle was destroyed by the waves, I'd amble along the beach, following a camel caravan of sand-diggers to the new city, gleaming in its whiteness. As darkness fell, I'd made my way home at a frightened run in an effort to reach the room before the creaking wheels of my grandmother's cart were heard as she came home from her day's work.

CHAPTER 7

Everybody was talking about the war that was rapidly moving closer to Eretz Israel. Avigdor Ben-Ari heard about it at the bathhouse next door to Widow Ziso's house, the smoke of whose chimneys filtered through the windows, blackening the fields of lace flowers that grew on her white tablecloths.

'The English are close and the war will surely come to Eretz Israel,' he ceremoniously informed Widow Ziso and my grandmother Simcha. 'Food in the market will soon run out and you must buy a lot of staples so you won't be short.' But my grandmother Simcha wouldn't hear of it. Even when the bands of pilgrims waiting for her at the edge of the citrus groves dwindled, and even when food prices shot up, she did not alter her ritual and continued the tradition of her former life. She made the farmers' *borscht,* spat her hatred into it and carried her dishes to the groves with the noisy creaking of her cart. And although she often came home with numerous dishes in the cart for which she had no buyers, she steadfastly refused to sell to people whose voices she didn't like.

'I throw food out and not sell to hooligans,' she informed Widow Ziso when she returned one evening with her cart still full. And when the number of poor unfortunates in the streets increased, she adopted a new custom and gave away the unsold food to beggars, the homeless and lepers, who were all drawn to our house by the aromas of her cooking. They all awaited her return, lying as if in a faint by the gate of the house, scratching their heads, fingering their beards and passing the time in idle talk. When they saw her from afar, they leapt up, surrounded her and her cart, baying like ravenous dogs, fighting for each piece of food, grabbing with their fingers everything she gave them and cupping their hands for her to pour some *borscht* into them.

The day she went to the port and the market to buy her provisions and came home with her cart empty, she knew that circumstances had indeed changed.

Avigdor Ben-Ari loved to tell horror stories about that war. He particularly enjoyed describing what he called 'the Eighth Plague' that beset the country between Passover and Purim, a year after the war broke out. Hot easterly winds brought with them clouds of locusts and the insects spread their transparent wings, exposing their reddish abdomens, covering the sun and darkening the world, so that my grandmother Simcha, who never went out of the house in the daylight hours, was able to go outside at high noon without fear. For twelve days the invaders plundered the soil, devouring everything it had germinated with much labour, stripping the citrus groves of their foliage and even using their knifelike mandibles to gnaw at the fleshy, thorny leaves of the *sabras*. Once the greenery that covered the land had gone, they comforted themselves with wooden fences, telegraph poles, verandah balustrades, boats and huts. In a desperate effort to get into the houses they smashed themselves against the window-panes and were squashed between the shutter slats. A terrible tumult filled the country; brutish sounds of chewing, crushing, grinding and gnawing mingled with the noise made by the landowners who beat on metal containers and pot lids in a vain effort to drive off the enemy. Then came a government order saying that each person had to fill three baskets of locusts every day, but after the first wave came a second, then a third, and the damage was calamitous.

After the locusts, further plagues were visited on the country's inhabitants. All the inhabitants who had come from countries hostile towards Turkey were ordered to either become Ottoman subjects or leave the country. When Simcha told me this story much later, she took out the small wooden box Fishke had made in which she kept old photographs, and asked me to find the *fotografia* of Fishke. I found it, a faded, hand-painted photograph of Fishke, a sheepish smile on his face and a red-painted tarbush, as befitting a Turkish citizen, on his head. Widow Ziso, whose late father was a Turkish citizen, was allowed to remain, and Simcha, who was 'manpower vital for the war effort', carried a certificate of protection signed by the pasha and sealed with his ring.

One morning, when my grandmother Simcha came to the port to buy fish, she heard women's voices raised in lamentation. A lot of boats were anchored by the jetty, she told me, as if she were able to see the scenes with her own eyes, and they were filled with gymnasium boys who had been abducted and impressed into the army. Each of them called to his mother in his own language and the mothers waded heavily through the water trying to follow the boats sailing towards the ship, wanting to embrace their sons one last time. Their wide, soaked dresses flapped around their thighs, the babies bound to their bodies wailed with awful cries and the waves broke against their chests. And fathers, their faces burned by the sun and twisted in grief and their arms outstretched in despair, followed the outgoing boats as ragged Turkish soldiers kept the weeping, screaming human mass at bay with their rifle butts, and there was no difference between the weeping of Jewish mothers and fathers and that of the Christians, Armenians or Moslems.

As the boats moved away, the exhausted parents stood in the water waving their arms in despair and vainly trying to get a final glimpse of their son, until the boats' passengers boarded the ship waiting for them.

'*Kulu min Allah*,' mumbled Moslem lips.

'With God's help he'll come back,' prayed the Jews.

And the Christians raised their eyes to heaven, crossed themselves and called upon Jesus and Mary in supplication.

Later, when Simcha came home with her empty cart, she angrily kicked Ben-Zion the Second who was standing in her way and who even pecked at her shin, and felt her way inside where she found Widow Ziso sitting on her bed holding some crumpled papers.

'What's happened?' she asked as she heard the rustle of paper.

'You're ordered to the army camp. Jamal Pasha, may his name be erased, is coming to tour Jaffa and they want you to cook for him.'

'Just not turkey's balls,' she said, frightened, and didn't even change her clothes before going to the camp.

From then on Simcha became head cook at the Turkish officers' mess, and Fishke's Latifa was her assistant. Because of the war, the School for Infants was closed down and from morning to evening little Yousuf and I were left in the hands of Widow Ziso, who tried hard to comprehend our private language that we had made up of fragments of Hebrew, Arabic and Turkish words. We spent the days in her room, playing with blocks and toys that Fishke had carved for us, and all kinds of games I invented. Sometimes I was a

115

princess and Yousuf, who never disobeyed me, was my slave. I'd command him to bring me a glass of water or a piece of bread, and he staggered along on his fat legs that had only recently learned to walk, eager to fulfil my wishes, and when he came back I'd reward him with a kiss on the top of his head.

Latifa and Simcha came home in the evening, bringing with them all kinds of delicacies they filched from the food they prepared for the officers. Lamb kebabs, aubergines in yoghurt, a peppered salad of wheat groats mixed with finely diced vegetables, aubergines fried in olive oil and garlic, potato casserole, and for dessert, sweet *baklawa* cakes made of very thin dough spread with honey and filled with greenish pistachio nuts. I found these wartime meals far tastier than the food my grandmother cooked in normal times. She always invited Widow Ziso and Fishke, and also Avigdor Ben-Ari and Zerach Levin, and when everybody had eaten their fill she'd pack up the leftovers, give them to Fishke and send them to Grandma Abulafia's house. Fishke told us that she took just a taste of the dishes he brought her, set some aside for her cats, and the dishes that were neither meat nor milk she kept on plates covered with other plates, 'For Yuda, when he comes home for Shabbat.'

In the evening, Latifa said goodbye to us and took Yousuf, whose heavy eyelids were already shuttering his eyes. Sometimes Yousuf fell asleep before their return and Widow Ziso laid him down on my bed and I had the privilege of sleeping with my grandmother in her carved bed.

The week after Passover, when the order was given to evacuate the city of Jaffa and its surrounding neighbourhoods of all their inhabitants, Jews and Arabs alike, Simcha petitioned the Turkish authorities, asking them to allow her to remain in her home. They gave her an official application form that she had to fill out in ten copies, appending a list of relatives and friends. Avigdor Ben-Ari rejoiced at the opportunity to write, sharpened a splinter of wood, dipped it into green ink, and in cursive lettering wrote a list headed by Widow Ziso, and her appellation: 'Mother'. He dubbed Fishke 'Husband' and me 'Daughter'. When he got to Latifa he hesitated, but Simcha had no qualms at all and told him to write 'Second Wife', and for Yousuf, 'Son'.

'Why are they doing *evakuatzia*?' Simcha asked Ali, the governor's secretary, as she handed him the form and list in ten copies.

'If the war comes here, it will be dangerous to stay,' he explained halfheartedly, and although he knew she was blind, averted his eyes.

'And why not possible to stay?' she persisted.

'It's impossible to make war in city with women and babies, but you can stay,' he said, mollifying her. He also obtained a special permit for Latifa, me and Yousuf, but Widow Ziso and Fishke were ordered to leave.

The inhabitants of Jaffa, Neveh Zedek and Tel Aviv hurriedly packed up some of their belongings, boarded up windows and doors, locked the rest of their property inside their houses, and took to the road. 'Look after the house,' asked Widow Ziso of Simcha as she said goodbye.

'And you to take good care of Fishke,' asked Simcha of Widow Ziso as she stuffed into her bundle some bread, hard-boiled eggs, wedges of cheese and olives she had taken from the officers' mess and hidden in her apron.

There was confusion and calamity on the roads, said the people who returned a month later. A huge mass of men, women and children wandering around aimlessly, the wealthier riding mules and donkeys, and those whose strength failed them lying on their belongings waiting for a miracle. At night, the wandering refugees sent their children to gather animal droppings that they piled up, ringed with stones, lit fires and heated kettles of water that they infused with tea leaves or coffee grains they had managed to bring with them.

A great silence descended then on Jaffa, Tel Aviv and Neveh Zedek. It was as if all the city's birds had been exiled with the uprooted population and not even a single chirp could be heard. Only the hungry dogs that had been left behind joined the hyenas and jackals, and under the moon that was covered with blood-red clouds at the late sunset, as though hiding its face in shame, straightened their necks and howled with longing until their jaws became dislocated and they lost their voices, and they could only grunt and moan.

The exiles reached Petach Tikva where they lived in shelters and tents put up for them by the local inhabitants. Some continued northward, passing Zichron Ya'akov and Haifa, and getting as far as Lower Galilee. Others changed their minds after a short distance on the road and stole back to their homes in the silent city. Then the cholera epidemic returned, besetting the poor unfortunates, and hunger struck the weak, joyfully completing the work of Death. The bodies were put into the roadside ditches as their relatives stood by in despair, begging a shovel from the passers-by to cover their dear ones with soil, lest they become prey for the hyenas and jackals that followed the refugees, waiting patiently for the weak to collapse, languish and die.

On the day that the city of Jaffa was emptied of its inhabitants and Fishke went with them to Petach Tikva, hoping like everyone else for the English saviour who would liberate the city from the Turkish yoke, Latifa brought little Yousuf to us as she did every morning. But that night she did not come back to the room with my grandmother and Yousuf stayed to sleep with us.

Next morning, and all the other mornings of that week, Latifa did not come to us or to the officers' mess kitchen. Every evening, Simcha put Yousuf, crying from missing his mother, into her bed, hugged his warm body and whispered soothing words in his ear until he fell asleep with thin trails of salt on his chubby cheeks, the marks of his dried tears. In the morning she found him snuggled up next to me with his thumb in his mouth. When she shook him by the shoulder to wake him up, he fixed his blue eyes on her, Fishke's eyes, remembered his miserable situation and woke me up, shouting, 'Mama, Mama, Mama.'

Latifa didn't come back to Jaffa, even when the English came to Tel Aviv and Jaffa and Simcha met them with her cart filled with warm loaves she had baked in the officers' mess kitchen at the Turkish camp, that was now empty of its former occupants. The soldiers, happy with the fresh bread, continued on their way to Tel Aviv where they were moved by the sight of a modern city, dazzling with its white buildings and straight streets, that suddenly appeared like a mirage in the heart of the sand dunes. A few broke into the fine houses whose inhabitants had not yet returned, went straight to the bathroom, filled the bath and washed their bodies clean of the dust and sweat that had accumulated over the long months of desert warfare. Then they oiled their hair with lavender oil they found in the perfume cupboard, splashed eau-de-cologne onto their cheeks, put their dusty uniforms back on and went out into the white, deserted city to find an outlet for their lust. When they didn't find what they wanted in Tel Aviv, they moved on to Jaffa, gathered in the city's brothels and with the prostitutes they celebrated the end of their many days of enforced celibacy in the desert.

When the city's inhabitants returned from their temporary exile, Fishke went looking for Latifa. First he went to her room, where he found nothing missing, as if the occupant had gone out for a moment and would be right back. Fishke collected Yousuf's clothes, stuffed them into the rocking cradle, and carrying his load limped to Madame Louisa's house.

Mush mawjuda Latifa, no Latifa, Latifa's gone, the girls welcomed him with their shouts. But as they were busy with English, Australian and New Zealand soldiers whose hearts were as open as their pockets, they had no time for him, so he left and went from hotel to hotel, visited the dens of the cardsharps and drug addicts, roamed the poorer buildings on the seashore that threatened to collapse, showed her picture wherever he went – but in vain, no one knew anything.

When he despaired of finding her, he went to the police station carrying her picture. The British policemen, who had just moved into their new headquarters, promised to help him, but when he answered their question about her previous occupation openly and honestly, they shrugged reluctantly and sent him on his way. Disappointed, he went to the Achim printing shop and had them print a thousand copies of her photograph, with his address at the bottom and, at the top, 'Missing Woman'.

Over the next few days scores of people came to tell him that they had seen her in all kinds of different places, miles apart, and all at the same time, as if Latifa had split into a multitude of women who were both here and there, just to confuse the searchers.

Chaim-Moshe the tailor, whose shop was next door to Fishke's carpentry shop, told him he had seen her during the great expulsion. He was ready to swear on the Bible that she had walked by him, asking the exiles if they had seen Fishke. She had done this for three days until she disappeared. Perhaps, he guessed, her longing for Fishke had broken her heart and she had gone looking for him, from column to column, until she had been taken by the epidemic, died, and had been buried nameless at the roadside. On the other hand, Sarita the whore thought that Latifa had gone off with a wealthy sheikh who had once loved her in the brothel, and had come back to Jaffa and tempted her with gold bangles with which he had manacled her ankles and wrists, and she had succumbed and joined his four wives and numerous concubines in the harem he built for them. And there were some who came to Fishke with the picture in their hands and told him they had seen her sailing off with the Turks when they left Eretz Israel aboard the big ship that had come to take them.

Simcha didn't believe any of these rumours.

'A woman doesn't leave her son and her man just like that,' she comforted Fishke in Russian.

'So where has she gone?' he grumbled.

'Latifa will come back,' she replied with certainty, and the dark cloud over Fishke's face immediately dissipated, to be replaced by a new look of hope.

But once a year had passed and Latifa had not returned, Simcha gave Yousuf, who had remained with us as the memories of his mother disappeared, the name Yosef, adopted him as her son and he called her 'Mama'. And when I went into the first grade, my grandmother Simcha sent Yosef to a kindergarten that had opened not far from our house. Fishke used to come to us every evening, as if to a regular ceremony, and bring with him complex wooden toys he had made. He sat with us on the carpet and made them move, ate supper with us, helped Simcha wash both of us in the washtub, put us to bed, and in his deep voice sang us a song he had heard from his mother when he was a child.

CHAPTER 8

My grandmother Simcha tied up clusters of secrets and hid them in the darkness, bound up in each other and dependent from one another in a chain of actions and events, that only when joined together would provide the whole story I so craved to hear. But she hid them from me, and only from time to time, on my birthdays, would she consent, giving in to my pleadings and, seemingly against her will, detach the cluster she had selected, loosening its tight grip, peering into it to see whether this was indeed the story she wanted to tell, and unfold it drily at the table adorned with my birthday cake. The secret that I had been spared until that moment would then fill the room and shake my soul with the new revelation it brought. When she was done, she would refasten the remaining clusters lest they disentangle and escape her control, and more painful truths would be prematurely revealed to me.

After every such revelation I would hurry over to Widow Ziso's, ask her for more details and seek hidden and unhidden meanings in the words that had been said and in those that had remained unsaid, and she, despite being surprised that my grandmother had disclosed what she had, would sit me down facing her and happily weave into the story colourful ribbons to replace those that had faded, infuse it with life and movement, adding details and interpretations of her own, and even get into the characters, describing their thoughts as they did what they did, not forgetting to include interpretations of the ever-meddling neighbours.

I would then go to Grandma Abulafia and, taking advantage of her strained moments of concentration at the sewing machine, ask her questions that she would answer absent-mindedly until she finished sewing the garment; then she would break off the thread attaching it to the machine, regain her senses, regretting the forbidden secrets she had revealed to me and start speaking of this and that, of mundane matters, in a futile effort to erase from my mind the things she had said earlier.

Later I added touches of my own to the stories of the three women, that even if some would then claim that this was not exactly how things had happened, I myself know that in this way and no other I have come to be what I am today.

If my grandmother Simcha had no choice but to tell me the first secret when I was three, she managed to delay the second until my sixth birthday when I enquired and asked how my father and mother had met. It was then that I discovered that if not for the contents of a pail full of dirty water being poured into the street from a balcony, I would not have come into the world. Although my grandmother accompanied this story with unexpected smiles, it did not amuse me at all. As soon as I heard it I ran out of the house, crying over the heavy pail and the water that had been thrown from it, a wave of pity washing over me. I heard the sound of the water splashing onto the street. I felt the cold burn of the wire handle of the pail weighted down with the water filling it, and the sour metal smell seeped into the pores of my skin. I stole a brief glance at the palms of my hands for a trace of the narrow red imprint, impressed deep into the soft flesh and the quivering transparent pressure blisters full of murky fluid, and I felt sorry for my mother, the little girl whose fingers my grandmother Simcha had worked to the bone. From the time this second secret was revealed to me, I pondered questions of 'if' and 'can you': can you love a person you have never known, can I miss someone whose voice I had never heard, whose smell I had never smelt, whose touch I had never felt? And if she were here, would we love each other as mother and daughter? More than once I would find comfort by telling myself that we would probably not have gotten on, just as my grandmother did not get on with my mother – after all, I had heard it from Widow Ziso and occasionally from my grandmother herself.

When I contemplated this story of my grandmother about my mother and the heavy pail, to

126

which colourful details were later added by Widow Ziso and Grandma Abulafia, I found it difficult to understand how my grandmother, who always tried to be soft as a down quilt with me, could abuse my mother so.

'Your mother was actually a good girl,' Widow Ziso told me. 'Your grandmother, you know, has the melancholy, God protect us, which is why Nechama tried to be good to her. She helped her in the kitchen, told her funny stories to make her laugh, combed her hair. But your grandmother never hugged or kissed her. She was always angry with her. About everything. Poor thing, she tried so hard to make her mother love her, and nothing she did worked. That's why she ran away from home and was in such a hurry to get married.'

The pail incident occurred when my mother was about twelve years old. As soon as she was strong enough to wring out a floor cloth and lift, even if with great difficulty, a pail filled with water, my grandmother made her wash the floor of the small room in Widow Ziso's house every day. When she finished scrubbing and washing the floor tiles, my mother found it difficult to climb down the stairs with the heavy pail to empty it, as instructed, into the gutter in the alley that collected rainwater and sewage. In a photograph of her from that time, her body looks thin and frail, her hands too small and fragile to bear the weight of the pail. That's why, after she had finished washing the floor, so my grandmother told me, she would stand for long moments in the middle of the room, deliberating whether to make the effort of going downstairs with the pail, as she had been instructed, or empty it from upstairs. When my mother chose the easier option, she would sneak out to the narrow balcony, lean over the balustrade looking right and left and right and left again, then turn her head for fear of her mother's prying eyes, that despite being extinguished were adept at discovering breaches of discipline and minor infractions. Then, if no one was walking in the narrow alley under the balcony and her mother was not standing behind her lying in wait to catch her red-handed, she would hastily pour the water into the street.

The dirty water would splash vigorously onto the ground and quickly collect into a small puddle that would immediately send out narrow rivulets to the sides. This I deduced from my personal experience following several observations I conducted, affected as I was by the story: I emptied several pails of water from the balcony into the street and observed the results. I discovered that there is always one stronger rivulet whose head breaches the puddle and while its tail is still stuck into it, sucking from it, gathers force and momentum, separating from the puddle and flowing down the slope to the steps of the alley not far from our house. There, in front of the top step, it lingers a while as if deliberating what to do, and because it has grown weak in the course of its brief journey down the alley, some of its water starts to trickle submissively into the loosened soil next to the flat stone step, watering the thin grey grass growing from it. Only one narrow and stubborn trickle continues resolutely on its way, skipping over the obstacle of the step, slightly elevated over the street, and crawls slowly down, one step after another until its water disappears, its strength drained.

My mother would perhaps have leaned on the iron railing worked with Stars of David, leaned over it just as I did, following the turbid water's journey down the alley, sinking deep into thought from which she would occasionally awaken in fright at the force of the blow to her buttocks. My grandmother, whose sharp ears could hear the sound of a needle falling to the floor in those days, would eavesdrop on her from the kitchen, waiting for the sound of spilling water that could be heard over the exhalations of the bubbling pots, then hurry to the balcony, to my mother, the upper part of whose body stretched over the railing as if she were about to jump down, and draw silently towards her, gauging the distance to her thin buttocks, and with her wet hands slap them sharply. When she turned around in alarm, the hand would swing onto her face, slapping it and imprinting on its translucent skin a red impression of five outspread fingers. At the sound of my mother's whimpering, my grandmother would threaten that if she caught her again she'd slaughter her just as a lamb is slaughtered for the Passover, or do to her what the hooligans had done to her family in the pogrom. And my mother would cover her face with her apron, sobbing, and promise not to repeat her wicked ways. For a week she would go downstairs to empty the pail, until once again her weary arms lured her into the forbidden act, and once again she would look fearfully in every direction, and pour, and get caught, and get beaten, and sob, and promise, and keep her word for a week, and so on and so forth. It was as if she did what she did and risked her life because she knew that this transgression would ultimately bring her beloved to her.

'Strong feelings of love,' Avigdor Ben-Ari once told me, and I do not remember in what circumstances, 'are born and grow under the influence of powerful dramatic events.'

But the love of my mother and father actually began in a very ordinary event. That day, after my mother had finished scrubbing the floor, she sneaked a glance toward the kitchen, saw that no one was there, and guessed that her mother was in the lavatory. This time, therefore, she was not afraid, did not even bother to inspect the street, and did not see Yehuda Abulafia, a student at the Herzliya Gymnasium, scion of a respected family from Neveh Zedek, striding down the alley in his festive clothes on his way to the nearby synagogue, to a relative's wedding celebration. She swung the heavy pail and quickly poured out its contents before her mother returned and caught her in the act. Yehuda stood stunned, his suit drenched in filthy water, his black felt hat, purchased especially for the occasion, flattened on top of his head, his stiff unruly hair, that he had spent a long time smothering in lavender oil before leaving his house, straggly and dishevelled, and his shoes stained with damp blotches.

When he recovered, he looked up towards the suspended balcony and through the Star of David railing and saw my mother's terrified eyes as she crouched in alarm behind it.

Wet and mortified, he climbed the stairs and banged on the door with his fists. My grandmother rushed over to him, sniffed the dirty water dripping from his clothes onto the clean floor, instantly understood what had happened, and her shouted 'Nechama!' could be heard as far as the synagogue, where guests had started to gather for the wedding.

Nechama had disappeared. Flushed with anger, my grandmother vigorously patted the young man's clothes with a towel she had used to wipe her hands when she came out of the lavatory, and set out to seek her hiding daughter. She found her huddled like a frightened hedgehog under the bed. She gripped her ankles tightly and dragged her out, pinching her legs and shrieking at the top of her voice, calling her names, most of which were her own invention, and some that she had learned from her Spanish neighbours: *pustema*, mischief-maker, filthy, lazy, shrew, troublemaker, Cossack, murderer, *shikseh*, devil's spawn. And when my mother tried to escape, she clutched her flaxen hair flecked with grey clumps of dust balls that had accumulated under the bed and escaped the water, dragged her behind her and flung her at her sodden victim. Nechama's body crashed into a startled Yehuda's, and the force of the collision almost sent them both tumbling to the ground.

Yehuda pushed Nechama away from his body in disgust and looked at the thin and frightened girl standing mutely in front of him, her eyes lowered to the shining clean floor, her face contorted with fear. His angry look wandered over her unkempt clothes, penetrated her dishevelled hair, glided over her hands, rough and reddened by water and laundry soap, and fixed onto her thick lips, trembling with stifled tears. And Nechama peered at him behind her damp, lowered eyelashes, shrugged in embarrassment, stuck out the tip of her tongue and rapidly licked her dry lips. Although she had no reason to be happy, she suddenly flashed a small inopportune smile at him, as if he were her partner in crime. They stood facing each other like that for a long and embarrassing moment, until the thing that made him realise that he had fallen in love happened. Nechama must have felt a strong itch on her right leg, because she raised her left foot inadvertently and pecked at the leg with her big toe. Fascinated, Yehuda looked at the toe scratching repeatedly at the unseen spot surrounded by countless orange freckles crowding on the leg's white, translucent skin. The girl's thin body, supported by one leg, lost its balance and started swaying in small motions as if participating in a primitive courting ritual, the rules of which were dictated to her without her understanding its origin, 'And they captured and mesmerised his eyes just as an Indian fakir mesmerises the snake with his movements, or as the swaying snake mesmerises its prey,' Widow Ziso told me, not understanding at all what had happened that day and how a young man who has dirty water poured onto him falls in love with the culprit. But Yehuda looked into her eyes once again, at her tongue fluttering over her lips, at her freckled legs, and forgot his stained suit and ruined coiffure, and the wedding also slipped his mind. Hoarsely he asked for a glass of water, and Nechama, who was happy to do something for him, skipped lightly to the perspiring earthenware jug in the corner of the room, poured some cool water into a chipped enamel cup, and handed it to him. Yehuda drank without taking his eyes off the girl facing him, a foolish smile plastered over her face. He then returned to his house, lay face down on his bed in his dirty, sodden clothes, his body sweating and burning like a critically ill patient. He lay there as if crucified, his hands tightly gripping the sides of the bed, and his nails digging into the mattress. That was how Mrs Abulafia found her only son when she returned from the wedding, and immediately screamed, calling for Dr Stein from Sha'arei Zion Hospital.

Since that incident, Yehuda tried to come to Jaffa every day and pass beneath that balcony at the very same time, the time when Nechama washed the floor of the room. 'It was as though he wanted her to empty a pail of water onto him again and he would have a pretext to come up to her,' Widow Ziso explained. But from then on, my mother made sure to go down and empty the pail in the street, and the red line etched by the handle into her hand increasingly deepened.

And when she went down, she would almost invariably see him lying in wait for her at the gate.

CHAPTER 9

Although Yehuda was only seventeen when my mother showered him with rain from heaven, and she herself was not yet thirteen, he decided that this girl would be his.

Every morning, when Nechama went to the school for orphans run by the Russian nuns, to which she had been sent by my grandmother to learn Russian and thus would be able to read Russian novels to her, and especially Chekhov's stories and plays, Yehuda would be waiting by the gate as if he had just happened to be passing, and their faces would redden as if they were standing in front of a hot oven. Then he would walk her to school, take his leave of her with great difficulty at the gate and then hurry off to the Gymnasium, arriving there breathless.

Quite a long time passed in this way and rumours of the suit pressed by Yehuda, and he the son of a good family, for the wretched girl from Jaffa, reached his parents' ears. They became agitated and angry and blamed one another for the calamity that had befallen them. Avraham Abulafia, manager of the Anglo-Palestinian Bank,

135

claimed that it was all the fault of Rashella Abulafia née Meyuchas, as she had not bothered to find a suitable match for their only son. And she excoriated her husband who, she claimed, could not see what was happening in his own home, right under his nose, because he was so busy all day at the bank. But despite their quarrel that raised old disagreements and dormant anger from the depths of oblivion, they finally reached a decision: Yehuda, who was an outstanding student at the Herzliya Gymnasium and a scion of the ancient Abulafia family, would under no circumstances stand under the wedding canopy with that impecunious, thin, ugly girl who besides everything else was an Ashkenazi and nobody knew who her father was.

Nechama, too, was given no encouragement. My grandmother Simcha, who claimed that from the moment the child had emerged from her womb she had known she would bring her only trouble, accused her of casting a spell on the heart of a fine young man and mockingly interrogated her about what she had done, who had given her advice, and what potion she had given him so that the eyes in his head had been extinguished, and he now desired her like a blind man desires a monkey. On the occasions she heard the two talking downstairs, she called to Nechama to come up right away, otherwise she would feel the weight of her hand. Their suffering went on for three months. Yehuda rejected all the girls that were offered him and Nechama did the best she could to protect her skinny backside from her mother's blows, which hurt her more and more.

Then one day they came to a decision and neither of them arrived at their respective schools.

Some say, so I was told by Widow Ziso after my grandmother's death, that they went to one of Jaffa's more dubious quarters, near the port, went into a cheap hotel and presented themselves as a brother and sister who only a few hours earlier had disembarked from a ship. Years later I filled in all the missing details with the help of my imagination. I saw them in my mind's eye, consummating their love in a shabby room smelling of lechery mingled with the sharp smell of salt and the stench of fish. There, at the foot of the bed, Yehuda knelt down, dirtying his trousers with grey dust balls mixed with sand from the shore, and his eyes and hands adoring every feature of her face and body. Joyfully he counted the freckles on her cheeks, carefully touching each one; longingly he ran his fingers over her protruding ribs, licked her rough, red hands, stroked her straw hair, gently bit her upturned nose, kissed her transparent eyelashes, caressed the arches of her brows with his tongue, and drowned his gaze in the murky pools of her eyes. And when his lips felt their way to hers and found them, she felt sweetness filling her mouth, pouring into her throat, descending to her chest and spreading through her belly. Circles of honey ringed her body like the wavelets from a stone thrown into a pool of still water, each one born of its smaller predecessor and bearing one wider than it, until her entire body was filled with concentric circles of sweetness that expanded to infinity. Shame-faced, Nechama looked at the boy kneeling before her, knowing that she loved him and not wanting to understand why, lest the magic dissipate and the mystery vanish. With trembling hands he took off her clothes, carefully, as though trying not to hurt her, gently laid her down on the sweat-soaked mattress, damp from the bodies of the people who had lain on it before them, and without taking his eyes off her, lay down beside her. And when his body met hers and they became one, their mouths opened in a loud moan, and the hotel-keeper sitting downstairs next to his brass cash register was shaken out of a doze, went up to their room and angrily banged on the latched door.

Some two hours later they went downstairs to the shabby lounge with dishevelled hair, embarrassed faces and sparkling eyes. The hotel-keeper looked frowningly at his head covered with its coal-black hair and at hers, as light as a day-old chick's down, and asked nobody in particular how two such unalike people could say they were brother and sister. Yehuda remained silent and with his face burning handed him the required sum, hesitated, and added another coin. Twisted fingers ravaged by rheumatism that had spread to the joints as a result of the hotel's proximity to the sea greedily grasped the coins and a hoarse voice told them, 'Come again whenever you want.' When he went upstairs to clear up after them he found a large bloodstain on the bed. Blood had soaked through the sheet onto the mattress, coloured its seaweed filling on the way, dripped onto the floor where it had collected in a red pool.

The couple went their separate ways home and Nechama bled for a week. The colour fled from her cheeks and she was beset by a deathly fatigue. In the end, Yehuda secretly took her to see Dr Stein at the Sha'arei Zion hospital who pricked her finger and squeezed out a drop of blood. When it didn't coagulate, he gave her a severe look through his pince-nez and informed her that she was suffering from haemophilia, the disease of kings that was prevalent among Russian nobles and princes, but rare in women. He said further that she must take care not to wound or cut herself, and that it would be best if she didn't become pregnant because giving birth would endanger her life. He managed to stop the bleeding only with great difficulty and Nechama forgot his warnings and only remembered the bit about kings and nobles, and amused herself with the thought that she was a captive princess.

About a fortnight later, when Nechama had recovered from her injuries, the couple went back to the hotel and found great love in everything around them: the stained sheets, the room's peeling walls, the waves breaking with a roar against the jetty, and the rattle of seashells on the beach as they clattered against one another with the movement of the waves. Nechama continued submitting to her mother's beatings while Yehuda remained unmoved by his parents' threats to disown him; in fact the two of them were actually fortified by their love and continued to visit the hotel in Jaffa as brother and sister.

Until they were seen by Fuad, the scouring sand seller, and as he was both curious and a terrible gossip, he had asked the hotel-keeper about them. The latter brought a thick finger to his lips and answered him in a single syllable that whistled as it emerged: '*Sha.*' But Fuad, despite his not being very bright, realised what it was all about and disseminated his discovery. The rumour ran through the neighbourhood, knocked on every gate, went into the houses, sat on the beds and armchairs, wafted into ears always pricked for any morsel of gossip, rang the bell wires strung from house to house, brought the tidings to the Neveh Zedek neighbourhood and the Abulafia family's big house. And there, under the angels' sky, among the cabinets with their carved cornices and the plump couches with their red velvet curtains, it hit Yehuda's mother with a brief swoon and his father with a headache so severe that they had to call Dr Stein to attend to him. And the rumour rang along the wires until it reached Widow Ziso's house as well, went up the steps and there encountered my grandmother Simcha. At the time, it had reached the ears of almost all the inhabitants of

Jaffa and Neveh Zedek, who discussed it every which way and rolled it around in all its details and said that God alone knows how that wretch had managed to capture Yehuda's heart; maybe it was her yellow hair, and maybe her translucent eyes that whoever looked into them was dragged down to the depths of the sea and drowned.

The rumour did a complete circle, ending up back with the hotel-keeper as Nechama and Yehuda were occupied with one another on the mattress in their room with its peeling walls. When they came downstairs, the hotel-keeper put on an angry face, upbraided them for misleading him, demanded – and was given – double payment for the room, and forbade them to return.

That night, Nechama and Yehuda walked on the shore afraid, embracing one another tightly and trying to calm their fears, and when dawn broke, they walked hand in hand, in full view of everybody, first to Simcha's room and then to Yehuda's parents' house, where they openly demanded the happiness that so far had been denied them. Sitting so close they looked like a body with two heads, first in my maternal grandmother's humble room and later in the splendid lounge of my paternal grandfather and grandmother, and Yehuda said his piece in halting sentences that fell to the floor flaccid and powerless, and one pair of hands, and two pairs of hands, dismissed them with an angry, contemptuous gesture. And as their harsh looks froze Nechama's blood in her veins, she searched for Yehuda's eyes, finding refuge in them and feeling the warmth returning to her flesh and thawing it.

Much against his will, Yehuda was sent to the home of relatives in Jerusalem. In the letters he smuggled out to Nechama he told her of a city lying on the putrid detritus of a gory history thousands of years old. He wrote of the high walls that bent the stature of anyone walking by them, the piles of garbage emitting the stench of fermentation of rotting fruit and vegetables, mixed with the reek of human and animal excrement. Winter had come to Jerusalem, he told her, earlier than it did at his Jaffa home, and Jerusalem looked wrathful and frightening. Cold winds whistled through the alleys, freezing the very bones of the passers-by, boards swept away in the wind, slapping their own faces, and hats threatened to detach themselves from heads and fly away on the wind. And the people of Jerusalem are white-skinned and red-eyed, with long gowns covering their dried-up bodies, and they roam the maze of dark alleys as though moonstruck. And there are people in this city whose flesh is disintegrating with leprosy, and all the maidens are lugubrious and ugly. One day, he wrote her, he went out for a walk in the hills surrounding Jerusalem and saw the city sitting there in its isolation, shrouded in mist and rain clouds that concealed the ugliness and filth. 'I am living here partly in a monastery, partly in a jail,' he added, 'imprisoned and suffocating in a place over which hangs a curse.'

Yehuda signed all his letters with the words, 'With a great love that no one can quench'. And when my mother read them in secret, she felt her legs folding under her with desire.

This enforced separation lasted for two months, until Nechama discovered that she was pregnant. Her belly had already swelled a little, raising her dress slightly in the front, revealing her skinny legs that played no part in the joy of her rounding figure. When my grandmother Simcha heard the news, she did not wait, as she usually did, until twilight fell and she could open her eyes wide without fear, but burst out of the house in the middle of the day and into the sunlight of a clear winter's day. All the way to the Abulafias' house, black circles of the extinguished sun danced before her eyes, her hands groped the way in the dark, and as she went she fanned the flames of her anger, angrily repeating the harsh words she would say to them bluntly the moment they opened the door. And when she arrived, she stood before them and demanded a wedding, immediately, for if not the belly would swell, and when it opened, a bastard would come out and bring shame on their family. That is more or less what she told them.

This is now my parents' secret was told to me by my grandmother Simcha and Widow Ziso, and I, as usual, have embellished it a little. But the two were reluctant to tell me any more than this. I pressed them to tell me about the wedding, where it took place, what food was served and what kind of a dress the bride wore on her wedding day, and they, as if they had joined forces, dug in behind their silence. They told me I was too young and that I'd hear that story too when the time was right.

But I didn't wait and went to extract the rest of the story from Grandma Abulafia. She was immersed in making a blouse for some poor girl or other, the needle racing before her eyes in tiny bolts of silver lightning and her head bowed over the material, and at first she, too, refused to loosen her tongue. Only when I threatened her with telling my grandmother Simcha about our forbidden meetings if she didn't complete the story, she shook herself like someone awakening from sleep, angrily bit the thread binding the blouse to the needle, and informed me that she was only prepared to talk about the gown she had made for the bride, my mother. In tears, she told me how she had wept when she had heard about my mother's pregnancy. And despite her not wanting Nechama as her son's bride, she made her a wedding gown. She made her a beautiful gown for there were none better than her for making bridal gowns. She measured my mother by sight, because what they said about her was true, that 'Mrs Abulafia sews by eye'. She cut the material on the dining table and joined the pieces on my mother's rounding body. And as she sewed the decorations of tiny pearls onto the silk dress and thought gloomily about the fate of her only son, her fingers were pricked again and again, perpetuating her sorrow on the shiny fabric in tiny spurts of blood, and her eyes leaking tears added pale stains of saltiness. Despite the urgency dictated by the bride's pregnancy, she was in no hurry to complete the work and each time my mother came for a fitting, she ripped stitches and hems to accommodate the dress to the belly in which the new life swelled and altered its shape and form from day to day. In my mind's eye I could see Grandma Abulafia's lips angrily clenched around long pins, and her hands tightening the material against my mother's body until she almost stopped breathing, as if she sought to kill the foetus in her womb. I could hear the silk rebelling: creaking, groaning and complaining and finally surrendering and moulding itself to the curves of the belly growing faster than usual. I could imagine Yehuda my father, who in the meantime had returned from Jerusalem for his impending wedding, looking at her with a great love, gently stroking her belly and whispering soft words in her ear. I saw him waiting for her to leave his mother so he could walk her to her house, paying scant attention to the evil glances of the passers-by that pinned him and his bride-to-be, but making every effort to prolong their walk in order to delay his taking leave of her. He probably stopped at a stall selling coloured sweets that attracted the eye and the flies, picked her flowers that grew on the roadside, twined them into her hair and begged her to slow down so as not to tire herself. At the gate to her house they would refuse to part, standing motionless and each immersed in the eyes of the other, until Bracha, the childless woman who lived opposite and who envied the happiness of others, screamed at them from her balcony, threatening that if they went on standing there like stupid clods, she would throw cold water down on them, 'And that water,' her voice echoed down the alley, 'will separate you like they separate a dog and a bitch stuck together in copulation.' Only then would my father shake himself, kiss my mother on the cheek and walk down the alley, gaily whistling the tune playing on the gramophone of Bracha, who was the rich children's music teacher.

When Rashella Abulafia finally finished making the dress, she asked Nechama to come for a final fitting before the ceremony. My mother stood before her embarrassed, enveloped in the white material sown with shining pearls and tiny flecks of blood, with her protruding navel looking like a thick button designed to adorn the middle of the dress. With lowered eyes she followed the movements of her future mother-in-law who was tightening the thick material against her body even more. It was then that Nechama felt the first labour pain that had come a month too early. And when she complained in a low voice of another pang, they rushed her, bridal gown and all, to the Heavenly Sisters Maternity Hospital in Jaffa.

The nuns, giggling behind their hands at the sight of the pregnant bride, told her to take off the dress quickly, but no matter how Nechama tried she couldn't manage it. Hidden hooks, of whose existence and location only Rashella Abulafia knew, imprisoned her body inside the dress and refused to release it. When the labour pains came more frequently and she was still imprisoned in the obstinate dress, the head midwife's patience ran out and she took a pair of sharp scissors, the kind used to sever the umbilical cord, and without warning slit open the dress from neckline to hem.

Like the curtain of the Holy Ark in the synagogue, the dress was split in two, revealing my frightened mother's belly and stilt-like thighs. As if at a command, two nuns in their white, flapping-winged coifs appeared at her sides, took hold of the dress by the sleeves, and tore it from her body. Nechama was left standing in her threadbare underwear in the middle of the white mound heaped around her in soft waves that lapped at her ankles, and she let out a groan. Not a groan of pain, stressed Grandma Abulafia, but one of fright because of a few shiny pearls that had fallen from the dress onto the floor with soft taps, rolled everywhere and hidden under cupboards, beds and chairs. My mother followed their flight and tried to skip over the pile of material to chase them, became entangled in its folds and was again engulfed in pain. The nuns grasped her elbows, pulled her from out of the tangled dress and bore her to a bed where they laid her down. But my mother refused to part from the dress that had not

147

fulfilled its mission, dragged it after her, and as the pain lashed at her she buried her face in the rustling silk, filled her mouth with it, stifling her screams, and on her cheeks the dress left the small, circular imprint of pearls arranged side by side in the form of a flower.

Yehuda ignored the consumptive figure of the crucified Christ that observed him from above in the derisory paroxysm of a martyr, and stood in the doorway swaying and praying with great devotion. And as the cries of the woman in confinement heightened, he tried to drown them out with his voice, roaring vows and beating his breast with his fist as one repenting his sins on Yom Kippur.

'Where is He, if here, then why He not come,' whispered Simcha who did not believe in God and who had also been called urgently and arrived in a carriage. And Fishke, who had come running from the carpentry shop, his face and hair covered in yellow sawdust, sat next to her in silence, gripping her hand.

Nechama's shouts finally shook Grandma Abulafia's nerves, which in any case were on edge, and she decided to make a 'tilifon' call to the Almighty so that He could hear the mother-to-be's cries without go-betweens and have mercy on the poor thing and her unborn child. Despite being bound in the corset that restricted her movements, she left at a run, with an agility that belied her size and condition, and got into the first carriage that passed the hospital gates, promised the driver to triple his fare if he hurried, and when they reached her house, told him to wait, went inside and came out again carrying several cardboard bobbins wound around with red embroidery thread. She climbed up heavily to sit next to him, ordered him to take her to Jaffa, to whip up his horse, and there, outside the Nitmachei Dalim synagogue, ordered him to stop.

In return for a few banknotes pushed into the treasurer's hand, they opened the velvet curtain of the ark, which she herself had embroidered throughout her own pregnancy in a masterpiece of filigree, and decorated in gold and silver thread with a relief of palm leaves holding a *menorah*. With a trembling fingernail she freed the end of a thread from one of the bobbins she had brought, bound it around the splendidly decorated silk and gold vestment of a Torah scroll covered with crowns and silver pomegranates. Then, clutching the bobbins to her breast, made her way back to the hospital on foot, staggering along with great difficulty with the thread paying out behind her, following on her heels, going around houses and shops, becoming muddied in the dirt, getting soaked in the sewage flowing down the sides of the alleyways, and becoming entangled round the ankles of people and donkeys hurrying on their way. When the thread came to an end and the bobbin was revealed in its grey nakedness, she joined the end to a fresh bobbin that she grasped strongly. By the time she reached the hospital she had unwound three bobbins, and the last length of thread pursued her up the hospital steps, wound along the corridor, skirted patients' chairs, beds and bedside cupboards, and reached the delivery room. With her fingers holding tightly onto the thread, she burst in breathless, ignored the nuns trying to eject her, and pushed the end of the thread into Nechama's mouth that was open in a scream of pain, and asked her to yell with all her might, for that was the only way God could hear her cries for help. Her cries would reach His ears directly and He would come to her aid. Then, clutching her chest and fighting for every breath, her body soaked in sweat, she leant weakly against the wall for a moment, and with faltering steps left the room. Silently she sat down next to Simcha, trying to diminish her presence, and looked with concern at her son Yehuda, whose lamentations and prayers were gradually subsiding.

Simcha paid her no heed, she sat there bent over on a wooden chair whose paint was cracked, waiting in ambush for whoever came out of the room. And when some of the nuns did come out, their aprons and shoes spotted crimson and their eyes refusing to meet the looks of the people waiting, with her fingernails she peeled off bits of white paint from the chair and made vows. With each piece she peeled off, she made another vow, fully intending to keep them if only her daughter were to come out of this place alive.

'If she not die,' she mumbled, trying to ignore her daughter's groaning and concentrate on her vows, 'if not die, like queen your wedding. If not die, no more beatings.' When the groans were replaced by a rattle, and only her ears heard the nuns' despairing whispers, she swore to never again call her a Cossack, vowed to care lovingly for the grandson about to be born, and when all hope was lost, she promised to do her very best to love her. And then the cry of a baby was heard distinctly, accompanied by a whispered plea, 'There's another one, there's another one,' but the baby's voice drowned out Nechama's weak one, that gradually faded away. In the terrible silence that suddenly fell, my grandmother's voice rang out: 'If dead, not forgive.' When the last nuns came out they found Yehuda in a faint by the door and Grandma Abulafia sitting upright in her corset, as white as chalk, and my grandmother Simcha sitting bent on a chair bare of paint, her dead eyes fixed on the floor and the bits of paint spread around her in a kind of white mosaic. And her fingernails, with flecks of white stuck under their crescents, scratched her thighs until blood flowed, and Fishke stroked her hair and whispered, 'Simchi *sha*, Simchi *sha*, Simchi *sha*.'

They brought Yehuda round with light slaps to the cheeks and by sprinkling water over his face. They brought Rashella Abulafia a glass filled with strong smelling salts, and ignored my grandmother Simcha. As though awakening from a particularly bad dream Yehuda sat on the floor in the middle of a pool of water, and asked to see her, and the sister, ready to fulfil his wishes, brought me to him, washed and sleepy.

'Not that!' roared my father, not wanting to look at me. 'Her,' he said, pointing at the half-open door. With great difficulty he managed to gather his stiff limbs together from his seat on the floor and burst into the room. They refused to tell me what went on inside, but he probably clung to her body and refused to part from her until they forcibly detached him from the young girl who had almost become his wife. Rashella Abulafia, who that day exhausted all her reserves of strength for a long time to come, just sat there unmoving, her eyes fixed on the space of the delivery room that was open before her like a gaping wound, and on her Yehuda who collapsed in front of her.

My grandmother Simcha adhered to her last vow and refused to part from her only daughter. She asked the sister for the bridal gown and when she put the dress with its crimson hem into her arms, she took it into the delivery room, feeling her way until she found my crib, lifted me up and wrapped me in the dress, and I lay there quietly against my grandmother's bosom, indifferent to the tragedy that had taken place because of me.

Many years later my grandmother Simcha told me that the moment she first held me in her arms and she stroked the down of my red hair and her ears heard my rapid breathing and her nose smelt my smell, the scent of babies, she loved me with a love so strong, the like of which she had never known, and she whispered murmurs of affection to me, and made promises and vows. Then she fastened the torn gown to my naked body and made to leave the hospital with me. The nuns tried to stop her but she strode through them and carried on walking, warding them off with her resolute look of the blind. Grandma Abulafia, too, who in the meantime had recovered from her catatonia, stood in her path and tried to talk some sense into her. Simcha paid her no heed and limped out of the hospital. She carried me to her room in Widow Ziso's house, feeling her way as she walked along at high noon, and Fishke hobbled behind her, worried that she might trip and ready to support her and gather her and me into his arms. And as she made her way past the police station in her dishevelled clothes, her face excited, her hair in disarray and her eyes fixed, holding in her arms an hour-old baby swaddled in a magnificent, blood-stained piece of material, she was stopped by the police who were convinced that this was a gypsy woman who stole babies, and they asked her where she had come from and where she was going. If Fishke hadn't slipped them a few *bishliqs* and told them the awful story, it's doubtful whether they would have let her and me go.

Since then, no one has ever dared lay claim to me from her, and my grandmother Simcha bound my destiny to hers.

CHAPTER 10

My grandmother Simcha was forced to go on working for her livelihood and mine, so she washed my mother's torn wedding dress, sewed it into a large pouch, attached shoulder straps, and secured it to her front, planting my bottom into it and binding my body to hers until I learned to walk on my own two feet. She tore the remaining material into square strips and made them into diapers for me, and with her teeth tore out the pearls that clung obstinately to the material, one pearl after another, and strung them on sewing thread. My grandmother Simcha managed to fashion three strings of pearls in this way, and sold them in the market in exchange for just a few coins after she found out that the pearls were actually mother-of-pearl that had been shaped into beads. She used the money to pay Mustafa the goatherd a retainer to bring a fine milking goat to her room every morning so that she could milk it, and feed the baby with fresh milk.

Hanging on my grandmother Simcha's chest, hunched like a foetus, I dozed inside the pouch, the burning smell of her body and the fragrance of the food she cooked delighting my nostrils, and the bubbling of soup sizzling in my ears. When I opened my eyes, I would see huge pots, dark beards, copper crucifixes gleaming in the rays of the setting sun, black robes, green citrus trees, the blue of the sea, and the orange orb of the sun sinking into it. My ears heard the sound of my grandmother's pounding heart straining to pump blood for me and for her, the chiming of the church bells, the cries of the muezzin, the squeaking axles of the cart being strenuously pushed, and the rustle of the dry leaves being crushed under countless feet. My grandmother's sighs and the calls of the hungry pilgrims kept me awake, and at night, after she detached my body from hers, extricating me from the pouch, she sprawled exhausted on the bed to sleep, and I would awaken in alarm to the sound of her screams.

Avigdor Ben-Ari chose the name Tamar for me. He and Widow Ziso maintained that 'The living should not be named after the dead,' and because they feared that my grandmother would name me after my dead mother, they persuaded her to give me a new name 'so that the fate of the baby should not be the same as that of the deceased'. The name Tamar, Avigdor Ben-Ari assured my grandmother Simcha, comes from the Holy Scriptures, and is the name given to the date palm whose fruit is sweet and tempting but whose pinnate leaves are sharp and barbed. 'There is no name more suited to a red-headed girl,' Avigdor said, 'because it won't be long before we all experience her fiery nature.' When I grew up and brought him hot loaves of bread from my grandmother's oven, he would recite the verse from the Song of Solomon to me, 'This thy stature is like to a palm tree,' and tell me that with my tall stature I justified my name: how fortunate that I was not given the name of some shabby, scrawny bush! And his fellow lodger, Zerach Levin, taught me that 'the date palm is a symbol of the Return to Zion' – which I wrote in my notebook of words of wisdom.

Throughout my childhood my name was pronounced in a variety of strange intonations and accents.

Grandma Abulafia pronounced it with the accent on the first syllable, stressing the 'Ta' as if sweet honey stuck her tongue to her palate, and rolling the 'R' at length. Whereas Avigdor Ben-Ari and Zerach pronounced my name with the accent on the last syllable, and it seemed as though a succulent brown date was actually dissolving in their mouths and they were rolling it around with their tongues, extracting its sweetness, prolonging the pleasure, and when only the hard pit remained, they hurried to spit it out to avoid chewing on it and breaking their teeth.

Only my grandmother Simcha called me Tamara, and all the softness of the Russian language that I never understood was imbued in that name.

No one in the neighbourhood understood what happened to Yehuda after the death of my mother Nechama. Until she was buried in the ground and during the seven days of the *shivah* mourning period, he conducted himself like a model mourner, in accordance with the instructions set out in the mourner's instruction booklet. He wept bitter tears when she was covered in soil, whispered the *Mourner's Kaddish* prayer, sat on the floor for seven days, did not change his clothes, did not shave his beard, did not wash his face, and responded with a sad nod to people who came to offer their condolences on the death of the bride who was almost his but who had slipped away and fallen into the hands of Death wearing her wedding dress. All that time he did not speak to the condolers about the healthy daughter that had been born to him, and they did not mention her existence either. On the seventh day the undertakers found him digging with his fingernails into the mound of earth bearing a small wooden sign, 'Nechama, daughter of Simcha and Fishke Mendel, Born 2 Tishri 5660 (1900), Died in childbirth 20 Tamuz 5673 (1913),' and they were divided regarding his intentions. Some thought that he wanted to bury himself along with her, and others maintained that he wanted to dig her out of the ground. One way or the other, Yehuda struggled with the soil and the undertakers, bit, kicked, scratched, and screamed, and returned again and again to dig into the mound. When they tried to coax him, he mumbled: 'I have sinned, I have sinned, I have sinned.' Finally, they practically dug him out with a spade and loaded him and the clod of earth he clutched to his chest onto a stretcher and carried him to his house. There they laid him down on his bed and he fell asleep, his face covered in earth and the smell of death he had brought with him hovering throughout the house, reminding the living of the dead.

Next day, when Grandma Abulafia woke him up for breakfast, she found him and his bed soiled with mud, for the tears he wept in his sleep all that night had dissolved the clod of earth. But when she wanted to change the bedding, he refused, waving his arms and legs to drive her out of his room. From that day on, Yehuda did not speak to anyone and did nothing but wander around the house all day looking for her and mumbling, 'I have sinned, I have sinned, I have sinned.' But when young brides came to his mother's parlour and she fussed around them with the dress she had sewn for them, the madness would take hold of him again. Furiously, he would sneak up on tiptoe behind the bride inspecting herself in the mirror. When she detected his frightening reflection behind her in the mirror, she would scream, and Grandma Abulafia would hurry to separate him from her with her thick body, trying to shoo him away with stabs of needle and pin. But he would respond by shouting, pushing her away and reaching out to try and pull the dress off the terrified girl. Once he succeeded and the poor bride stood facing him in her undergarments, wretched and trembling, covering her bosom with her arms, and watched him in terror as he trampled the material, screaming at the top of his voice: 'I have sinned, I have sinned, I have sinned.'

Yehuda's madness quickly became public knowledge and the brides were afraid to come over, and asked Grandma Abulafia to take the trouble of coming to them. When Grandma Abulafia saw that her son was not recovering from his illness, it occurred to her to show me to him, the baby that had been born to him, and perhaps he would cheer up and return to the land of the living. She sent many emissaries to my grandmother Simcha's room, but she refused to grant her consent: 'Don't want Nechama, don't get Tamara,' Simcha repeatedly said with satisfaction. Then Grandma Abulafia came in person and candidly related Yehuda's gloomy situation to her, omitting nothing, and tried to arouse her compassion. 'Perhaps the baby will bring a smile to his face,' she entreated. But my grandmother Simcha stood her ground, and now she had a new excuse ready and waiting: she feared, Widow Ziso later told me in her defence, lest my father, who had lost his mind, would lay the blame upon me for the death of his beloved, and harm me in an act of desperation.

Day after day, my grandmother Simcha hauled me around in the pouch she had sewn, to the port and the market at daybreak, and at dusk to Jaffa's citrus groves. Until Widow Ziso, feeling sorry for me, reproached her and offered to look after me herself during the mornings and afternoons. Then, on the days that she was charged with looking after me, her loyalty to Grandma Abulafia overcame her loyalty to my grandmother Simcha, and after my grandmother Simcha left the house, she would watch the cart as it drew away through the alleys and, while Simcha argued loudly with her pilgrim customers, the widow betrayed her trust, wrapped me up in a blanket, covered my red hair with a hood, and slipped out with me, taking circuitous routes and hugging the walls of the houses, to Grandma Abulafia's house. Rashella Abulafia would be waiting for us impatiently at the door, and the two women would look to the sides like partners in crime, lest anyone see them, and would only calm down after they had been swallowed up into the house. There Grandma Abulafia would take me in her arms, draw the blanket away from my face, remove the hood from my head, breathe in my scent, click her tongue at the sight of my red chest, and display me in front of Yehuda's impassive face.

'This is Tamar, Tamar. Tamar your daughter, look at her, she looks so much like Nechama.' When she said the name Nechama, Yehuda's ears would prick up, an expression of weeping spreading over his blank face, and he would beat his breast and cry, 'I have sinned, I have sinned,' and refuse to look at me. Even when she drew me up to his nose so that he could smell my baby smell, he did not flare his nostrils, and when she laid me in his lap, he sat unmoving as though against his will. 'He looked at you,' Widow Ziso told me, 'but he did not see you; as far as he was concerned you did not exist.'

Yehuda lived his life lonely and morose, wearing his grief thin, until his mother had her fill of his presence, took action and sent him off to the lunatic asylum.

During all the years of my early childhood, my father was a faceless man to me. Only his gaunt and bent back, the back of his scalp with its thick black hair flowing from it to cover his shoulders, the tip of his straggly beard, its brittle strands sticking out at the sides, and his bony hands that continuously fluttered over his clothes as if searching for something lost, only all these I knew well. Sometimes I would see the tail of one of Grandma Abulafia's cats that had curled up on his lap rising up and swaying from behind his back, but I never saw my father stroking the cat's fur or playing with it.

He always sat this way during his short visits with his mother, his back to me and his face to the window. It was only several years later that I realised that he wanted to see the sky outside and not the sky inside, the one adorned with the chubby angels it was forbidden to see.

'This is your father,' Grandma Abulafia introduced him to me in a whisper when he came home for his first leave from 'there', and I talked to his back and asked him to turn around to face me. But Grandma hurriedly put her finger to her lips and whispered at me 'Shhh . . .' as if afraid that I would wake him up from a deep sleep, even though I could tell he was awake by his hands fluttering over his body. Later that day as I sat in her kitchen swinging my legs from the chair and nibbling candied orange peels, she asked me not to bother my father, and explained tersely that he was ill and that when he felt better he would surely be happy to speak to me. From then on I yearned for that moment, imagining the meeting with my father, his face that I had never seen, his voice that I had never heard, and his hands that I had never felt stroking my head.

And he would disappear just as he had appeared, and I never knew where from and where to.

About a year after my father had been committed, one Saturday afternoon a few hours after the meal of *hamin*, my grandfather Avraham Abulafia broke wind noisily and at great length, belched and hiccuped loudly, and expired. It was said of him that he died of a broken heart over his only son, who did not live up to the high hopes he had for him.

But Grandma Abulafia, after burying him in the new cemetery, suddenly held her head high as if a heavy burden had been lifted from her, and when she returned to her home she vowed that she would not rest until she released her Yuda from the prison

162

of his soul, extricated me from Simcha's clutches, and united the three of us into one family of three generations. Then she took in a pair of cats so she wouldn't be so lonely, and decided to devote most of her spare time to her granddaughter and to making wedding dresses for poor brides.

Then Grandma Abulafia went to my grandmother Simcha, promised whatever she promised, and obtained her consent to visit me once a week. Many years later I discovered that she undertook to care for all my needs should anything befall my grandmother Simcha, and this promise softened Simcha's stubborn objections. Every Thursday afternoon, our regular visiting day, Grandma Abulafia would take her leave of her cool parlour and beloved angels clinging to their musical instruments, lock the door to her house, get into a carriage and make the journey to our house, wobbling up the stairs to our room on her swollen blue-veined legs. Panting from the strenuous ascent – 'That one she's fat,' my grandmother Simcha would mock her, 'like climbing many stairs with many sacks of flour on body,' – she would fall onto the narrow chair in the room, legs spread and stretched out in front of her, her tiny feet tight inside her velvet shoes embroidered with flowers, and clutch the flounces of her dress, fanning her face to catch her breath. This was the moment I waited for. I liked to peek through the numerous petticoats she wore under her dress and discover the luxuriant linen knickers edged in stiff lace. I was especially fascinated by the slit gusset that revealed a sliver of her black pudenda. 'This way I can pass water without removing my knickers,' she explained to me without embarrassment when I enquired.

Memories of Grandma Abulafia's visits evoke a sweet taste in my mouth, the taste of the 'sweeter than sweet' confectioneries she would secretly feed me until I became nauseous.

On her visiting days she would measure my body with her eyes, imprinting my measurements in her mind, and, to ward off the evil eye, search for any flaws. She would then stroke my ridiculous hairdo, uttering a plaintive '*Wai, wai, wai,*' but not daring to say a word to my grandmother Simcha, lest she anger her and the quota of weekly visits she had allocated to her be reduced. The freckles dotting my skin and crowding my face were included in her list of flaws that could keep the demons away from me. On each of her visits she would ask me to uncover my arms, ceremoniously place her pince-nez on her nose, peer through it and inspect the new freckles that had appeared. She would then brush the locks from my forehead, meticulously scrutinise my face and, with her chubby fingers emitting sugary fragrances, tap my nose and my cheeks as if counting the freckles that had appeared there one by one. She would slowly remove her spectacles, hold me close to her chest until my freckles were crushed in the valley between her breasts, utter another wail of '*Wai,*

wai, wai,' and whisper in my ear as if confiding in me: 'Tell Grandma Simcha to put a hat on your head when you go out. The sun loves you and gives you many kisses, and each kiss leaves you with an orange freckle, and it is not becoming.' Then she wold sigh morosely that I was growing too fast, that the speed was consuming my flesh leaving me thin and shrivelled, pinch my arm, imprinting red squeeze marks on it, grope my thighs and my buttocks and whisper bitterly: 'Only in height, only in height you're growing, and what about a little flesh on the bones?' blaming my grandmother to herself. 'That Simcha is neglecting the child and doesn't feed her as she should. For strangers she cooks, and to her grand-daughter she denies her cooking.' And when she was done counting the flaws in my body, she would gaily complain, loudly and very deliberately, to our Father in Heaven: 'Ah, Señor del Mundo, how will she find a bridegroom with such thinness, such red hair, and so many spots on the skin.'

And then, far from her rival's eyes, she would open the bag in her lap and take out a tin box packed with candied orange peels, a jar of quince compote, a bowl of fig jam, crispy wafers, fried sugar biscuits, and a handful of nuts mixed with pale raisins. From a small pocket on the front of the bag she would take out, as if by magic, a shiny silver teaspoon and two linen napkins scattered with small lace flowers. She would spread the napkins on my knees and hers, ask me to 'Open nice and wide like a lion, because only sugar can put flesh on bones,' and patiently feed me all this sweetness, and she was not content until everything she had brought vanished inside me. I would consume so much sugar during her visits that bitter nausea sometimes spread through my stomach and a terrible dryness would irritate me, and I would drink all the cool water in the earthenware jar that stood in the room, and immediately after she left the house I would hurry to the lavatory and quietly vomit up all the sweetness and everything else, not telling my grandmother Simcha, lest she decide to curtail Grandma Abulafia's quota of visits.

Once a month Grandma Abulafia also brought me a garment she had made herself: an embroidered silk dress, a cotton blouse with lace edgings, stiff linen knickers similar to hers, a nightdress made of Egyptian cotton, and colourful kerchiefs. My grandmother Simcha would take the garment from her with a sour demeanour, thank her politely, and wait impatiently for her to leave. And when Grandma Abulafia's body was finally swallowed into the dark interior of the carriage, she would listen to the sound of the squeaking wheels drawing farther and farther away from our house, then she would pack the new item of clothing I had received into a tight bundle, and bury it in the rusting hope chest next to her bed, and mumble as if memorising to herself: 'Little girl not can be pretty. Mens look and wanting to touch.' She would dress me in simple cotton clothes that she purchased from the Arab women in the market, and in thin grey woollen pullovers that Widow Ziso knitted for me from worn-out socks that she unravelled.

Then, when Grandma Abulafia returned to us for her weekly visit, she would look sorrowfully at my shabby clothes and embark on a whispered dialogue with me as if she feared my grandmother Simcha's hidden presence in the room.

'Tamar my love, did you like the dress I sewed for you?'

'Yes, Grandma.'

'So why aren't you wearing it for me?'

'Simcha told me that we should keep it for Shabbat,' I lied so as not to sadden her further.

'Then perhaps you can come to see me on Shabbat and wear the dress, and perhaps your father can see you? He's coming on Saturday.'

'Simcha forbids it,' I had to reply.

I never wore the clothes Grandma Abulafia brought for me. Sometimes, when my grandmother Simcha took herself off to her citrus groves, I would lift the lid off the chest and inspect the bundles of garments that had accumulated there, take out one of the new dresses, try it on and get a shock at the sight of my reflection in the mirror. The dress would always be too small, and my thin legs stuck out of it, long and unattractive. I knew that Grandma Abulafia was telling the truth, that I was growing too fast and 'who would want a red bride covered in spots, long and thin as a pole?'

Indeed, in cunning and devious ways my grandmother Simcha convinced me that I was ugly, and Grandma Abulafia innocently collaborated with her, only wanting to ward off the evil eye from me.

In those days I did not understand that my grandmother Simcha wanted to sabotage my beauty. She particularly victimised my hair and would shear it into a boy's haircut. Twice a month she would sit me down on a chair, wrap a sheet around my neck, place a chipped enamel bowl on my head, and mow my hair in a straight line along the rim of the bowl. When my head got bigger and it was no longer possible to put it into a bowl, this custom came to an end, but she did not give up and tried to coax me into allowing her to cut my hair, because head lice love long hair, she said, and if she were to find even one louse on my head, she would be forced to shave my head and I would look like a waif who had run away from the orphanage. It was only when I grew older and became obstinate too that I succeeded in lifting this punishment. My hair was saved from the scissor blades: it grew long and was braided into a plait that swung coquettishly on my back. The plait grew so long that I could sit on its end, thick as a housepainter's whitewashing brush, and it was always wet due to the nasty habit I had acquired of sucking it at times of embarrassment.

In the last year of her life Widow Ziso told me that I was actually a pretty baby. Even then, when my grandmother took me with her to the citrus groves, the women of Jaffa peered inquisitively into the splendid pouch she carried on her chest and which supported my bottom, and a new question presented itself: how is it possible that the ungainly Yehuda and the pallid Nechama produced such a pretty girl. And Widow Ziso contended that the blend of two blood types that had never been mixed before, Sephardic blood and Ashkenazi blood, for instance, bestows on the offspring only their parents' good qualities. But I, with the ignorance and innocence of a little girl, believed the words of my grandmothers, and when I looked into the mirror I would see a gaunt and awkward girl facing me, elbows angular, her nose too small, and her feet too wide and too big. Once, I made a list of fifteen features and body parts that I wanted to change, to give them to my friends in return for theirs, which were perfect in my eyes. I particularly hated my big toes that to me seemed as swollen and graceless as the head of an ageing sea turtle. But I didn't like my cheekbones either: they were high and protruding like those of a Tatar, so my grandmother Simcha said, nor my rusty hair, that was cropped into a boy's haircut, and not the freckles scattered across my face and body. I would inspect my reflection with anxiety at every opportunity – any mirror, puddle, or darkened glass that I happened upon were forced to accept my image and reflect it back to me. Again and again I would be taken aback at the sight of myself and made a vow, which I never managed to keep, that I would not look at my reflection for a whole week. When I started going to school I would disobey my grandmother Simcha and make a detour to Grandma Abulafia's house, where in her parlour I would be multiplied endlessly in the four mirrors, one on each wall, that were set in elaborately carved wooden frames. And once, when I was bored, I decided to count all the Tamars I could see: an entire class of girls, all with red hair, freckled, thin, and stubborn, looked back at me, insolently sticking their tongues out at me. When I had counted a hundred, which was the highest number I knew, I vowed yet again that I would not look at my reflection for a week. The next day, when I looked into the mirror over the little basin in our room, I promised myself that when I grew up I would never have mirrors of my own, and that I would paint the mirrors fixed to the wardrobe doors black, to spare myself undue distress.

Now, as I write these words and look at photographs of myself, I see an attractive little girl who grew up to become a pretty young woman, and I had no idea. My hair was thick, sleek and red, a successful fusion of my father's hair, which was black in his youth, unmanageable and wild, with my mother's hair, that was wondrously light and soft as down. I inherited my wide lips from my mother, which on her gaunt face appeared crude and twisted, and on my face looked succulent and enticing. The colour of my eyes, blue with tiny flecks of brown and yellow, was inherited from my mother's soft, watery eyes, and was intermingled with my father's brown gaze. My height I inherited from my father, and from my mother my small hands and upturned nose strewn with orange freckles, and since I liked to run about in the sun, the freckles on my face merged to almost entirely cover it like a permanent tan. One by one I could go on counting the parts of my body in this way and enumerate which part I inherited from whom, if not for the embarrassment that gripped me, as though I was undressing and standing naked in public. Despite the embarrassment I cannot omit a description of my belly, that despite my thin figure was always round and bloated, and all those years I believed that it stuck out because of my unborn brother. And had my mother been alive, she would surely have claimed that my beauty was nothing but the spoils I plundered from my brother, because one measure of beauty was granted to us both and should have been equally divided between us. And since only I came out, I took it all.

CHAPTER 11

I concocted the tale of the unborn brother when I was six years old, immediately after I was told the second secret. Nechama, Widow Ziso told me, was convinced that she was carrying twins in her womb. Anyone hearing her say as much dismissed her words out of hand, but she was unwavering in her belief. When I asked Widow Ziso what made my mother think she was carrying twins, she told me it was because of the hiccups. Babies hiccup in the womb and Nechama could feel hiccups on both sides of her belly. First the left side hiccuped and the right side rested, and then the right side hiccuped and the left side rested, and sometimes she would feel two hiccups at the same time, on either side of her belly. At night she would complain that 'the twins were now quarrelling about who would be the first to come out.' Consequently she knitted two white woollen jackets – one edged in pink yarn for the girl, and the other, for the boy, in blue. And my grandmother would tease her and say, 'Two bastards you want, eh? One bastard not enough for you?'

Indeed, when I was born in that savage birth that ripped my mother's organs from within, she could be heard entreating: 'There's another one, there's another one.' When the midwife mopped up the blood with towels and sheets her voice gradually faded. 'Another one, another one.' Even when her lips turned blue, she was heard wheezing, 'Another.' Widow Ziso told me that even as her drained body was being lowered into the grave, the sound of her voice echoed in the ears of the handful of people who gathered around the pit that gaped like an open wound in the red loam: 'There's another one, another one, another.' She herself could hear that desperate cry of 'Another one' for several days, and the hyenas that roamed the fields surrounding the neighbourhood laughed mockingly. 'You wept,' she said, 'and the hyenas laughed like lunatics. That's the way it was every night, until we almost lost our minds too.'

One day Zerach Levin, who would come to peep at me as if he were witnessing a miracle, so he told me, angrily called me 'Bint d'ba'a' over some mischievous act. When I asked him to explain the meaning of this name to me, he became evasive and seemed to regret losing control of his tongue. Finally, when I told him that I would ask Avigdor Ben-Ari, he capitulated and agreed to explain the origin of the nickname that I had heard several times before from the gypsy women of Jaffa and the washerwomen at my friend Leah's house. 'You are called daughter of a hyena,' he said, lowering his eyes to the ground, 'not only because of their laughter that echoed your cries, but especially because your birth was the same as that of hyenas.' And he told me the tale that he himself had heard from Abu Khalil the water carrier, who filled his water skins at the well on the edge of the citrus grove Zerach Levin guarded. One night they both heard the spine-chilling, mocking laughter of a band of hyenas. Abu Khalil told him that every gravid female hyena carries two foetuses in her womb, and they are hostile towards each other even before birth. Bitter rivalry exists between them in their mother's womb, and they fight each other for primogeniture: they squabble, and scratch and bite each other's tiny bodies. Sometimes, the stronger of the two kills the weaker one while they are still in the womb and, if he fails, he pushes himself out first at the end of the pregnancy, then lies in wait in the lair for his weaker brother to emerge behind him, and immediately bites him to death. 'Hyena cubs, unlike other predators,' added Zerach as if in confidence, 'are born with their eyes wide open and they have sufficiently strong teeth to crack bones.'

'Why does he want to kill his brother?' I asked, taken aback.

'Because like a woman, the female hyena has only two teats, and the stronger cub wants to have them both. You should know that in nature only the strong survive.'

For a long time after my birth, which ended in my mother's death, that terrible tale still made the rounds in the neighbourhood and terrified pregnant women and fathers-to-be, who whispered it to one another behind closed doors and in their beds. Women gossiped about it together in small shadowy kitchens over bubbling pots, repeating the words: 'There's another one, there's another one. She said there's another one.' And when I grew a little older, the nickname 'Tamara another one' clung to me like a leech together with the other more derogatory ones 'Carrot-head' and 'Tamara rooster'. Sometimes they were all flung at me together: 'Tamara rooster carrot-head another one,' and also 'Your ma is your grandma,' and the Arab women selling their wares in the market would lower their eyes when I passed them, covering their faces with their black veils, and whispering the terrible nickname *'Bint d'ba'a, bint d'ba'a.'*

After I heard this story from Zerach Levin, my punishment became greater than I could bear. In my haste to be first, I told myself, I had ripped a huge hole in my mother causing a fatal haemorrhage until she dried up and died, and my brother died inside her. But when I looked sorrowfully at my bloated stomach, I feared that perhaps things had turned out differently and in one of the eternal power struggles waged between twins in the womb, I had ingested my brother into my body, and his tiny body was now concealed in my belly, becoming my own flesh and blood. I am a walking grave, a living monument to my twin brother, and over there, where his spirit wanders, he sometimes takes vengeance on me for the wrong I did him, striking me and trampling me from within until my entire body is shaken. It is because of him that my stomach hurts, until my grandmother lays us down on my bed with a fresh loaf of heavy, steaming rye bread bound to my belly, and the bread soothes and comforts him and me with its warmth and fragrance. Beneath the covers I would peck at its hard crust, penetrate its soft heart with my fingers, tear out crumbs and gnaw its insides. Warmth would spread throughout my body, silencing my stomach and my brother and easing my pain. And my brother would be appeased, draw close to the side of my belly, stroke me from within my depths with his fluttering touch, reassuring me with his closeness. Then I would see him in front of me, red-headed, his nose dotted with freckles, his nature like mine, and I knew that had he lived we would have dreamed the same dreams, felt the same feelings, and thought the same thoughts.

One night I asked Yosef to put his ear to my belly.

'I've got a baby there and no one else knows, only you,' I whispered to him beneath the covers.

'Little girls can't be pregnant. First they have to be big,' he replied.

'I'm not pregnant but I do have a baby in my belly,' I said adamantly, 'and I can even hear it crying inside.'

'You don't have a baby because you're not

married, and anyway, little girls don't get married,' he insisted.

Eventually, he reluctantly agreed to listen to the baby crying inside me. He hesitantly put his cool ear to my bare belly and listened attentively.

'Well?' I urged him.

'You've got noises in your belly,' he admitted in embarrassment.

'What noises?' I enquired, 'what do they sound like?'

But Yosef did not respond. He turned his face to the wall and pretended to be asleep.

Next morning he avoided my eyes and was quieter than usual.

All her life my grandmother Simcha blamed herself for her daughter's forbidden pregnancy and for the suffering her tyranny had caused her in the short course of her life. That is why she was so gentle with me, easily appeased, and attentive to all my whims, as if that could atone for the wrongs she did to my mother. She never reprimanded me over mischievous behaviour, not even when I risked breaking my bones by rapidly sliding backwards on the outer iron railing of the house that twisted from one storey to another, landing abruptly on my backside in the garden courtyard where it suddenly ended. Widow Ziso saw me sliding this way, straddling the railing with legs spread out on either side, wrung her hands and mourned my virginity. But my grandmother Simcha hushed her and said, 'It no matter, only bones matter.' She asked the blacksmith from the blacksmiths' market to solder a shining copper ball onto the end of the railing to break my descent, and indeed from then on, my buttocks always came to a sharp stop with a forceful jolt.

My grandmother Simcha was strict with me about only one thing. Her greatest concern was that my fate would be like hers and my mother's, and she would follow me like an elderly spy and watch over me with her extinguished eyes when I played with boys. Once she found me in the wardrobe, wetly kissing the neighbour's boy. It was her keen hearing that sent her hurrying from the kitchen to the bedroom and to the half-open wardrobe. When I saw her grave countenance peering at me through the mirror on the door, I realised I was in serious trouble. I had never before seen her face so terrified, as if her dead eyes had seen an angel of destruction rather than two eight-year-olds secretly exchanging kisses on a soft pile of heavy quilts covered in silk that was cool to the touch and strewn with pungent mothballs. She slapped my face for the first time and the last. When I dissolved into tears enfolded in her arms, she wept tearlessly with me and warned me to beware of men because they are dangerous. They have a stick, she explained to me, a flesh stick, and when this stick enters a girl's body, it brings forth babies.

That night, after she had fallen asleep with a sigh, I conferred with Yosef on the subject. We whispered and inspected the lower apertures of my body in the dim light of the streetlight, and deliberated on the matter. We made assumptions and rejected them, and finally selected the navel. I drilled into it, first with my index finger and then with my little finger, and Yosef did the same. Because we failed to penetrate it, I drew the conclusion that this flesh stick must surely be more adept at the task than my finger. It was only two years later, when I heard my girlfriends' version of how children come into the world, that I understood that we had been inspecting the wrong place, and that was also when my ambition to be pregnant took root. I would secretly put on my grandmother Simcha's dresses, tie large pillows to my belly and inspect my profile in the mirror. My grandmother hated my pregnancy games, reported to her with grave concern by Widow Ziso, and repeatedly cautioned me to beware of the danger of boys: 'We just look at a man, and already we have a baby.'

In those days I remembered that Fishke's Latifa, who had vanished from our lives, was apparently of the same opinion. Because one day when she took time off from her cooking, she glanced at baby Yousuf lying on his back on my bed, then sat me on her lap, touched my lower belly and asked in a whisper, '*Shu hadha?*' What's this? And when I did not know how to answer her, she said with a sheepish smile, '*Hadha ibbiq.*' She repeated this ritual with the devotion and patience of a mother trying to teach a slow-witted infant, until I learned to recite the two words, whose meaning I only learned many years later, and when she touched my crotch, I would precede her and announce: '*Hadha ibbiq*,' 'This is your shame,' and she would smile at me contentedly and stroke my hair.

My genitals were my shame, Latifa taught me, and I had to conceal them and safeguard them against the boy's flesh sticks, my grandmother Simcha cautioned me.

And wherever I went, the warnings of the two women went with me.

CHAPTER 12

As if by design, on my first day in first grade my grandmother Simcha decided to be cruel to me. Many years later I was still trying to erase those troubling scenes from my memory and they, as though etched on the inside of my eyelids, repeatedly popped up at unexpected moments to taunt me and remind me of that day that played a significant role in the shaping of my miserable sense of myself.

In honour of my first day at school, Grandma Abulafia made me a blue dress adorned with a starched, whitened linen pinafore and bought me a pair of soft, pearl-coloured kidskin shoes that gently hugged my ankles, climbed halfway up my calves and wound themselves around them warmly, where wide silk ribbons held them in place. On a chair by the bed I put the dress and shoes together with the sugar candy shaped like the letters of the Hebrew alphabet she had made to sweeten my first day at school. 'I made candy like this for your father when he went to the first grade,' she said, and asked me to come and see her in my new clothes right after school so she could show me off to the neighbours.

Yosef lay next to me that night, hugging me with his chubby arms and wailing straight into my ear, pleading with me not to leave him, begging me to take him with me to school. After I had comforted him by holding him close to my body and whispering words of love and promises and he fell asleep, I lay there wide awake listening compassionately to the sounds of the soft snores and snuffles he made through his nose blocked with the mucus of crying.

In the morning, and after a sleepless night, as my grandmother rattled her pots and pans in the kitchen, I hurried to put on my festive clothes and kidskin shoes and stole into the kitchen from behind, to surprise her in my new outfit.

'Simcha, look at me,' I shouted triumphantly, lifting the hem of my dress and putting a coquettish foot forward.

My grandmother turned to me, ran her hands, damp with beet juice, over the clothes, felt my shoes, and the look of aversion that spread over her face I will never forget.

'Not go like that,' she quietly hissed, as if to herself.

'But why not, Simcha . . .' I pleaded, looking horrified at the purple-pink stains left on the pinafore by her groping fingers.

'That's for whores,' she replied, delivering her verdict on my new clothes and giving me to understand that the subject was closed for discussion and negotiation. It was then that I first heard that word, whose meaning I didn't yet know, and that later would be heard from her lips ever more frequently, accompanying my growing-up from little girl to young girl and from young girl to woman.

'But Simcha . . .' I protested.

'Quick, take off dress and shoes and put on new trousers,' she ordered impatiently.

I hesitated, and as I deliberated on how to soften her heart, with tears or simply by pleading, Simcha grasped the lace collar and ripped it from the dress, and the scream of the tearing material sent a shudder through me. I burst into bitter tears and ran to the room with her on my heels.

'This to wear,' she said, first throwing at me a shirt and a pair of simple cotton trousers, the everyday dress of the Arab boys, and then my well-worn and dusty sandals.

I was frightened and did as she said. And I went on my way, crying as I walked and followed by Yosef's eyes, who was standing on the balcony, his head just about reaching the balustrade, waving and crying quietly as though afraid to rekindle her anger. Ben-Zion the Second pushed his red neck through a triangle of one of the Stars of David that decorated the balustrade, crowing loudly after me and bristling his feathers in excitement.

Thus I was accompanied by my grandmother's haranguing, Yosef's wailing and Ben-Zion the Second's crowing, and their gloominess prevailed over the revelry of the children who were also on their way to school, happy and gay, and who paid me no heed. In the schoolyard I joined a group of festive boys and girls who were holding the hands of their young, fresh-faced mothers, wearing light, colourful summer clothes.

Only one girl came to school by herself that first day – me.

Two by two the children formed up in a long line, and I remained at the end without a partner. I stood there, wallowing in my suffering, reliving the calamitous morning, ashamed of my pitiful clothes and ridiculous haircut, and I was filled with self-pity because of my loneliness. But I was quickly consoled, telling myself that it was better this way than to be shamed by my miserable grandmother Simcha in front of all these well-dressed children and their good-looking mothers.

Ruth the teacher sat me down next to a dark-eyed girl with long plaits, the flounces of whose dress splendidly enveloped her body and invaded my seat. She hurriedly gathered her dress to her lest I sit on it. At first I buried my face in the desktop and then I raised it timidly and began inspecting the girls in the classroom, all of whom, so it seemed to me, were sitting carefully so as not to crease their beautiful dresses, gracefully tossing their long hair or the plaits in which silk ribbons had been twined by a mother's loving hand. The teacher's words buzzed around in my head but did not register in my brain at all.

While I was still indulging in self-pity, and

infatuated by the sense of inferiority that was deepening its hold on me, the classroom door burst open. My grandmother was standing there in her threadbare clothes, her eyes fixed straight ahead and the smell of burning that came from her scorched the air in the room. Her hands, whose fingertips had the particularly well-developed pads of the blind, were hugging a small pot covered with a plate wrapped in a cloth.

'Tamara?' she said, breathing heavily.

I shrank into my seat.

'This for Tamara,' she said, extending her loaded hands. 'Where Tamara? Tamara forget take food,' she shouted.

'Tamara,' called the teacher, who had not yet had time to put names to faces, and looked from bench to bench, searching for me on the name cards pinned to our lapels.

'Where Tamara? Where Tamara?' the children mimicked my grandmother's cracked voice with loud laughter.

I froze on my bench.

'Tamara!' proclaimed my grandmother like a market woman.

'Which of you is Tamara?' repeated the teacher.

I raised my hand hesitantly and, with my face red and burning with shame, stood up and went to my grandmother, took the pot and plate from her and returned to my place, ashamed.

'Eat all,' her voice lashed my retreating back, 'All, all, all, all,' her words echoed in my head.

'I thought you were a boy,' said my neighbour on the bench, 'that's because you're wearing boy's clothes and your hair is like a boy's,' she added in a polite excuse for her mistake.

Again I buried my face in the desktop and studied the deep scratches in it and the ink blots that floated between them like blue butterfly wings.

'Who's that woman who brought your food?' she asked when the teacher turned her back on us to write the word 'Shalom' on the blackboard.

'Her? Her? She's an old woman who works for us. She's our cook,' I whispered as my insides turned over with nausea from the lie and the smell of fat rising from the pot I had put into the desk.

'No she's not, she's her grandma and she's an orphan,' came a loud, clear voice in dissent from the back. The wounding secret echoed around the room and went on pounding in my head for hours afterward.

At lunch break I swapped the contents of the pot for a *pitta* full of the flavours of goat's cheese and pitted olives with my neighbour on the bench. Her name was Leah, she told me, and I asked her to call me Tamar. And as I chewed her *pitta* and she sipped my soup with gusto, she turned her round eyes to me for a moment and whispered, 'It must be good being an orphan, because everybody feels sorry for you.' I mused on what she had said and just as I was about to reply, she added, 'And besides, you can do whatever you want because nobody tells you what to do.'

For a long time after she went to skip rope with some other girls who had invited her to play but not me, I wondered if she was right, but even if she were, what is it that I want to do, I asked myself, and didn't know what to answer.

On that first day I made myself a habit to which I adhered throughout all my years at school: in order not to be suspected of lack of concentration, I would focus my eyes on a certain spot I chose on the teacher's forehead. Sometimes I lowered the spot to the tip of her nose or even the centre of the depression in the lower part of her throat, and I'd stare at it for a long time until the teacher became two, and once I'd perfected my focusing power, I saw three and even four teachers. And once, during a particularly boring lesson, after I had been staring at her for a whole hour, I counted eight of her.

At the end of that first day at school, my grandmother Simcha was waiting for me at the school gate, her eyes blinded by the noon glare that mercilessly robbed her of the little sight she had left. I skirted her in a wide arc, adopting a faltering gait so she wouldn't recognise the sound of my footsteps and then began walking quickly in the direction of the house.

'Tamara!' she called, groping in the unfamiliar surroundings, her arms spread wide and her fingers outstretched, trying to hold onto the rough stones of the school wall. 'Tamara! Tamara!' she pleaded as she followed me. I dug my heels into the burning sand that poured through my light sandals, kissing the soles of my feet with a burning biting, kiss.

'Don't follow me,' I ordered her.

'Tamara, wait for Grandma,' she said, ignoring me.

I quickened my pace until I was almost running along the neighbourhood's dusty paths, and she limped after me, tripping and calling after me in a strangled voice. 'Tamara wait, Tamara wait.' At the entrance to the neighbourhood, the houses closed in on me, they too breathing heavily like asthmatics and following me with the compassionate look of their open-window eyes.

'Tamara?' she panted as she came into the room after me, looking with her blinded eyes towards where she imagined I was.

'Don't you dare come to the school,' I shouted angrily. 'Do you hear? Never again, never!' I screamed. Angrily I took off the wide trousers and fell onto the bed, burying my face in the pillow and weeping bitterly.

My grandmother didn't answer but sat down heavily on a chair and buried her head in her hands, her shoulders quaking. For the first time in my life I saw her really weeping. Yosef came quickly, frightened out of his mind, and stood stock-still between us until he decided to take action, and ran from me to her and from her back to me, trying to console her, and me, and again her, and then me, until he finally gave up in despair, sat down on the floor between us and he, too, started sobbing. I got up and hugged him and dragged him to my bed and calmed him down in my arms, stirred by his black eyelashes that were stuck to one another in small points, lighting up gleaming stars, damp with tears, around his eyes.

From that day onward I never forgot to take the meal she prepared for me every morning, so she would never again surprise me with a visit to the classroom, God forbid, and I made a food pact with Leah, whose mother's dishes were far tastier than those made for me by my grandmother.

I don't really know if it was that incident that made me loathe school from the outset, or whether I was fated to hate it with no connection to it at all. In any event, I was never able to get used to the rigid timetable imposed on me, to waking up at a predetermined time, the ringing of the bell that always interrupted me in the middle of something and disrupted my thoughts about my miserable existence, and my envy of my classmates who all seemed prettier than me, happy and gay, the rustle of their dresses driving me out of my mind. For three years I stared at the teacher, doubling and quadrupling her, or decorated my exercise books with coloured butterflies until I was able to draw almost any species with amazing precision. At the end of every term my reports bore the legends, 'Disgraceful', 'Beneath criticism', and 'Bad', while the words 'Perfect' and 'Good' were never to be seen.

In my third year at school Yosef joined me. With a serious expression, as if all the troubles of the world rested on his shoulders, he walked with me hand in hand, my old leather satchel containing the big, rough, wooden pencil box that Widow Ziso had given him, just like the one she had given me on my first day, ruining his shoulders too.

Yosef, who was curious to know what was written in my books, taught himself to read and write before he entered first grade, and he also learned addition, subtraction, multiplication and division. So a month later he was advanced to second grade and in the middle of the year he joined my class and I found myself sharing a bench with him. Despite my complaining that I didn't want to study with babies, I enjoyed Yosef's diligence. Within a short time he, the little one, became the best pupil in the class. And when he was bullied during break time and they called him 'Arab and Arab, Arab and Arab', and sometimes even 'Your mother's a whore and your father's a cripple', I wrestled with the bullies and fought his battles by scratching and pinching and hitting. And when they finally retreated, their clothes torn and faces bruised, they yelled at me from a distance, 'Tamara Carrot-head! Your ma's your grandma and your dad's mad!'

But Yosef repaid me very generously, and when I went on my secret visits to Grandma Abulafia, or to play with Leah, or to wander on the seashore and through the alleys of Jaffa, he did both our homework. At night we'd snuggle up together in one bed and he'd tell me horror stories he had read in books, about man-eating, bloodsucking vampires and about people who lived on other planets, while I would tell him about enchanted princesses who fell in love with the prince who came to free them from captivity.

I would sometimes ask him to put his ear to the left side of my chest, hold my breath and tell him to listen to the sounds of my murmuring heart. Then I'd ask him to describe the heart murmurs, and in return I would put my ear to his chest, listen to the beating of his heart, that would heighten, and by clicking my tongue against my palate, tick off his heartbeats. Then we'd compare the sounds and try to discover the difference between my sick heart and his healthy one.

We continued playing our nocturnal games until I was eleven and my breasts began budding. Then Yosef demanded that Fishke make him a separate bed. Our room became crowded and Fishke closed off the balcony with beams, leaving a little opening, and I had room of my very own.

CHAPTER 13

Fresh white paint covered the ceiling of Grandma Abulafia's parlour, and the plump cherubs, they and their musical instruments, had been blurred under a thick layer of paint, becoming faceless and nondescript blotches.

There I found my father, thin and stooped.

Six years after he had been committed, and three years after the end of the war, my father was discharged from the asylum. The British doctors who had come in the wake of the victory examined him, asked him numerous questions and decided that as he was harmless, even to himself, it would be better for him to go home.

'He's vowed to become a monk,' Grandma Abulafia whispered to me solemnly at the door of her house when I came to visit, but I was so excited that I forgot to ask her what a monk was and why she'd covered my angels with paint.

My father was sitting down, but contrary to his habit of years past, he now had his back to the window and faced me. I could finally see what he looked like. His face was like that of 'the gypsy who kidnaps little girls' who appeared in my nightmares and in my grandmother Simcha's warnings, who forbade me to go to the market without her, because 'There are many black *tzigane* there, take bad girls.'

I stood before him and scrutinised his face with interest.

My father's cheeks were sunken as though he had sucked them into his mouth, dark hollows had been dug out under his eyes, his nose was aquiline, and the long, tangled hair of his head and beard gave him a threatening look. I looked at his hands scuttling back and forth over his clothes that hung on him pitiably. His fingernails had grown wild and were tipped with dark crescents. I was surprised that Grandma Abulafia, who always insisted that mine be cut down to the quick, had not said anything about this to her own son.

My father looked at me with interest and his lips twisted, as if in a malicious smile, but his eyes were clouded and serious, as though he had just heard some bad news.

The awful impression he had made on me dissipated when I heard his voice. 'Tamar?' he softly spoke my name in a gentle, melodious and pleasing whisper that won me over completely.

I nodded happily, thinking to myself that it was exactly in this tone of voice that fathers were supposed to talk to their daughters.

But my father's look froze and his lips suddenly began trembling, shaking his overgrown beard in strange movements, and the shock slid down from his beard to his chest that rose and fell rapidly, like the chest of man who has run a long way. His whole body rapidly contorted in ludicrous dancing movements. Enchanted, I watched the act he was doing especially for me, to amuse me, so I thought, until he buried his face in his hands and I heard strange gnashing and the sounds of the snuffling of a runny nose.

Grandma Abulafia gently patted his back, as though trying to pacify a baby with wind, and told me to leave the room with her.

'Let him get used to you,' she begged me outside, 'don't be upset by him. He's hurt. He cries at everything just like a little boy.'

'But the angels, where are the angels, why aren't there any angels on the ceiling?' I asked, grieving for my chubby childhood friends who had suddenly vanished.

'That was his condition for coming home.'

'To cover them with paint? Why?'

'It's because he's a monk.' She repeated the word I didn't understand as she pushed me towards the door and asked me to come back to visit again next day, 'For a short while, so he can get used to you little by little.'

That evening, equipped with a loaf of rye bread and my red notebook, I knocked at Avigdor Ben-Ari's door, eager to hear his explanation.

I took a big bite of bread and with my mouth full announced the startling news: 'Grandma Abulafia says that my father is a monk.'

Avigdor's eyes widened in surprise. 'Yehuda? A

monk? Impossible,' he mumbled as if to himself. 'I know him, he can't be a monk.'

'But that's what he is, that's what Grandma told me,' I said, hurriedly swallowing the dough filling my mouth and giving the remainder of the loaf to Avigdor. I wet the point of my indelible pencil with the tip of my tongue and later saw in the mirror that I had accidentally drawn purple dots and lines on my tongue and lips. On tenterhooks, I opened my notebook at a fresh page, wrote the title 'Monk', and asked Avigdor to explain the word to me.

Many years later I found his definition in my notebook: 'A monk is a man who mortifies himself by suppressing his lust thus intensifying his powers.' And beneath that line there was another sentence, as obscure as its predecessor, that I didn't understand then either, despite my writing it down word for word as Avigdor dictated it, with no mistakes, because Avigdor willingly and patiently always spelled the difficult words for me: 'The monk converts the vague suffering of life into meaningful pain.' And then, in a fresh paragraph, came a whole lecture: 'A monk is a man who mortifies himself, that is, he torments his body and soul. Sometimes he tortures himself to atone for a sin he has committed, and sometimes to set himself apart from this world and its vanities, that stand between him and God. Some monks do not cut their hair, like Samson in the Bible, others do not drink wine, and there are those who live without any property and shut themselves off in tiny caves in the desert. A small number of monks go as far as taking a vow of silence, and from the day they do to their dying day, they do not utter a single word.' And I remember that he hesitated for a moment before adding, 'And almost all of them do not take a wife.'

'That means that you're a kind of monk too,' I shouted triumphantly when he finished dictating, happy that I had finally discovered Avigdor's secret.

But Avigdor lowered his eyes and this time, totally out of character, he remained silent.

Next day I went back to visit my father who spent a long time looking at me and only with difficulty held back his tears. Later, I went to visit him every day and our meetings gradually lengthened. After a few weeks had elapsed, he whispered with trembling lips, 'If Nechama could only see you, the way you are, she would be so proud,' and that was the first and last time he spoke my mother's name to me.

One day, when I felt particularly comfortable with him, I suggested we play father and daughter. 'When you come home from work,' I said, explaining the rules according to what I'd seen at Leah's house, 'I ask you, "Father, what have you brought me?" and you answer, "I've brought you a little present."'

'A present?' he asked, astonished.

'Yes, you always have to bring me something small, like a sweet, or Victorian cut-outs you've bought just for me.'

And really, over the next few days, waiting for me in his pockets as deep as a well were little gifts: transfers of pictures of the Land of Israel, cards from the 'Our Greatest Poets and Writers' series, a coloured pencil, a new pencil box, and I'd climb onto his lap, pulling his beard and kissing his cheeks in gratitude.

Despite my father not having to work for a living, because my grandfather had left a great deal of property and money, he made up his mind to become a greengrocer. Fishke built him a wooden cart like the one he had built for my grandmother, and like her he went out first thing in the morning to the wholesale market, filled his cart with fruit and vegetables and pushed it around the alleys, shouting his wares and stopping to talk with the people he met on his way. Everybody liked him and they said he was 'the most honest and generous greengrocer in Jaffa and Tel Aviv'. Because after he finished weighing the produce on his scales, he would always add another piece of fruit or a vegetable, while he never added even a penny to the price. That was because he feared, so he once told me, that the second-hand weights he had bought had become heavier after years of use and were inaccurate, and that in the Abridged Code of Jewish Laws, the *Kitzur Shulchan Arukh*, it is written: 'Measure should be given generously, there should be more than the just measure, as it is written "give full measure and righteousness shall be thine", and what is the meaning of the word "righteousness".'

It was also said that the scales should always be in good working order, he told me further, and so he always wiped them clean between customers, between weighings, lest a grain of soil stick to the pans and tip the scales adversely for the customer.

In the evening, when his cart was empty, he went to the synagogue in Jaffa and on his way came to our room with vegetables and fruit he had set aside for us. And my grandmother Simcha accepted them with a sour look on her face and mumbled her thanks through clenched lips. Throughout her life, so it seemed, she blamed him for her daughter's death and nothing he did to conciliate her or to come closer to her, would help.

A long time afterwards, when I lived in the church with Christodolos – and I never told my father about him so as not to break his heart – I finally plucked up the courage to ask my father why he had decided to become a monk. My sudden question took him by surprise and at first he answered me vaguely, that he lived a life of abstinence so as not to cause injustice to pure souls. But when I persisted, he went on to say that life in this world arouses man's drives, his lust, brings him constant suffering and does not allow him to serve the Lord wholeheartedly. Only through celibacy can he be free of them and give himself over completely to a spiritual life and the fear of God.

When my breasts started to bud, my father began avoiding me and our meetings were no longer as frequent as they had been. When I tried to sit on his knee or hug him, he would push me away and tell me to stop that, it was for little girls and not for a grown-up girl who would soon be a woman. He once even raised his voice at me when I brought my lips close to his and asked for a kiss. Later, he would often shut himself up in his room when I came to Grandma Abulafia's house, and she would apologise for him and ask that we leave him alone and not disturb him in his seclusion. But I still knocked on his door, informing him in a loud voice that I was there, hoping that perhaps he might change his mind and come out to be with me, and before I left I would always say goodbye through the closed door and receive a dry, weak 'goodbye' in return.

On one occasion, when Grandma Abulafia was not at home and was unable to protect him from me, I insisted on seeing him. I hammered at the locked door with the lion's-head doorknocker and shouted through the keyhole that I missed him and that I wouldn't budge until he came out and talked to me. In the end he let me in and we sat facing one another for a long time, and he was silent, fixing his eyes on the floor as if afraid to look at my face, and his fingers combed his beard in embarrassment.

His words hit me like a thunderbolt, and I felt that all my loved ones were conspiring against me and a noose was tightening around my neck. 'Keep away from men,' he told me, pleading as if his life depended on it, 'it mustn't happen to you as well.'

CHAPTER 14

My grandmother Simcha was a heretic. I first heard the word from Avigdor Ben-Ari in a long conversation I had with him about religion and God. In my notebook, under the heading 'Religion', I quoted him as saying that 'A heretic is a person who refuses to acknowledge the existence of God, like your grandmother Simcha. And she doesn't believe in Him,' he added, 'so much so that she doesn't even complain to Him about the hard life He has given her, for only people who believe in God are allowed to address Him with protests and complaints.'

And indeed, Simcha never lit Sabbath candles, never went to the synagogue, didn't celebrate the festivals and never mentioned the name of God. Actually, she did mention it now and again: '*Bozhe moy*', my God, she used to cry in Russian, either when surprised or angry, but she didn't mean the Almighty.

My grandmother's heresy did not have many supporters among the inhabitants of Jaffa of that time. All of them, so it seemed to me, worshipped one Supreme Father, and only His name on their lips – Theos, Allah or Adonai – varied in accordance with what their origin dictated at the moment of birth. And although at the time people liked preaching to their fellows, especially if they were different from them, and liked interfering with their fellows' activities, nobody dared to try and change my grandmother Simcha's philosophy or to try and bring her into the fold of their belief and religion.

'Where's God? Why not come? Where was He when Nechama died?' she once yelled at my father Yehuda when he brought her fruit and vegetables one day, and suddenly and accidentally mentioned the name of God. And he lowered his eyes and kept silent.

Only once did I raise the matter of my grandmother Simcha's heresy with Grandma Abulafia. And on that occasion, much to my surprise, she took her side, thus breaking the rules of their age-old dispute, the seeds of which had been sown with the ruining of the splendid wedding dress that Grandma Abulafia had lent my grandmother Simcha, and which had germinated with the senseless falling in love of their children, and then blossomed with my birth and the 'disgraceful act of kidnapping you', as Grandma Abulafia put it. But on this occasion her round face wore an expression of great misery, as if someone had tightened the laces of her corset to the point of suffocation, and she told me in a serious tone: 'A woman who has gone through what your grandmother has, has no reason to believe in the Creator. Not ours and not our enemies'.' And when I asked her what she meant, she sealed her lips and wouldn't agree to say any more or tell me when and why my grandmother had lost her faith.

I couldn't extract any precise details from Fishke either. When I went to see him at the carpentry shop and asked him about it, he stuffed a handful of nails into his mouth, silently imprisoned them between his teeth, and with maddening slowness took them out one after the other, and hammered their slender bodies into a plank with short, sharp, angry blows of his hammer, until they all stood in a straight, crowded line like a battlement. I would lie in wait until he took the last one from his mouth to get back to the purpose of my visit, and once more Fishke bent over his box of nails, stuck his fingers into it unhappily, took another handful into his callused palm, again stuck them between his teeth, choked back a cough deep in his chest, and I kept quiet lest he suck a lethal nail into his lungs on my account, God forbid.

I didn't give up and interrogated Avigdor Ben-Ari. He once dictated into my notebook a scholarly reply, which back then was beyond my grasp. 'Religion demands that a person worship it, and it rewards him by providing his spiritual needs, brings succour to the travails of his soul, supports him at times of uncertainty and provides him with answers to questions of essence and existence. And the fact that your grandmother is a heretic is perhaps a good sign, a sign she has a robust soul, that she has all the answers and she doesn't need the kindness of religion.' And in a fresh paragraph I wrote down his words, 'In all matters pertaining to God, our world is divided into two types of people: those who believe that God created Man, and those who believe that Man created God. Your grandmother apparently belongs to the second kind.'

'But if God exists and she doesn't believe in Him,' I remember asking him, frightened, 'then perhaps He may punish her for it?' And he replied, 'Your grandmother has already been punished so severely that it's enough for ten sinners and even more.'

'But why has she been punished?' I asked, but he did not answer.

My last chance was Zerach Levin, and it was he who taught me a new word: 'Atheism', and for my notebook dictated the words of Pushkin, his favourite poet: 'Although there is no consolation in atheism, it is, unfortunately, the most reasonable world-view to hand.'

My grandmother's heresy was particularly noticeable in Jaffa for belief resided in everything in the city: its sounds, smells, scenes, the people's clothing and even in their faces. Everybody belonged to a defined group of believers that was delineated by language, customs and houses of prayer, and these distinguished them from other groups. And although everyone was united in bearing the heavy yoke of religious faith, in a kind of unity of contrasts they created a unified city in which everybody and everything combined together and merged, like the vari-formed, -shaped and -coloured pieces of a mosaic, that despite everything create a single, whole picture.

And at that time I tried to hold onto the overall faith as a counter to my grandmother's heresy and wandered the alleyways of my city, among its numerous churches, mosques and synagogues. The churches raised their bell towers on high, the mosques pricked the sky with the needles of their minarets, and the retiring synagogues lay hidden among the limestone palaces.

A cacophony of voices, ringing, hymns and melodies called upon the One God of many names. The church bells rang out in honour of the Holy Trinity, from their pinnacles the minarets sent out the muezzins' splintered cries of woe to Allah, the One and only God and Muhammad his Prophet, the thunder of the cannon made no distinction between Jews, Arabs and Christians, waking everyone up in the dead of night to inform them of the obligation of the fast of Ramadan, and the blasts of the ram's horn announced to all that the Jewish Days of Awe had arrived and Yom Kippur was in the offing. All these sounds stubbornly vied with one another over which of them would rive the heavens and reach the ears of God.

It was on one of my many meanderings through the city that I became aware of a new religion, that of the prostitutes, and of their flock of believers, men. I discovered the sites of its ritual, the ritual of the flesh, whose temples were spread over the lower town, near the port. Rising above the other buildings and distinguished from them, these holy places stood out in their loud colours and fluted columns supporting round balconies enclosed by balustrades blossoming with iron flowers. In contrast with the apertures of the rest of the city's houses, whose eyes were always closed with layers of wood from behind which glinted the jewels and eyes of women hiding from the lustful glances of men, the windows of Jaffa's temples of pleasure were open wide. Plaster flower stalks adorned them from above and the stained-glass windows blinked at the passers-by with their open shutters and winked at them with their panes. And the prostitutes who leaned out from them, Christian, Arab and Jewish, dressed in the apparel of their faith, the faith of harlotry, solicited the believers with the language of seduction known to all: their red mouths agape, their fleshy tongues swinging like a pendulum between their teeth, and they smacked their lips and whistled and cooed in hoarse voices to raise the men's heads to the décolletage and the breasts above the windowsills.

Long queues wound in front of these temples and members of all religions and statuses stood there side by side with a most impressive restraint: Christians of all persuasions, Moslems, Jews, Armenians, and even representatives of His

Britannic Majesty in their white suits, topees and magnificent moustaches. They went upstairs one at a time and came down a short time later, bodies fatigued and faces glowing.

On one occasion when I was standing at the foot of such a house, watching all that was going on around it, I saw Fishke limping along. He didn't have to wait in the queue because a well-dressed *matronita* suddenly appeared, wearing coloured fathers stuck into the tower of her coiffure, pushed her way through the men thronging the doorway, ploughed through them until she reached him, linked her arm through his and led him inside. And then his wooden leg was drumming on the marble floor, a piece of which I saw each time the door was opened, tapping on its black and white tiles arranged like a chessboard.

I waited there a long time until he came out. The tapping of his foot was swallowed up by the banging of the metal shutters as they were closed on the market shops, and the creaking wheels of food-sellers' carts as they got up from their resting places and made their way home, aromas of unsold food still rising from their pots. The sweet-potato cooks, the lupine-seed and sugared-almond sellers, and the children offering prickly pears and corn on the cob slowly disappeared from the alleys. A cool wind was already blowing from the sea, drying the sweat of the day and, with their scythes, dozens of silvered crescents rising from the domes of the mosques kissed the reddening sky, seeking to join the pale stars that had just come out.

I tiptoed behind Fishke, whose face was shining in the last rays of the setting sun, and followed him until we reached my grandmother Simcha's house.

'I saw you coming out of there,' I called, surprising him.

Fishke turned around and looked at me, perplexed.

'I saw you coming out of there,' I repeated, 'and I'll tell Simcha and Yosef on you – unless you tell me why Simcha doesn't believe in God,' I added threateningly.

Fishke looked through me as if I wasn't there and shoved an imaginary fistful of nails into his mouth. At a fast limp he climbed the steps to the house and went into our room, with me on his heels. We sat down to eat and I glared at him in silent rebuke. But he avoided my hostile glances, swallowed his soup and chewed his food in silence, and as he got up to leave he asked me to accompany him. He limped heavily down the steps and I slid rapidly down the banister, banging myself as usual on the copper ball that had been fixed to the end, and waited eagerly for him by the gate.

'Not now,' he told me when he finally reached the bottom.

'Why not?'

'I can't tell you now, you wouldn't understand. As soon as Simchi wants to, she'll tell you,' he said, dismissing me and limping away from the house as if fleeing for his life. I followed his disappearing back and it seemed to me that his walk was particularly heavy and his limp more pronounced than usual.

Frustrated, I went back to the room, looked into my grandmother's eyes, and yet again dared not ask her why she didn't believe in God and what was the secret they were concealing from me, and when would she finally agree to make me part of her secrets.

'A man who needs women sometimes buys their bodies,' I wrote in my notebook under the heading 'Prostitute'. That is what Avigdor Ben-Ari said to me when I told him about the new temples I had discovered, holding myself back from blurting out Fishke's secret. 'That is woman's degradation at the hands of man. If the woman has no money to live, the man pays her for the temporary enslavement of her body.' And I remember him adding angrily, 'Disgraceful,' as if my question had aroused in him a great, accumulated anger that burst out at that moment. But when I asked him to tell me more, he silenced me and suggested that we didn't talk about things like that, which 'are inappropriate for the pure ears of little girls'. And he tried unsuccessfully to go back to delving into the black handprints of the Arab youths he met at the bathhouse.

CHAPTER 15

My grandmother Simcha forbade me to go into the Turkish bath, possibly because Widow Ziso, whose house was next door to the bathhouse with its smoking chimney that made her life a misery, called it 'a den of iniquity' and added ominously that 'all our troubles will come from there'. At the time I didn't understand what she meant. I asked Avigdor Ben-Ari, but he shrugged uncomfortably and grumbled into his beard that Widow Ziso was possessed by demons and it would be better if I didn't listen to her.

The bathhouse, that was a meeting place for the neighbourhood's residents, was open seven days a week. Men and women flocked there, carrying soap and a towel under their arms, and coming out with their bodies perfumed with scents of rose-water and lemon, their hair pomaded with lavender oil and their backs bearing the sweetly painful red stripe marks left by the bathhouse attendant's twig switch.

Widow Ziso was revolted by the bathhouse and complained bitterly about it to anyone willing to listen. Her house was there first, she said, and the

209

bathhouse was built years later, and had she known it was to be built, she wouldn't have built her house there. The noise of the bathers heard in her rooms drove her out of her mind, and the smoke from the chimney blew into the house showering the furniture with flecks of soot and dirtying the laundry hung out to dry on the roof. And when she closed the windows on Fridays and on holy day eves, which were particularly busy days, everybody roasted in the heat of the sun. The soot reached everywhere, even into my shorn hair, and when my grandmother Simcha washed it in the washtub she complained that the water turned black, even though she was unable to see it.

Thursday was bath day in Widow Ziso's house. She lit the Primus stove in the lavatory – that was also the bathroom – put a big pot on it, and when the water boiled we held the bathing ceremony one after another. When it was my turn, I stripped naked, took the dipper, scooped some water from the pot and splashed it onto my feet to test its heat. If it was too hot, I'd add some cold water from the big tub in the corner whose water was used for washing behinds and hands. After soaping my body with the heavy laundry soap, which sometimes slipped from my hands, fell onto my feet and sent a dull shock of pain through my body, I'd scrub my skin over and over with the bristly loofah lest my colour be insufficiently red and then I would fail the test and be sent back to the lavatory. From behind the door, Widow Ziso and my grandmother

Simcha persistently reminded me, in chorus, to wash behind my ears, scrub my neck, my stomach, and most especially 'wash down there'. The lavatory was dark and narrow and the wheezing of the Primus stove sounded like a barn owl and a snake hissing at each other in the darkness. I would sometimes splash water onto it by mistake and the wheezing would fade and thick, stinking black smoke would darken the room even more, choking me. Red and scratched I would flee right into the big sheet held open wide by Widow Ziso, and she would wrap me up in it and rub my body until I pleaded for my life. Widow Ziso loved bathing and drying me. 'It's because she got no babies,' explained my grandmother Simcha, and in her voice I could hear a pleading note, that I agree to sacrifice my skin for her.

In contrast to the mortification of my skin and flesh that I suffered in the lavatory, I imagined the bathhouse next door as paradise where beautiful, plump women lay supine on warm velvet divans, and Sudanese servants, whose bodies gleamed with fragrant oil, splashed lukewarm rosewater onto them and caressed their bodies with soft, fluffy towels. I had heard about the place and its wonders from my friend Leah, who went there once a week with her mother and sisters. 'Because they have no place to wash body in house,' my grandmother Simcha informed me firmly when I complained and asked, 'Why is Leah allowed and I'm not?' and gave me to understand that I should be happy with my lot and that I would never see the bathhouse from the inside.

The bathhouse was a centre of gossip: '*mikveh neiess*', bathhouse news, is what Avigdor Ben-Ari called the tidings he brought us from there before they were spread around the city. In the women's section, so Leah told me, you could see a swelling belly before you saw it in the street. And only in the bathhouse were you able to know, by the marks on the body, which of the women had been beaten by her husband. In the public bathroom, Leah said, the women were occupied with all manner of treatments. With hands encased in rough gloves they scrubbed each other's backs, helped one another to cut their nails or remove hard skin from the soles of their feet. One woman there removed the pubic and underarm hair of brides on the eve of their nuptials with the help of strong sewing thread held between the teeth. The thread is twined around the curly hair, and she pulls it out by the roots to the victim's screams. On betrothal or wedding days, the bathers are given bowls of red henna, and they would rub the bitter-smelling stuff onto each other's heads, while the experts, using thin twigs, drew delicate designs of dots, flowers, birds and butterflies on the hands and feet held out to them.

When Yosef was eleven, he was taken to the bathhouse by Fatima, his mother's best friend from 'there'. Fatima came to visit him once a month when she would also visit the bathhouse. On one of these occasions, and that one time only, she managed to smuggle Yosef inside without Simcha's knowledge. He later described for me the horrific sights he had seen there: huge backsides spotted with red pimples, folds of fat falling from bellies that covered private parts like an apron of flesh, heavy breasts hanging down to the navel and swinging to and fro with each of their mistresses' movements. And the smell was acrid, sickening and strange, he said, totally unlike anything he had ever smelt. And when I teased him, asking how he felt standing naked among all those women, he answered joylessly that they looked unashamedly at his penis that suddenly hardened and stood erect, and pointed at it, giggling. And one of them, who Fatima said was called Allegra and who was the most famous madam in Jaffa – and at the time he had no idea at all what a madam was – bent over him until her nipples tickled his head, grasped the head of his penis and tugged it gently as if testing how far it would reach and, to the raucous laughter of the women there, told him affectionately not to worry, it would grow.

When I compared Yosef's testimony with Leah's, I couldn't understand how the two of them had provided me with such vastly different descriptions of the same experience from the very same place.

Of all the people who lived in our house, only Avigdor Ben-Ari fully enjoyed the bathhouse and its facilities. Every evening, when he finished his day shift at Mr Horowitz's citrus grove, he crossed the narrow path separating Widow Ziso's house from the bathhouse, and was swallowed up in the large crowd of men congregated in the main bathroom in the men's section, that was spacious and tiled with pinkish Carrara marble. Stories of pleasurable intercourse were heard there as well as stories of the city's new and beautiful prostitutes. On the wooden benches, profitable business deals were sealed with a handshake and a kiss on the cheek, and important political messages were whispered surreptitiously.

An hour after he went inside, Avigdor came out with a purified smile on his face. His hair and beard were washed and pomaded and his steaming, pallid body bore the red marks of the switches. From the bathhouse he took the young men he had met there right up to his room, to fully investigate their skulls and bodies for the racial theory he had developed.

Our Jewish neighbours, who could no longer suffer the bathhouse's soot and tumult, left Jaffa and moved to the clean, white city where pretty gardens separated the houses and flowers bloomed and green trees provided shade. But Widow Ziso and my grandmother Simcha kept faith with the old house and despite the trouble the bathhouse caused them, they stayed in Jaffa. Every now and again our former neighbours came for a Sabbath visit and told us of the wonders of the new city, all of whose inhabitants were Jews, where there were no smoking bathhouses, nobody pushing and shoving and cursing and spitting, and even if you left your door wide open, no thief would go inside and steal your property. And the air there was fresh, the houses had spacious rooms and the lavatory and kitchen were not outside, but actually inside the house, and, wonder of wonders, fresh water sprang from a spout in the wall. So when our visitors came they looked contemptuously at our ramshackle water pump standing in the yard on its one leg, wretched and ashamed, as though it was to blame for the emptiness of the cistern from which it sucked. The exiles wrinkled their noses when they recalled the sight of the ruined cistern in the dubious service of Abu Khalil the water-seller, and the water-skins he brought them in the summer, filled with water that had a stench and the depths of hell rising from it. They even mentioned to Widow Ziso the small stones, bits of mould, dead beetles and the red mud-worms that Abu Khalil always poured with the water, but she defended his honour fiercely. 'Even in summer he never missed a day,' she said in his defence, 'and you,' she fired at them, 'who will guarantee you that water will come out of the wall every day? Perhaps the spout will dry up one day, and you'll come to drink at my house so you won't die of thirst.'

Avigdor Ben-Ari and Zerach Levin didn't even give a thought to leaving the room they rented from her. Avigdor in particular spoke about Jaffa with great sweetness, as if describing a beloved. And when he was asked why he didn't move to the new city, he answered with a question: 'And why should I leave Jaffa? Is life bad for me here?'

Sometimes, when my grandmother was busy in the citrus groves and Yosef was bent over his school books, I'd knock on their door and in the doorway, that was wide open, one of them would always be standing before me because when one went off to his shift in the grove, the other one would return from his, and vice versa. Two folding canvas beds stood there on the coloured tile floor, dozing under old, woollen blankets, thin and holed from much washing. Orange crates standing unsteadily one on top of the other served to hold the few clothes and books they had brought from over there, and three more crates had been converted into a pair of chairs and a table. The room had two balconies, one facing north with a green landscape of blossoming citrus groves and tall palms bursting through it into the room, and the other facing west, revealing golden sands and a broad, sparkling strip of sea. On that balcony stood a single straw stool, on which each of the room's two occupants sat in turn, thoroughly enjoying the cool breeze blowing from the sea, whose gusts dispelled the heat. I especially loved the smell that hung in the room: in the spring the fragrance of citrus flowers that the two brought with them in the folds of their clothing, and in the winter the sourish smell of ripe oranges that rose from their tunics and pockets.

The evening was Avigdor's time for rest and

relaxation and when I knocked on the door, with Ben-Zion the Second at my feet, swaying impatiently, I would find him there clean and composed after his visit to the bathhouse. If he had no other visitors, he would spread a white handkerchief on one of the box-chairs and gallantly invite me to sit down. And Ben-Zion the Second, who was also a welcome guest at Avigdor's, would spread himself at my feet, indulgently close his eyes and wait for our host to stroke his head affectionately and call him Feigeleh the Second. Avigdor would sit down on the other box and ask how madame, that is me, was, peel an orange and divide it into perfect quarters, lay them out on a plate in the form of a lucky four-leaf clover, and offer it to me. In return for his oranges and the words of wisdom I put down in my notebook, I would bring him fresh rye bread on weekdays, straight from my grandmother's *tabun*, and on Fridays and festival eves – a light-coloured plaited *callah* sown with plump raisins that had been soaked in sweet wine, from the *challahs* my grandmother had baked to sell to the city's Jews. Avigdor would lovingly clutch the *challah* to his chest, circle the room with it in a slow dance, whisper secrets to its plaits, and as he did so would tear off plait after plait and stuff them into his mouth. Again and again he would tell me the story of the *challah* of his childhood, forgetting that he had already told it to me on numerous occasions, how he used to take home the *challah* that had just been taken,

217

hot and sweet, from the baker's oven, and by the time he reached home its plaits were torn and its body was full of holes, and his mother would smack his bottom until in the end she sent his younger brother to the baker's instead of him. Avigdor treated the rye bread with the greatest consideration and respect. With a blunt knife he sliced slice after slice, gathering up the crumbs that fell like dark manna from heaven onto the orange crate with a spit-wetted finger, while quoting apologetically, 'He who leaves crumbs on his table is as an idolater.'

Ben-Zion the Second followed suit, pecking up from the floor the fallen crumbs that Avigdor had missed. The three of us had a common passion, a passion for bread. 'For one loaf of bread we are even prepared to steal, aren't we, Tamar? Aren't we, Feigeleh the Second?' he asked with a wink, for all we needed was to smell the aroma of a steaming loaf as it was taken from my grand-mother Simcha's oven, and right away we felt so good. And my ravenous hunger would be so acute that on many occasions I would snatch the still-hot loaf, tear off pieces and swallow them without chewing, even before the bread mingled with my saliva. I sometimes devoured a whole loaf this way and then had a stomach ache, but perhaps my stomach also hurt because of my grandmother Simcha who held that 'hot bread is hurting in stomach'. And yet she didn't stop me. On the contrary, she was happy to see me so eager for the bread she baked; 'It's your Russian blood,' she joked, calling me 'my Russian girl'. The tone of her voice told me that this was a compliment, the only compliment I received from her, and to this day I recall it whenever the smell of fresh bread fills my nostrils.

Avigdor, too, was convinced that our excessive excitement over bread, and our longing for it, stemmed from the Russian blood flowing in our veins, because, after all, we were not pure Jews, so he claimed, and he adopted bread as part of his personal ideology, added the required refinement, and accorded his longing a philosophical, universal meaning.

At the time, I regarded Avigdor as an extremely old man. Today I know that he was only in his mid-thirties. 'Avigdor the romantic' was what Widow Ziso called him, despite us never having seen him in the company of a young woman. He had green eyes – 'Because he looks so long at the green of the groves,' said the widow – with the fresh, damp gleam of a leaf covered with morning dew. With an expression of wonderment, like that of an infant investigating the world around him, his eyes opened before me, framed in a network of fine flat lines that gradually deepened when he smiled, until they became rays coming from the sun in the drawings of little children. His cheekbones stood out in his thin face, whose skin was as taut as a drumhead, his hair was yellow and sparse and his long beard that was streaked with white, brown and yellow hairs gave him the air of a Greek philosopher. Widow Ziso, who knew him well, said of him that back in the Ukraine he had been a *yeshiva* student and a prodigy, and he had come to Palestine because of the pogroms there. Here he was introduced to secularism, divested himself of his long *kapote*, removed his velvet skullcap, and joined up with some dubious characters from whom he learned Arabic and Turkish, in which he was now fluent. Avigdor sat for hours in the room he shared with Zerach Levin, putting his thoughts down on paper with a curved quill that etched them onto the thin paper used for packing oranges. He once told me about his sensational discovery on which he had laboured for many years, ever since he came to Palestine.

'The Arabs in the Land of Israel are Jews,' he disclosed to me.

'But Arabs are Arabs and Jews are Jews,' said I, daring to disagree with him.

'You're right,' he replied, 'but the Jews and the Arabs are from a single origin, and that is my discovery.' He added that the noble, powerful and proud Arabs of the Holy Land of our time were a recreation of the Jewish farmer of Biblical times. But he went no further and promised that when he had made more progress with his studies he would present his complete theory, point by point.

About a year before the disaster that befell him, he told me about the history of the Arabs of Eretz

Israel since the time of the Romans. 'Although the Romans took thousands of Jews captive, men, women and children, sold them into slavery or ordered them to fight in the arena as gladiators for the people's amusement, thousands of Jews remained in this country. The majority of the Jewish People, brave farmers, did not go into exile but held onto their land and continued working it,' he told me solemnly. 'Under Christian rule some were forced to convert to Christianity, and many others converted to Islam when the country fell into the hands of the Arab conquerors. And the Palestinian Arab,' he trumpeted with a grand flourish, 'Abu Khalil the water-seller, Khaled the greengrocer, Ra'if the bath attendant, and handsome Moussa, are all the offspring of those same Jews, and are quite possibly pure Jews, purer than you and me at any rate. And if you roam through the villages and look carefully at the bold *fellahs*, you will see they resemble Sephardi Jews, there is absolutely no difference between them.' At the sight of the disbelief in my face, he had the good grace to admit, in a low voice, that 'Perhaps some have a sixty-fourth part of Arab blood.' He later taught me a new word, 'race', and quoted from the Bible, 'And there shall come forth a rod out of the stem of Jesse', and on a paper before him he drew a tree trunk, giving it a lot of branches to illustrate for me that 'The Jews and Arabs of this country are the branches and rods of this one trunk, and so the close relationship between the Palestinian Arabs and Jews is even closer than their relationship to the Arabs of the neighbouring countries.'

I wrote down all of the above in my notebook under the heading, 'Avigdor's Arabs are Jews'.

When I pressed him on how he could say that the *fellahs* are purer Jews than me and him, he got up and took the broken piece of mirror hanging from a nail on the box-cupboard, and held it in front of us: our heads were reflected in it, his yellow one next to my red one, and his green eyes roamed over my face and his.

'Take a good look at our physiognomy – my hair is yellow and my eyes green, and your hair is red and your eyes are blue. We both have high cheek-bones, which is common in Tatars and rare in Jews,' and he ran his hand over my cheek as if seeking to emphasise my cheekbones. Then he brought the broken mirror up to my nose and added, 'And I've forgotten the most important thing. Please look at your snout.' I sorrowfully focused on my freckled nose until I was squinting, and I suspected him of just wanting to tease me. 'Your nose is upstretched to the sky,' he said, interrupting my morose thoughts, 'it's unlike a Jewish nose. Our looks are not those of the children of Shem. You can see right away that we have a mixed racial heritage and, indeed, in exile our Jewish blood was mixed with other blood. And it is actually the Arabs who are the true Jews, for they remained in this country over all those years and their blood was not mixed with the blood of Khazars and Tatars and Cossacks.'

I was ashamed to ask him who the Khazars and Tatars and Cossacks were, and in any case, as he had spoken with such absolute authority, I assumed he was right and only the mention of my nose bothered me, the nose that together with another fifteen organs I would willingly have exchanged for others.

'My nose isn't a Jewish nose?' I asked, insulted, as though asking him to at least withdraw from this particular observation.

'You have a nose upturned to the sky, a gentile nose, a snub nose, *kournosaya*,' he said, affectionately mocking me in Russian, and declaimed: 'Thy nose is as the tower of Lebanon which looketh toward Damascus.'

'And it's not a pretty nose,' I said, making an assumption I hoped he would refute.

'God forbid,' he replied with a pretend shudder.

'But they say my nose isn't pretty,' I wailed.

'And who is the scoundrel who says your nose isn't pretty? Show him to me, let the villain stand up and face me!'

'They all say so,' I lied.

'Then send them to me, I beg you,' he suggested, 'and I will prove to all of them that there is not, without a shadow of a doubt, a prettier nose than yours.'

But when he looked at me and saw my crestfallen expression, he was sorry that he had touched upon such a sensitive subject and rummaged in his box of books, took out the Socrates volume, blew clouds of dust from the author's likeness and showed me his snub nose – see, his is upturned as well!

'Listen to what Socrates had to say about noses,' he said, amused, and told me that Socrates had held a mock beauty contest with his young friend Critobulus, 'who was as handsome as an angel fallen from heaven,' noted Avigdor with a deep sigh, and read me what the two contestants had said, which in the book he held had been translated from Greek into Russian, from which he translated for me into Hebrew, and I wrote it all down in my words of wisdom notebook under the heading 'Nose'.

'Critobulus to Socrates: Whose nose is more beautiful, mine or yours?

'Socrates to Critobulus: Mine. If we agree that the gods have given us noses with which to smell, then your nostrils point downward whereas mine are wide open and turned outward, so as to catch odours more efficiently.

'Critobulus to Socrates: How can you say that an upturned nose is more beautiful than a straight one?

'Socrates to Critobulus: Because an upturned nose is no obstacle to vision, and the eyes can see without impediment anything they want to. But a high nose walls off the two eyes.'

Avigdor banged the book closed, stroked the tip of my nose, tickled the top of Ben-Zion the Second's head, and said, 'And this is the proof. Socrates, whose wisdom is beyond doubt, held that an upturned nose is more beautiful and useful than a straight nose, albeit he forgot to mention that it's hard to blow an upturned nose. For in the straight nose, the nose juice drops straight down of its own volition, while in yours, *kournosaya*, it is sucked into the throat.'

When I took my leave of him, he remembered what he had said earlier about the Jews and Arabs, and in the doorway he said, like a kind of prophet: 'Look, with the advent of the Messiah, they will all become Israelites again.'

'And what about Yosef?' I asked during another talk, 'is he a Jew or an Arab?'

Avigdor thought about this for a few moments and then replied that according to the Jewish religion, Yosef is considered an Arab as his mother is an Arab, because with us a child's religion is determined by its mother's religion. But the Arabs hold that the child's religion is determined by the father's religion, so Yosef is considered a Jew.

'And what about you?' I asked. 'What is Yosef for you?'

Avigdor scratched his head, perplexed, and again deliberated a while before replying, then finally delivered his unequivocal verdict: 'Yosef is a perfect Jew, more than me or you.'

At the time that Avigdor was working on his studies, he used to bring Arab youths he met at the bathhouse to his room, and conduct 'racial examinations' on them. He asked Fishke to make him a big wooden clamp, the jaws of which were separated by a metal screw, and he would open the jaws wide and then gently tighten them on the youths' heads, thus measuring the circumference of their skulls. Then, like a tailor, he would measure the circumference of their waist, chest, calves and thighs with a tape he had filched from Grandma Abulafia. Finally he would pour a little ink onto a pile of paper, grasp the hands of the youth being tested, and press the palms onto the inksoaked pile and, once the hands were black, he would ask the youth to place them, fingers outspread, on a white sheet of paper he placed on the orange-crate table. 'So I can thoroughly examine the lines on the palms of the hands and the fingerprints,' he explained, adding that, 'On the palms and fingertips of every human being there are lines and whorls that are unique to him or her.' Avigdor told me further that he sought to complete his study by comparing blood samples taken from Jews and Arabs, and that he had already approached Yehudit, a nurse at the neighbourhood clinic, to lend him a syringe for taking the blood. But he later gave up this plan when he remembered that he didn't have the money to buy the instrument that would enlarge an ant into an elephant, or even a magnifying glass, so he consoled himself with the fact that blood is blood, everyone's is red, and that perhaps no real difference would be found between Jewish and Arab blood.

Meanwhile he had accumulated huge piles of

papers containing the measurements, drawings, and fingerprints of scores of Arab youths.

At the end of the tests the youths fled his room on unsteady legs, with blackened palms and greenish faces, but with pockets full of biscuits and coins, and Widow Ziso would see them coming out and bite her lips, saying to my grandmother Simcha that she didn't like the whole business of Avigdor's measurements, he'd only bring down trouble on his head, and perhaps on all our heads.

Most of the youths who came to Avigdor's room never went back, because having their body parts measured once sufficed. Only handsome Moussa, who sold corn on the cob at the seashore, the handsomest young man I had ever seen, came back regularly. His skin was dark brown and smooth, his face narrow, his eyes the eyes of a young deer, brown and glistening, adorned with long silken lashes, and his pomaded hair was combed back and smelt of lemon blossom. His red lips were fleshy and sweetly impudent, and when opened in a smile they revealed even, white teeth. He and Avigdor sequestered themselves in the room for hours deliberating on matters of race, so Avigdor told me and Yosef, warning us not to dare open the door of his room when handsome Moussa was there. At the end of the consultation handsome Moussa would come out of the room, flash his fresh smile at us, run his hand over my head and Yosef's, look long and hard into Ben-Zion the Second's evil eyes, and ask him the question usually asked of turkeys, '*Aymta shaher Ramadan?*' When is the month of Ramadan? And when the turkey answered with an excited crowing, handsome Moussa would burst into a ringing laugh and sail off on his way, whistling gaily. I once went into the room immediately after handsome Moussa had left and found Avigdor completely exhausted from so much work. He lay on the bed in a deep sleep, his chest bare, covered in a thin wool blanket drenched in sweat that he refused to part with summer and winter.

Not everyone endorsed Avigdor's theory. The first and most critical of its opponents was Zerach Levin, the co-occupant of his room, whose face became flushed with anger when I once asked him whether it was true that all the Arabs are Jews.

'He's been talking to you about the powerful and proud Arab, the noble savage, eh? He told you that this Arab is the Jewish farmer of ancient times, didn't he?' fumed Zerach. 'Just look at them,' he wheezed in contempt, 'their eyes are covered with the pus of trachoma, they're savages, weak and spineless, cruel and ignorant. They're even crueller than the Russians who ran riot against us. Only a lunatic like Avigdor could say that they are the ancient Hebrews of yesteryear.' And Zerach raised his voice to me angrily, as if it were me who had invented this theory, and warned me not to let Avigdor fill my little red head with all kinds of mouldy rubbish, and I remember how his face contorted in anger and white froth showed at the corners of his mouth. 'The Arabs want to spill our blood,' he told me, and I wrote down what he said in my notebook, under the heading, 'Zerach's Arabs'. 'There will always be clashes between Jews and Arabs. They see us as invaders and will constantly try to throw us out and we will always be obliged to fight them. In every way. That is why we must not intermingle with them or allow them to intermingle with us, and Jewish society here in Palestine must remain separate and distinguished from their national and cultural environment. Because we have come from peoples with *kultura*, and if they become assimilated into us, we will descend to the level of the savage peoples' *kultura*. For all these reasons there is no point in learning their language, because that language, like the Arabs' culture, is poor and we have no need of it.'

I wrote down Zerach Levin's words verbatim, but I still didn't fully understand them. Not even when I heard him say to Widow Ziso, about a week before the riots, this frightening sentence, which I hurried to perpetuate in my notebook as well: 'They may be many and strong, but the Arab only respects those who stand against him heroically and courageously, and we will overcome them, but only in a war in which both our blood and theirs will be spilt, until we are victorious – and thus our nation will also be built.'

At that time, when Zerach came home in the morning from his shift at the citrus grove, my grandmother Simcha used to invite him to join us for breakfast. He had managed to gain her affection, mainly because he always brought with him a basket full of oranges and lemons, and he offered her this gift of fruit with great solemnity, as though he had won Ali Baba's treasure trove for her, which Latifa had once told me about, and not fruit he had filched from the very trees he was supposed to guard. When we sat down to eat, he would kick Ben-Zion the Second under the table, who, unlike Avigdor, he detested for some reason or other, and to my grandmother he would quote, like an ardent suitor, whole stanzas from Pushkin's poems, especially *Boris Godunov* and *Eugene Onegin*. And as he chewed her rye bread with his strong teeth and repeatedly shooed away Ben-Zion the Second who tried to snatch the bread from his hand, and sometimes even from his mouth, he would tell Yosef and me stories of heroism from the citrus grove. One night, he told us, he heard a rustling from among the trees, gnashing of teeth and loud, coarse laughter. And despite being frightened half to death, he approached the source of the sounds grasping his heavy club, ready and willing to strike the intruder.

'And then . . . ?' we asked with bated breath.

'And then I saw two hyenas, mother and cub, gnawing at the carcass of a jackal by the light of the moon. When they saw me, they showed their fangs, as long and sharp as nails, and their hackles rose from head to tail.'

'And do you know why hyenas usually have only one cub?' he asked, bragging, as if trying to impress us with his knowledge and forgetting that he'd already told me the story. 'Actually, she carries more than one in her belly – two, and sometimes even three cubs. But she only has two teats. That's why the cubs try to kill one another before they emerge from the womb. They bite, scratch, kick and thrash around, and even if they are all born alive, the strongest, that manages to be born first, kills the cub that follows him, or seizes one teat while at the same time preventing his weaker brother from suckling from the other, and the poor thing dies of hunger a short time after its birth. So the female hyena almost always hunts with one cub, and that one cub will always be fat and pampered, because it suckles a double ration of milk and gets all the attention, that was intended for its brothers as well, that it didn't allow to live.'

When he told this story to the three of us, it seemed to me that my grandmother looked at me with an accusing look in her empty eyes, and in my round belly echoed the frightened cries of the Arab washerwomen, '*Bint d'ba'a*', and the vicious teasing of the kindergarten children, 'There's another one, Tamara another one.'

Another time he told us about a lorry that drove into the grove without lights, and two men jumped out and began picking oranges and loading them onto the lorry. He managed to scare them off by imitating the hair-raising laugh of the hyena, and not only did they flee, they left behind the lorry and the small amount of fruit they had managed to load. One night, he told us further, by the silvery light of the moon, he met Lilith, the queen of the demons, a beautiful woman who tried to seduce him with her long, golden hair, red lips and lewd, whispered suggestions. But he was not tempted and drove her off with the words, 'Lilith, be off,' and she fled shamefaced to the adjoining grove where she tried her luck with Shimon the watchman.

On the few occasions that Zerach Levin and Avigdor Ben-Ari met in their room, one after his shift and the other before it, loud shouting could be heard. In the main, the two of them argued bitterly about Avigdor's 'theory of race'. Avigdor tried to convince Zerach about the merits of his claims and the accuracy of his studies, while Zerach yelled at him that he was wasting his time, and called him a lunatic and a false prophet. When the argument became heated, all I could hear were the words Jews, Arabs, Moslems, Sephardis, blood, war, separation and *kultura*, and a shudder of fear would pass through me. And Widow Ziso would stand outside the locked door, biting her lip and predicting that no good would come of those two, only disaster, and she could already smell it coming.

CHAPTER 16

'For I the Lord thy God am a jealous God, visiting the iniquity of the fathers upon the children, and upon the children's children, unto the third and to the fourth generation of them that hate me,' our second-grade teacher, Ruth, read aloud with enthusiasm and explained that in this fifth verse of the first of the ten divine commandments, God punishes the sons of the sinning father up to the fourth generation. And I, afraid to appear stupid, did not have the courage to ask her whether this terrible verse, written in the masculine gender, also applied to mothers and daughters. In which case, if the mother sinned, her daughter, granddaughter, great-granddaughter and great-great-granddaughter would pay the price for her crime, even if they themselves had not sinned.

That year, we decorated the school with placards of the sayings of the wise, and one of them that proclaimed in red letters that 'Like Father Like Son', particularly worried me. Once again I did not have the courage to ask if this also applied to mothers and daughters.

This matter worried me to such an extent that I had difficulty concentrating in class. I was convinced that one of my ancestral mothers had committed a terrible sin, and as a result my grandmother was blinded, my mother died, and who knows what would befall me, my future daughter, and perhaps her daughter too: the punishment would be carried down, from mother to daughter for ever and ever. I viewed the conspiracy of silence maintained by the people around me regarding our family's past, my father's request that I beware of men, Avigdor's talk about my blood being mixed with foreign blood, and my grandmother's frequent nightmares that made her scream in terror, as further testimony of an unforgivable crime undoubtedly committed by one of my grandmothers.

After much hesitation, I shared my concerns with Avigdor Ben-Ari. His eyes narrowed as if he was about to fall asleep, but I knew that he was listening to me attentively. When I finished he smiled, his eyes encircled with that delicate web that rose to his eyebrows and spread sideways all the way to his temples.

'The mothers have eaten sour grapes and the daughters' teeth are set on edge,' he said and laughed. 'An interesting conundrum to which I have never given any thought,' he confessed.

'It's true, then,' I said in horror.

'Perhaps . . . there are such stories.'

'Tell me one,' I asked.

'Have you heard of Andromeda?'

'There's a rock by that name in the sea.'

'And have you ever heard the ancient Greek myth about the princess?' he asked and sank into a deep silence.

For a long time we both sat on the orange crates in his and Zerach's room, with Ben-Zion the Second squatting at my feet, eagerly tearing one plait after another from the steaming *challah* I had brought with me that day, chewing silently, blissfully surrendering to the warmth spreading through our stomachs. Afterwards, with a sombreness he reserved for special occasions, Avigdor moistened the tip of his finger with saliva, silently gathered the crumbs that had fallen onto the box, and blew out the paraffin lamp. Soft, creamy moonlight filtered through the latticed window and sketched delicate lines on the floor of the room, which looked to me like the inscrutable markings of an ancient arcane code. Suddenly Avigdor's voice thundered as if someone else was speaking from his throat. Only the name Andromeda was whispered sweetly through his lips, like the name of a long-lost lover.

'One evening,' he said, 'Princess Andromeda was shackled hand and foot with cold iron chains to the black rock in the sea. Her father Cepheus, who loved her more than anything, shut himself up in an inner room so that his eyes would not behold the death of his beautiful daughter.'

With frightening clarity I saw Andromeda shackled to the rock: green seaweed was entangled around her legs, binding her with slimy velvet manacles, and small hermit crabs peered at her surreptitiously in their aimless, diagonal scurrying across the surface of the rock. Her fettered hands embraced the rock, which was covered in a plumage of pinnate sea vegetation swaying back and forth with the movement of the waves like a miniature jungle on a winter day. Her ears rumbling with the sound of the surf breaking softly on her body as if taking pity on her, and drops of salt water glimmering in her red hair like pearls that had been fished from the depths, her eyes the colour of the calm sea, weeping. 'Andromeda had to die because of a sin committed by her mother,' Avigdor's voice permeated the image I had created. 'She knew that the sea monster would soon come, break the iron shackles binding her to the rock, and carry her down to the depths.'

'And why did she have to die?' I asked, in a choked voice.

'For the sin of pride, hubris in the language of Greek mythology.'

'You mean they wanted to kill her because she was conceited?' I insisted.

'Andromeda was not punished for her own sin,' he reminded me, 'her mother Cassiopeia was the one who sinned.'

'And what did she do, her mother?' I asked.

'Cassiopeia boasted that there was no one as beautiful as she in the whole world, that her beauty even surpassed the beauty of the Naiads, the nymphs of the sea. The nymphs heard this and were deeply offended. They complained before Poseidon, the ancient Greek god of the sea. Poseidon was very angry and resolved to punish Cepheus and Cassiopeia's kingdom.' And I saw Poseidon the god of the sea rising from his emerald throne in his azure palace, its roof inlaid with shells that opened when the tide ebbed, revealing magnificent pearls, and multicoloured fish peering anxiously through amber windows that had been polished until they were translucent.

Once again Avigdor's voice rose and echoed through the splendid rooms of the palace and told me how Poseidon raised his voice and high, dark waves flooded the kingdom of the father Cepheus, sweeping away people, possessions, and livestock, threatening to engulf the entire kingdom and send it down into the depths of the sea. Then Cepheus consulted with Ammon the god of Egypt, who told him that only sacrificing his beloved daughter Andromeda and offering her to the sea monster could save his country. So Andromeda was shackled to the rock on Jaffa's coast and she waited heroically for her death, a death that would bring salvation to her country. For a long time she stood fettered until the dreadful sound of flapping wings was heard, and the frightened Andromeda closed her eyes and prepared to die for her country to atone for her mother's sins. But nothing happened to her, and as she opened her eyes she saw a handsome man before her – the valiant Perseus who had returned from his battle with the monster, Medusa – hovering in his winged sandals, carrying a heavy sack on his back with the monster's head in it.

Even before Andromeda had a chance to tell him her tale, the sea suddenly roared, drowning out her voice, and a terrible dragon rose up from the deep. When Perseus beheaded it, a terrible scream could be heard and the dragon's decapitated body plunged into the sea, turning the water red for as far the eye could see.

At that point, I already knew the tale's happy ending: 'And Perseus broke the chains that bound Andromeda to the rock, flew off with her to his homeland and they were married.'

'How did you know that, my clever, daydreaming little girl?' Avigdor asked, and did not wait for a reply but invited me to join him on the western balcony to look at the silhouette of the rock Andromeda had been shackled to. 'Andromeda Rock,' he announced and pointed to a black and gloomy-looking rock that protruded from the sea, faintly lit in the moonlight. 'If you swim close to it,' he assured me, 'you will surely hear the dim sound of the broken iron chains clanging against each other in the depths of the sea.'

'And what happened to the monster?' I remembered in terror. 'Where is it now?'

'The monster was swept to the Jaffa shore, buried in the shifting sands and forgotten. Until Scaurus, the commander of Pompeius' army, arrived and discovered the huge skeleton and transported it by sea to Rome. There he paraded it proudly in a victory procession on a wagon drawn by a hundred oxen. But some of its bones may still be buried in the sands, and if we search carefully we may find them.'

'And what happened to the coquettish Cassiopeia?' I asked, wanting to draw out the tale just a little longer. Avigdor pointed to a constellation of stars twinkling right above the rock, and told me that after Andromeda died, the goddess Athena set her in the heavens next to her beloved Perseus and her mother Cassiopeia, and the three of them hang there together to this very day and light the northern skies in that constellation, united in one legend. My gaze lingered on them, as it did on the teacher during particularly boring lessons, until they multiplied and shone and twinkled in their thousands, with strips of white clouds intermingling with them like cotton wool, and Avigdor explained to me that this was a nebula and in fact a constellation of stars. He then showed me the Milky Way and said that it too was a nebula, and that the two nebulae, Andromeda and the Milky Way, were twin sisters. Now I scrutinised the twin nebulae that had not been forced to part, and I thought of my twin brother who was possibly imprisoned in my belly.

This mythological tale about the courageous princess who was prepared to pay with her life for her mother's sins, and the valiant and handsome prince who had delivered her from death, captured my heart, especially its romantic ending, so unlike the uncompromising curse of the Jewish Torah, 'The mothers have eaten sour grapes and the daughters' teeth are set on edge', in the masculine gender of course. This tale of theirs that ended happily raised my hopes and Andromeda became my heroine. I frequently went all the way to her rock on my walks, swam out to it, and strained my ears to hear the iron shackles clashing against each other in the depths of the sea. Once I even dived around the rock and amused myself with the notion that I would perhaps find the chains and bind myself to it until my saviour arrived to deliver me too from my imminent death, a death that I had been condemned to by God for a sin committed by one of my grandmothers, and that everyone hid from me in a conspiracy of grown-ups.

CHAPTER 17

Cruel and fickle fate, that produces deceptive and unfitting coincidences, played one of its jokes and with a tightly bound knot of joy and sorrow tied the day of my birth to that of my mother's death, for the moment I first filled my lungs and screamed my first cry she sighed her final sigh and returned her soul to the Creator.

From the time my grandmothers told me about this, on my sixth birthday, the happiness of my birthday has been mixed with the grief of death. My grandmother Simcha, resolute to mourn and rejoice on the same day, insisted on making me a part of that accursed day in two ceremonies: the anniversary of my mother's death and my birthday, and she would not countenance my request to postpone my birthday celebration by a few days.

'It's good to mix joy and mourning, like boiling and cold water poured into the same bowl,' said Widow Ziso in an effort to console me, 'because together they give us lukewarm water.'

And on this matter Avigdor Ben-Ari told me that: 'In tears Man comes into the world and in

241

tears doth he depart it,' and he added another sentence that I remember without even referring to my notebook, because until the disaster befell him he repeated it to me another three times: 'A birthday is not a time for joy, for each passing year brings us closer to our end.'

A month before the tragedy, Avigdor told me – and his words on this occasion were the last of his that I wrote down – that 'Life is like a string of beads. Each bead signifies an important event in a person's life, and there are good ones and bad ones. As the years go by, the beads are joined to one another, clustering together and forming a unified chain that cannot be broken and whose beads cannot be separated, because each one hangs from its predecessor and leads the one following it. At the head of your chain stand two beads, one good and one bad, and they have stuck to one another and become a single bead, because they both signify one event, part joyful and part sad.'

To illustrate what he meant he looked for his favourite book that was well known to me. Because quite often, when Avigdor was on guard at the grove, Yosef and I, looking for excitement, would steal into his box-cupboard and, under the sleeping Zerach's nose, take out this book with its worn covers. Then we'd hide in the lavatory and leaf through it as we stifled shrieks of fear and astonishment at the sight of the horrific photographs looking out at us from its pages: men, women and children stood there naked, unashamedly displaying their deformed bodies. There were dwarves and giants, children with six toes, black women whose legs were as solid as an elephant's, and others whose skin was covered with boils or repulsive sores. One man had a head the size of a pinhead, and next to him stood a man with a huge head, as blown up as a balloon. We couldn't read the explanations beneath the photographs because they were in Russian.

Avigdor leafed through the book and showed me the photograph that had already aroused my curiosity more than all the rest: two smiling children joined at the abdomen, as if they had been sewn together, giving them a single, fat and ungainly body from which came four legs, four arms and two heads.

'Chang and Eng,' announced Avigdor proudly, as though introducing me to two particularly successful relatives, 'Siamese twins.' He explained that Siamese twins are twins joined together by part of their body, and because they did not manage to separate in the womb they are born joined, stuck together at the abdomen, chest or back. They sometimes have only a single heart, liver or stomach, and then one cannot exist without the other and if, God forbid, an attempt is made to separate them with the surgeon's scalpel, they will both die.

'And why are they called "Siamese twins"?' I asked.

'Because Chang and Eng were the first twins of

this kind we knew of, and they were born over a hundred years ago in Siam,' he replied. 'They were joined together throughout their life, and yet they married and had children. The first two of your beads that stuck to one another are like Siamese twins: under no circumstances can they be separated.' And when he saw gloom spreading over my face, he hastened to pacify me: 'But those beads, your Siamese twins beads, are joined by other ones, a chain of events that have transpired and will transpire, and all of them together make up your life.'

But now I was interested only in the fate of the joined twins:

'But if one wants to sleep and the other wants to play, what do they do?'

'Well, then they have to discuss matters and decide.'

'And if one of them has to get to the lavatory quickly and the other one wants to eat?' I persisted.

'They have to learn to live together, in a single body, they have no choice.'

I studied the photograph and was afraid to ask Avigdor if there were cases of one twin swallowing the other in the womb and absorbing it into its own body. I didn't want him to recall the story of the hyena, the one Zerach liked so much, because then the nickname given to me by the gypsies, '*Bint d'ba'a*', daughter of the hyenas, would suddenly be heard in the room.

It was as if Avigdor had read my thoughts:

'Are you thinking about your twin who wasn't born?' he asked, amazing me, because I had never spoken to him about it.

I bent my head to Chang and Eng who smiled at me in a friendly way, and did not reply.

'Now listen to what I have to tell you,' said Avigdor, breaking the silence, and with a solemn expression asked me to reopen my notebook with his words of wisdom. 'Greek mythology,' I wrote as he dictated under the heading 'Twins', 'tells that in bygone days human beings were round and whole because they were joined in couples: a man to a man, a woman to a woman and a man to a woman. They lived this way happily and peacefully until Zeus, king of the gods, came and cut them into two and, from a whole, every couple became two halves.'

'How can you do that?' I remember asking him.

'It's very simple,' he replied, 'just as you take a knife and slice a fig or a hardboiled egg into two equal parts, and just as Simcha slices open the belly of a fish and divides the fish into two. From that time to this day, every one of us, who is a fraction of the whole, longs to return to the ancient state of unity with his or her partner from which he was separated by the god, and throughout our lives we search for the second part of ourselves. And until we can find the part we have been separated from and join up with it, we will never be whole. Because the two parts are the single whole.'

'So what happens when the two halves meet after a long separation?' I asked.

'Well, then the two halves meet in friendship and love, with a deep sense of belonging. And when you meet your other half, the one cut from you, you will forget the twin that troubles you so much.' Avigdor added afterwards that all those words of wisdom appear in *The Banquet* by the Greek philosopher Plato. In it, questions of belonging and love are discussed at length, and the words on the two halves were spoken by a man called Aristophanes.

Many years later, when I read Shaul Tschernichovsky's Hebrew translation of *The Banquet*, I discovered that Avigdor had concealed Aristophanes' most beautiful and impressive words from me, on a woman's love for a woman and a man's for a man, and that 'After the division the two parts of man, each desiring his other half, came together, and throwing their arms about one another, entwined in mutual embraces, longing to grow into one . . . and they are themselves the best of boys and youths, because they have the most manly nature. Some indeed assert that they are shameless, but this is not true; for they do not act thus from any want of shame, but because they are valiant and manly, and have a manly countenance, and they embrace that which is like them.'

In an annual ceremony, whose rules were strictly observed by my grandmother Simcha even at times of war and anguish, she would wake me up early in the morning on my birthday, order me to wear my Sabbath blouse, wash my face well, not forgetting the back of my neck and behind my ears, and brush my shoes. A carriage harnessed to a horse with protruding bones, whose hire was considerably cheaper than hiring a better one, drove us along the seashore for a long way, rocking us over shifting sand hills that sometimes were in one place and sometimes moved to another. On the way my grandmother asked the driver to stop by wildflowers that grew here and there, and while the horse bent its scrawny neck and nibbled at bushes with its yellow teeth, we picked poppies with flimsy, crinkled petals, whose picked stalks exuded white spit and a nasty smell. With arms filled with the red flowers, we finally reached the iron gate of the new cemetery. My father always got there before us and we always found him standing at her side, his eyes veiled as if the many years that had elapsed since her death had only made his love for her stronger. With bowed head and in silence, I stood at his side and tried to fill myself with yearning for the girl who had been my mother and who had never held me in her arms. With her fingertips my grandmother traced the gravestone's surface, and with loud snorts of dissatisfaction wiped the stone clean of the accumulated dust and sand with her sleeve. Then she would scatter the flowers, light a memorial candle and ask me to put a small stone on the gravestone, so that 'Mother know her girl come.'

I fulfilled her wishes obediently, waiting for

another few minutes by the grave before rejoining her at the place where she stood waiting by the carriage near the *sabra* bushes, a strange expression on her face that I never managed to decipher. And Fishke, who had popped up from out of nowhere in his Sabbath clothes, stood some distance away, looking at her, and she faced him staring, and they did not exchange a word. And when my grandmother hurried me to get into the carriage, he slipped through the cemetery gates as though it was now his turn to visit her and he had been waiting patiently until we left.

In the afternoon my grandmother Simcha baked a big cake and covered it with hot chocolate, seeking to make me happy with it on my birthday. We held this party as if it were an event to be ashamed of. My friends were never invited, she sent Yosef out of the house on some pretext or other, and she even forbade Fishke, the person closest to her, to come to our house on that day. Just the two of us shut ourselves up with Ben-Zion the Second in the dark room, and celebrated my birthday in secret. We sat facing each other in silence, and I would look into her extinguished eyes, waiting for the slightest movement in her face, for the moment she would notice that I had grown and was worthy of hearing her great confession, her secret of secrets. The chocolate cake and Fishke's vodka bottle stood between us, because only on my birthday would she allow herself to drink one glass, and raise it in honour of the double event. First, she used both hands to grope for the bottle containing the transparent liquid that I was forbidden to even smell, then with her fingertip she would touch the rim of the glass I placed in front of her, and finally pour some vodka into it with great skill, never spilling a drop, as if she had previously calculated the exact capacity of the glass. Then she raised the filled glass, wished me *mazal tov*, threw her head back, and with a grimace poured the drink into her throat in one.

Then, her face burning, she cut four slices from the cake, threw one to Ben-Zion the Second who was crowing excitedly at her feet, put another aside for Yosef when he came home, took one for herself and gave one to me. I swallowed my piece hurriedly, waiting impatiently for her to announce that the party was over. Then I took the cake, less four slices, and generously offered some to Widow Ziso, Avigdor Ben-Ari and Zerach Levin, while they were still with us, went to Fishke's carpentry shop, gave him a slice and received in return a kiss redolent with the viscous smell of glue, and a birthday present he had made for me, continued to Neveh Zedek, to Grandma Abulafia's house, gave her her piece and and waited for her presents. Grandma Abulafia would always prepare two packages for me, one small, one big. Into the small one she put a gift of little value that I could take home and show my grandmother Simcha without risk, while the big one contained expensive gifts: a beautiful festive blouse with a rose embroidered on it in crosses so small that even my perceptive eyes were unable to distinguish between them, a leather-bound notebook for writing down the thoughts of the wise people I met, white cotton stockings and petticoats, a new book, a big box of *Caran d'ache* coloured pencils, and things like that. I was forced to leave these presents at her house so as not to anger my grandmother Simcha, who always claimed that, 'That one from Neveh Zedek buys girl with presents.' My father was never waiting for me there on my birthday, and it was even forbidden to remind him that it was my birthday, because for him that day was a day of tragedy.

When I got back home with the empty cake tray, my grandmother Simcha would demand to know 'what that one from Neveh Zedek gave you'. And when I described the modest gift I had brought, she would feel it grudgingly and say, 'That one is rich and much afraid for her money. Even to her granddaughter doesn't give.'

My mother was thirteen years older than me, and a few days before I turned thirteen I was afraid I'd die just like her, because if 'like mother, like daughter', this birthday would also be the day of my death. I quickly wrote down a list of the property I had amassed in my short life, including the clothes that Grandma Abulafia had made for me and which I had never worn, and the presents she had bought me and which had remained in her house. Next to each item I wrote the name of the beneficiary. I directed that my words of wisdom notebook should be buried with me. On the morning of the thirteenth anniversary of my mother's death I adamantly refused to go to the cemetery, and when my grandmother Simcha left the house, grumbling to herself in Russian, I took from the chest the white batiste dress that Grandma Abulafia had made me for the approaching Jewish New Year, put it on and lay down on my bed. To hasten the end, I shut my eyes tightly and held my breath. As I wasn't dying I pinched my nose between my thumb and forefinger so not even a whiff of air could get in. I awoke to the sound of my grandmother Simcha's dragging feet as she came up the steps, and when I heard her groan as she came into the room on her return from the cemetery I knew I had been saved.

I got up with a feeling of relief and sat down at the table with her, and ate my slice of the cake she had baked in honour of my birthday.

From that day forward, Death preserved my mother in my mind as a little girl whose arms and legs were dotted with freckles. A year later, when I turned fourteen and she remained a year younger than me, I finally decided to put an end to the custom of marking my birthday by visiting the grave of my mother who was younger than me, and my grandmother was forced to visit the cemetery on her own. When she returned that time she told me that she had put a stone on the gravestone for me as well, and apologised to my mother for my absence.

CHAPTER 18

'The English brought her wealth and the Arabs robbed her of it,' Widow Ziso mourned Simcha's temporary fortune that had gone up in the smoke of the riots.

Several years after the war ended, the traffic of ships from the port of Odessa to Palestine stopped almost entirely, the flow of pilgrims turned into a trickle and Russian speakers vanished from Jaffa's citrus groves. Through force of habit my grandmother Simcha continued preparing the royal *borscht* in the small pot and the farmers' *borscht* in the big pot and, when she could find no customers, she distributed the farmers' *borscht* to the '*Lumpenproletariat*', as Avigdor Ben-Ari called the beggars who crowded at the gate to the house, awaiting her return. Later, when her savings were exhausted, she decided to confine herself to baking, because 'Bread everyone always eat.'

'Your grandmother is the bread alchemist,' Avigdor Ben-Ari praised her to me and said that Simcha reminded him of the naturalists of old, those eccentric scientists who tried, using weird and wonderful experiments that took them their whole lives, to transmute base metals into gold. 'But they failed and died despondently, and she succeeds.'

'*Tvoy khleb zolotoy*,' your bread is gold, Avigdor would compliment her, his mouth full of warm bread, and she, who never liked receiving compliments, would dismissively wave her hands that were burned from the heat of the oven.

Sacks of rye flour from the cold northern countries were delivered from Jaffa's market, and in the evenings she would dilute the yeast with water and milk and pour it onto the dark flour, which she mixed with white flour, adding the ingredients of her own secret recipe, which she did not reveal to a soul for fear of her as yet nonexistent competitors, just like the alchemists of old. She would leave the dough standing the whole night, because a prolonged leavening improved the flavour. I would stand next to her in the kitchen for a long time, watching the mixture seething with life, fermenting and moving and expanding and growing before my very eyes, and in the morning I would find in its place a tall mound of dough that swelled over the rim of the bowl and brimmed over it in all directions, an intoxicating and addictive aroma rising from it that I could not describe in words.

Once I asked Avigdor Ben-Ari to tell me what the smell of dough was, so that I could write it down in my notebook, but he replied that 'Our language is poor in smells, and most smells are named for the substances that produce them. Hence, even if I were to search the dictionary I would not find words appropriate for a smell as rich as that of dough because there is no *definitzya* for this thing in which the soul, and not the body, delights.' And he further added that 'Every dough is different in its smell from all others; the smell of your grandmother Simcha's dough is not the same as that of Widow Ziso or that of Rashella Abulafia.'

But I insisted on finding a definition for the aroma of my grandmother Simcha's dough and did not rest until I came up with an idea, and one day squeezed a small lump off the mound of dough, tore it in two and stuffed my nostrils with the sticky concoction. The two chunks of dough remained in my nostrils for the whole of that day, separating my nose from the air and its smells, overpowering and satiating me with their aroma. In the evening, after plucking them out with difficulty because in the meantime they had dried and hardened, I could tell Avigdor that the aroma of Simcha's dough was composed of a large number of smells that combined with each other and intermingled: it was a blend of the green fragrance of grain and harvest, dissolved in the scent of the first rain of the season, mixed with a dash of tart green apples, stirred with the sweet and intoxicating smell of sweetened lukewarm milk, sprinkled with the saltiness of the sea and the bitterness of unripe fruit.

Apparently, my grandmother Simcha also placed

great importance on the smell of the dough, for she would not start baking before pinching the dough and sniffing at the large mound. When she was satisfied with the aroma, she split it into equal chunks, rolled them into twin balls, as if they had been cast from one mould, repeatedly rolled each ball between greased hands, lengthening here and shortening there, and loaves of kneaded dough identical to one another rapidly spread out before her as if by magic. She would then pick them up one by one and score two deep, criss-cross incisions with a sharp knife, 'So that crust open and let bread grow,' she explained to me and then explained to Yosef too, so that we would not think, God forbid, that she was marking her bread with crosses out of belief in Christianity. A short time later new smells emerged, smells of baking, from the small clay *tabun* in the yard and from the oven, from which soon after that hard steaming brown loaves burst forth one after another, the cross on top of them swelled and split, leaving a wide scar. And I would fill my lungs with the warm smell, a blazing, friendly and filling smell, and try to calm Ben-Zion the Second as the aroma of the fresh bread drove him out of his mind, and bite my lips lest I myself surrender to the temptation of tearing off one or two hunks and wolf them down while they were still hot. My grandmother Simcha would immediately hasten to sell the warm loaves, because the crust of bread left standing in the humid air of a house starts to blister and the steam trapped within the bubbles seeps into the heart of the loaf and dissolves it into spongy, moist and bland dough, and the bread raises mould and is no longer fit to eat, and then she would be forced to sell it for a penny to the donkey-drivers who fed it to their beasts.

From force of habit my grandmother would first wend her way with her heavy sour loaves to the outskirts of Jaffa where she sold them to the handful of Russian pilgrims, remnants of the vast groups of recent years who had stayed in the country, because they opposed the Communist Revolution, and congregating in cheap hostels, they had their fill of the bland, thin and pale *pitta* breads and they would buy all her produce from her. Later, aroma, rumour and flavour were passed by word of mouth and customers began arriving at our house when my grandmother was still removing the loaves from the oven. Hands trembling with the restrained passion of hunger and longing for the tastes of their childhood, they dropped their coins into her hand and clutched the loaves to their chest in awesome reverence, and then placed them in the sacks they had brought with them. Others followed the Russians, and my grandmother Simcha's customers grew in such great numbers that Fishke built a small kiosk for her at the edge of the neighbourhood, on a tiny plot of land she had purchased very close to the seashore. It was constructed of wooden beams, the edges of its ungainly roof adorned with wooden scales made of lattice artwork. She stood there for hours every day, until the veins in her legs swelled, selling her breads. In the hours and days when I was free from my studies, I helped her, handing loaves of bread and bags of biscuits to the customers, pouring lemonade from large glass jugs with chips of ice and slices of lemon swimming in them for the thirsty. Yosef stood on a raised wooden platform that Fishke had installed for him and collected the coins. My grandmother Simcha's breads gained such a reputation that Fishke purchased a pair of mules and built a cart, and in the early morning, before going to his carpentry workshop, he would transport warm breads to Tel Aviv and sell them to the grocery shops and restaurants of the white city. And because he was as parsimonious as they come, he attached jute sacks to the mules' rumps and when they filled up with dung he would feed it to the *tabun* in the yard and stoke the fire with this fuel that, despite its rather unpleasant stench, burned long and well. When the English also began to frequent the kiosk, demanding other kinds of pastries, my grandmother was quick to learn their tastes and prepared vanilla slices, butter biscuits, ginger snaps and sweet buns for them.

But the demand for 'Simcha's bread' continued to grow and my grandmother employed out-of-school boys and girls to work with her, sifting the flour, dissolving the yeast, rolling out the dough and moulding it into a variety of shapes and forms.

When she did not want to be dependent on the merchants for flour, she leased the mill near the Yarkon River where the donkey and mule owners stopped to water their beasts, and the water turned the millstones and ground the wheat for her. My grandmother became a wealthy woman. And although according to Widow Ziso she could have bought up half the neighbourhood, she preferred to continue living in the small room that the widow had bequeathed to my grandmother and me and to all our descendants for as long as we lived.

What did she do with the money? 'Money should be kept in the bank, in an iron treasure house,' Grandma Abulafia declared repeatedly, but to no avail. She patiently explained to her that a bank is the only truly safe place, as one explains the facts of life to a young and wilful child, and who knew that better than she, whose late husband was an important manager in a bank and they never kept even one *bishliq* in their home for fear of robbers. But my grandmother Simcha did not heed her advice and did not deposit anything in the Anglo-Palestine Bank except for a small sum to pay for my studies when I grew up. With the rest she purchased heavy napoleons of pure gold and hid them where she hid them, not revealing their hiding place to any of us, not even to Fishke. But the rioters who broke into the house found the treasure and took all the gold, to the last napoleon. From that day my grandmother Simcha refused to speak of it, of the gold that was gone. Even when Widow

Ziso probed her after the event, in case she did not remember exactly and had hidden it somewhere else, where it could yet be found. She dismissed her with a scornful wave of her hand and proclaimed that money was only money and the most important thing was that we ourselves had survived, and in any event shrouds have no pockets. When I heard this conversation between the two women, one mourning the lost treasure and the other placating her, it seemed to me that my grandmother was somewhat relieved that the riots had fallen upon us leaving her empty-handed.

Widow Ziso was the first to warn against the impending catastrophe. Rumours spread through the city that a great evil would descend upon us on the First of May and anyone valuing their life would shut themselves off in their homes, lock the shutters and pray for the best – so I heard her say to my grandmother Simcha, and she, who hated the word 'prayer', mumbled: 'Not more pogrom. Once see pogrom never see pogrom again.' When she went out to the market to buy the spices for her bread, I asked the widow the meaning of the word pogrom, but she refused to answer. 'Why did Simcha say that she was not going to go through another pogrom?' I later asked Fishke, but he did not answer either, and hurried to stuff nails into his mouth, pretending that he was too busy to talk.

Left with no other choice, I asked my grandmother Simcha herself for the meaning of 'pogrom'.

She blanched as if a demon had appeared before her blinded eyes and made me swear to never utter that terrible word again, because in the Land of Israel there is no pogrom and there would never be a pogrom, she announced and did not explain.

In those days it seemed as if everyone was conspiring against me on the matter of the 'pogrom'. They all used the word extensively, but when I asked them to tell me already what it was, they became tongue-tied. Even Avigdor Ben-Ari, who could usually explain difficult things to me clearly and fluently, became befuddled this time. The explanation he gave me was so awkward and vague that I shut my words of wisdom notebook in despair, and to this day the word 'pogrom' is inscribed in it as a heading at the top of an empty page. Later I heard him talking with Widow Ziso, saying to her that indeed he had heard things in the bathhouse and noticed that hostile looks were being directed at him, and handsome Moussa had secretly advised him to keep away from the bath-house. 'But even if something does happen, we will not be hurt,' said Avigdor, trying to calm Widow Ziso. And when she asked him how he knew that we would not be hurt, he told her that sightless Simcha was sacred in their eyes, and as for him, well, everyone knew him and his research, and his credit and Simcha's credit would stand us all in good stead.

But Zerach ridiculed him and his comforting words. And when he saw agitated Arab youths crowding together around the citrus groves he guarded and at the entrance to Neveh Zedek, he warned Widow Ziso that 'These youths presage imminent riots, for the Arabs always send children and youths as a vanguard to a *provokatzia*, so that if one of them is hurt it serves as a pretext for an act of reprisal. And if they hurt us, the adults can plead innocence and claim that they were just youthful pranks.'

To prepare for the worst, he decided to attend to the heavy and rusty old rifle he had found in one of the citrus groves during the great retreat of the Turks before the British. He secretly invited me and Yosef to his room. Waving his hands, he drove away Ben-Zion the Second, his bitter enemy, who had followed me as always, spread a white sheet on the floor and disassembled the gun, boasting of his ability to perform the task with his eyes almost closed. When a bizarre pile of rusting metal parts heaped up on the sheet, he applied cooking oil he had drawn from Simcha's oil jug to each and every part, and spent a long time rubbing, polishing and buffing the rust spots that dotted the barrel and breech. When he was done, he laid all the cleaned parts on the sheet and laboured to assemble them into a whole rifle. We sat next to him on the sheet for a long time observing him, as he assembled and disassembled, disassembled and assembled, and then Ben-Zion the Second, who had meanwhile stealthily returned through the half-opened door, and while

Zerach was absorbed in joining the trigger, sights, and safety catch to the breech, moved towards the pile of rusted parts and pecked at it greedily. With my own eyes I saw him pick up a screw in his beak, tilt his neck and swallow it greedily as if he were swallowing a succulent worm. Zerach noticed him only after the fact and screamed at him 'Shoo!' and 'Get out of here!' The admonished rooster bristled its feathers, swelled up its reddening gullet, gave Zerach a terrifying glare and prepared to peck at his leg. Zerach picked up the half-assembled rifle and pointed it at the formidable fowl. They stood like that, facing each other, bristling and furious, until I picked up Ben-Zion the Second in my arms, apologised to Zerach, and took the troublemaking bird out of the room. After I returned on my own, Yosef and I still had to wait patiently for some time until Zerach finally managed to produce the rifle intact, splendidly oiled and polished. He waved it proudly, cocked it and listened joyfully as it clicked in response, put it down, and when he lifted the sheet to fold it, discovered a tiny spring he had overlooked. Zerach picked up the spring and gazed at it confused and bewildered, wanting to attach it to the gun but not knowing where, despaired and gave up, and flung it out through the door that opened onto the northern balcony.

Widow Ziso actually heeded Zerach's warnings and invited Fishke to her house and asked him to fix the wooden shutters firmly to the window frames. Fishke went from room to room, his mouth full of nails, a heavy hammer in his hand, and in thundering silence fixed each shutter to its window frame before moving on to the next one and vigorously rattling the shutters to inspect the firmness of the join. Then Widow Ziso asked him to repair the front gate that dangled on a single hinge. Fishke lifted the heavy iron gate with ease, fitted its lugs on all three hinges, oiled the lock and made sure it could be locked, and when he finished all his labours kissed me and Yosef and limped off to the carpentry workshop, that was now entirely his.

In the newspapers that were full of black obituary notices, opinions were divided on the chain of events that led to the riots and those to blame for them. They carried extensive reports of two May Day parades that went out on a hot, dry, presummer's day to demonstrate in the empty sand dunes which in those days separated Tel Aviv from the Arab Manshiyyeh neighbourhood – one procession of the Achdut Ha'avoda labour movement, who had an official licence to demonstrate, and the other by the *mopsim*, members of the Socialist Workers Party, who demonstrated without a licence and even dared to wave banners in Arabic, English and Yiddish calling for the toppling of British rule and the establishment of a soviet in the Land of Israel. They came from opposite directions until they met face to face. One group mingled with the other, calling each other names, and eventually the situation deteriorated into fist-fights, and then into blows with the nail-studded poles that had carried the banners, and the *mopsim* retreated from the police and fled to Jaffa.

From this point, opinions were divided. Some of the reporters claimed that had it not been for the *mopsim* who insisted on demonstrating, there would not have been so much bloodshed, because they ignited the flames that led to the bloody clashes when they wandered through Jaffa bearing the remnants of their banners. The *shabab*, Arab street hooligans who had prepared themselves and were armed with rifles, daggers, sticks and axes, took advantage of the riot that ensued and attacked every Jew they happened upon. They wounded and killed until the alleys were empty of Jews. Then the rioters broke into shops and homes followed by a swarm of screeching women who came in and plundered anything and everything: foodstuffs, clothes, jewellery, religious artefacts, carpets and household utensils – all stuffed haphazardly into sacks they dragged behind them where they jangled irritably. Later, after the women had emptied the plundered homes of their cheap and expensive household utensils, the rioters attacked the bedclothes, system-atically slashing mattresses, quilts and pillows with their daggers, and shook the slashed quilts out of the windows. The air filled with fluttering down and feathers that fell to the paving stones in the alleys in a sprinkle of white, as if it had started snowing in the middle of a hot and dry day.

In the midst of the shouting multitudes, some in anguish and others in passionate zeal, stood Fuad, the one-eyed, hunchbacked knife sharpener, peacefully and diligently sharpening bloodied knives and blunted blades on the knife grinder he had inherited from his father, who had inherited it from his father before him. Before returning the weapon to its owner he would inspect the blade's sharpness by passing his heavily scarred thumb over it, and only then handed it to him, offering wishes for success. The tiny sparks emitted by the grindstone encircled his head in a blazing aura of cold fire that was reflected in the eyes of the rioters. On that day, Fuad did not demand payment for his labours. He was labouring for Allah and not for lucre, aiding the rioters, who he could not join because of his disability, to carry out their holy mission and massacre the infidels.

When the rioters arrived at Fishke's carpentry workshop, threatening to put it to the torch, he waited for them at the door, blocking it with his stocky body, his heaviest hammer in one hand and sharp-toothed saw in the other. Anyone bold enough to get too close received a heavy blow from the hammer or was treated to a deep gash from the saw whistling through the air. And when the rioters tried to stone him from a distance, he flung at them whatever he could lay his hands on: planks, planes, mauls, clamps, files, stools and chairs. Eventually they gave up and fled, frightened, beaten and bleeding, and went straight to my grandmother Simcha's wooden kiosk. They kicked in the flimsy wooden door, went in and plundered everything they found there – a few loaves of bread, biscuits, and a few coins that were hidden in a metal box under the counter – then dropped a lighted torch and left. With a merry crackling sound the fire spread upwards, hungrily consuming the ornamental latticing of the roof edge and the cone-shaped roof covered in wooden scales, wriggling crimson tongues through the latticework as if mocking those who had set it ablaze, and rising in a huge flame, like a giant beacon reflecting in the mirror of the flat sea. Much later, the fishermen and seamen who had happened to be there in their boats and ships said that the reflection of the fire could be seen from a great distance and had the appearance of a lighthouse, as if it wanted to entice distant ships with fiery flattery to draw near and shatter against Andromeda's Rock.

On that day, the sounds gradually drew near our house. I took my words of wisdom notebook, shoved it deep into my trousers, forcibly pulled Yosef and my grandmother Simcha behind me and fled with them to Widow Ziso's room. Trembling and cramped inside the widow's wide wardrobe, we listened in fear to the cries of '*Allahu akbar*' and '*Idbakh al-Yahud*' that could be heard drawing closer and closer. Yosef clung to me and curled against my body and we hugged Simcha with our four arms, encircling her lean body from both sides, our hands touching one another's. But my grandmother did not imbue us with a sense of safety, and for the first time in my life I saw her dazed and scared. She whispered long sentences in Russian, as if praying, and the word 'pogrom' was repeated again and again. Suddenly, her voice was that of a little girl begging for her life, until Widow Ziso, whose nerves were a wreck anyway, admonished her to be silent. Simcha obeyed and her body shrank as if it was about to disappear. We heard the rioters running wild in the adjacent new immigrants' house and the screams of the people being slaughtered there. Suddenly, heavy pounding was heard on the iron gate of our house and loud whispers: '*La takhafu, la takhafu* Simcha. *Iftakh el-bab*,' do not be afraid, do not be afraid, Simcha, open the door. Widow Ziso ventured out of the wardrobe to peek between the slits of the shutters and I followed her. We saw Khaled, Simcha's greengrocer, pounding on the gate with his fists and we could hear him begging in despair as if he were the persecuted party: 'Simcha, leave everything, come with me, you'll be slaughtered.' Widow Ziso went down to him apprehensively and I saw her fall into his arms. Then I hurried to crouch and ordered the scrawny Yosef, who was crying and trembling all over, to hold onto my neck and climb onto my back, and I galloped with him down the stairs, neighing like a horse to amuse him. Khaled had to forcibly remove Simcha from the house, her eyes wide in terror, and her body rigid as if paralysed. '*Ta'alu, ta'alu*,' Khaled invited Avigdor Ben-Ari and

Zerach Levin to join us too, waving the curved *shabariyya* dagger tied to his belt to hurry them along. But they declined. Zerach apparently trusted the rifle he carried, and Avigdor probably put his trust in his theory and his youthful friends.

At that instant I imprinted the image of Avigdor in the album of my memories, the album preserved in my head, containing a collection of scenes, images and moments that I have not forgotten and never will: Avigdor standing calmly on the exterior staircase of the house, one leg thrust slightly forward, and his moist, boyish green eyes looking fearlessly as if all hell was not breaking loose in the surrounding alleys. I see him calmly taking a packet of cigarettes out of his pocket, lighting one, drawing the smoke deep into his lungs, and waving us goodbye, even winking at me as if seeking to hearten me.

Khaled led us to his house, a distance of just a few strides, and pushed us into an arched alcove that had hastily been emptied of the blankets and mattresses stored there. He gently closed the doors of the alcove and bolted them. I peeked through a crack in the door and saw him standing at the entrance to the room, puffing up his chest, ready to fight for our lives, and I heard him ordering his wife and young children, who were huddling fearfully behind him, to be silent. I put my hand over Yosef's mouth and nose as he clung to me sobbing in the darkness, and pressed it hard to silence him until he almost suffocated.

It was already nightfall when Khaled let us out of the alcove and we went out into the street that was now deathly silent. We made our way home, our feet stepping in the darkness over a layer of feathers, tripping over slashed quilts, broken furniture, shattered household utensils, fragments of cups and plates and ripped clothing. At the corner of the alley near our house, Fishke stood waiting for us, holding a lamp in one hand and a maul in the other. He lifted Yosef onto his back with ease, supported Simcha's elbow and led her between the obstacles of wreckage. The iron gate was broken open, and when we made to climb up the stairs we bumped into Avigdor Ben-Ari sprawled on his back, his head facing down and his legs facing upward, as if he had climbed the stairs backwards. His hair and beard were dishevelled, his chest bare, his trousers down, exposing his bloodied genitals, and dark puddles stained the stairs. At the sight, Widow Ziso erupted into screams the likes of which I had never heard coming out of her mouth before, and my grandmother Simcha joined her, faintly sobbing, without knowing why or what about. And Yosef and I exchanged amused glances and burst into uncontrollable laughter. We tried to stifle it with our hands but the choked laughing seeped between our spread fingers and turned into roaring laughter, until Fishke raised his hand and slapped me hard and then Yosef too, and the manic laughter turned into hysterical weeping.

In an angry voice, as if we were responsible for

the killing, Fishke ordered us to go and stand by the gate, avert our heads and not look. But I could not restrain myself, and peeked back surreptitiously. I saw him load Avigdor onto his back and go down the stairs with him, and I saw Avigdor's legs and long arms dangling-swinging like the limbs of a big rag doll. Fishke laid Avigdor down in the yard under the pomegranate tree and, as if seeing to a living person whose body was in agony, gently pulled up his trousers, covered his chopped-off privates, and repeated his order, 'Don't move, don't look', and then went up hastily to look for Zerach. I later discovered that he had found him hanging by his wide belt from the railing of the northern balcony, and in my mind's eye I envisaged his body like an effigy of Haman the Wicked dangling from the rope the children strung from house to house during the festival of Purim.

I saw Fishke come out again carrying Zerach's body wrapped in one of the thin wool blankets that had covered the beds of the two men in their room, and another blanket rolled up under his arm. He slowly came down the stairs, bent under the weight of his heavy burden, and laid the blanket-covered Zerach in the yard next to Avigdor. Immediately, like a concerned father fearing for his child on a particularly cold night, he covered Avigdor with the extra blanket, but Avigdor's feet persisted in sticking out as if refusing to disappear. Now Widow Ziso's two lodgers were laid out wrapped in blankets next to

270

each other at the foot of the pomegranate tree, whose buds blazed like red stars in the light of the lamp Fishke had hung on one of the branches.

Then, Fishke drew water from the pump in the yard into a pail, went up the stairs again and poured the water onto the puddles of blood that had almost dried, wiped them with his shirt, which he had taken off, and only then did he permit us to go up into the house.

Abdul Abu Hassan, the neighbourhood policeman, who witnessed the massacre but was unable, so he said, to stop the rioters because there was just one of him and so many of them, later testified before the British police that Avigdor had been killed by handsome Moussa. He was able to describe the terrible incident in minute detail, and much later when I read him quoted in the book *When The People Willingly Offered Themselves* by Shmaya Lev-Zion I added my own personal touch to his testimony, and in my mind's eye I saw the rioters uprooting the iron gate and breaking in through the gap that opened before them in a gesture of Eastern hospitality, and Avigdor standing on the stairs, a cigarette in his mouth, and he welcomes the rioters with greetings of *ahalan wa sahalan*, as if they are guests coming to visit in his room. Among them he sees handsome Moussa and he smiles in relief. Handsome Moussa does not return the smile, but calls out '*Allahu akbar!*' as he climbs the stairs towards him with his bloodied *shabariyya*, and stabs him in the groin. Avigdor's eyes widen in bewilderment, his hands clutching at the wound, blood gushing from it – the policeman swore that he heard him mutter 'Why?' – and handsome Moussa slits his belly. The young man he loved is the last thing Avigdor sees before falling on the stairs.

Abdul Abu Hassan, who came into the house with the rioters, testified that Zerach Levin also greeted them at the entrance to his room, and I could see Zerach standing there with murder in his eyes, clutching a rifle that could not fire. One of the rioters effortlessly takes the gun from his hands and slams the butt onto his head with great force. Zerach's skull cracks and a jet of dark blood spurts out of his mouth as if from a fountain. Then the rioters hang his body with his wide leather belt, which held bullets that did not even fit the gun, over the point of one of the Stars of David that adorn the railing of the northern balcony.

Finally, we were allowed to go up into the house and I saw that the edges of the damp stairs had pinkened from the blood which had been diluted with water. We made our way from room to room between the broken furniture and dishes, and Simcha groped her way to the kitchen. We found her standing there, her feet wallowing in a puddle of red liquid, the spilled *borscht*, her hands groping around the devastation. When she went out to the yard she discovered that her clay *tabun* had been smashed and all the sacks of flour and jugs of oil had vanished. That night my grandmother also searched for her treasure of gold coins among the ruins of the kitchen. 'To hell with the money, more important we live,' I heard her saying the next day to Widow Ziso, who mourned her smashed furniture and her valuables that had all been plundered.

Wind billowed in Avigdor's and Zerach's room, whistled through the opening to the western balcony, the door to which had been ripped out, played with Avigdor's papers, scattering sheets soiled with black handprints, the hands of the Arab youths he had loved, and covered the floor with wrapping paper from oranges, inscribed with his dense handwriting in the green ink he liked. A book cover peeked at me between the papers and I picked it up: as always Chang and Eng smiled at me, oblivious to the appalling catastrophe that had come to pass. I took the book with me for safekeeping and went into our room, and was surprised to find everything in its place, especially my grandmother Simcha's carved bed, beautifully intact as before.

The rioters had left our room untouched.

It was only some time later that I noticed the absence of Ben-Zion the Second who had been left to his fate, and with pangs of conscience I searched for him everywhere, among the broken furniture, and in a number of crates that had remained intact in Avigdor's and Zerach's deserted room. I called his name, smacked my lips and promised to give him anything he wanted if he just showed himself. But I could neither find him in the house nor when I went out to the yard equipped with an oil lamp, despite my grandmother Simcha and Widow Ziso's warnings.

When I returned empty-handed, Widow Ziso, who was also one of his despisers and even feared him, told me that 'That disgusting rooster is probably splashing about in the soup the cursed ones made from him, and may the dry flesh of that ferocious old bird stick in their throats and may all the enemies of Israel perish.' And when I told my grandmother Simcha that Ben-Zion the Second might also be among the slaughtered, she hissed at me: 'Better dead.' Suddenly, a loud rasping, grating and screeching sound erupted from her mouth, as if she had not used it for a long time: she laughed, she laughed heartily, and even slapped her thighs in merriment. I looked at her in astonishment and saw the laughing mouth and the shaking body and her dry eyes, but despite the laughter the anxiety and sadness that always dwelled there did not vanish. The laugh lines adopted the furrows of the worry lines, and the laughter itself was eventually replaced by prolonged coughing that almost choked her. I had to support her and lead her to our room, which without the oppressive presence of Ben-Zion the Second now actually seemed spacious, pleasant and welcoming.

That night we all – Widow Ziso, my grandmother, Yosef and I – slept in my grandmother Simcha's wide bed. Fishke watched over us, dozing on the chair with the heavy hammer clasped to his chest. All that night my grandmother Simcha wept in her dreams, sobbing like a baby and rejecting my arms outstretched to hug and comfort her, and around the house vulgar voices could be heard mocking and deriding, and the howls of hyenas wandering the citrus groves, attracted by the smell of death, searching for fresh carcasses and laughing their repulsive laugh in chorus. And in my mind's eye I saw their boil-infected bodies, their stooping rumps, like those of a dog cringing in fear of being whipped, and their hind legs, shorter than their forelegs, frenetically scratching their flea-infested bristly fur. I curled up next to Yosef and remembered what Zerach had said, that only one cub, the stronger one, remains after killing its brother, and that I should know that in the wild only the strongest survive.

News of the riots in Jaffa reached the soldiers of the Jewish brigade, the 'First Judeans', who had not yet been officially disbanded, and they hastily left Sarafand Camp and arrived in Jaffa the next day armed with rifles and knives. The day they arrived was a day of vengeance in the spirit of the Torah: 'Whoso sheddeth man's blood, by man shall his blood be shed,' and 'Eye for eye, tooth for tooth.' The armed Jews broke into Arab homes, beat, murdered and did not spare women and children either. Streams of Arab blood mingled with the Jewish blood that had been spilled the day before, and the red river of atrocity flowed thick and heavy in the gutters and into the sewers that welcomed it with gaping mouths as dark as the caverns of hell.

To no avail my grandmother Simcha sought to save her greengrocer, Khaled, our benefactor, from the hands of the Jewish rioters. When she arrived limping at his house to bring him and his household to take refuge in Widow Ziso's house, she stumbled into his gaunt body, which had already been trampled by numerous feet, sprawling shot on the threshold. Stumbling and groping inside the house she found his dead wife and five children. The killers did not even spare his donkey and dog, which lay dying next to one another, the gaping ugly wounds on the sides of their bodies covered in a shimmering blanket of green death flies. In Khaled's clenched hand a letter was later found, written in Hebrew in Widow Ziso's spidery handwriting and stained with his blood, informing whomever it may concern that 'Khaled is an honest and compassionate greengrocer who risked his and his family's lives to save two Jewish families and gave them refuge from the rioters. Therefore, he and his family should be treated with mercy and respect, for he loves Jews, and whoever harms him will be severely punished.'

Khaled, his wife and his children, like all the

other murdered Arabs, were buried in the Moslem cemetery near the sea, while the Jews were carried in funeral processions all the way to the new cemetery, where my grandmother was married and my uncle and mother were buried, and were interred in a large common grave, the gravestone inscribed with 'Common Grave For Pure And Holy Souls', which can be read to this day in the cemetery in Trumpeldor Street in Tel Aviv.

From that terrible day our lives changed radically. Many children no longer came to school, either because they had been murdered or because their families had moved to Tel Aviv; this I learned from the teachers' whisperings in corners of the school playground and corridors. All the survivors were gathered into one small classroom. Leah, my comrade in food, was also lost to me, and I was told that she had moved with her family to live in Tel Aviv. And to the end of my primary school days I could not find one girl who would agree to exchange her *pitta* for my grandmother Simcha's cooked meals, which I had already had my fill of, but was forced to continue eating during breaks.

After my grandmother Simcha became impoverished and lost her sources of income, she decided to work as a cook for a British officer's family whose Jewish cook had been murdered in the riots. From then on, her hair, hands and clothes emanated new smells – of vanilla, ginger and cinnamon – which immediately merged amazingly well with the smell of smoke and burning that always rose from her body and which she could not rid herself of to her dying day.

Following the riots Widow Ziso vowed never to leave her house again, and she broke that vow only three times: when she accompanied me to my grandmother Simcha's funeral, when she gave me away under the wedding canopy a few weeks later, and when she was carried on a stretcher to the purification room, shrunken and weightless as fruit that has withered on the branch for too long during autumn, shrivelled and vanished into its skin.

Fishke then decided that Arabs were no longer to be trusted, because among the rabble that had laid siege to him, so he claimed, he saw some of the lads who worked for him. So he went to El-Hanud market, where swords and other weapons were sold, and equipped himself with a long, sharp *shabariyya* dagger, suspended it from his belt for all to see and fear, and announced before Simcha that when the next pogrom came, he would rout all the rioters.

If my grandmother Simcha is to be believed, the riots also caused a change in Yosef, because it was solely due to them, so she believed, that he decided some years later to devote himself to the God of the Jews and study in a *yeshiva*. Had those appalling atrocities not occurred, he would probably have

278

grown into an ordinary youth, playing football and going to the cinema, and not buried himself in those ancient books that were written by who knows who.

Grandma Abulafia, whose neighbourhood had escaped the riots, tried to appeal to my grandmother Simcha to allow me to move in to live with her, because it was safer in Neveh Zedek, and in so doing reignited the flame of the old feud between them. For many months they did not speak to one another, and each forbade me to mention the name of her rival in her presence.

For a long time after the riots I wandered the alleys of my city, confused and hurting. More than anything, I missed Avigdor who I suddenly realised would never come back into my life. I wore out my brain in an attempt to guess what interpretation he would have given to this terrible thing that had happened, how he would have justified handsome Moussa's betrayal, and whether even now he would have upheld his belief that the Arabs are Jews. I repeatedly opened my notebook, reading and rereading his words of wisdom, his definitions of difficult words and his views on the subject of the Jews and the Arabs, seeking a hidden clue, a prophecy or an explanation after the fact, while trying unsuccessfully to banish Zerach's words of warning that filtered audaciously between the lines, as if sticking their tongue out at me and teasing: 'I told you so.'

'Just look at them,' against my will I reread Zerach's words in my notebook, 'their eyes are covered with the pus of trachoma, they're savages, weak and spineless, cruel and ignorant. They're even crueller than the Russians who ran riot against us. Only a lunatic like Avigdor could say that they are the ancient Hebrews. There will always be clashes between Jews and Arabs. They regard us as invaders and will try to throw us out and we will always be obliged to fight them. In every way.'

But actually I wanted to believe Avigdor's words.

After the riots I no longer wrote words of wisdom in my notebook, and to this day I have not found a worthy substitute for Avigdor, who could clarify at dictation speed the incomprehensible in places where it overshadowed the comprehensible. On the days that my yearning for Avigdor was particularly deep, I found comfort in his wisdom preserved in my notebook and which I allowed to continue shaping my opinions and preserving the memory of a world that was gradually drawing further and further away from me. As a substitute for that world I also cultivated the album of photographs engraved in my mind, and squeezed into it more and more important scenes and images that should not be forgotten, so that I could pull them out when the longing pinched at my heart.

Despite the riots, which the prophets of doom claimed would recur many more times, Widow

Ziso and my grandmother persisted in their refusal to leave the house in Jaffa, like old women refusing to go through even one more upheaval in their lifetime. In the evenings, when Simcha returned from her work, bringing with her a few buns and butter biscuits that she had baked for her employers, she would first go into Widow Ziso's, and the two women would sit facing each other silently for a long while. Nonetheless, Widow Ziso told me that even from my grandmother's silences she managed to learn what was new in and outside the neighbourhood.

My grandmother did not like to go into details about her work in the English family's home, but I knew that she prepared other dishes for them; different to those she had been accustomed to cooking. Every morning I would watch her put on the clothes they demanded she wear: a crisply starched, white pleated linen apron over a black dress. Seven days a week she worked for them, from morning to night, but she continued to cook for us all the same: two pots of *borscht*, royal and farmers', early on Sunday morning, and a loaf of rye bread that we would find in the oven every day. At noon, when Yosef and I came home from school, a carriage would stop at the gate to the house and Grandma Abulafia, stifling in her corset, would alight heavily from it with trays of food and sweetmeats. She would only leave a few moments before my grandmother Simcha returned, leaving behind her a trail of sugary aromas, a clean and tidy room, dishes washed, and us in our beds, clean and bathed too. My grandmother Simcha would return exhausted from her day's work and never asked us, not even once, about Grandma Abulafia's visits, although she knew about them from the neighbourhood gossips as well as from Widow Ziso.

CHAPTER 19

A few years after the riots, old age fell upon
Fishke without warning. It happened with
brutal rapidity, not the long drawn-out
process that goes on for years and helps us get
used to the changes taking place in us. One
morning, when he got up from his wood-shaving
mattress in the carpentry shop, he felt that his
soul was tired and he wanted to rest.

To all appearances nothing much had changed:
his shock of hair had neither thinned nor
whitened, but had simply faded a little, his eyes
had kept their clearness, his face was not wrinkled, he had not lost his teeth, and even his body
remained upright and sturdy as before. It was the
nails that revealed his disgrace: he frequently
forgot that he had nails in his mouth and would
open his mouth to speak, or worse, fall asleep with
them still stuck between his lips. One evening he
swallowed a nail in his sleep, awoke with terrible
pains in his guts and, frightened to death, rushed
to Simcha. She sat him down at the table and cut
him a thick slice of stale, dry black bread that she
spread with a thick layer of butter, and ordered

him to eat it right away, 'so that it will mix down there with nails'. And indeed, not a day passed and the nail exited through the back door, leaving only a small wound in his anus.

His tendency to forget his customers' requests caused him far greater damage. Although he meticulously wrote down their orders in great detail on bits of paper lest he forget what they wanted or one of their whims, he couldn't find the notes. And while he did his best to put them in one place, his arms and hands began betraying him as if they possessed a will of their own. When I visited him in the carpentry shop one day, I saw him holding a nail to be hammered home, while the hand grasping the hammer, as though out of spite, brought the hammer down in a different spot. His amputated leg bothered him more and more, too; he would scratch the stump of his phantom leg at night until the blood flowed, until it drove him out of his mind.

Then he began collecting all kinds of things for which no one had any use. The carpentry shop soon filled up with scrap iron, worm-ridden planks, dusty jars filled with bent nails, rusty tin receptacles, stinking rags and piles of old newspapers. Simcha found out about this and tried to persuade him to let her get rid of these unnecessary things. But he held onto the huge amount of property he had amassed and refused to part from his junk. In the end, she asked me to go to the seashore with him on the pretext that he should get some fresh air, and then invaded the carpentry shop with Yosef. They made huge piles of all the rubbish, loaded it onto Simcha's old cart and took it to the dump, once, twice, until the shop was almost empty. When Fishke returned with me he looked silently at his empty shop, and next day he went out to roam the streets and again started to collect old rags and newspapers and planks and nails, and refilled the place that served him for both work and lodging. 'I use the rags and papers for polishing,' he explained to Simcha, 'I mix paint in the jars and I straighten the bent nails with a hammer.' And Simcha listened and looked at him sorrowfully and murmured, '*Kazhdei s uma skhodit po svoyemu*,' everyone goes mad in his own way.

The carpentry shop filled up more and more until Fishke no longer had room to lie down. Then one day he fled his shop and came to our room at noontime, laid himself down on the bed he had once carved for him and Simcha, said he was very tired, and asked Yosef and me not to disturb him. When Simcha came home in the evening she didn't throw him out but next day went to the carpentry shop, locked the doors, returned the deposits the customers had paid for furniture they had ordered, and compensated those who proclaimed that they had suffered damages. Since then Fishke stayed with us, shared Simcha's bed, ate the dishes she cooked for him, and added to the room the fresh smell of wood shavings and the stinging smell of cabinetmaker's glue that mingled with the smell of burning that came from Simcha's body and the smells of vanilla and cinnamon that came from her apron.

In the evenings, when Simcha came home from work, she would look at him affectionately, caress his face and whisper in his ear, '*Moy rodnoy*,' my one and only, and he would kiss her prematurely white head and murmur softly, 'My Simchi.' And sometimes they went out arm in arm to walk on the seashore in the cool evening breeze, and return with a basket filled with seashells they collected on the beach. Fishke had found himself a new occupation: he made little wooden boxes and inlaid them with gleaming shards of seashells, Damascene works of art. The boxes, some of which were adorned with Stars of David and seven-branched *menorahs*, Yosef sold to the tourist shops on the main streets of Tel Aviv.

And indeed, a miracle happened to Fishke when he was with Simcha: his hands steadied and he was once again able to do painstaking work. His phantom pain also eased, his memory improved, his clear eyes gazed at Simcha with the look of a young man desiring the charms of his beautiful wife. And she, with all the sensitivity of the blind, sensed his glances roaming over her and smiled to herself, and I once even heard her humming a Russian melody as she kneaded the dough.

Despite the deep lines etched into her face by all the hard years, Simcha was still a beautiful woman. Her white hair was braided into two long, thick plaits rolled around her head, endowing her with the shining aura of a saint, and her unseeing eyes were more translucent than ever.

Fishke once told me that her wrinkles were a testimony and memento of all the pain and trials that had hurt his Simchi and wounded her soul. The wounds of the soul had healed, but the scars became apparent with memories that were suddenly aroused, and etched lines on the face. Each line is a memento of pain and all of them, the entire dense network of lines on her face, were evidence of a life filled with pain.

I looked at Fishke's still-smooth face and asked him, 'You had troubles too, so where are the wrinkles?'

Fishke laughed: 'Simchi took my troubles upon herself and some of the wrinkles on her face are there because of me.'

But despite his declaration that his Simchi's wrinkles were beautiful and didn't bother him at all, I found them one day sitting facing one another and his fingers, rough from cabinet-maker's glue and from the splinters lodged in them, and dripping oil, were gently massaging her face. He kneaded and massaged each wrinkle, as though trying to erase all the painful mementos from her face. He first softened her forehead, whose lines stretched from temple to temple and whose ends disappeared into the roots of her hair at the sides. She sat facing him in silence, her eyes closed, giving herself up to the pleasure of his touch, her face softening under his oiled fingers and her lips open in a gentle expression. His fingers then moved down to her cheeks, and as they reached the lines of bitterness at the corners of her mouth I knew that I shouldn't be there and I got up and left the room on tiptoe, keeping that scene forever in the photograph album of my mind – a scene of the belated happiness of two people whose whole lives had passed until they were finally united in a great love. It was a scene that told me that fate sometimes desists from its despicable habit of misleading us, shows mercy and also bestows upon us days of grace. And then all we can do is hold onto them and not let go, lest fate changes its mind and once again shatters all our hopes.

The country was quiet for seven years after the riots and in my own life there were no further events worthy of preservation in my memory. Only amorphous secrets, fears and worries roamed the darkness of the house, settled in Avigdor Ben-Ari's and Zerach Levin's deserted room and maliciously aroused harsh memories from hibernation. During those years, on the anniversary of my mother's death that was my birthday, I would again ask my grandmother about her secret, and whether it was connected to a pogrom, and she would shake her head and say that the time had not yet come.

I sometimes think that everything that has happened to me since then took place as a result

of the conspiracy woven against me by my grandmothers, who feared that my fate would be like
my mother's, and that the disaster that had
befallen her would befall me as well, because they
also apparently believed that, 'like mother, like
daughter'.

So when I reached *bat mitzvah* and the boys of
Tel Aviv and Jaffa had difficulty ignoring the
flames of my red hair, I was summoned to a
serious talk with both of them, who in this matter
had joined forces, and they informed me that I
was forbidden to associate with boys.

'Your mother became pregnant and gave birth
before she was thirteen, and that must not
happen to you,' Grandma Abulafia warned me,
and my grandmother Simcha kept silent and
nodded her head in agreement. With her face on
fire, Grandma Abulafia described how a baby
gets into its mother's belly, which was something
I had already discussed with my girlfriends and
with which we had been preoccupied ever since,
to the accompaniment of giggles and excited
shrieks. Then my grandmother Simcha informed
me in a long, rambling and tedious speech that
men would try and exploit my innocence, and
this time Grandma Abulafia kept quiet and
nodded in agreement. In the end, when they
thought I did not understand the seriousness of
the situation, they mentioned the rheumatic fever
I had contracted when I was three, and the words
of Dr Aberbuch, that it was doubtful if I would

be able to have children because my heart had been irreparably damaged and apparently would be unable to withstand carrying a foetus and the burden of pumping blood for two.

When the first signs of puberty appeared in my body, Simcha watched over me like a hawk and did not let me go out with my girlfriends in the evening. And when I rebelled and announced that I was going out, she would burst out and shout that she didn't have the strength to raise a bastard great-grandchild too, and even threatened me with, 'You'll die giving birth like your mother.'

Every time I disobeyed her and went out dancing with a joyful group of boys and girls, either she or Grandma Abulafia, in ways that were beyond my comprehension, would find out where I was, and so that I wouldn't be walked home. God forbid, by one of the boys who might touch my private parts with his lustful fingers, they instructed Yosef to wait for me as I came out and he would accompany me home in silence, like a jealous husband, angry with me and himself for neglecting his studies to safeguard my virtue.

'Wait, not now, you mustn't now, it's dangerous now,' the warnings went with me everywhere. But the body has its own set of rules, and at age fourteen at the Eden Cinema I had already hungrily kissed one of my suitors, who had even stuck his tongue into my mouth, struggled there with mine, caught it between his lips and sucked it, and cut my lip with his teeth. Afterwards I spent a sleepless night frightened that I had got pregnant. It was at that time that my belly began rounding and sticking out, and Grandma Abulafia got frightened and rushed me to a lady doctor who determined that, 'The girl is still a virgin, but perhaps it would be prudent to examine this swelling of her belly.'

And I felt that everybody who loved me was conspiring against me to watch my movements, and their reproachful looks, if not they themselves, were always with me, and I sought refuge in daydreams. When the sun was at its zenith and shimmering mirages rose from the sand dunes, I would wander around Jaffa and let my imagination run riot. I am Cleopatra, Queen of Egypt, and I have just immersed my body in a bath of asses' milk, sated myself with pearls dissolved in vinegar, my handmaidens have wrapped my soft, smooth skin in a many-pleated golden robe and hung a gleaming, heavy pendant of precious stones around my neck. From among the ragged market pedlars I selected the one who will be my beloved Mark Antony, from his head I removed the stained tarbush and replaced it with a chaplet of gold leaves, and now he gracefully offers me the gift of a lover – the city of Jaffa, with its walls, turrets and houses. And I wander in it starry-eyed, keeping close to the walls lest I be crushed by the camels wending their way through its narrow alleys, enjoying the lustful glances darted at me by my subjects, the café frequenters. My heavy gold jewels slow my steps, and my twin sons, the fruit of my love for Antony, swim around in my womb and I speak to them softly. I rule my kingdom and subjects with a rod of iron – until up pops Yosef who is always lying in ambush for me somewhere or other.

Yosef's look was enough to make me remove my royal garments, get rid of the jewels and rip the twins of love from my womb. By the time we got back to our crowded room in Widow Ziso's house, I was once again Tamara Carrot-head, Tamara Rooster, Tamara Another One, and Daughter of the Hyenas.

By the time I completed my high-school education, I had had enough of the gloominess of the house, of Yosef who watched my every move, and the edict 'The mothers have eaten sour grapes and the daughters' teeth are set on edge' that had threatened me from my elementary school days, in the feminine gender. It occurred to me that if I were to change my abode, my luck would improve, as in the old adage 'A change is as good as a cure', that also hung on the dining-room wall at my elementary school, right next to 'Like father, like son'.

A small sum of money from the errands I ran for Grandma Abulafia and the notes my father pushed into my hand every now and then that I had managed to put aside over the years gave me the false sense that I was ready for independence, and after harsh and bitter arguments with both my grandmothers I left my grandmother Simcha's room and for a pittance rented a tiny window-less room in Jaffa's Old City, near the sea. A musty smell stuck to the peeling walls and scraps of azure, like flakes of blue sky, fell on me from the curved ceiling, filling my hair and the mattress I spread on the floor with grains of bluish dust and flecks of brittle plaster. Deep cracks in the walls revealed innumerable coats of paint, one for every year, like the annual rings of a felled tree to which each winter added a new, thin hoop to thicken its hips. On my first night there, by the light of a lamp that cast shadows onto the ceiling, I tried to count the coats of paint in one of the cracks that hung threateningly over my head. When I reached the nineteenth layer, whose colour was bright pink, a great tiredness fell upon me. And yet that night I couldn't fall asleep and I don't know what troubled my sleep more: the know-ledge that for the first time in my life I was about to go sleep on my own, or the upsetting parting from my childhood home and the terrible fear that perhaps I had made a mistake, and that by running away I would not be able to change my fate. To these thoughts and fears were added the nocturnal tumult that filtered through the gap between the door and the jamb: the heavily breathing sea, the waves breaking with sobs of pain against the jetty, threatening to flood my room with salt water, the drunkards' singing coming from the inns near the port, and the cracked calls of the muezzin who hastened the faithful to the mosque before sunrise – all those sounds were in my room, lying with me on my mattress and driving sleep from my eyes.

Next morning Fishke knocked on the door of my room. Silently, he sniffed the sour air that stood in the small windowless space, which after the long night had absorbed the smell of my fear, nodded at the sight of the cracks in the walls and ceiling, and left, dragging behind him his wooden leg whose worried tapping on the pavement I could still hear for a long time after he had gone. He returned about an hour later with Levi, the Kurd porter, whose back was burdened with a disassembled wooden bed, a small table, two chairs and some shelves. The two silently assembled the bed, placed the table and chairs in the middle of the room, fixed the shelves to the crumbling walls and left. Not a moment had gone by, and I heard the creaking axles of my grandmother Simcha's old cart, as if the three of them had arranged it all between them. I peeped through the open door and saw my two grandmothers unloading a paraffin stove, a large pot, a kettle, eating utensils, a tablecloth, sheets, cushions, and a quilt stuffed with sheep wool. They came in without a word, ignored me as if I wasn't there, and arranged the room as if it was theirs. Together they made the bed, spread the cloth on the table, heated the food they had brought on the paraffin stove and infused tea leaves in the kettle. Together they set the table without saying a word, laid out on it one plate, one cup, a spoon, fork and knife, ladled the heated food onto the plate, next to it placed a dark, dense loaf of bread, and they, too, left without even looking at me.

I sat down on one of the chairs that Fishke had brought and examined the plate. Steaming *borscht* winked at me with reddish-purple eyes and tried tempting me with the chunks of meat and the big bone that lay in it. I was hungry and so I suppressed my stubborn disgust for this liquid, fished out the meat and chewed it without much enthusiasm. I tore bits from the loaf and dipped them into the soup until they were as soft as sponge, and when I sucked them in my mouth a longing for my grandmother Simcha's room and her smells awakened in me. I wiped the plate clean with the last bit of bread and a feeling of fullness spread inside me, suffusing my body with a sweet weakness as a result of a full, exhausted stomach and a sleepless night. I lay down on the fresh sheets and fell asleep immediately.

Next morning I shoved open the door and through it burst a strong light that expelled the darkness, and the strong smell of an ancient city assailed my nostrils. Like a suffocating blanket impossible to shake, a haze hung over the city, mixed with strange stenches and all kinds of pleasant aromas that intermingled and competed for domination of my nostrils. The stink of refuse fermenting in the main street was salted by the smell of sea and fish, stirred into the columns of smoke escaping from the blacksmiths' tents and the dung fires of the street cooks, peppered with a pinch of the odour of donkey and camel excrement, spiced with a grain of the scent of incense coming from the church doors, and the sweetness of the citrus blossoms, insolent and stinging, that rose from the vast orange and lemon groves that encircled the city in a fragrant ring.

And as if my senses had become over-keen, to the extent of giving me a headache, I was suddenly hit by a terrible noise and sounds I had never heard invaded my ears. Murmured syllables and words, the echoes of ancient stories, the notes of songs and melodies, the prattling of idlers on the street corners, the groans of lovemaking, the braying of donkeys and grunting of camels. The shoe-shiners drummed loudly with their fine-cut brushes on metal boxes decorated with feathers and shining nails, a rhythmic tapping came from the feet of the street tailors as they energetically treadled their sewing machines, and amber beads clicked through the fingers of the *nargileh* smokers as they rolled them incessantly. Scissors clacked in the hands of barbers drumming up custom, coins rattled in the battered tin cups of the beggars, copper bells rang in the hands of the tamarind-sellers who also banged their cups to arouse the thirst of the passers-by, and donkey-drivers cursed their stubborn beasts and the camel-drivers cursed theirs, and all these sounds blended into a tumult that encompassed me until my ears rang and my head spun.

I turned my back on the Old City and the sea of people swaying heat-stricken in the alleys, and went up to the exclusive Bostoros Street. Idly, I walked the length of the street where a domed arcade provided shade on both its sides, and went from one display window to the next. I pretended I was examining the merchandise on show, but more than I looked at the merchandise I glanced at myself, at my reflection in the window, and tried to assess my attraction for the dapper men walking down the street and for the shopkeepers sitting in their shop doorways, half-fainting from the heat and in a weak voice inviting the passers-by to come in and inspect their wares. Rivulets of sweat stuck my dress to my body and the humidity played havoc with my hair, curling it around my head. Flushed and overheated, I took refuge in the dimness of a shop over which a sign in three languages, Hebrew, Arabic and English, announced 'Salim – Latest Ladies' Fashions'. I walked around the shop, fingering the beautiful dresses hanging on hangers and stroking the blouses folded in piles on the shelves.

'Try it, why not, try it on,' encouraged a voice from behind me. Small, shining eyes sunk into a round face were fixed on me. Mr Salim, the owner, scrutinised my body with an interest devoid of male desire, curiously looked at my red plait, and his sparse grey moustache trembled above his upper lip.

'No, there's no need, thank you,' I blushed.

Mr Salim ignored my stammerings. With his short-fingered, meaty hands he energetically ruffled through the coloured dresses that were crowded, puffed, splendid and rustling in an obedient straight line, like beautiful, curvaceous, headless and legless women happily waiting, while gaily gossiping, for an important event. With a triumphant shout he pulled out a red dress dotted with white flowers, spread it out on the counter, asserted that it suited the colour of my hair, ordered me to try it on and, when I hesitated, he pushed me behind the screen. I quickly took off my old dress, whose armpits were damp and exuded a sour smell of sweat, with its hem I wiped my sticky skin, pulled the new dress, whose colour burned, over my head, smoothed my wild hair, and shyly slipped out from behind the screen. Looking at me bashfully from the mirror were a crimson face and body that were not mine. The dress had a plunging neckline and it revealed the cleft between my breasts, accentuated my freckles, narrowed my hips, and showed my knobbly knees and thin arms.

'Bella, bella, bella,' Mr Salim choked and rubbed his hands. 'I knew it. This dress is yours. It's as if it was made for you. It's you,' he said and asked me to take it off quickly so he could wrap it up.

'But I haven't got any money,' I whispered.

'No matter. For you, it's free,' he replied immediately. 'You go in this dress and they'll all know that it's from Mr Salim's shop and they'll come and buy from me,' and again he pushed me behind the screen.

I was afraid he would peep at me so I took off the dress with my back to the screen and hurried to put on my old one. As if it were a very fragile object, Mr Salim carefully took the dress I held out to him. 'It doesn't even need altering,' he said with satisfaction, and sniffed the dress as though following the traces of my sweat, smoothed the pleats, put his hand into the neckline and I blushed again, as though he was doing all this to my body. Then, with gentle movements, Mr Salim wrapped up the dress in rustling tissue paper.

'It's yours,' he smiled, putting the parcel into my hands.

'But I've got no money,' I persisted.

'I told you that there's no need to pay,' he said, waving his hand generously.

'It's out of the question. It's expensive. I'm not taking it,' I said insistently as the heavy parcel weighed down my arms as if it were a lump of lead.

'When Mr Salim gives, you have to take,' he said, tightening my hold on the parcel.

'No, I can't,' I answered weakly, 'I must pay.'

'When you have the money, you can pay,' he said, and asked my name and proposed that I come to work for him. I made a quick calculation and saw that with the wages he promised me I would be able to pay for my room and one meal a day, so I accepted.

'I open at nine o'clock in the morning,' he announced to my retreating back.

I walked down Bostoros Street with the parcel pressed to my chest. Merchants with nobody to sell to sat idly in their shop doorways, their legs apart, roasting in the sun, but with their heads in the shade, in the cool darkness of the shop, and they waved to me with tired, soliciting gestures and invited me to buy from them as well. I didn't stop again but walked quickly, the dress searing my hands, and I sang all the way to the Old City. At the entrance to the alley leading to my room, I thought I saw Yosef. I called him, but he turned his back and walked away quickly until he disappeared.

The smell of cooking wafted into my nostrils at my doorway. I was amazed to find that my bed, which I had left unmade that morning, was perfectly made up, the paraffin stove was burning on a low flame, and on it sat a heavy iron pot. Although it was a Tuesday, in the pot I found *hamin* rich with potatoes and brown eggs, just the way I liked them, and the smell was the smell of Grandma Abulafia's Sabbath *hamin*. But despite my great love for her *hamin*, I sat down to eat it filled with anger. I realised that the two of them would never leave me alone, even if I moved even further away, even if I travelled to far-off lands.

When suitors began flocking to my room, I was unable to silence the warnings reiterated by those who had loved me throughout my life. 'Not another bastard,' I could hear my grandmother

Simcha screaming into my ear when a new boy knocked on the door. 'Be careful, don't let them touch you,' remonstrated Grandma Abulafia when lustful hands stole under my blouse and felt my breasts. 'Only after the wedding, not a moment before,' they unanimously screeched at me as inquisitive fingers insinuated themselves into my underwear, pleading to touch the softness between my legs. And even Latifa the prostitute did not keep silent: '*Hada ibbiq*,' she whispered softly. And in the background came the echo of my father's voice. 'Keep away from men, it mustn't happen to you, too.'

A few dozen boys visited me in my room, walked with me around Jaffa Port, watched uncounted sunsets with me on the seashore, bought me corn on the cob on the beach and spoke words of love to me. But not one could say I was his alone, until my notoriety gained currency among the boys of Tel Aviv-Jaffa: it is forbidden to touch her until her wedding night, the rumour spread, and one by one my suitors left me alone and walked out of my life. A few months after I acquired my independence, I found myself constantly alone in the dank room by the sea, counting the coats of paint on the walls at night by the light of the lamp. On each layer of paint I counted I would weave a new plan to extricate myself from my fate and the siege laid upon me by my grandmothers.

The solution I once came up with at the tenth layer was amazingly simple. On one of my weekly visits to Grandma Abulafia I asked her to make me a wedding dress. Her round face beamed in happiness. I knew that she would hurry to bear the glad tidings to my grandmother Simcha and Yosef, and then, perhaps, they would all leave me alone.

'Who is the boy?' she asked excitedly, 'Which family is he from? Do I know him? How long have you known him?'

'There's someone, and I think this is it,' I stammered.

'I hope you haven't let him touch where it's forbidden,' she said, her face clouding.

'No, Grandma.'

'And you're sure he wants to marry you? He's asked for your hand? Have you met his parents? Have you told your father and Simcha? Why haven't we had the pleasure of meeting him? Are you ashamed of him? He's ugly perhaps?'

'No, Grandma.'

'Are you pregnant?' she asked, suddenly afraid.

At that moment I gave up. 'I haven't got anybody,' I screamed. 'They all run away from me because of you, nobody wants me.'

'So what's the dress for?' she enquired drily.

'If you make me a dress, he'll surely come,' I said, trying to convince both of us. 'First a dress, then you'll see that a bridegroom will come, too.'

'You're mad,' declared my grandmother, 'You don't make a dress before there's a boy. It will bring you bad luck.'

'If you don't make it, I'll go to Alla,' I said, threatening her with the name of her hated rival, Mr Salim's seamstress. 'Alla will be only too happy to make it for me, and I've got the money to pay her,' I said, provoking her.

My threats bore fruit. 'All right,' she grumbled, 'I'll make you a dress you can also wear on holy days,' she said, proposing a compromise.

'Only a wedding dress. One you wear only once in a lifetime, magnificent and long,' I replied, rejecting her proposal.

My grandmother sighed and capitulated. The preparations went on for months: one month she measured me over and over, and as she was dissatisfied with my extreme thinness she fed me with sweetmeats so I would put on a little weight, because who would want a bride so long, so thin and pallid. Then she ran around for two whole months looking for a suitable fabric, and when she finally found it another few months passed until she dared to cut it according to the pattern I wanted. More than six months elapsed until she asked me to come for the first fitting.

'Look, not one of the dresses I gave to the women of your family brought luck – not to your grandmother and not to your mother. And now you're tempting fate and asking me to make you a dress before you've even found a bridegroom,' she muttered pleadingly, despite the long pins stuck between her teeth. 'What do you need it for? You can still change your mind, nothing's happened yet.' But I stood my ground, pressing her to complete the work and assuring her that the moment the dress was ready, I would find the boy for me.

But it seemed that my grandmother was not satisfied with her work. She undid stitches and re-sewed them, again undid them and again re-sewed them, and so on and so forth, until I felt that the dress was perfect and hugged my body softly and lovingly.

'No, this stitch is crooked and loose,' said Grandma Abulafia, showing me a straight, tight stitch. 'This button's not in the right place, and the hem is a real zigzag, and this sleeve is too long.' Until one day, when I put on the dress for one more fitting, I informed her that she must not touch it any more, ignored her protests, and the moment I took it off I folded it carefully and took it to my room in the Old City of Jaffa, knowing that I would very shortly find myself a man.

He appeared the next day at 'Salim – Latest Ladies' Fashions'.

CHAPTER 20

I first saw him as he crossed the threshold of 'Salim – Latest Ladies' Fashions'. In a flash his presence filled the shop that was full of women, hangers, dresses and loaded shelves. I was unable to take my eyes off the tall man, and when he turned his back to me for a moment to talk to Mr Salim, my eyes lit on the knot of hair resting on the nape of his neck that emerged, shining and perfect, from beneath the circular hat whose top was like a flat roof. For a moment I was troubled by a thought: who brushes the mane of his hair, I wondered, and if he does it without assistance, how does he manage to gather it together and coil and bind it so tightly that not a single stray hair escapes. When I finished deliberating over the knot, I went to straighten the summer dresses on their hangers just so I could steal a glance at him from the front. Against my will my eyes glided towards and became caught up in the stranger's beard. My fingertips felt the tickle of the soft, auburn fur of his chin that presented an amusing colourful contrast with the black hair of his head. As though mesmerised, I traced the dance of his hair that curled with a spring-like pliancy, and I followed it from where it joined his chin to where it had been cut at the middle of his throat, above his Adam's apple, in a straight, precise line. And I could not but compare the beard of the stranger with that of my father, which was bright yellow around his mouth because of the cigarettes he smoked, and wild, plucked and dry locks, in tones of pepper and salt, hung from it in curled shame, until it seemed to the observer that many and varied insects and vermin had found a hiding place in the tangle.

I awoke from my daydreaming when Mr Salim met my gaze and winked, as if he had read my thoughts, and turned the young man over to me.

From within the beard fleshy lips were suddenly revealed, teeth flashed at me in wet enticement and a soft tongue moved inside it as he spoke. But I didn't hear a word he said and inspected his clothing in embarrassment. He was wearing a simple black habit that hung loosely on his frame, covering and revealing grey trousers. I suddenly felt the saliva bubbling in the depths of my mouth – a childhood habit I had adopted under Yosef's influence: you collect saliva in your mouth, roll it into a ball and spit it out to the sides in an expression of disgust whenever one of those black-garbed men passed us, men who slipped through the alleys of Jaffa like walking statues, tall and silent, with an expression of gravity fixed on their faces. I was frightened by my involuntary action and hurriedly swallowed the saliva, chewed the end of my plait in embarrassment, and told myself that this was the first time in my life that a monk was actually addressing me, and I tried to concentrate on what he was saying and get the shining knot out of my mind, the curly hairs of the beard, the fleshy lips, the wet teeth and the flickering tongue.

'Please, I want to buy a coat for my sister,' I heard an unfamiliar foreign accent, soft and melodic.

'What size is she?' I asked like an experienced saleswoman.

'Like your size,' he replied, and I suspected him of blushing behind his thick, auburn beard.

I moved over to the coats with the 'elegant walk' that Mr Salim had taught me, and came back with a few coats in my size that were heavy in my arms. A colourful melange of coats were piled on the counter and with a gesture I invited him to look through them.

'Please, will you try them on?' he asked in a hesitant whisper.

I pulled out the black coat that lay on top of the pile and put it on with an expression of purposeful indifference on my face, as though my position in the shop obliged me to demonstrate for the customers how the garment looked on the body. I buttoned the coat that fell to my calves, and it itched, oppressing me with its warmth and heaviness, and I could feel the beads of sweat gathering at the nape of my neck under the high collar, lining up one behind the other as though waiting impatiently for their turn to slide down in the pleasant shiver that gripped me, over my spine until they reached the elastic of my knickers.

'Please, this coat,' he whispered, pulling out another garment from the top of the pile. He gently removed the black coat from my body and helped me into the other one. A foreign scent invaded my nostrils when he came close, a tender smell of the resin of a fragrant tree that burned slowly, spiced with cinnamon and the sweet scent of jasmine, a smell that later would be with me wherever I went. I felt his eyes pinned on the coat that covered my knees in greenish folds, slicing through the heavy wool weave, stiffening my skin, meeting my flesh and invading my body. He removed the coat from my shoulders and his touch made my body shiver in the awful summer heat, and he put another coat on me, that burned in orange.

I don't remember how many coats I tried on that day or which one he finally bought for his sister, but I remember well that I thought only of him all the way through the winding alleys to my room. And at night the smell of burning resin invaded my bed and the burning hands of the man in the black habit wandered over my skin, his full lips met mine and his tongue roamed inside my mouth.

I tried to drive him out, his smell and his hands and his image, that had somehow imprinted itself on my retinas, like the sun that doubles when you look at it for too long, and then you can't get rid of it, because even if you escape to a darkened room, you find it there in dozens of dark suns.

About a month later, when the memory of the smell had dissipated and the touch of his burning hands had cooled, I met him again. That day I was walking through the alleys of Jaffa with Ruth Abulafia, a relative on my father's side of the family of about my age, who had come on a visit from Jerusalem.

'Just like the alleys in our Old City,' said my bored guest, and urged me to take her to where she could look at the sea, because a Jerusalemite who visits Jaffa wants to see the spume of waves, smell the saltiness of the sea and feel drops of cool water spraying onto her face and hair. I led her in the wake of tiny scraps of wet blue that glinted in tiny flashes through the cracks in the partly ruined ancient city wall. The blue scraps led us to a pink-painted church whose façade blocked our view of the sea. A strange feeling pervaded me, as if I knew what was going to happen to me there. In an attempt to prevent what had been decreed for me, I sought to go around the church and continue on our way, but Ruth insisted on going inside.

We went in through a wide, inviting door directly into the darkness of a nave, and my pupils dilated to take in the scene we had been forbidden to see. By the light of candles and lamps and between paintings of saints who transfixed us with reproving looks at the uninvited guests shone the knot of hair at the base of the head bowed before the altar. A presence of a kneeling man dominated the large space.

'Let's get out of here,' I whispered fearfully.

But Ruth did not budge, her eyes were fixed on the back of the monk absorbed in prayer. I tried to drag her away, and was already on my way through the columned vestibule towards the door. But then the monk shook off his stillness, as if he had eyes in the back of his head and could sense our presence behind him, he turned his head and his glance hit me. In the terrible silence of the church I could hear my wildly beating heart, the fizzle of the candles and the rustling of his habit that struck his legs as he walked towards us. What little light that came through the coloured windows joined the glow of the flickering candles, sharpening and lengthening his nose, deepening the shadows beneath his eyes and the hollows of his cheeks, and he looked much older than I remembered him in daylight, in the shop. I was embarrassed and feigned interest in the murals and the portraits of the saints, letting my eyes roam up and down just so that I wouldn't have to meet his. On the wall opposite me I saw a huge painting of a man whose face was like that of the monk who stood facing me. He, a very thin man whose ribs stood out, was hanging on a cross, a kind of grey towel covering his loins, his eyes closed in anguish and on both sides of his narrow face his hair fell in untidy locks and merged with the halo around his head that lolled onto his left shoulder. I looked at the monk standing before me and again at the figure of the crucified man on the wall. Suddenly, I heard Ruth's excited voice, who apparently was also looking at both of them.

'It's that man!' she whispered.

Later those who loved him were to say that God, in a prank whose deep meaning only He knew, created Archimandrite Christodolos in the image of Jesus. And the proof, they were to say, is that if we scrutinise the tens of thousands of portraits of Jesus painted both by renowned and anonymous artists in every period and throughout the Christian world, we will see that the vast majority are identical to or resemble Christodolos' face. And it makes no difference if it is a black Jesus painted in Ethiopia, or a flat-faced, slant-eyed Jesus as in the Alaskan Eskimo paintings – it's as if the monk who stood facing me in the Jaffa church had sat as a model for all of them.

'Thank you very much,' he said, breaking the silence and into my thoughts, 'the coat suits my sister,' and his calm voice was somehow out of kilter with his lips that trembled through his beard and revealed an emotional storm.

He turned on his heel and moved away from us like a huge black butterfly in his wide habit, fluttering away and leaving behind him a scorching trail of charred resin and strong emotion that gradually spread throughout my body. I glanced at his back and could swear then that his every movement revealed heart-stopping simplicity that gained one's respect.

Some might say that I had been hit by what is known today as 'love at first sight'. Today, from a distance of the years that have passed, I know that the impression left on me by the monk, even during those few moments when I watched his retreating back, came from 'charisma', a word I had once learned from Avigdor Ben-Ari, it and its definition he had given me and dictated for my notebook: 'A god-given gift of mysterious power, for which you will not find a good dictionary definition. An illusory power, chimerical, that cannot be measured or seen, and it hovers transparent around the person who has been given the gift, trapping in its hidden web the innocent victims from among those he meets in the course of his life.'

The monk had been given this gift in abundant measure.

A long time after I met him for the second time, I again felt the burning touch of his hands that penetrated the thick cloth of the coats I had tried on for him in the shop, and despite the hot easterly wind outside, I again shivered.

In silence I went back to my room with Ruth and we didn't mention the monk again. Next day I took Ruth, who was about to return to Jerusalem, to the bus station and on the way home I found

312

myself walking in the direction of the church. With a previously unknown confidence I went inside and felt relieved when I didn't find him there.

But at night I again nestled up against his beard, undid the knot at his nape and smoothed his long hair with my fingers. I separated it into curling tresses, oiled each one with fragrant oil of rosemary, gathered them in my hand and retied them into a tight, glistening knot.

As the days went by the aroma of resin incense diminished and when I did not succeed in reviving it in my memory, one Sunday I put on my red dress, the gift from Mr Salim, rolled my long red hair into a knot like that other one, and walked to the pink church by the sea. A foolish act, and I'll never know whether I did it because of Christodolos' bewitching charm, or because it was predestined, even before I was born, as I was to learn later from my grandmother Simcha when she revealed her last secret to me. I sat near the door on the last in a row of worn wooden pews, knowing that I stood out with my bright red hair and loud red dress. The monk gave his sermon in Greek and Arabic and the congregation looked at him and listened as though hypnotised. When he finished, he descended from the pulpit, walked among the faithful who knelt and at his feet opened their mouths like fledglings in a nest, put out their tongues, and on them he placed a thin wafer. When he reached me, I smiled and was happy to see his eyes shining at me and his teeth gleaming through his beard.

I waited impatiently for the ritual and the service to end, and it was an eternity until his flock finally lifted their heavy behinds from the pews and broke up into groups that lingered to chat in the columned vestibule, and the last of the congregants slowly departed.

Just the two of us stood in the empty nave, like a pair of grasshoppers in a huge bowl, extending their antennae towards each other before mating. Variegated sunbeams, painted in the colours of the rainbow as they passed through the stained-glass windows, were turned into a kaleidoscope of giddying shapes on the floor, crazily chasing one another. My eyes, that feared meeting his, roamed the vast space of the church in embarrassment, until they came to rest on a bald and bearded saint holding a key in his hand while at his feet a big, fat chicken floundered, its tail adorned with red, orange and green feathers, its bright red comb lying flat, reminding me of my beloved rooster, Ben-Zion the First.

The monk's eyes smiled at me.

'And he said, I tell thee, Peter, the cock shall not crow this day, before that thou shalt thrice deny that thou knowest me,' his voice suddenly burst into my consciousness, tearing me away from my memories, and he was silent for a long moment before adding, 'I am Christodolos.'

'I'm Tamar,' I answered, and again we fell silent for a long moment, looking at one another like wrestlers before a deciding bout.

'Ta-mar,' he repeated my name with the sweetness of his strange accent.

And again we were silent.

'What's the connection between that man and the cock?' I asked, unable to resist the question, for after all a rooster had been my first love.

'That saint's name is Peter, but in your religion he is known by his Hebrew name, Shimon Ben-Yochanan. He came from a family of fishermen on the shores of the Sea of Galilee and he was Jesus' favoured apostle,' Christodolos was happy to relate. He told me that the cock was connected to Passover eve, the Last Supper held by Jesus with his twelve apostles, including Peter. It was at that supper that Jesus foretold his death the following day and hinted that one of them would betray him. Peter said that he would never fail him, and then Jesus told him that that night, before cockcrow, he, Peter, would denounce him three times. That night, after the meal, Jesus and his apostles gathered at Gethsemane on the slopes of the Mount of Olives, and a great multitude came armed with swords and staves. On behalf of the leaders of the priestly sect they came, and with them Judas, the traitorous disciple. Judas went up to Jesus and kissed him, the signal that this was the man to be arrested. Jesus was arrested and taken to the high priest's house, and the concerned Peter also went there to see what was to happen to his teacher. And there, in the high priest's courtyard, he denied three times that he was Jesus' apostle so that he, too, would not be harmed. And then the cock crowed. When Peter recalled what Jesus had said, he rose and left, weeping.

I don't know how long we stood there facing each other after he finished his story, and I don't know how my naked body finally ended up in his narrow monk's bed, with a small statue of the crucified Christ, his face the face of the monk, looking at us from the wall with his dead eyes, his head lolling on his left shoulder.

Many things have been erased from my memory; details, scenes and feelings have been cast into oblivion.

Years later I sometimes still wondered whether he had undressed me, if he had kissed me, what the touch of his hands felt like, when had he loosened his long hair, what he had said to me, had he hurt me and, most of all, had I enjoyed the touch of our bodies at all. From that first time, only one scene always surfaces in my mind: the gold crucifix on a thin chain he wore round his neck that swung from his chest, hovered over my face, tickled my cheeks and danced between my breasts.

Next morning I woke up in his bed, wrapped in his shining, fragrant hair that covered my body like a warm and splendid silken mantle. Christodolos was awake, lying on his side and scrutinising my face. 'You're beautiful,' he said in wonder, as though seeing me for the first time in his life.

'Do you really think so?' I asked in trepidation.

Christodolos confidently poured the words

directly into the depression of my navel: 'You're beautiful.'

'Are you sure?' I said, still unbelieving.

'Beautiful,' he said for the third time, and to impart greater force to his words he took the blanket off me completely and let his eyes roam over my body – his look caressed my neck, slid gently over my breasts, stroked my belly, fingered my pudenda and pleasured my legs from thigh to feet. Then his fingers joined in and crawled over me, sending a shudder of pleasure through me as he counted the freckles on my face and breasts, kneaded my round belly and moulded my thighs.

'You're beautiful,' he declared again, ruffling my already uncombed hair and getting out of bed, his member distended and hard. With great difficulty he pushed it into his underpants, squirmed into his trousers, put on his white shirt and over it the black habit that finally concealed the swollen bulge. Then he took a handful of long hairpins, inserted them between his teeth, mischievously pursed his lips around them, like someone about to whistle gaily, haphazardly combed his long hair, rolled it onto his nape into a loose knot, and bound it to his skull with the pins he took from his mouth one at a time.

When he finished, he hustled me to get dressed, but only after a long search was I able to find my dress thrown forlornly between the bed and the wall. As I put it on I discovered that three buttons were missing from the front, which had apparently been torn off at some point. I crawled under the bed to look for them and found there dust balls, candle ends, faded rigid moths, their wings spread, a few hairpins, and even a cockroach that had breathed its last while lying on its back. But I couldn't find the buttons. I hugged my chest to cover my breasts that were showing from the unbuttoned neckline, as if Christodolos had not seen me in all my nakedness only minutes ago.

'Come tomorrow at six in the evening,' he whispered, despite there being no one else there, and he walked me to the heavy wooden gate of the church where he slid back the heavy bolt for me.

'Tomorrow at six in the evening,' I heard him whisper anxiously to my back, lest I forget.

I did not answer. I grasped the open neckline of my dress, and uncombed and blushing ran through the churchyard towards the fence, and fled through the wicket in the iron gate. Scorching air seared my lungs, expelling the dark coolness I had inhaled in Christodolos' thick-walled room. My ears, that had earlier enjoyed the quiet, were now deafened by the shouts of the pedlars, and the stink of donkey and camel dung drove out the scent of incense that still lingered in my nostrils. Barefoot children dressed in rags thronged around me, shoving filthy hands into the folds of my dress, stroking my body filled with sweetness and asking for *baksheesh*. I flowed with the crowds of people thronging the alleys, my hands clasped to my bosom and my back against the walls of the houses as a camel caravan passed me in an alley, leaving piles of dung in its wake and sending into the narrow space between the two rows of houses the guttural shouts of the camel-drivers, and I suddenly found a wondrous beauty in everything around me. The sun beating down on my head stood with wonderful precision in the middle of the heavens, the people crowding around me were handsome and smiling, and even the touch of the children's hands on my skin, which at any other time would have sent a shudder of revulsion through me, was now pleasing. The world smiled at me, took me lovingly into its bosom, and my eyes could not get enough of it.

For a moment a new chapter in my life had been opened. I believed Christodolos and felt I was a woman, a woman loved for her beauty, and the bad opinion I had of my looks, a view that was the loathsome fruit of my grandmothers' conspiracy against me, dissipated and vanished.

I lay on my bed in my tiny room and vainly tried to picture what had happened to me. Only the sweet smell of slowly burning resin that still came from the pleats of my red dress, from my finger-tips and rose into my nostrils, sent waves of pleasure right through me and they reminded me of the thing that had happened to me.

But by next morning when I gazed into the depths of the mirror, from which a woman had looked out at me the previous day, I again saw the young girl I had been, a girl with an upturned nose, too prominent cheekbones, her red hair thick and wild, skin dark and freckled, and her body skinny – a real bag of bones.

So I returned to him that evening and again he loved me with his body and again I was beautiful, in his eyes and mine. Until the morning, when my beauty again faded, and so on and so forth. That is how my days with Christodolos passed, I became beautiful and returned to ugliness, I was ugly and became beautiful again, until it sometimes seemed that without Christodolos I would never be beautiful in my own eyes. For a short time after our lovemaking I would again see in the mirror the ugly young girl I had always been, and I had no doubts that the woman I had seen in it earlier was not me.

CHAPTER 21

All day I would wait impatiently for the evening when Archimandrite Christodolos would be mine alone. Then we would seclude ourselves in his house, the temple of our love. The house, adjoining the Church of St Ioannis, was painted stark white like the houses of Greece, as Christodolos described them to me. The roof was covered with scales of orange Marseilles tiles and had two small rooms, a small bedchamber and a living room whose narrow arched windows overlooked the sea, and a tiny alcove adjoining it served as the bathroom.

We used to sit facing each other on the narrow bed covered with a purple coverlet whose material had sprouted stains of dried semen and was dotted with stiff waxflowers, and I would sit there looking at him looking at me. Every movement I made, even a yawn, scratching the tip of my nose or crossing my legs, spellbound him as if I had worked a miracle. He used to say that my eyes were so transparent that through them he could see what was happening inside my head, while in his brown eyes, by the faint light of the lamp, I found red sparks of an evil nature and the dampness of tears.

They are tears of exaltation, he once explained to me, like the tears that sometimes gather in the eyes of someone studying a magnificent work of art. Because I was so beautiful that he was elated with gratitude to the Lord who had created me. And to reinforce his words he would touch my body, part by part, and praise them all, even the fifteen I hated, because he only found beauty in me and ignored the ugliness. He especially praised my freckled breasts, my small hands, my upturned nose and the big toe of my left foot, that I thought looked like the head of an ageing turtle, while in his eyes it was the acme of perfection. And once he even knelt at my feet, nibbled and licked their soles with his warm tongue, stuck the graceless big toe into his mouth and suckled on it with great pleasure. At those moments of grace, that endowed me with a little of the robustness I so lacked, I felt that Christodolos was creating me anew with his gaze, his words and the touch of his hands. From my image in his eyes came an intimation of the life I might have had had my mother not disappeared on the day of my birth, had she stayed with me to kiss and extol every part of my body just as he did, even though it be flawed.

Then for just a moment I would be filled with a feeling of consequence: Someone loves me so much! And immediately came the doubt: Can it be?

The moment I loved most of all was when Christodolos put his head into my hands, and I would gently, so as not to hurt him, pull out the long hairpins stabbed into the knot of his hair. And each time I was amazed afresh by the sight of the nape of his neck as soft and vulnerable as a baby's, with a deep fold etched in it and thin hairs curling softly from it. His mane joyfully escaped its narrow prison, surged down his back, kissed his waist and spread in soft, black, shining, flowing waves around his body. Then Christodolos would undo my plait and three thick flaming snakes would fall onto my chest as if vying with the length and thickness of his hair. And he would bend over me, enveloping me in his flesh and mane, lower my body onto the bed and lie at my side, and our hair would merge into a single mantle of intertwined black and red. With one arm I would cradle his head and the fingertips of my other hand would plough through the shock of flowing hair, borne on the softness of its waves. And Christodolos would purr like a grateful, satisfied cat, his head on my breast and his hands undoing my clothes and invading my limbs.

First the hands would describe circles on my round belly, the way someone does after a good meal, circling, caressing, and sending waves of pleasurable excitement coursing through my body. One hand would stop as though deliberating and then send an inquisitive finger into my navel, feeling around its depression as if I'd hidden a treasure there. When the hands had had their fill of my belly, they would cunningly and restrainedly crawl under my blouse to my breasts, each hand cupping a breast, embracing it, encircling and pinching the nipples between forefinger and thumb. And when a groan escaped my lips one would go on with its work up above, while the other withdrew, moved downwards, pushing away my underwear and sliding into my softness. The investigating finger would be withdrawn and again sent into my depths, almost accidentally stroking my mons on its way. And as my pelvis was aroused, revealing its desires and answering the movements with rhythmic movements of its own, Christodolos would throw off his habit, open his trousers, loosen his pants and burst into me powerfully. He stifled my cry of surprise with his hand over my mouth, because sometimes people would be walking around the church on the other side of the door. And I noticed that when the tapping of the flock's shoes and the murmurings of the novices sounded closer, his passion mounted, his erection hardened and his member became an instrument of destruction, thrashing and pulsing inside me until I was forced to plead with him to stop.

'That's for Theotokos,' that is, the Mother of God, he would hiss between clenched teeth as he pounded at my pelvis, 'That's for Christos,' and again stick his member into me, 'That's for Petros,' taking it out and sticking it back, and until he had mumbled into my ear the names of all the apostles and a few more saints, he would not calm down. And when he climaxed he would groan 'Theos,' God, come out of me, roll over and lie on his back at my side.

Only on Sundays, feast days, weddings and requiem masses would he release the gag over my mouth and let me groan and shout as much as I wanted, and then my shouts would accompany the ringing of the church bells. And he would shout with me and together we would create such a tumult that our voices would rise to the chapel roof, climb the tower, penetrate the belfry and be swallowed up in the bells' ringing. Then our noise and theirs would meld into a huge sound that would burst from the tower, come down and land on the heads of the passers-by in the alleys, thunder in their ears and shatter in a jumble of hard, metallic notes. And until that deafening turmoil fell silent, we lay on our backs side by side, hoarse, exhausted and emptied, listening tensely to the shuffle of feet in the church and the sounds of talking coming from there, afraid lest this time we had been heard.

During those moments of our loud lovemaking I used to listen, as though eavesdropping, to the sounds we made, to his groans and my moans mingling with increasing amplitude until they reached a shout, and I would think to myself that if a member of the congregation were to put his ear to the door, he was liable to take fright and think that a fight was going on behind it, that desperate enemies were grasping each other's throat to the death. And when we got up, fatigued and wet, and hurried to the bathroom, we seemed like a murderer and his victim hastening to wash their bodies and erase all traces of the crime.

About a month after our first meeting, I arrived at Christodolos' house carrying a suitcase whose contents I spilled out onto his narrow bed. For a long time Christodolos fingered the clothing and underclothes piled up in a colourful confusion of dresses, blouses, trousers, brassieres and under-wear. He passed his hand over the fabrics, felt the brassieres, sniffed the dresses with obvious pleasure, except for the wedding dress made by Grandma Abulafia, which he ignored, and then put everything into his wardrobe, making sure to hide my dresses and underclothes behind his colourful robes, trousers and shirts. His camou-flage was so good that had a stranger peeped into the wardrobe, he would not have discovered my clothes.

Like children planning their next prank, we looked for hiding places where I could conceal myself when priests and nuns or members of his flock came to see him when I was there. As we did so, Christodolos showed me hidden escape routes and dark hiding places that even the most suspicious person would never think of searching. At Passover I lay in one of them for five hours when he was visited by the elders of the Greek community led by the consul from Jerusalem, and I listened helpless and silent, my limbs stiff and

326

my bladder close to bursting, to the musical Greek being spoken right next to me, and to Christodolos' happy voice telling his guests an endless story. Only after he escorted them from the church and came back to make sure that none of them had forgotten anything did he free me from my prison.

From the day I moved in with my beloved, Yosef abandoned his studies and laid siege to the church. He would sit in Abu Ali's café at the corner of the street, downing scores of tiny cups of bitter coffee, and lie in wait for me. One day, so I was told by Christodolos, who never imagined who the young man was, he spat at him in disgust. 'But I am not angry with him,' he said, 'I even forgive him as our church commands, for it is written, "Whosoever shall smite thee on thy right cheek, turn to him the other also."'

But Yosef chaperoned me in particular. Every morning, as I slipped out of the church on my way to 'Salim – Latest Ladies' Fashions', I would see him hiding behind the smoke of the *nargileh* he sucked on in the café. The moment he saw me he would put down his coffee cup and the *nargileh* mouthpiece, put some coins on the table and accompany me in silence. He never said a word to me, never rebuked me, never preached to me, and this silent denunciation that fanned the flames of my guilt feelings was harder than a thousand reproofs. Once, as he accompanied me to my grandmother Simcha's room, I was unable to restrain myself any longer and attacked him, pummelling the broad chest he had inherited from Fishke, screaming, weeping and squirming in his arms that pinned me to him, and begged him to shout at me, hit me, rebuke me, say something. But Yosef just looked at me with Fishke's calm blue eyes, wiped the tears from my eyes and cheeks with his hand, smoothed my plait that had come undone, and walked on with me in silence.

Even when we were all gathered in my grandmother's room for the Sabbath meal, he would not utter a word; he sat opposite me in silence and, like a partner in crime, lowered his eyes and avoided looking at me. As we ate, he sat there silently chewing his special dish: unpeeled fruit and walnuts and almonds that my grandmother Simcha piled on a glass plate that was his alone, for he strictly observed the dietary laws, and he would wash his plate separately in water he drew from the pump in the yard. When we finished eating and I got up to leave, Yosef would also get up and announce that he would walk me to my room. At the door I would thank him politely, kiss his cheek, lie down on the bed fully dressed and blow out the lamp. A long time after the echo of his footsteps had been swallowed up at the top of the alley steps, I would get up, look out of the half-open door, make sure that no one was there, and leave. I walked to the church by a roundabout route, staying close to the walls of the houses, finding cover in their darkness and warmth. But in the alley leading to the church I would always see him, standing and waiting for me by Abu Ali's café, his eyes gleaming in the darkness like the eyes of a starved jackal. And again he would accompany me in silence, the sound of his footsteps swallowed up in the sound of my own, to the stone wall with the cross carved on it. There he would stop, spit in loathing, and follow my back with his eyes until it disappeared into the blackness of the courtyard. At lunchtime next day he would be waiting for me at the café and walk with me to Grandma Abulafia's for our Sabbath *hamin*.

At that time, when my love for Christodolos was full to overflowing, I sank into a slow and protracted process of decline and detachment from the world. Yosef, who was apparently waiting for the moment I would sober up and come to my senses, became my one tenuous connection with my past and with life outside. A few months after I moved in with Christodolos, I left my job at 'Salim – Latest Ladies' Fashions', despite Mr Salim's pleas that I stay and his promise to raise my wages and give me a new dress as a gift every six months.

I knew that just as Christodolos had to conceal his relationship with me, I, too, was unable to announce my great love to my loved ones. In the house we choked back our voices, we dared not be seen together in the street, and the future quickly began teasing us, firing darts of jealousy, suspicion, anger and agony. Our difficulties proliferated uninhibited, like rats in a barn, and with obscene sounds of chewing and gulping they gnawed at our love.

My love for Christodolos was desperate and tied with a Gordian knot to a sense of loss. Love and loss, loss and love walked with me and with us during all that time, tangling themselves around our feet and tripping us again and again. Each time Christodolos went out about his business, even for only a few hours, a fear awoke in me that I would never see him again. And as the hours went by it was as if my body shrank and was about to disappear, it and my entire being, because without him I had no existence, even the mirror on the wardrobe door showed no reflection, and when I went outside I was afraid of looking into people's eyes, of haggling with the pedlars and of ridding myself of bothersome children. At that time I only saw the filth and the vile in the world around me: the dirty puddles on the way to the church, the tattered laundry hung out to dry in the yards, the runny noses of the ragged children running in the streets, the heaps of stinking refuse piling up in the alleys. And at Christodolos' house I would sit for hours on his bed in the little room, my eyes fixed on the gaunt crucified man, whose face was the face of my beloved, my ears pricked to hear the creak of the opening door and the rustle of his habit.

Only the moment he came in would life return and revive me, the way a blood transfusion brings a casualty bleeding to death back to life. In his arms I would thaw, and when we became one flesh, all my past was forgotten and the future was no longer important – there was only the present making my body and soul tremble. And when my beloved awakened from his sleep after the act, his face happy and his arms embracing me, his mouth breathing me to him and whispering words of love, then the face of a beautiful woman would look out at me from the mirror. Then I would walk through the church, smiling to myself and joyfully lighting the sacred candles and the incense, stroking the faces of the martyrs with a feather duster and singing the hymns I heard him sing on Sundays, and go out into the street to the pleasant, slightly sticky sweetness of the liquorice and tamarind and their splendidly garbed sellers, the *booza*, ice-cream stands and those selling golden *ambar* sweets tasting of burnt sugar, and *salep* in glass jugs and rosewater dripping from the *baklawa* cakes filled with almonds and doused in honey.

At those moments I tasted only sweetness and didn't see or hear either the swarms of flies loudly buzzing around the piles of sweetmeats or the waving arms and the curses of the pedlars trying to drive them away.

Once, after my beloved had been away for a particularly long time, and not for the first time, either, I could no longer contain myself and bothered him with questions and interrogated him about what he had been doing outside for the many hours he had left me by myself. But he closed himself off inside his habit, withholding from me both his body and his soul, and he even adopted a new custom of shrouding himself in a vow of silence for hours, even whole days. Then he would distance himself from me and I saw him sullen and ill-tempered, so I tried to diminish my presence because I knew he was angry because of me. Like a shadow torn from a body I walked after him on tiptoe, humbly offering him my love, my body and soul, and he didn't even look at me but angrily waved his hand as if I were a bothersome insect buzzing at his ear, and without a word he would order me to shut up. The more frequent his silences became, the more he distanced himself from me and I wanted him more than ever, seeking to bind his body to mine, to join him to my belly with invisible glue, until we became that whole being as yet undivided by Zeus, and like the Siamese twins in the photograph Avigdor Ben-Ari showed me in his book, that was now mine.

I longed to go whither he went, to see the sights he saw, to draw air into my lungs for him and with my heart to pump blood for him too, and I knew that should he die, I would die as well because we had a single heart, and when it ceased pulsing, both his body and mine would die.

But his self-imposed silences increased and silence reigned between us like a malicious ancient monster, lying with clenched lips and fouling the air with its stinking breath, and sentencing me to a terrible loneliness. I lived as if in a world of nightmare. Christodolos would answer my unspoken cries with silence, hear my pleas and seal his lips. And in this awful silence I would hear the whispering of the tiny flames flickering in the church and consuming the candles' wicks, and the rustling of the moths' silken wings as they were drawn to the flame, and the creaking of the wooden beams in the ceiling. And when, one morning, from within the silence I suddenly heard the whisperings of the saints hanging on the walls and the angry beating of my hurting heart, I hit my beloved with the brass candlestick that stood next to the altar. Christodolos sat down on the floor, arched his back and submissively took the blows raining down on him. An expression of great tranquillity spread over his face and his eyes were closed in sweetness, like someone taking spiritual pleasure from physical affliction. Then a sharp pain pierced my body, as though the blows were landing on me, and I dropped the candlestick and sat down next to him on the floor, buried my face in my hands and burst into tears. Christodolos got up, straightened his stricken back and stepped over me as if I were an obstacle in his way. That night I rubbed his bruised back with paraffin oil, kissed the blue bruises spread over his flesh, and I wept and promised and begged him to forgive me and not to leave me.

Thus my days with Christodolos were hurled between beauty and ugliness, joy and sorrow, love and hostility. And the contrasts deepened and the swinging back and forth increased until it was like the swinging of a swing to which I was tied, with him standing behind it controlling its movement, pushing it hard and resting, pushing and resting, pushing me away and bringing me closer, bringing me closer and pushing me away, time after time, ever harder, and the swing soared high and touched the sky, and then came down and touched Hell, again soaring and again descending, and I was screaming in panic high up, even in the depths, begging for my life, and he closed his ears and pushed and rested, pushed and rested.

CHAPTER 22

As my suffering increased and my life with him became unbearable, I decided to confess my love for a monk to my grandmother Simcha. I know today that it was a cry for help. I wanted her to be angry with me, to place obstacles in the way of our love, order me to return home and extricate me from Christodolos' clutches. I knew that were she to demand that I leave him, I would have obeyed her and then I would have been able to justify the separation to myself, to view it as an act imposed upon me. And perhaps I also told her about Christodolos because I feared that Yosef, her faithful Yosef, was liable to unintentionally give the game away, and I wanted to pre-empt him.

But from day to day I put off talking to her. In my mind's eye I could see myself sitting facing her in her room, pleading and promising, and she filled with anger and even getting up and slapping my face as she had once, and only once, done when in my childhood she had caught me in the wardrobe kissing the neighbour's son. Over and over I practised what I was going to tell her and

335

how I would answer her questions, how I would try and appease her, until I finally sat down opposite her and, stammering and tearful, told her the story of my love for Christodolos.

She kept silent, her beautiful face darkened and it seemed that she was far away from me, wandering in her thoughts in other times and places. Her hands shifted restively and appeared to be fingering the clusters of secrets she kept from me.

'Simcha, say something,' I begged.

'I know,' she said, stunning me.

'Who told you?'

'No matter, I know.'

'But if you knew, why did you keep quiet?'

My grandmother twisted her lips in pain.

'Say something to me!' I screamed.

My grandmother turned her head aside.

'Do you want me to leave him?' I wept, 'I'll do anything you ask. I'll leave him if you just ask me to.'

'Do what you want,' she replied, got up, left the room and shuffled to the kitchen, and I could hear her mumbling angrily to herself in Russian, as was her wont when she was in a particularly gloomy mood.

It was a Friday when I came to her, and in the evening we were forced to eat burnt food: the soup had evaporated almost completely and all that was left were the ruins of potatoes and carrots that had been reduced to a purée, the rolls of stuffed cabbage were burned at the edges, the meat had suffered fatal burns and was tough and stringy, and even the salad looked like a mixture of vegetables that had been picked up haphazardly in the market at closing time.

My secret, now freed of its manacles, hovered over us, prattled, mocked and stuck out a long dripping tongue at me as my grandmother Simcha told it to Fishke in Russian. But now the Russian words did not sound caressing, sensual and soft as they usually did, but escaped her lips hard and rough in the way she used the language to hiss curses, tell secrets and express fear.

At the end of the meal Fishke, with a serious expression, asked me to step outside with him and I immediately realised that Simcha had authorised him to speak for her and to conduct the required talk in her place. I sought to forestall the danger and opened my mouth to reason, explain, promise, but he silenced me with a gesture, and without preamble informed me that my grandmother had not been surprised and that she wasn't angry with me. 'It's God's will,' he said without looking at me, 'Simchi knew it would happen to you, and it doesn't matter to her that he's a Christian or even a monk, because she has no faith. She only wants what is good for you, and if it's bad for you, then leave him. But no pregnancy,' he added in a whisper, despite there being nobody there but us, 'be careful. There mustn't be another bastard in the family. Simchi will die if it happens to you as well.'

I was so amazed that I forgot to ask him what my grandmother Simcha knew, had she known that I would fall in love with a monk of all people? And only when she was on her deathbed and told me her last secret was I to recall this.

That night, when I went back to the house next to the church, I didn't find Christodolos. As was his custom in recent weeks he told me before leaving the house that this evening he was going 'to give charity'. From his slip of the tongue a week earlier, when he came home tired but I still didn't let him close his eyes until he had told me where he had been, I knew that he was giving charity at Beit Sarah, the new pioneer women's hostel that had been built in Tel Aviv. So I went there, too, to find out what business the abbot of a Greek Orthodox monastery had in a hostel for Jewish pioneer women.

The smell of rutting hung in the air by the hostel, mingled with an acrid pinch of laundry soap coming from the underwear and brassieres hanging out to dry in the big front yard. In a fragrant, insolent and inviting defiance and with a fawning tongue, the perfume lured the passing men and they followed their noses to the yard and stood by the laundered undergarments that preserved the curves of the female body, and flared their nostrils to catch the scents of lust. I saw the women in the evening, coming and going in shorts fastened to their tanned thighs with an elastic band, embroidered blouses that were rounded over full bosoms, their laughter impudent and loud and their movements free, and they shook their washed and fragrant hair, and the many men gathered there followed them with a look of longing – from British policemen with their magnificent moustaches and red noses to Jewish workers in their rumpled and sweaty work clothes.

And I tortured myself with these scenes and fed my soul with my hate: how I hated those pioneers that Christodolos pleasured with his hot tongue, his hands and sensitive fingers, while they probably stroked his hair admiringly.

In Christodolos' dark room that was filled with the heavy smells of incense and candle wax, I felt that the eyes of the martyred saints, painted in every colour, were glaring at me with sanctimonious looks and boring into my flesh, burning with the flames of envy. And I lay down on his hard monk's bed with its narrow mattress, I cursed him and the women and raised my eyes to the pitying gaze of Theotokos, Mother of God, that rested on me in compassion, as if mutely expressing the common destiny of women. On many occasions I lay on the bed and she was hanging on the church wall facing the open vestibule door, and we both watched Christodolos as he oiled his hair with lavender oil, tied it into the tight, shining knot, combed his auburn beard, straightened it with sharp scissors, and sprinkled rosewater on his face and over his black habit from beneath which a pair of dandified trousers peeped. Then we would watch him standing in front of the mirror, examining his face from the front and in profile, and enjoying what he saw. He would bend over me, flutter a light, dry kiss of guilt onto my forehead, and leave. And as his merry whistle, whose tune he borrowed from the Sunday service, moved away with him and was swallowed up in the darkness, I would lie on the pillow and shed tears onto the oily halo left by his hair on the starched pillowcase, and the tears dotted it with dark stains whose edges were white with salt. Then I returned my gaze to the Mother of God and she would look at me sorrowfully and embrace the infant in her arms even more strongly.

I was jealous, not only of the faceless pioneer women, but of Christodolos too; of the freedom he enjoyed to do whatever he wanted, while I was bound to him and his bed, and I knew that even if I were to get up and leave, I would still be shackled to my grandmothers, my adopted brother who was constantly lying in wait for me outside the church, and the fate that had been decreed from the moment of my birth.

On one of those evenings when he left me on my own and time stood still, I wandered restlessly, upset and angry, around the church. And when the colours of the stained-glass windows were dimmed and the nave darkened, the candles cast giant shadows on the face of Jesus painted in gay colours on the walls, and with my own eyes I saw how it was replaced by Christodolos' face. And around me I saw my beloved surrounded by whores and seductive women. On the eastern wall he looked at Pelagia, the dancer from Antioch, and on his lips a tiny, lewd smile, and on the western wall he lusted after Mary Magdalene. And the paintings multiplied and spread and were everywhere: on the dome, the floor and the altar, and when I covered my eyes with my hands they looked at me through the gaps between my fingers. I saw Christodolos moving from one woman to another, to a third and a fourth, his naked body bent over them, over their breasts, their bellies and pudenda, and his buttocks rose and fell in the rhythm so familiar to me. And when a thick, green, viscous poison of envy started to bubble in my veins, I knew that I must exact vengeance on him and his saints.

That night I urinated into the font, scooped up some of this holy water in my hands that I joined into a small bowl, splashed it onto the altar behind the screen, and then went back, took up more water and wetted the Eucharist lying in its prothesis. Then I dipped the smouldering incense into the font and it let out a poisonous hiss as it came into contact with the water. Thin wisps of white smoke rose from it, bringing tears to my eyes. One by one, between finger and thumb, I snuffed out the flames of the candles burning in the brass candlesticks and tranquilly observed the fluttering wings of the obtuse moths that were attracted to the flames and thrashed in their death throes in the pool of melted wax. And as though Theotokos were to blame for all my travails, I stood facing her and her son, who looked like an adult miniaturised to play the role of the baby in her arms, I bent over before them in a mocking genuflection, stuck out my tongue at them, turned my back on them and again bent over, revealing my bottom. Before I left, I tore down the heavy green velvet curtain from above the altar, on which one big cross and lots of little crosses were embroidered in gold thread in relief, went back to Christodolos' room and spread it on the bed, undressed and lay down on it, naked. When I awoke at dawn and went to the bathroom to relieve myself, I found red depressions imprinted on my skin in the shape of one big cross and lots of little crosses all around it.

While I was still admiring the crosses embossed on my flesh, I heard the church door opening and I went out into the church and saw Christodolos genuflecting at the altar and his hands, that still held the smells of other women, were grasping an icon, and he was kissing the forehead of the crucified Christ with a mouth whose tongue had danced inside other mouths and titillated private parts. Then Christodolos reverently crossed himself before the portraits of the saints whom I had profaned the night before, got up and went to the font where he dipped his hands into the holy water, diluted with my urine, and splashed his face with it and crossed himself again. I hurried to get back to the room before him, and there I welcomed him naked on the bed, but he put a finger to his lips signalling that he was observing a vow of silence, and warned me with his eyes that I should not address him.

But that morning I paid scant attention to his vow and his exhausted body and forced him to make love to me, and he, his member flaccid, buried his face in my shoulder. I could smell the smell of the other vaginas on his fingers, remembered the crosses indented in my flesh, and a sudden fear shuddered through me. I got up from the bed, left Christodolos lying impotent on the velvet curtain and went back to the church.

I fished the pieces of incense from the font and took some fresh flakes that I lit, I revived the dying candles, begged forgiveness from Theotokos and her son, and with a light flick of the feather duster I cleaned the heavy layer of dust that had accumulated in the cracks of her face, the folds of her robe, and the corners of her son's grave eyes, and clouds of dust hung in the air, rose upwards towards the roof, glinted in the colourful morning sunrays, floated over the heads of the saints, tried to leave the building and shattered against the locked windows.

When I finished, I tiptoed back to the room, pulled the velvet curtain from under Christodolos' sleeping body, returned to the church and spread it in its place on the altar. When Christodolos awoke from his long sleep in the afternoon, he showed me the crosses impressed on his flesh and said a miracle had happened to him, and that it was a sign that he had been completely forgiven by the crucified Christ.

Once, after Christodolos had not returned to the church for three days, I waited for him in his room, hurt and miserable and wearing the wedding dress that Grandma Abulafia had made for me. I don't know why I had decided to wear it. I only remember that on the third day I was lying on the bed in it, half asleep and frequently awakening in fright, as though something terrible was about to happen. Towards evening, when eventually I heard him opening the church door, I got up onto wobbly legs, went to him and blocked his way to the altar. Christodolos looked at the beautiful white dress, was momentarily confused but immediately came to his senses and pushed me aside. He sought to genuflect, confess and beg forgiveness for his sins, but I forestalled him and lay down on the altar. The skirt of my dress fell from both sides of the altar and flowed in folds, like a magnificent lace curtain, and my nails dug into the curtain spread over it.

'You have no shame!' I screamed as he silently tried to prise my clenched fingers from the edges of the altar.

'You have no shame!' I spat at him. 'Every day a different girl, is that what you want? I won't let you ask for forgiveness here, first ask my forgiveness!' But Christodolos again put a finger to his lips to remind me that he was under a vow of silence, and didn't say a word.

I burst into tears and cursed and insulted him in Arabic with curses I had heard from the washerwomen, in Ladino I had been taught by Widow Ziso and her Sephardic neighbours, and in Russian, with the vicious curses my grandmother Simcha used when she spat into her farmers' *borscht*, and which I had learned without knowing what they meant.

Christodolos' burning eyes bored into me in disgust. I was shocked to suddenly hear his voice raised in the church despite his vow of silence. As if seized by madness he screamed at me, accusing me of the collective sin committed by my people: 'Murderess! You Jews are all murderers, you killed Him, He died because of you!'

Stunned, I slid from the altar and attacked him with my nails bared before his face like the talons of a bird of prey swooping down from the sky, ready to sink them into his beard, his eye sockets and cheeks, leaving a mark of disgrace there. Christodolos grasped my elbows and as my fingernails vainly scored the holy air, he gazed at me in horror. Then he freed my arms, gathered up the hem of his black habit and tucked it into his belt, revealing his best trousers, and fled. Through the open door I saw him slipping quickly through the gate in the churchyard wall, looking over his shoulder in terror every few steps. I rushed after him in my wedding dress, picking up small stones and throwing them at his retreating back, my sick, hurt heart pounding in the cage of my breast and sending daggers of pain through me. Yosef, who as usual was in the café waiting for me, got up and came towards me wide-eyed in astonishment at the sight of Christodolos passing him at a run, and at the sight of me pursuing him in my white wedding dress, and he put out a hand to stop me, bent down and grabbed the hem of the dress, but I turned and kicked at his hand and when he released it with a cry of pain I continued after Christodolos, who was running towards the sea.

When I reached the shore, I knelt on the wet sand and watched him approaching the waterline where he stopped for a moment like someone afraid of allowing himself to change his mind, and then resolutely walked into the wavelets lapping the sand and darkening it, and they licked at his toes with flattering, ingratiating tongues, and then he moved out into the taller waves that assailed him as their foam swirled around him, and with broad tempting movements of convocation, they invited him into the depths. Together the waves bore Christodolos on their backs, billowed his habit around him until it became a black bell and his body the clapper. They toyed with him for a long time, like giants amusing themselves with a rag doll, throwing his body from wave to wave in a cruel game of life and death, and he gradually dwindled until all that was left was a distant dot. I stood facing the sea as it panted with passion, and screamed in terror, calling him to come back, but my voice was lost in the argent screeching of the gulls and the roar of the breakers. I sat down heavily on the packed, damp sand, covered my eyes with my hands as my heart tore the left side of my body with stabbing pains, until I dared to look again through the gaps between my fingers: the black dot had vanished. I was horrified by the thought that Christodolos had drowned and I got up to join him, charging into the waves, but their buffeting repulsed me and again I went back into them, with the weight of my soaked wedding dress dragging me to join my beloved in the depths.

An eternity passed and then I saw him from afar, walking on the water. The surface was now as flat as a mirror and its roaring had subsided into a submissive whisper, and Christodolos came closer, striding gently on the water, his wet habit flapping between his legs, the glistening snakes of his hair writhing around him like tangled seaweed, and flakes of salt decorating his beard and the lashes of his closed eyes.

By the time he reached the shore a magnificent backdrop awaited him: the orb of the setting sun radiated the scintillating beams of the last light that burst over his back and head, and a brightness shining like gold burst out from behind his body, surrounding him with the aura of a saint.

When Christodolos reached dry land he ignored me and continued walking on the beach as before, like he had walked on the water, this time towards the church. I ran after him, estranging myself from Yosef who stood amazed as he looked at Christodolos, even forgetting to spit at him as he usually did, and again he grasped me, pleading with me to speak to him. But I wriggled out of his grip and hurried after Christodolos, straining to keep up with his long strides. This time, Yosef did not give up and tried to come into the church-yard with me, but I shut the iron gate in his face, bolted it, picked up the hem of my dress and ran to the church door that Christodolos had left ajar. I went inside, closing the door behind me and leaned my back against it, panting heavily and looking for Christodolos. I couldn't see him anywhere, not behind the screen in the apse, not in the prothesis, not before the altar and not on the bema. Frightened, I ran to his room where I found him standing naked in front of the mirror, calmly combing his wet hair and absently running his fingers through his salt-caked beard.

'You walked on the water,' I wheezed, fighting for every breath.

But he apparently had again taken a vow of silence and did not reply. He lay down on the bed, covered himself with the blanket and with a finger beckoned me to join him. I slowly took off my wedding dress that was heavy with water and sand, put it on the back of the chair over his soaked habit, and lay down next to him. I whispered words of love into his ear, kissed his still-wet body, licked the salt crystals from his beard, and moaned when he came into me, harder and stronger than ever.

'Don't you fear God? You're a monk. You took a vow of celibacy. 'It's forbidden,' I rebuked him next morning, setting myself apart from the rest of the women he was forbidden to touch.

Christodolos looked at me as if seeing me for the first time.

'Aren't you afraid of hell?' I said, trying to frighten him, 'You're breaking your priestly vow, you'll end up in hell.'

'And do you believe in hell?' he asked with a mocking chuckle.

'You taught me to believe in it, and I believe that you'll be burnt because of your sins,' I threatened him, and at that moment I truly wanted him to be consumed by fire or some equally terrible punishment.

Christodolos burst into wild laughter, a superior laughter that emphasised my ignorance and naivete and turned my anger into a fleeting feminine caprice.

'I am not subject to rules or regulations,' he told me when he calmed down.

'Why?' I persisted.

'Because I'm different,' he replied.

'What makes you different?'

'The story of my birth.'

Later, after he had told me the story, I never dared to rebuke him, but I'd bite my lip until it bled on the nights he went roaming and waited for him, awake, in his bed. But when the tragedy befell him, I had no doubt at all that it was because of me, for tempting him to break the vow of celibacy he had sworn to his God, and perhaps also because of the vile curses I had screamed at him then in the church, and also out of his hearing, in my heart, in the long days and nights he left me by myself and went to dispense charity to other women.

CHAPTER 23

'The story of my birth was a miracle famous the world over,' Christodolos told me as I snuggled in his arms after our love-making. He nibbled my earlobe, sending shivers of pleasure through me, and I gratefully reciprocated by tickling his protruding ribs, separated from me by only a thin covering of skin, and I expected to hear his laugh. But Christodolos became serious, extricated himself from my arms, got out of bed, sat down on the chair after removing the pile of clothing we had thrown onto it in our passion, and told me, far from my intrusive fingers, the story of his birth and life, and I, in my way, added my own dapples of colour.

Christodolos was born to a family of vine-growers in the small village of Rodia, whose name meant 'village of roses', not far from the ruins of the palace of Minos, King of Knossos, at the edge of the big town of Heraklion in Crete. The village's white houses were set into the slopes of a small hill and drowsed as though drunk with wine among the vine trellises, pomegranate orchards and rose bushes in whose branches multicoloured sunbirds nested. At summer's end the village was redolent of the sweet fragrance of raisins, and in winter the sour smell of young wine fermenting in pinewood barrels in the dark rose from the cellars. At the heart of the village, in the square, stood the church, resplendent with its red-tiled roof and belfry whose bells rang softly. The house where Christodolos was born stood next to the church wall and the ringing of the bells and the sounds of prayer on Sundays and feast days echoed throughout the house, rattling the window-panes, arousing pangs of conscience in its dwellers for things they had and had not done, and reminding them again and again of their Messiah.

It was on one of these Sundays that Anastasia's groans came from the house, through the blue windows and penetrated the heart of the church, mingled with the prayers of the congregation, and so distracted Father Diodoros that he changed the regular version and offered up a special prayer to God that he should ease the mother's pain and bring a healthy babe into the world from her womb – the mother who at that moment was lying on her back with the mound of her belly before her as though it was about to burst.

For many hours the father, Andreas, waited outside the room listening helplessly to his wife's groaning and screaming, and when his firstborn was long in coming, he rolled his eyes heaven-ward and swore that if he had a son, he would dedicate his next grape crop to the church. And when the groaning stopped and the wail of an infant was suddenly heard, his knees weakened and he was unable to take even one step, until Ofrosini came out to him, virtuous Ofrosini, the widowed midwife, with a squalling, moving, diaper-wrapped bundle in her arms. In a triumphant gesture she raised the large newborn babe over her head and called to the father, '*Ios*! It's a boy!'

She then went back into the bedroom, and while the mother rested from her labours she removed the diaper and washed the baby's body clean of the residue of the placenta and blood in a tub of luke-warm water she had readied. Nothing in the circumstances of the birth, neither mother nor child, had prepared her for the shock that gripped her as she gently scrubbed off the oily layer that had protected the infant in the amniotic fluid. At the sight of the marks she screamed in terror, the baby slipped from her hands like a piece of slippery soap, fell into the water where it sank up to its soft, pulsing fontanelle, immediately surfaced like a cork, and then began stroking with his tiny arms like an experienced swimmer. In an unthinkable act, Ofrosini left the infant to its fate in the tub, knelt, crossed herself in panic, mumbled the names of all the saints and called upon them to come to her aid. Andreas the father and the rest of the family, who were waiting patiently for the festive entrance of the bathed infant, burst into the bedroom in fright on hearing Ofrosini's cry to find her kneeling by the tub, with a chubby infant floating on the surface of the water.

The father wanted to call his firstborn Dimitrios, and while the foetus was still kicking in its mother's womb he promised him all his vineyards and the small winery he had built with his own two hands. But now he could see and knew that another vocation entirely had been ordained for his son. God has no need of my wine, he later told everyone who asked him about the grape crop he had promised to give to the church. God wanted his son, and so he had marked the newborn babe with the four burning red stigmata on his wrists and ankles, as though he had just been taken down from the cross. The excited father knelt before the tub, and as the baby swam in the water he vowed to dedicate his firstborn to the priesthood.

Father Diodoros was rushed to the home of the new mother to see the miracle with his own eyes, and Ofrosini the midwife, who was well known as a God-fearing woman, swore in the name of the crucified Christ that despite the strong, prolonged labour pains, the confinement itself had been very easy and there had been no need for any instruments whatsoever, and not even to pull the baby by his head, feet or hands, as in many other births, because, despite his size, the infant had slid out easily between his mother's thighs, just like a newborn kitten. And when the priest examined her fingernails, lest she had inadvertently scratched the infant when she was bathing him, he found that they had been cut down to the quick.

The priest duly recorded the story of this particular birth in all its details in the village records. He set down every detail of the midwife's description: the mother's big belly, the prolonged, strong labour pains, the easy birth (he even quoted her words, 'just like a newborn kitten'), the miracle of the baby floating in the water and the wonder of the stigmata revealed on the baby's wrists and ankles.

At his baptism and at the priest's suggestion, the baby was christened Christodolos, Servant of Christ, and everybody regarded him as a saint. So much so that even his mother did not dare to look him in the eye as he suckled at her breast, and she changed his diapers apologetically and with true awesome reverence. When the baby learned to sit, his father would sit him at the head of the table on a cushioned chair at mealtimes, and ask him to save his vines from the mildew spreading through them.

Diodoros was very proud of the miracle that had taken place in his village, and would relate the story over and over at religious convocations to which he was invited as a result. The story of the crucified baby quickly spread throughout the archipelago, reaching as far as Russia and Asia Minor and Palestine, and was discussed at archiepiscopacies throughout the Orthodox world where they searched for signs and omens in it.

One day a journalist from the *Ta Nea* newspaper came to the village with his camera and tripod. He put his head under the black cloth, set off a sodium flare to dispel the darkness from the room, and the photograph of the chubby baby lying naked on a sheepskin with his marked arms and legs waving in the air appeared in the paper, bringing in its wake visitors from all over the archipelago who arrived in ships, small boats and on donkey- and mule-back, until they were able to knock on the door of the house and see the baby. They knelt before him, crossed themselves and called him 'the Son'. And Anastasia the mother demanded five *taliari* from each one and hid the coins in an oil jug. When the jug was filled to its lip and oil dripped down its sides, she slit her mattress and hid the coins inside.

The baby became so famous that Giorgios I, King of the Hellenes, decided to abandon his throne, his wars with the Turks and the rest of the archipelago's troubles, and sail to Crete to see the baby as well.

It was then that the excited mother who, in anticipation of the king's visit, examined the four stigmata each day, discovered that they were gradually fading, gradually blurring, to the point that if you wanted to see them you would have to look very closely indeed. So without a word to anyone, neither to the priest nor her husband and despite the baby's loud protests, she stood and scrubbed the stigmata with a dry sponge until they reddened again. And when, two days later, they again paled, she boiled a beetroot and used the stock to highlight them. But the beetroot juice, too, was erased, so she squeezed some pomegranates, took a piece of cotton cloth, dipped it into the dark juice and dabbed it onto the four fateful spots. Excitedly, the king looked at the blackened pomegranate stains on the baby's wrists and ankles, brought his left eye close to it using a gold-handled monocle, and received, directly into his face and in a graceful arc, a stream of urine. With a pristine white handkerchief proffered by one of his counsellors, Giorgios I embarrassedly wiped the urine from his face, polished the lens of his stained monocle, presented the baby's parents with a gold coin bearing his likeness, commanded them to sell it when the time was right and with the money provide the child with an education that would prepare him for monastic life.

For a long time Anastasia continued to nurture the stigmata with pomegranate juice, until Christodolos grew into a stubborn and rebellious toddler who refused to subject his body to this ritual, and the stigmata faded and then disappeared completely. The mother hid the gold coin in a flour jug, and every few days she would go to it, slide her hand into its narrow mouth, extract the floured coin, blow it clean and bite it to ascertain, again and again, that it was indeed made of gold, and then reluctantly return it to the jug until the next time.

Christodolos abused the people's reverence for him and became a mischievous rebel. At school he liked to look up the girls' skirts, pinch their budding breasts and stroke their behinds, while the teachers ignored this and took no disciplinary action.

Christodolos fostered another hobby in his youth: on numerous occasions he would play truant from school and go to the Labyrinth, the maze-like, haunted ruins of King Minos' palace that had been destroyed, so they said, in the great earthquake that had shaken the neighbouring island of Tara. There he would jump over the broken red columns and the piles of stones, wander from room to room, make his way from hall to hall and hunt for the kingdom's treasure. He sometimes dug into the palace's floor with a two-tined fork, dug out coloured mosaic stones and put them into a cloth bag. Many times he would come home with verdigris-covered copper coins, shards bearing the likeness of bulls, fragments of glass whose sharp edges had dulled with the years and whose surface was spotted with age stains of every imaginable colour, clay tablets covered with unfathomable writing, and bits of plaster with parts of crocuses, monkeys, bulls and dolphins painted on them. He would sit in his room for hours and very patiently try and put together the pieces and fragments he found to create a whole picture, and he would seclude himself with the clay tablets, copy the etched markings onto paper, trying to decipher the writing in the stubborn belief that it would lead him to the vanished treasures of King Minos, son of Zeus and Europa. When he failed to decipher anything, he consulted the priest and the village elders but they, too, did not know how to read the marks. When his collection grew so much that the house was too small to hold it, his father built a shed in the yard, fitted it with shelves, and Christodolos arranged his entire collection on them and also drew each item in a thick note-book, noting by each description the date on which he had found it. One day they were visited by the priest and at the sight of the impressive collection he told Christodolos that his hobby was called archaeology and it could be studied at the University of Athens.

Later, when Christodolos had grown into a young man whose beard had sprouted, the priest dis-covered, much to his astonishment, that his face bore an amazing resemblance to the face of Jesus in the painting of 'the Mandylion', the mantle or shroud he had seen at one of the convocations to which he had been invited as a result of the miracle that had taken place in his village. It was as though Jesus' countenance, preserved in the mantle offered to him by St Veronica on the road to Golgotha to wipe away his sweat, had been copied in Christodolos' face. The resemblance was so great

359

between his joined eyebrows, long, thin nose, wavy hair and beautiful large eyes and those of the Mandylion that it seemed to the priest that if Christodolos were allowed to spread that mantle – against which Jesus' likeness had been preserved down the generations in blood, sweat, tears and pollen – on his face, his eyes would be reflected through Jesus' eyes, brow would rest on brow, mouth would kiss mouth and Christodolos' nostrils would breathe the air from the place of the crucified Christ's nostrils.

Thanks to his reputation gained by the legend of his birth and the efforts of the village priest, Christodolos, who was not among his school's outstanding pupils, was accepted by the University of Athens to study theology and archaeology. Kyprianos, the monk who studied with him in Athens and who later lived with him at the Greek Orthodox monastery in Jerusalem, told me after Christodolos' death that he had used his studies in Athens to excavate and examine the bodies of the city's girls, who sacrificed their virginity for him and loved him loudly on his wide, creaking bed in the room he rented in the Monastiraki market. On completion of his studies he was sent to the Monasteries of the Air at Meteora to learn to be a monk. It took him ten days on horseback through the fertile valley of Thessaly to get there. To the east the mountains of Ossa towered over him while from the west he was threatened by the Pinaros range. When he reached the town of

Kalambaka he was amazed by the sight of the monasteries that had been excavated from the giant black catapult rocks that had fallen from the skies and landed on the bald mountain summits. There, at the Moni Aghias Tridas monastery, Christodolos grew his hair long and secluded himself with his God. Every evening he went up onto the monastery roof that was sprinkled with stardust and shrouded in a cloak of low-lying clouds that hid the scenes of the world from his sight, and there on high, close to sanctity, he repented the sins of his youth, made vows and swore oaths, and would not return to his cell before his hair and beard were drenched by the white mist that enveloped him. It was at that monastery that he took the three vows: to live a life of poverty, to forego carnal love and to obey his superiors, and with love he accepted that he must keep away from the vanities of this world and devote himself to the love of God that was boundless. Three years later he was lowered out into the world below in a basket that swung on a rope between heaven and earth, and then, at the mercy of the iron pulleys creaking with his weight and the books he had brought with him, he made one more vow – to go to the Holy Land.

First he went to Jersualem, to the Greek Orthodox monastery, but Jerusalem was oppressive in its gloom and torment, the chill penetrated his very bones and frequently made him ill, and he missed the sight of the sea and the caress of the sunshine. The order finally took pity on him and sent him to St Ioannis' Church in Jaffa. When the rumour spread that the stigmata of the crucified Christ had been imprinted on the flesh of this man of God while he was still in his mother's womb, the small congregation of Orthodox Christian Arabs and a handful of Greek merchants who had settled in the city welcomed him with ululations of joy.

Christodolos had no difficulty in learning Arabic, Hebrew, English and Russian and took pride in his achievement, and he took pains to talk to the city's inhabitants in their own mother tongue. When the carnal lust of his youth and early manhood returned to beset him, so he told me, he would clench his fists until his fingernails dug into his palms and imprinted a line of four crescents there, and the pain would help him to drive out forbidden thoughts and tempting scenes.

Until he met me.

When I led him astray with my red hair and blue eyes, it was revealed to him, so he confessed to me, that it was his vocation to pleasure women until they lost their senses and that this was his charity and mission in this world, and so he was forbidden to allow his love for me to stand between him and other women. Not only that, he must give his charity to as many women as possible in penance for all the years of celibacy and devotion to study and prayer in the cold, damp clouds that shrouded the monastery at Meteora.

Christodolos had faith in God's compassion and the wounds of the crucified Christ that had been imprinted on his flesh at birth, and in his confessions and pleas for mercy at the altar, and he believed that no evil would befall him as a result of his breaking the vow of celibacy. And when the disaster befell him, his friend Kyprianos, who was chosen to replace him at St Ioannis' Church, told me that 'In the desert, in a cave high on a cliff, one can perhaps lead a life of abstinence, but certainly not in this city of sin, with its sun, sea, and its multitude of temptations.'

CHAPTER 24

Like a delegation of messengers of evil, three perspiring men in khaki suits with many pockets stood at the doorway to the church. Wide breeches covered in a fine dust brought from another place hung over their high boots, and their faces were burned and flushed despite the white topees, which they hastily removed as they entered the church. The tallest of the three carried a large, bulky satchel with a heavy copper buckle that locked its lips closed.

Christodolos pushed me into the small bedroom, and I peeked curiously through the crack in the door. I watched him hurry to pour them cool water from the large earthenware jar that stood in the corner, as the tall one extracted a bundle wrapped in newspapers from the satchel and placed it carefully on the table. Christodolos peeled off newspaper after newspaper, and finally looked ashen-faced at a small object. Then an animated discussion ensued, but much as I pricked my ears, I could not make out what the three wanted from him.

After they left, I found him standing at the altar

in a pool of brightly coloured light that flowed from one of the stained-glass windows, holding a stone in one hand and looking at it, deeply immersed in thought. I called out his name, tried to rouse him, battling for his attention, but he looked right through me with hollow eyes, as if concentrating on some kind of secret ritual, and I knew that a new rival had entered my life. Christodolos had decided to return to his old lover, the one he had betrayed, whose appeal was the dust of excavations, ancient potsherds, and an assortment of relics left behind by the dead. After being temporarily pushed aside in favour of the smoke of incense, the chimes of bells and the adoration of the faithful, she had returned to him in a leather satchel, carefully carried by a red-faced, heat-tormented Englishman.

Christodolos devoted long nights of strenuous effort to deciphering the characters engraved on the small stone, and when he finally managed to decipher them the Englishmen returned with a pile of potsherds that were also adorned with strange and bizarre lettering. When he had deciphered these too, word of his new occupation spread through the markets, and Bedouin in dark robes, their hair white from the dust of the desert, storm-sand nestling in their deep facial furrows, came and stood with him in the pool of light in front of the altar, and took out scraps of scrolls, copper statues, coins and potsherds from deep within the folds of their robes. The Bedouin were followed by antique dealers from Jaffa, Jerusalem, Hebron and Bethlehem, who opened boxes full of valuable relics before him. Christodolos now devoted himself to periods and people that had been and were no longer, completely forgetting the present and the living. In vain I would wrap my arms around him and whisper words of love deep into his ears – he would stroke my hair distractedly, drag me to the bed, love me hastily with his body while his thoughts were preoccupied with the potsherds and their markings. Afterwards, he would return to his other lover, commune with her, and only then lie down to sleep, satiated and peaceful.

He frequently disappeared for several days at a time, returning with face bronzed, blistered hand, and the crescents of his nails darkened with earth: yellow loess when he excavated in the south, red loam when he dug in the central region of the country, from Jerusalem he brought heavy, dark earth, and muddy black peat from the region of Lake Huleh and the Jordan River.

Once, when I stretched myself across the doorway and tried to block his flight to ancient times with my body, he stepped over me and left, but when he returned he brought me a peace offering: a tarnished copper bracelet, the clasps on either end fashioned into stag heads with curved antlers. He found it in the grave of a Persian soldier, he proudly informed me when he gave it to me. But I never wore the bracelet, and to this day it rests idly in the wooden box inlaid with shells Fishke had given me. A month later, he brought me small gold beads that he found in a grave from the Herodian period, and then bone combs and brooches that he unearthed in even more ancient tombs and did not know what period they were from, and then a blue bead adorned with a pinkish-white patina. A great many beads from a medley of places and periods accumulated in my jewellery box – beads of gold and silver and mother-of-pearl, of rubies and transparent crystal, copper beads beaten into shapes of discs, and also clay beads moulded into the shape of small barrels. I collected them one by one, my beads of the dead, and never strung them together on a thread when Christodolos asked me to, and did not wear them around my neck. The smell of devastation clung to them, and memories of the plundered graves, and the dust of the dead who had once worn them, and the lost time Christodolos spent with them, preferring them to me.

And when he returned from the regions of death and oblivion, he would take off his clothes and drop them to the floor of the small bedroom in a dusty pile, and I would inspect the suntan marks on his body, and see again and again that he had been digging with exposed chest and bare knees. Then he would heat some water on the Primus stove and fill the large tin bathtub that stood in the bathroom, carefully lowering his body into it, staining the water in the hues of the earth he brought with him from one place or another. And when he wanted to indulge me, he would let me wash his hair. Locks of wet snakes, dark, writhing and slippery would drop onto his back and I would take them in my hands one by one and scrub them with soap and water, trying to remove the smell of dust of the dead. 'Grave robber,' I would whisper into his lather-filled ears, and he would be shocked and make me swear by Jesus lest I repeat that name. 'I am an archaeologist,' he would say; '*Archaeologos*,' he recited time after time and taught me that the word 'archaeo' means 'ancient' in Greek and 'logos' means 'wisdom'. In other words, he was engaged in the wisdom of the ancient.

One time, he revealed his great dream to me: to find the Holy of Holies, which apparently had been buried by the Jews in the deep catacombs beneath Temple Mount. He told me about the treasures that had been found and taken to Rome, and showed me a photograph in a book of the plundered Temple *menorah* engraved on the Arch of Victory in Rome. But, he said, the Jews had hidden the Holy of Holies, the pure-gold Ark of the Covenant with the tablets Moses received on Mount Sinai, beneath the Temple itself, which was built on arches, the spaces beneath which were designed to separate it from the impurity of the dead. Whoever found it would gain eternal fame and would be written about in the history books, he said repeatedly as if possessed, and I stopped my ears with wet thumbs, refusing to hear, and continued to call him grave robber in my heart.

When he had finished bathing, when he lay beside me clean and peaceful, he liked to describe to me the labour of excavating, how the past is revealed layer after layer, that each exposed layer reveals a new-ancient tale, and conceals beneath it an even more ancient one, as if trying to stand out and erase what had occurred before it. That is why, he explained, it is necessary to first decipher it, then remove it, and dig beneath it to reveal the layer that preceded it, which also has a tale that requires deciphering and it too zealously covers what preceded it. All this is very important, he explained, because in order to understand the end, it is necessary to arrive at the beginning.

'And what remains after all the layers are peeled away?' I asked.

'The findings. Everything that is found in the ground, that is what's left, a testimony to life of yesteryear.'

'Robber and destroyer of graves,' I would repeatedly tease him, and Christodolos, who was in good spirits at these moments, would reply by touching my body, like a merchant in the market inspecting a leg of lamb.

'For me to love you,' he once told me, 'you should have been ancient, shrivelled and dry as parchment. And truth to tell, would that you were a skeleton, then I would embrace your beautiful skull, and your mouth that is always open in complaint would smile at me with a final wide smile of death.' And I, not knowing whether to take offence or not, pulled at his beard, ruffled his hair, bit his dry lips, cracked from heat and dust, and begged him to never leave me again, to stay with me always, to forget the church, the women pioneers, and the excavations. But weary Christodolos turned his back to me and fell asleep, and I wrapped my arms and legs around his sleeping body and listened to the sounds rising from him, and in my heart I could already sense the pain of separation that had not yet come to pass.

From the day I told my grandmother Simcha the secret of my love for the Greek monk, we both kept it well hidden so that it would not reach Grandma Abulafia and my father. She herself never demanded that I put an end to this love affair, but she did not hide her disapproval from me. 'He not make you happy,' she would always grumble when I came to visit her. She would sit me down at the table, and without being asked would pour one bowl of royal *borscht*, place a pile of steaming *piroshki* on a plate and then slam the two dishes onto the table in front of me. 'Now not talk, food,' she would order. 'Your body no blood, crazy Greek suck your body, in end only shell be left,' she declared as if she could see my pallor.

But Fishke, after talking to me on that evening

when I told Simcha my secret, thought that he had done his bit and there was no reason for him to interfere any further, so was satisfied with mumbling a few vague words about predestination. Simcha, who seemed to always understand him, even when he spoke with his mouth full of nails, would silence him with a loud '*Sha*', and I would get up and say goodbye, a steaming loaf of rye bread, heavy and fragrant, in my arms. I would clutch the bread to my belly to soothe it with its warmth, and go to my beloved, accompanied by my grandmother's voice calling after me, 'If he doing bad, coming home quick.'

One day Christodolos returned carrying a black metal box with a circular piece of glass fixed to it and the name Leica inscribed above it in clear Latin lettering.

'That is a camera.' He presented it to me.

'And what do you need a camera for if you can be photographed in a studio?' I asked Christodolos, who seemed very pleased with the new toy he had acquired, kissed my forehead, and hastened to initiate me to the possibilities it presented.

'The role of a camera is to perpetuate,' he said 'and I will use it to photograph antiquities, especially the buildings I uncover. After I photograph them and they are preserved in photographs, I will be able to dismantle them and reach the layer beneath with greater ease. And again, I will photograph and dismantle and penetrate deeper and deeper until I reach the very first period of life of the ruins I find. Then I will publish an account of the place I have discovered, accompanied by photographs, in the *British Journal of Archaeology*.'

I followed his hands as they stroked the black box, and adored him for his expertise and ideas: 'Photograph me,' I asked.

'You can't photograph in the dark,' he smiled indulgently, 'there is not enough light here.'

'Then let's go out,' I suggested, grasping his hand and trying to pull him to the door.

'Later,' he promised.

But he never kept his promise.

From then on, he always returned from his excavations with rolls of film. He would take the rolls of film to be developed at Michael Moussaieff's photography shop and, when the photographs were ready, he would bring them back in a paper bag, sit me down on his bed beside him and shuffle them as if they were a pack of cards, then pull out one photograph after another and show me: 'This is a ruin,' he would say, and I saw a low mound strewn with dry thistles. 'And this is a house from the Hasmonaean period,' and I saw stones scattered haphazardly on the ground. 'And this is a statue of the god Poseidon,' he said with particular pride, and I saw a fragment of a foot wearing a strip of sandal.

One day Christodolos decided to treat me to an excursion. I put fresh *pitta* bread, goat's milk cheese, olives and a bunch of spring onions into a basket, and when the muezzin's call pierced the chill air of dawn we set off in the patriarchate's elegant motor car. Several hours later we reached Nazareth, surrounded by its mountains, the city of his Messiah, and Christodolos sought to infect me with his religious fervour.

'In this very place the history of mankind changed,' he declared ceremoniously, pointing to a modest church, and related to me how the archangel Gabriel appeared before Mary, a virgin who was betrothed to a man named Joseph of the house of David, and said to her: 'Blessed art though among women.' And when the virgin was horrified, he calmed her and said: 'Fear not, Mary: for thou hast found favour with God. And, behold, thou shalt conceive in thy womb, and bring forth a son, and shalt call His name Jesus. He shall be great, and shall be called the Son of the Highest.' And when Mary asked in surprise how she would conceive seeing she did not know a man, he replied with the famous answer: 'The Holy Ghost shall come upon thee, and the power of the Highest shall overshadow thee: therefore also that holy thing which shall be born of thee shall be called the Son of God.'

Christodolos examined my face as if fearing to discover hints of a mocking smile. But I was happy with his excursion that took me out of the darkness of the church in Jaffa, and indeed I gazed at him with interest. He immediately roused himself and added that only we, the Jews, call Jesus the Nazarene, because his mother was informed of his birth in Nazareth, where he was also brought up.

Later, by a spring, the water of which gathered into a well called Mary's Well, to commemorate the appearance of the archangel before Mary, I watched young women squatting to draw water in their cupped hands and drink it eagerly.

'Any woman who drinks from the waters of the spring will conceive and bear children,' Christodolos whispered in awesome reverence.

'I'm thirsty too,' I announced and squeezed between the drinking women, knelt down, cupped my hands, immersed them and sipped from the cool water that was very sweet to my palate. I drew more water and it flowed down my chin, dripped into the décolletage of my dress, and trickled down my belly. Christodolos watched me in embarrassment and apprehension.

'Enough, you've drunk enough, let's go,' he urged me.

'No, not enough, I'm still thirsty,' I gurgled, teasing him, and immersed my face in the spring, and my plait that had freed itself of the pins floated on the hallowed water. I drank more and more in noisy defiance until I felt Christodolos' hands tightly clutch my wet arms, and he pulled me out of the water and dragged me behind him to the motor car.

We drove in silence. At noon, the Sea of Galilee glimmered in the distance, and we drove for a few miles until we reached the ruins of Capernaum.

There Christodolos climbed onto one of the rocks, stood and recited: 'And when Jesus had heard that John was delivered up, he retired into Galilee: And leaving the city Nazareth, he came and dwelt in Capernaum on the sea coast.' He climbed down from the rock and wandered among the ruins reciting, and I stumbled behind him, listening to the stories of the miraculous deeds of Jesus in those days. Until I tripped over a basalt rock, sat down on it rubbing my injured heel, and saw him lean towards a pile of hewn rocks, select one, lift it up over his head and cry: 'The stone which the builders rejected is become the chief cornerstone, and whosoever shall fall on this stone, shall be broken: but on whomsoever it shall fall, it shall grind him to powder.' He quickly put the rock into the basket he carried, like a thief, and I turned my face from him, preoccupied with the pressure in my bladder, full of the hallowed water from Mary's Well, got up, searched, and found a hiding place behind a rock adorned with buds and flowers. I squatted and urinated with great pleasure to the sound of verses soaring from Christoldolos' lips: 'That thou art Peter; and upon this rock I will build my church, and the gates of hell shall not prevail against it.' But he suddenly noticed my absence and fell silent. I saw him go in one direction and then another looking for me, and then I got scared, and got up quickly, not managing to cover the lower part of my body that stood out in its pale nakedness. Christodolos saw me and was filled with fury, turned on his heel and trudged away. He returned to the motor car almost at a run and I ran after him, tripping over the holy stones, entreating him in vain to wait for me. I tried without success to mollify him all the way to Jaffa: I lightly tweaked his hair and beard, kissed the soft nape of his neck, stroked his thighs, took his genitals in my hands, but we drove in silence, his face grim and his lips tightly closed in rage. That night he fell asleep his face to the wall, and even his member did not respond to my hands as they sought to bring it to life.

The next day he got up and went to Jerusalem on his own and came back only three days later. When he returned, he pulled a strip of stained threadbare cloth from his pocket, and carefully spread it out in the palm of his hand, revealing a thick, crooked and rusty nail. 'This is apparently one of the nails used for the crucifixion of Jesus,' he announced excitedly. 'It belonged to the monks of the Franciscan Monastery in Jerusalem, and now it's mine.'

I looked at the find he had brought and told him that our Fishke had hundreds and thousands of those in his old carpentry workshop. The next day he asked me to go with him to Fishke, coaxed him to come with him to the workshop, ensconced himself with him for a long while, and returned carrying a glass jar stained with congealed varnish and full of crooked, rusty nails. He patiently photographed them one by one in the yard, with the church as a backdrop, and then wrapped them in pairs in tattered squares of cloth, kissed me goodbye on my forehead and left. Two days later he returned with his pockets full of money.

From then on, Christodolos and Fishke became allies and frequently sequestered themselves in the carpentry workshop. Fishke was glad for the occupation that had suddenly come his way, and joyfully pulled old nails out of rusted lock mechanisms, from wood beams that in ages past supported houses that had collapsed in the days of Napoleon, from dilapidated fishing boats that were no longer in use. And when he returned to my grandmother Simcha's room, aromas of glue, varnish and wood shavings once again emanated from his clothes. Christodolos wrapped the nails in strips of tattered cloth, disappeared with them for a few days, and always returned with his pockets full of coins, of which he always gave some to Fishke. Until one day two British policemen knocked on the church gate, withdrew with him, raised their voices at him, and the flourishing trade in nails came to an end.

But it wasn't long before my beloved found a new source of income – he was going to baptise pilgrims in the Jordan River, he informed me, and an ominous shiver ran through my body.

CHAPTER 25

That Saturday that fell about a month before Passover was particularly wet and wintry. It had rained incessantly for a whole week. Cellars filled up with muddy water, a silt of earth and dead fish, and the floods crumbled the ruins of the ancient walls and washed away sections of the city's paving stones. The rain penetrated the tiled roof of the priest's house, staining the ceiling with stubborn, grey, damp spots, and trickled with an irritating drip into the receptacles we had put down throughout the house.

The night before Christodolos left for Tiberias, the news on the wireless reported that the Jordan River was in full flow, the Sea of Galilee was flooding and that the next day was expected to be as rainy as the previous ones. All that night we argued in whispers under the heavy winter blanket that trapped beneath it the fresh smell of our last act of lovemaking. I told him that the pilgrims would not come out of their hostels on a day like this to subject their bodies to the icy gushing waters of the Jordan River. I begged him not to go, to stay in bed with me. 'Just a little longer,' I pleaded and embraced him from behind. But he extricated himself from the restraining grip of my arms, and at dawn, when the smell of my body was still infused in his, he threw off the blanket, abandoned my naked body to the cold of the room and deserted the bed. Sullen and irritable, he put on his clothes, combed his hair, tied it into a knot, grumbled between his teeth that were clenched around hairpins which he pulled out of his mouth one at a time and angrily stabbed into the knot. Then he was swallowed into the darkness to the sound of gay hooting from the patriarchate's motor car horn that Abdullah the driver sounded to hurry him along. That morning I rejected the cool kiss he sought to plant on my forehead, and turned my back to him.

After Christodolos had hastily departed, I discovered he had forgotten to take with him the camera from which he never parted for even a moment, and was now cast forsaken on the bed beside me, its single eye open wide and sparkling, gazing at me baffled. I pulled the blanket over me, covering it and me, clung to the traces of our warmth and wallowed blissfully in my jealousy and anger. I listened to the clanging of the church bells swinging in the blustery wind whistling outside, and waited impatiently until the roar of the car's engine faded into the distance. I waited a little longer, lest he remember the forgotten camera and order the driver to return, and then I put on my red dress and went into the church in my bare feet.

Flashes of lightning flickered through the stained-glass windows, and for an instant they lit up the gloom of the nave, gilding the icons of the saints. I tripped on the base of one of the many wood scaffolding beams that had been erected for the renovation of the ceiling for Easter, and cursed Christodolos and his God. With my bare foot I kicked the scaffolding that had tripped me, the force of the kick crushing my big toes, and then when the shock of pain spread from my foot to my head, I suddenly knew what I had to do to free myself of him.

In the cold brilliance of the storm raging outside, the frightened eyes of Theotokos bearing the child bored into me anxiously as if she could foresee what was about to happen. I surveyed the wide nave of the church and peeked through the grille separating me from the apse, and when I saw that not a living soul was there, I slammed the doors of the church that Christodolos had neglected to close when he departed, and secured them with the iron bolt. Now I was imprisoned alone in the darkness that was sporadically illuminated by the flickering lights of candles and lightning, which created around me a ghastly theatre of the silhouettes of ghosts and martyred saints. And like gallows patiently waiting for their victim, head bowed, the scaffolding stood serenely waiting for something to happen. I ignored the reproving looks of the icons and set out to wreak vengeance on Christodolos' God and his saints, who meant more to him than I did. First I did all the things I had already done once before, and with a sweet sense of revenge I stuck out my tongue and bared my bottom at Theotokos and the baby, I mocked Peter's bald spot and John's beard and the camel-hair cloak draping his body, I cast words of blasphemy at the crucified Christ, whose face was that of my beloved, I spat into the font and scattered flakes of smouldering incense into it, that once again let out a deadly hiss as they came into contact with the water until their dying breath and, not fearing the flames and the heat of the hot wax splattering my hand, I throttled the candles between finger and thumb. Then I took the tallest and thickest candle of them all, engraved with crosses and an inscription in Greek with the names of the benefactors, and carried it like a torch to light my way back to the room.

Opinions are divided about what occurred next. Some said that it was the storm that caused the blaze: lightning struck the church and ignited the top of one of the wood scaffolding beams inside the church. But police records, that cleared me of all suspicion, stated that this was an act of arson – a lighted torch that was deliberately thrown from outside smashed one of the stained-glass windows, penetrated the church and set fire to one of the wood scaffolding beams.

The only thing I remember is taking that thick candle, of which it was said that it could burn for several months before its wax was consumed, bringing it with me to the room, and clutching it tightly as I stood in front of the lectern beside the bed. Mesmerised, I watched three moths haplessly circling above the flame, getting caught in the fire, their wings going up in smoke, while the fourth, which managed to escape the blaze, sank into the melted wax and drowned in the boiling cauldron.

Was it possible that this candle accidentally fell from my hands and landed on the bed? Or perhaps I dropped it deliberately?

In any event, after the fact, when I saw the inferno from a distance, I was swept into a raging maelstrom of emotions: joy, sorrow, passion, envy, revenge, anger, love, hate, excitement, grief, and they all clashed with one another, fighting each other for control over me, choking me and tearing me apart bit by bit. And I, wet from the rain, shivering from the cold and burning from the heat, darted around on the beach, weeping and laughing like a lunatic.

At that moment I was prepared to admit that I had started the fire, even if not deliberatcly, for deep in my heart I knew that my true wish had been fulfilled. If I were to be questioned today, I would admit to nothing more than plotting to burn the bed that cherished our love, so that no other woman would lie there with him and wallow in my memories after I was gone. I believed that with the bed the fire would also consume our love and nothing would remain but a small pile of embers and ashes, and then, and only then, would I be able to sever myself from Christodolos. I remember well that I stood by the bed, the candle whispering in my hands, and I wanted to burn it but did not dare. I saw the springs that had trembled under our entwined bodies, the mattress that had submissively absorbed our perspiration, seed and tears, and the pillows I had used to stifle my groans of pleasure and pain, and did not dare to burn but a few objects that I brought close to the flame: Christodolos' writing block, which I found on the lectern, imprints of Greek words visible on its top page, testimony of the last letter he sent, was consumed immediately. The snuffbox blazed merrily, spraying tiny sparks and emitting a strong smell that effortlessly overpowered the smells of resin from the incense that had died out in the meantime. I then tested the strength of the huge candle's flame on the azure silk cassock, hanging on the headboard, which Christodolos liked to wear on Sundays. With tiny crepitations, the cassock surrendered to the burning tongues avidly licking it, strips of blazing cloth fluttered in the air like butterflies venturing too close to a flame, their wings caught by it, and fell softly onto the bed, covering it in red sparks. I bent to remove the blanket and quickly picked up the camera, so that it would not be destroyed by the fire as well, clutched it to my breast, calmly watching the bed's purple bedspread as it, too, willingly surrendered to the fire, sharing its fiery joy with the blanket and pillows and the mattress. The repugnant stench of singed rooster feathers spread as they caught fire, and aroused in me wistful memories of my beloved Ben-Zion who had ended his life in a soup.

It was this stench that eventually saved my life. I watched the eager tongues of fire on our lovers' bed, my nose filled with the repulsive stench, and nausea gripped my bowels, sending bitter gastric juices to my throat, and I retreated from there in alarm and ran into the nave, clutching the camera. Theotokos beseeched me from the wall that I save myself, her gaze was imperious and her mute lips cried and implored me. I wanted to save her and her baby, but the painting was hung too high, as if she too refused to depart, choosing to burn and become one of the martyred saints herself. I begged her forgiveness for everything I had inflicted upon her, crossed the nave at a run, shaking dying sparks and singed feathers from my hair and clothes. Through the smoke the frightened eyes of the martyred saints gazed at me, and they stretched out pleading white arms that had never been exposed to the sun, and lamented their ill fortune. I ignored them and ran on, my ailing heart shooting piercing pains from within my chest, pursued by a gushing river of fire skirting the font, feeding on anything in its way: Virgin Marys, Jesuses, Johns, Peters, angels, crucifixes, pews, prayer books, communion wafers, bottles of wine, candle wax, bags of incense, velvet curtains, paraffin oil, pulpits, flowers that had dried, wood scaffolding, and splendid priests' cassocks. In a blanket of thick smoke I groped my way to the outer door, choking and coughing, forced open the red-hot bolt that left a searing burn on the palm of my hand, and fled outside.

I looked back and saw the thwarted tongues of fire, blocked by the heavy door I had slammed shut behind me, climb up the scaffolding, their heat shattering the colourful stained-glass windows that sought to halt them, wave at me with red arms, ascend higher and higher to the beams of the roof and the tiles that were already charred, climb up the stairs to the belfry, creep into the bell chamber and melt them, those bells whose chimes had masked the sounds of our lovemaking.

I pushed the wicket in the churchyard's iron gate and ran terrified down the path, leaving behind me the church being sacrificed in a huge torch of fire and columns of smoke, until I reached the sea that coupled with the gloom of the sky and welcomed me, dark, raging and hostile. I dipped my burned feet and hands into the water, and cold tremulous tongues licked at them in salty greed, burning my scorched skin. I could not calm down, and darted back and forth along the shoreline alternately crying and laughing until I was overcome by heart pangs, and, my mind empty of thoughts, sat down exhausted on the wet sand and watched the enormous bonfire and the tiny, helpless figures that were now running to and fro, fighting a lost battle. I stayed on the beach until the fire was extinguished, leaving in its wake a charred, roofless skeleton and curlicues of fine smoke, until a pale light appeared in the east revealing the sleeping countenance of the city emerging from the sea, and the chill wind blowing onto my face, filling my eyes and nostrils with grains of sand, drove me away from there. I returned to my tiny room purged of my sins, lay on the bed in my wet dress that emitted smells of burning and smoke, and fell asleep. I woke up at noon with a sense of someone watching me: the camera's glazed eye beside me peered at me in cold reproof. I wrapped it in a corner of the bed sheet, and again fell into a feverish and delirious sleep.

Next day, the daily *Ha'artez* carried a report of a church in Jaffa that had gone up in flames in a fire that was apparently caused by a *yeshiva* student. Yosef's eyes peered at me from the photograph of the suspected arsonist, and beneath it the caption: Yosef Mendel, nineteen, resident of Jaffa. The headline announced that Yosef Mendel had confessed to the deed and claimed that he had done it 'for the sanctification of God's name'. The report described how Mendel had expressed no remorse for his deed and was being remanded in custody for a further nine days. He was apprehended, so it said in minute detail, dancing and prancing in front of the burning church, singing Lag Ba'omer bonfire songs in the light of the fire, and had even obstructed the work of the firemen. The police presumed that Mendel broke into the church, plundered its valuable treasures, and then set it on fire to cover the traces of the theft, and was now presenting himself as a religious zealot. The newspaper further reported that officials of the Greek Orthodox Church stated that no one had been hurt, but the church had suffered extensive damage and it was doubtful whether it could be restored. Following the incident, the newspaper reporter noted, the police had reinforced its patrols around Jaffa's churches to prevent further cases of arson.

Below this report appeared another one of only three lines that might easily have been missed, drily announcing that a Greek monk of thirty-three had drowned as he pulled a pilgrim from an undercurrent near the Jordan River estuary into the Sea of Galilee.

I asked Abdullah the driver, who had chauffeured him to his death, whether Christodolos had told him the story of our love during their long drive. But Abdullah just handed me an antique gold ring that had been found in Christodolos' trouser pocket, and repeatedly stated, so that I would finally believe him: 'Christodolos drowned.'

But I refused to believe it.

'That's not possible,' I insisted, 'Christodolos was an experienced swimmer, he couldn't have drowned.' Then Abdullah capitulated and recounted to me the chain of events in great detail, accompanied by hiccups and tears. And I could see Christodolos before my eyes, towering in his black cassock over the people waiting to be baptised as they surrounded him trembling and helpless, their long, white cotton robes clinging to their skin in the torrential rain coming down relentlessly. And Christodolos slowly descending the riverbank and going into the icy waters that collected snowmelt from the peak of Mount Hermon. The water reached his waist, surging in gloomy swirls, sketching rings of silvery spume around his body, his teeth chattering and his arms spread out, urging the pilgrims to join him. One by one they come down to him, entrusting their bodies with faith and love to the cold and his arms, and he supports their back and baptises them one after another, time after time, and his lips, blue from the cold, mutter the holy prayers.

Ofrosini was last, Abdullah told me, the midwife who had severed the umbilical cord that had joined Christodolos to his mother and, seeing the signs of the crucifixion on the baby's hands and feet, had let him slip in alarm into the tub of water. After Christodolos had settled in the Holy Land – this I heard after the fact from his friend, Kyprianos – Ofrosini saved her drachmas and sold her vineyard so that she too could come to the Holy Land to see the holy baby she had delivered, to dip in the Jordan River and atone for her sins before the good Lord summoned her to Him. But when she descended the riverbank with heart pounding in excitement in anticipation of meeting the man she had delivered, her feet stumbled on the slippery peat mixed with the silt of mud and slime. She tried to clutch at the reeds growing on the riverbank but lost her balance, fell heavily onto her backside, and slid screaming in terror into the water. She quickly sank to her knees in the muddy riverbed that sucked her in, and a ruthless whirlpool caught and spun her around. Christodolos, who was standing in the river, his arms widespread to receive and baptise her, saw her drowning and stumbled heavily towards her, grasped a strand of her hair, pulled her out and draped her, spluttering and vomiting turbid water, over a large rock that had miraculously appeared next to them on the riverside. But when he too tried to climb out of the water, the lap of his cassock became entangled in stems of water lilies and skewered on reeds, and the more he tried to disentangle it the further his legs sank into the marshy, loam riverbed.

Petrified with fear and cold, the pilgrims watched from the bank as their baptiser gradually drowned. After members of Kibbutz Degania, who had been alerted to the scene, managed to extricate his dead body from the mud, the pilgrims crowded around him in a mass in their white robes, and mourned him bitterly. And Ofrosini even threw herself on the body and screamed: '*Christodolos phethane, Christodolos phethane,*' – 'Christodolos is dead!' The rumour rapidly spread that the drowned monk had been born with the stigmata imprinted on his body. Then the pilgrims thronged to the Jordan River carrying pails, bowls, kettles, pots, and plates, and drew water from the place of the drowning, to bring it in sealed jugs to the churches where they lived, so that the sick and crippled could touch it and be healed.

A British police officer charged with writing a report on the incident recorded that two pilgrims testified that they had actually managed to reach the drowning Christodolos and wanted to pull him out, but he had begged them to let him die peacefully, meet his Maker and serve Christos. Ofrosini, whose testimony the policeman also took, insisted that the drowning man wished to serve Theos and not Christos. But the author of the report determined that this witness, who blamed herself for his death, was very confused; hence her version should not be trusted.

Next day, Christodolos was returned to Jaffa. On the day he was buried the rain stopped and a warm sun dried the blackened puddles that had collected on the floor of the roofless church. Abdullah the driver told me that Christodolos' body, washed and perfumed in a new purple cassock, was laid out in a shiny mahogany casket lined in white silk that had been specially brought from Nazareth. Six men from the community held the gleaming copper handles and bore him to the pit that had been dug in the yard of the burned church next to the charred limestone skeleton. That day the church bells did not ring in his honour, because their clappers had melted in the fire and stuck to the inside of the bells.

On the first anniversary of his death the church

commemorated him. Near the place of his drowning a marble crucifix was erected to mark his heroic deed, and at the inauguration ceremony deacons, protodeacons, protopresbyters and archdeacons vied with one another to bestow upon him the highest praise. They all said that he was a humble man, an ascetic and a great scholar, a humanitarian and a benefactor, and that he followed God's path. Later, the faithful in their white robes would make the sign of the Cross in awesome reverence in front of the marble crucifix, and Christodolos' name and heroic deed spread by word of mouth. Soon it was said that this saintly man had saved a hundred men and women from drowning, until a white arm emerged from the depths and pulled him into the abyss. It was further said that anyone kissing the marble crucifix before descending to be baptised in the river would not be swallowed up by the water even during a storm, and the drowned man's blessing would stand them in good stead until they emerged from the water onto the riverbank safe and sound.

Much later the church in Jaffa consecrated the anniversary of Christodolos' death. On that day worshippers appealed to the man who had been my beloved to be their advocate with God and His Son. When they rebuilt the church in Jaffa, they painted his image on one of the walls, and I could see him standing there, his face that of the martyred Jesus, the edges of his black robe dipping into blue waters surrounded by green water plants, one hand gracefully raised to Heaven, his head crowned with a golden halo, his long hair encircling his body in soft black waves and his eyes twinkling at the gloomy Mary Magdalene on the opposite wall.

I gazed at my Christodolos, who had been elevated to the status of a saint, and whispered to him in my heart, far from Mary Magdalene whose ears had heard everything about sin: 'You succeeded, my beloved. Death and suffering become you.' And I left that place without begrudging Mary Magdalene, who never takes her eyes, painted in harlot's kohl, off him. Because I knew that he was mine no more, his holy water had taken him away from me forever, and now he was a member of the painted congregation on the walls of the church. He belongs to the church-goers who gaze upon him and believe in him, and to the pilgrims who kiss the marble crucifix on the riverbank and then faithfully entrust their bodies, at the spot where he drowned and died, into the arms of another monk.

CHAPTER 26

In the first days following Christodolos' death a great tranquillity descended upon me. Like a dead woman I walked in the world of the living, observing them and not mingling. My mind emptied and my senses were clouded and sealed to external stimuli, as if they sought to protect me from physical and mental anguish. At first the sounds disappeared: the ringing of church bells, the muezzin's call to prayer, the shouts of the market traders, the children's laughter, the sound of the waves, all reached my ears dulled, as though my head was immersed in a vessel of water and I could only hear the thumping of my heart racing in my chest. Then the sights became blurred, flowing through my vision like transparent veils of vapour, and my brain did not know how to decipher them. And finally my sense of taste vanished, too, and for many days I did not want to eat.

Only my sense of smell remained, and as though it had become more finely honed at the expense of its dulled counterparts, for a long time I could smell the smell of burning that relentlessly stuck to me; it came from my hair, it was on my clothes, it rose from the sheet and blanket and even managed to overcome the smell of darkness that always hung in my alcove of a room.

I shed no tears at that time because I felt no sorrow, I felt no pain in my burned fingers and toes, and hunger did not trouble me. Only some time later, when I realised that Christodolos had left me never to return, did I want to die as well. I roared like a wounded animal with its leg caught in the jaws of a trap, and the sound that burst from my breast and seeped into my ears bore no resemblance to my voice. One moment my body shivered from the coldness of water and the next from the heat of flames. One moment I was freezing and the next I was sweating from the heat, and so on and so forth, as if I had contracted a deathly fever and had become addicted to it.

On the seventh night I strode fearlessly into the dark sea that panted at me in hostility. I was undeterred by the silhouctte of Andromeda that suddenly arose from the waves, nor by the slippery tentacles of the seaweed that tried to shackle my feet to the cold sand of the shallow water, but continued to walk towards it, as if driven by the magic of the moon that shone on me doubly, both from on high and from the depths. Water tasting of tears flowed into my gasping mouth, flooded my nose, stung my eyes and tightened around my waist like a vice. The waves broke onto my face from above, slapping me angrily, while below my body was caressed by chilly currents as if in a parting blessing from she who was about to die, and they licked at my breasts and hardened my nipples, climbed up my neck and gently encircled it.

I don't know how much time passed until I suddenly felt a sting like a whiplash on my behind, and I looked and saw a translucent jellyfish glinting in the moonlight, its tentacles swaying together with the waves, and I took fright and began swimming until a big wave came along to carry me, light and empty, on its back and mercifully cast my body onto the beach, my backside afire, lungs burning, eyes blinded, and my mouth spewing jets of seawater that had been warmed in my guts. After it had vomited me up the sea became quiet and its breathing calmed. Christodolos is again toying with me, I thought as I made my way back to my room on weak legs.

I did not get out of bed for a few days. My body was racked with fever, my mouth screamed Christodolos' name, my arms flailed in the stormy waters that threatened to cover my head, my nostrils filled with the smell of burning and my eyes saw only the pleading expression on Theotokos' face before she voluntarily went to the stake. I blamed myself for Christodolos' death: it was me who had tempted him with my red hair, I had led him into sinning, into breaking his vow to his God, because of me he had become a man who deserved to die.

When I did not go for Sabbath eve dinner at

my grandmother Simcha's or for Sabbath *hamin* at Grandma Abulafia's, they came to me bearing pots and pans. Afterwards they both liked to tell and retell how they found me in my dark and stinking room under the sweat-soaked blanket, wrestling with ghosts and demons.

'Just skin and bones, skin and bones,' said Grandma Abulafia over and over again.

'Hair, dry, smelly, dirty,' said my grandmother Simcha, for my long red hair had always been the root of all evil for her, as if I used it as a net for catching men.

The day they found me like that, my mouth emitting the stench of empty, dried-up bowels and my clothing stained with excrement, they hurried to heat water, undress me, and their four hands scrubbed my body from top to toe. They joined forces and laid me down on the bed whose sheets they had changed, and I lay there helpless on the cool sheets and under duress opened my mouth obediently to sip my grandmother Simcha's royal *borscht* and nibble at Grandma Abulafia's sweet confectioneries, only to open it again a short while later to unwillingly vomit it up all over the clean bedclothes.

My grandmothers took care of me for some ten days: while one slept the other stayed awake, and when one went out to bring food and clean bedclothes, the other would make sure I was still breathing. One cleaned up my vomit, and the other combed my hair and they both bathed me and changed the bedclothes and so on and so forth. This time the two bitter rivals joined forces, and all to save my life.

Thin, pale and stumbling, I finally emerged from my den with Christodolos' camera dangling on my chest like a lead weight, and made my way to Michael Moussaieff's photography shop. I asked him to quickly develop the film hidden in the camera for me, and three days later I went back and came away carrying the brown paper bag and my heart forecasting doom. Ten enticing women, some in bathing suits and others even further unclothed, smiled at my beloved who was unseen in the photographs I took from the bag. I was troubled most of all by a particularly beautiful blonde girl who was puckering her lips in an eternal kiss. And when the kiss freed itself from the girl's lips, took wing and landed on my forehead, the suspicion that Christodolos was still alive arose in my mind, alive and still playing tricks on me. He had apparently had enough of our frequent quarrels and fled to Jerusalem. In the daytime he roamed the narrow alleys of the Old City, a crown of thorns on his head, and at night he frequented the women pioneers' hostel in Rehavia.

Next day I put on the dress that Grandma Abulafia had made for me after all my clothes had gone up in flames, a white dress with a whole field of sunflowers and poppies flowering on it, around my neck I hung his camera into whose belly Michael Moussaieff had fed a new film, and went off to Jersualem.

For three and a half hours the bus drove along a circuitous route between chasms, roiling my insides, until it set me down at my destination. There I quickly joined a group of black-garbed Greek Orthodox widows on their way to the Church of the Holy Sepulchre. On their breasts glinted the crucified Christ on a gold chain, their eyes were tear-filled and in their arms they clutched bundles of gold-rimmed white candles, and in their hands they held tin boxes with a glass window in which they would take back to their countries the holy flame that would descend upon them this day in the Church of the Holy Sepulchre, in memory of Jesus' resurrection.

With dry lips I listened to the familiar prayers that the women mumbled in pain, and saw how our group joined up with another, and yet another, and we were swallowed up into black waves of the faithful as they flowcd through the narrow alleys of the Old City of Jerusalem, and me, so conspicuous in the flowered dress I was wearing in honour of Christodolos. At each of the Stations of the Cross along the Via Dolorosa of the Son of God, the women in my group stopped with expressions full of pain to hear the explanations of their guide, as if they themselves were experiencing all the awful tortures on their own bodies. And I clicked away on my vanished beloved's camera, that had become mine, heard his voice speaking to me from the guide's lips, and I could feel his breath on my cheeks and his sometimes playful tongue worming its way into my ear, sending shivers of pleasure along my skin.

'This is where Jesus walked,' slowly and directly into my ear, giving life to those scenes of ancient times. 'Here He walked in His purple robe, a crown of thorns on His head, and a very heavy cross burdening His shoulder. Here the Jews cursed Him, mocked Him, spat at Him and threw rotten vegetables at Him. And here the soldiers stopped one Simon of Cyrene and ordered Him to carry the cross. And it was here that St Veronica offered Jesus the mantle to wipe away His sweat. And here Jesus saw His mother standing weeping in the crowd.' The weeping black widows around me kissed the niche in the wall against which Jesus had leaned to rest, and the invisible Christodolos whispered to me, 'Father, forgive them, for they know not what they do.'

Suddenly, a huge mob of pilgrims with blurred features came rushing towards us from all sides, my feet were lifted from the ground and I was swept along by the huge wave into the turbulent courtyard of the Church of the Holy Sepulchre. This was immediately followed by another human wave that pushed me against my will into the church itself that was already full to overflowing. Like refugees clutching the remnants of their worldly goods, the thousands clasped the candles and lamps and waited expectantly for the holy flame that would descend upon them from heaven. The suffocating stench of unwashed bodies and fetid breath enveloped me, mingling in my lungs with the little air I was able to breathe, the foreign exhalations of those around me. Heavy clusters of black-garbed people hung from the walls, oozed along the aisles, fought over every chair, struggled for every foothold and trampled on each other's feet. Back hit back, nose rubbed nose and eye met eye, until they all became a single entity, one body with thousands of heads baying and moaning in anticipation. And when the oxygen in my lungs ran out, I heard Christodolos' indistinct voice from within the cavern: 'And when the sixth hour was come, there was darkness over the whole land until the ninth hour. And Jesus cried with a loud voice and gave up the ghost. And behold, the veil of the temple was rent in twain.'

A new human wave suddenly swept me into the depths of the church, flinging my body against the wall. I clutched the camera and with my fingers felt the cold walls closing in and choking me. Crushed in the crowd, I stood on tiptoe, stretched my back, craned my neck, raised the camera over the whirlpool of heads, aimed the lens at them, pressed the button, and the camera responded with a familiar pleasing click.

And then I saw her.

Illuminated by the light of a paraffin lamp, clasping her Son the Messiah to her glowing bosom, Theotokos was looking at me, smiling her sad smile and on her face a soft expression I had not seen before. Her look sharpened and stabbed me, split my belly and penetrated my womb, and it seemed that her smile had opened her lips a little.

'In the end of the sabbath, as it began to dawn toward the first day of the week,' intoned Christodolos' voice, and again my skin shivered with pleasure, 'came Mary Magdalene and the other Mary to see the sepulchre. And, behold, there was a great earthquake: for the angel of the Lord descended from heaven, and came and rolled back the stone from the door, and sat upon it. And the angel answered and said unto the women, Fear not ye: for I know that ye seek Jesus, which was crucified. He is not here: for He is risen, as He said.'

'Ye are with child and shall bring forth a son,' interrupted Theotokos and a great roar rolled in echo of her words, and the holy flame that they all expected stormed down from the church ceiling, ignited the torch held by the Patriarch, that was under a canopy. 'O Lord, creator of light who hast brought us out of the bottom of *Sheol* and led us to the wondrous light of knowing Thee. O wondrous light that told the light to shine from the darkness, that said "Let there be light" and there was light,' cried the Patriarch in Greek and Christodolos hurried to translate his words into Hebrew for me. With a loud cry the Patriarch lit the first candle offered to him and this candle lit another's candle, and candle suckled on the flame of candle and torch lit torch, flame lit flame, and all at once thousands of candles were burning held by upraised hands with knuckles whitening from the effort. And the flames spread in ever-widening circles, like the ripples from a stone thrown into a quiet pool. And the sea of fire came closer to me with tens of thousands of flashing, glimmering and dancing eyes of tiny tongues of flame that blackened my face with soot. I waved my arms repelling the waves of flame, with feet and hands forced my way towards the lighted opening and was carried along with the huge human mass clutching its candles, onward towards the light of day coming in from outside. But the tidal wave of burning that surrounded me sent sparks onto the flowered field of my dress, burned my face and clutched the rope of my plait like a drowning man. I screamed Christodolos' name and fell exhausted into the hundreds of hands outstretched to help me as I burned. The hands outstretched to choke off the flames that sought to devour me probed my clothing, slapped my head, ran over what was left of my plait and poured lukewarm tea over me from little kettles hung on belts. The smell of charred flesh and the stink of burned feathers filled my nostrils. Then the arms lifted me above the sea of heads, rocking me from side to side, passing me forward to other arms eagerly raised to receive me, craving to perform on me a Christian act of mercy. Then finally, stripped bare of hair and clothes, my face and body blackened and the camera still swinging on my chest, the hands bore me through the lighted door to the church courtyard.

With the raised hems of their black habits, soft-handed and palefaced nuns shielded my naked body, supported me by the elbows and led me step by step up the stairs of the Greek Patriarch's house opposite the church. There they laid me down on a narrow bed whose headboard was protected by the crucified Christ.

'*Thoma, thoma*,' a miracle, a miracle, they said, wringing their hands after cleaning my naked body of the thin, dark layer of dust that covered it, and probing the length of it and not finding a trace of burns. With great compassion they gave me very sweet tea and again washed my blackened face. As evening fell I slipped away, shrouded in a nun's black habit from which rose the smell of incense, twingeing and painfully familiar, and my bald head protected by a cowl. I made my way up the market steps towards Jaffa Gate, emitting smells of smoke and sanctity, and with the habit of years I ran my hand over my head and found a bald scalp. At that moment I had no regrets over the loss of my hair, I knew that I had been punished in that fire and I believed that in it I had expiated my guilt over Christodolos, and now he had finally been driven from me and would never dare to trouble me, neither in my dreams nor in my waking hours.

'Ye are with child and shall bring forth a son,' I hummed Theotokos' words all the way back to Jaffa, and I hugged the camera. 'Ye are with child and shall bring forth a son,' I tossed and turned all that night. 'Ye are with child and shall bring forth a son,' I announced to my eyes bare of brows and lashes, and they looked back at me from the mirror, from a bald, sooty head adorned by charred bristles like a prickly chaplet of black thorns. 'Ye are with child and shall bring forth a son,' I announced, and made up my mind to live.

A week later I sat on my bed and examined the photographs I had taken on my trip to Jerusalem. A vast crowd of men and women carrying crucifixes and lighted candles surrounded me, and I scrutinised the faces, searching among them for Christodolos' face that was hiding from me. In one photograph I saw a suspicious hand gesture and I brought the photograph closer to my eyes and saw a priest secretly lighting the torch held by the Patriarch. In the next one the congregation had moved towards the flame, seeking to light its candles from the holy flame, and I thought I could see his silhouette there, close to the Patriarch's torch, with the knot of his hair at his neck shining in the light of the candles. But the few strands of hair that escaped the knot made me think that it was someone else. Then in the lamplight I looked again at the photographs of the women he had taken, and again envy tormented me and I was filled with tremendous anger at him. I made a decision and tore those smiling pictures into tiny shreds, went outside and threw them into the cold night wind blowing from the sea which cooled my anger somewhat.

Next morning Michael Moussaieff from the photography shop knocked at my door, and with him was a short, balding man. 'Shmuel Bar-Chaim,' he introduced himself, 'editor of *Eretz Yisrael in Pictures*.'

For a long time after they had left I held in my hand the banknotes Bar-Chaim had given me in an envelope, hardly able to believe my luck and hearing again his compliments and promises: 'Nobody has ever managed to capture the ceremony of the Holy Fire from inside the church as clearly and sharply as you. Carry on photographing as much as you can, and my magazine will pay you handsomely.'

CHAPTER 27

Yosef, who was suspected of setting fire to the church, was incarcerated to await trial in the Acre citadel. He later told me that he had been held in one of the stone citadel's huge dank halls together with scores of Jewish, Moslem and Christian detainees. A window with a rusty grille, layered with bird droppings and plastered with seagull feathers, was his sheet anchor. Yosef stood there for most of the day, his back to the other detainees, pushing his nose through a small hole he bored through the filthy grille using a soup spoon he hid under his mattress, reviving his soul with the smell of the sea, whose spume sprayed onto his face. The blue open spaces, the screaming of the gulls and the rumbling of the waves dispelled the stink of the jail, the sight of the prisoners and the weeping of those under sentence of death, and helped him to maintain his sanity.

At mealtimes and during exercise in the prison yard, Yosef, who stood out with his side-locks and beard, held conversations and hot debates with the members of all the races and religions who were with him: to the Jewish underground detainees, those in red suits, sentenced to death, with the blood of British soldiers on their hands, he preached that God, not they, would save the People of Israel. He chatted with the Moslems in Arabic on the fellowship of cousins and the need to live in peace, while he tried to convince the Christians, including the British warders, that Jesus had remained a Jew, kept His faith with the Jewish religion and died for it. He reminded them that the Romans crucified Him as 'King of the Jews' and claimed that Christianity had come into being only after His death, and had He seen the ritual founded in His name and had He known that many generations of Jews would be murdered in the name of His teachings, He would surely have turned in His grave.

Some thirty people were executed every month at the jail, one prisoner a day. In the early morning they would hear the noise of the trapdoor dropping, the scream of the iron pulley and the creak of the wooden scaffold as it bent with a horrifying sound under the weight of its prey. And when the victim was taken away on a stretcher, silence would reign throughout the cells. Then the silence was broken by sighs, the rattle of manacles, the murmuring of supplications and prayers to God and the screams of the prisoners as they were bastinadoed, caned on the soles of their feet. During the beatings all the detainees would hold their breath and count the screams – one scream, one stroke. They sometimes counted six strokes and sometimes twenty-four. The warders who administered the punishment would then carry the semiconscious prisoners, their feet bleeding, under their arms and throw them back into their cells where they would collapse onto the stone floor like marionettes whose strings had been released by the puppet master.

Every Sunday, when I came to Acre by bus and alighted at the station, a smell similar to that of Jaffa, my city, permeated my nostrils. I would hurry through the alleys that wound without rhyme or reason, wending my tortuous way between the food stalls and haberdashery pedlars, taking care to avoid being hit by the donkeys and lowering my eyes before the penetrating looks of the idle men lounging on straw stools much smaller than their bottoms. They scrutinised every contour of my body, holding their looks for a moment on my cropped head and then moving their eyes back greedily to my breasts.

At the prison gate I waited my turn in a long line of anxious women who were loaded down with bundles and packages. I, too, carried a reed basket filled with goodies: *pittas*, cream cheese, spring onions, Syrian olives and crumbling sesame biscuits from Grandma Abulafia's kitchen. There was also a closed tin containing my grandmother Simcha's royal *borscht*, but Yosef, who continued to observe the Jewish dietary laws, used to swap it in the jail for cigarettes.

Before I was allowed through the prison gate,

my naked body was subjected to a thorough search by a cold-eyed British woman soldier who examined me from top to toe in menacing silence. She stuck her gloved hands under my arms, ran a finger between my buttocks and then inserted it into the slit of my vagina. When she finished burrowing between my toes she gestured with her head, telling me to get dressed and get out, and I gathered up my clothes, dressed quickly and went into the visitors' hall where I was greeted by a miasma of mould: the stench of mildew mingled with the acrid smell of disinfectant, the stink of rotting vegetables, the pungent acidity of the prisoners' sweat and the smell of death. On one occasion I was unable to control my churning stomach and the moment I entered the hall I ran into a corner, bent over and vomited. A warder who saw me came over with an angry look on his face, shoved a filthy floor cloth into my hand and ordered me to clean up the filthy mess that had spread over the floor.

At the sight of Yosef's silhouette striding towards me from the other end of the hall, from force of habit I ran my fingers over my cropped hair that no longer needed a comb. His face cracked into a broad, compassionate smile as he sat facing me on the other side of the dusty grille separating us, and I sat looking at the new silver threads that had prematurely appeared in his black hair. His serious eyes, that always examined me in minute detail as if seeking to reveal right away what I was going to tell him, were always inflamed. In the great commotion in the hall, the lamenting and complaining and wailing and weeping of babies and adults, we secluded ourselves inside a bubble of tranquillity that was ours alone. With his eyes Yosef would caress the soft red down that had already taken hold on my skull, as if it were trying to sprout for him, and like a lip reader his eyes were glued to my lips to draw from them the words I wanted to tell him amid all the tumult. And when he spoke, my legs trembled under me and my heart went out to him, to that lean boy who had sacrificed his freedom to save me.

When visiting time was over, as I went back the way I had come, once again the looks of the men sitting in the cafés awaited me, the eternal coffee cup in front of them, their fingers holding the yellow beads of amber, their thumbs rolling the beads interminably and their eyes stinging my behind.

Yosef was imprisoned for a month and a half before he was brought to trial. On the day of the trial I sat in the last row in the courtroom, the bristles of my hair covered with a kerchief like the Orthodox women, my eyes lowered, trying to evade Yosef's wandering glance that passed over the faces looking at him and that tried to meet my eyes. The trial lasted for only a few minutes. The judge asked and Yosef answered him with verses from the Book of Books while swaying back and forth like a devout worshipper.

'Is your name Yosef Mendel?' asked the judge.

'And the house of Joseph shall be like a flame,' he answered.

'Tell me what happened that night,' ordered the judge.

'Thunder, and with earthquake, and great noise, with storm and tempest, and the flame of devouring fire,' answered Yosef excitedly.

'Did you, Yosef Mendel, set fire to the Church of St Ioannis in Jaffa?' asked the judge despairingly, and Yosef rocked back and forth and replied joyously, 'Behold there came fire down from heaven.'

'Do you admit to setting fire to the Church of St Ioannis in Jaffa?' he asked again, wording his question differently.

'And he burnt the house of the Lord,' he mumbled.

'Did you steal ritual artefacts from the church before the fire?' enquired the judge.

'Ye shall burn their graven images with fire,' he answered with a foolish smile.

Silence fell in the courtroom and the judge put a finger to his temple, hinting as to his opinion of the accused before him.

'The accused will answer his honour,' the clerk of the court reprimanded Yosef.

I was looking at Yosef from the side as he stared with a stupefied expression on his face. He then turned his back on the judge and as he faced the courtroom he began shouting, 'Behold a smoking furnace, and a burning lamp, thou shalt not kindle a flame on the Sabbath day, and when he had set the brands on fire, but this shall be with burning and fuel of fire, and the sight of the glory of the Lord was like devouring fire, for wickedness burneth as the fire, and he burned like a flaming fire, and I will kindle a fire in his cities, the shining of a flaming fire by night . . .' until two warders rushed at him, one grasping his waving arms and the other gagging him with his hand so that only a few choked syllables escaped his lips. The embarrassed judge again pointed to his own temple, ordered the accused released due to lack of evidence and recommended that he be committed to a mental hospital. Yosef heard his words with a shy and sheepish smile, turned again to the people in the courtroom and shouted his parting words in loud and solemn tones: 'Then take of them again, and cast them into the midst of the fire.'

Pale, he stumbled to freedom, his eyes, which had become used to the gloom of the jail, blinking in the bright light that suddenly assailed them, searching for me through his dazzled vision. I called his name and he fell into my arms. I supported his wasted body and led him to the bus station. All the way to Jaffa we sat in silence on the wooden bench in the smoking, juddering bus. In silence we walked to Widow Ziso's house, in silence we climbed the steps, and I looked on amazed as Simcha, most uncharacteristically, burst into cries of joy and hugged and kissed Yosef again and again. She stopped suddenly, as if caught red-handed, turned to me and sent me to look for Fishke and tell him that his son was back.

I found Fishke on the beach. His face paled when I gave him the news and he hurried home at a fast limp. I felt that nobody needed me at this three-sided reunion and went back to my own room. There I changed into a swimsuit and went for a dip in the sea to cleanse my body in the salt water of the smells of the jail and the dust of the journey. I returned purified, sprayed some fragrant lemon water onto my neck and arms, put on my best dress, put fresh sheets on the bed, swept the floor, put on the kettle and sat down to wait for him. When dusk fell and he had still not come, I dragged a chair into the alley and tried to calm my raging spirit with the sunset. The sun, almost touching the sea, rode on it for a moment like a gold earring. I got up and went inside, leaving the door open wide. The pale glow of a tired day came through the opening, illuminating the room with its pink softness. When darkness prevailed and I lit the lamp, Yosef came.

We sat facing one another, he on the low stool and me on the narrow bed. We exchanged a multitude of words without speaking, and when he took my hand into his broad ones, I knew what I had to do.

I pulled my hand from his, got up and began unbuttoning my dress. One after another I undid them before him and he followed my every movement with bated breath. I threw off the dress and stood on it in front of him hesitantly, not knowing whether I should remove my undergarments and pull him with me into bed, or if it would be better to give him time to respond. Yosef sat frozen, vainly trying to take his eyes from my half-naked body he had been forbidden to look at ever since my breasts began to bud. And then, before his pale face, I reached behind me, unhooked my brassiere and let it fall with a soft rustle onto the mound of the dress. I moved closer to him, took his clenched fists that hung unmoving at his sides, drew them to my mouth, kissed the clenched knuckles, opened them without difficulty and put my breasts into his hands, one breast into each hand.

'It's forbidden, forbidden,' he whispered, and his soft fingers, the fingers of a *yeshiva* student, curled around my breasts and began kneading them gently, and they extended their nipples in his honour.

'It's allowed, allowed,' I confidentially assuaged his fears without knowing exactly who had permitted us to one another, but knowing in some way that it felt unquestionably right.

With my breasts cupped in his hands and tears flowing down his cheeks, I bent over him and took off his Sabbath shirt revealing a broad white chest adorned with a single curl of hair, then I moved my hands further, to his trouser buttons, and felt his erection respond throbbing to me.

I don't know who guided whom to the bed and

who led whom in the carnal dance, but the sweet taste of our act of love then, as sweet and soft and pink as a ball of candy floss, lingers in my mouth to this day. I remember how, when his body became one with mine, hesitantly at first and then forcefully, all at once the memory of our common childhood was erased, the days when Yosef-Yousuf was my adopted brother, the son of my grandfather Fishke and Latifa the whore. The memory of his small, trembling body held close to me on the day of the riots was erased, the nights when we lay side by side and he put his cool ear to my chest and listened to the murmur in my heart were also gone. And the memory of much later times was erased, too, the days he followed me and stood guard when I was Christodolos' beloved. I knew it was in the power of those old pictures that filled our common photograph album locked in my mind, to force their way into my bed and come between us. And when I drove them away we were man and woman who were one flesh, without memories and without baggage from the past. Then I suddenly knew that Yosef was my lost twin, the foetus I hadn't allowed to be born. We had been created in one womb and a single umbilical cord had fed us with oxygen and nutrition. Until I had been separated from him with the slash of a knife, just like a fish or a hardboiled egg is sliced. I had searched for him all my life and now I had finally found him and become joined to him in love, and in a flash 'Tamara Another One', the hyena's only daughter who had killed her rival in the womb, had vanished from my life.

Exhausted, we lay in each other's arms and Yosef's hand stroked the mound of my swollen belly, soothing it. That night I cried in my sleep and Yosef woke me up, stroked my face and calmed my body with his.

'Do you have any regrets?' he asked.

My answer was to cover his mouth with mine and I did not move it away until the sun rose in the sky and the heat of the room became unbearable. Weak from loving we went to the beach to cool a little in the sea breeze, and I decided to tell my grandmother Simcha everything that had happened to me with Yosef and compel her to tell me her last secret that she had so far kept from me.

CHAPTER 28

A few days after I confessed my love for Yosef to my grandmother Simcha and she repaid me with her last secret, she fell ill. Her head and body ached, her temperature rose and she was unable to get out of bed. Influenza, said the doctor and ordered her to drink a lot and cover herself with three quilts, 'to sweat it out'.

Fishke, helpless and concerned to the point of tears, paced the room. With his heavy carpenter's hands he kept opening and closing the windows, saying it was too hot for her, too cold, there wasn't enough air in the room, there was a draught, the smoke from the bathhouse made it hard for her to breathe, until Yosef, who was always respectful towards him, could no longer restrain himself and told him to stop, because if he didn't both she and we would go out of our minds. And Fishke, who could not see her suffering, went to her kitchen, shut himself in, made her black tea, came back and vainly tried to make her drink it, plumped the pillows beneath her head, wiped away the sweat shining on her forehead and placed cold pads on it. At night he sat at her bedside, protecting her

417

soul lest it fly out of the window, God forbid, and disappear. On the fifth day her condition worsened and Yosef came to my room to tell me that she wanted to see me right away.

'They took everything, nothing to leave,' she told me apologetically, and her hands that had never known a day's idleness moved purposelessly over the quilt, feeling and searching for something that I too couldn't see.

'I teach you *rezept* to make *borscht*.'

Then, as she dictated the recipe to me, I wondered at her decision to reveal the recipe for the soup I had never liked, on the eve of her death. Only later, when I made it myself in her kitchen, I realised that this soup, in which she had invested all her love for me in my childhood, was the most meaningful thing she could have left me before her death.

That day she ordered me to take pencil and paper, and as I wrote her sharp ears were pricked to hear the whisper of the pencil point on the paper, to make sure I hadn't missed a word.

With great precision she first dictated the recipe for the czars' *borscht*, and then hastily added the recipe for the farmers' *borscht*, that differed from the royal version only in the number of cloves of garlic to be added to it, and the quality of the meat that was somewhat inferior.

When she finished dictating with great difficulty, she demanded that I read her what I had written, and she listened, nodding her head during the brief pauses at the end of each stage. Her eyes were closed and only her hands, patchworked with the red haematomas that heralded the approaching end, came back to life every now and again: her fingers twisted by rheumatism peeled beets and potatoes, cut the meat and potatoes into small cubes, quickly sliced the turnip, carrots, cabbage and celeriac into thin strips, grated the cooked beet, skimmed the dirty froth with a spoon from the surface of the bubbling water, threw in a pinch of salt and pepper, gently poured in the vinegar, and when I read the instruction 'stir', she made stirring movements in the air.

'You make soup like this for your son,' she said, and repeated her request that I should not give birth to a bastard because she had no more strength for bastards.

When I rose to say goodbye, I kissed her forehead and for the first time in my life called her 'my grandmother', and she waved like a queen commanding her citizens to leave her in peace. I quickly obeyed her and left the room, and when I peeped through the half-open door I saw her extinguished eyes shedding tears.

That same day I bought all the necessary ingredients and prepared the soup. I remembered every detail of her instructions and did not need to look at what I had written even once.

(Much later, so that her soup would not fade into oblivion, I rewrote the recipe in my words of wisdom notebook under the heading, 'Grandma

Simcha's Czars' *Borscht*', and I translated the quantities, the names of the ingredients and the various stages of preparation, that had been taken from her world and language, into modern Hebrew. As I did so, I wondered how she could have dictated the instructions so precisely, because she herself never cooked that way but used the traditional, mysterious method that Widow Ziso called 'cooking by' – 'cooking by eye, by hand, by heart, by colour and by thickness'.

Wash three beets well, cut off the root hairs and the top with the leaves, and cook in water for a long time until they are soft and their colour changes from dark purple to noble crimson. Meanwhile, put half a kilogram of beef, cut into cubes, into a pot for the soup, four pieces of shin bone full of marrow, two onions sliced into rings, a teaspoonful of black peppercorns and two bay leaves. Add twelve cups of water, bring to the boil and leave to simmer on a low flame. After about an hour, put into the pot three peeled potatoes cut into cubes (*'And not forget take dirt off top with spoon,' my grandmother told me on reaching this stage of the recipe*), and continue to simmer for about half an hour. Then peel the cooked beets (*'And the skin come off very easy,' she said, showing me how the cooked beet popped out of its skin, shedding it*), grate them on a coarse grater into bowl, on to the grated beets pour very slowly, with sensitivity, while sniffing *(my grandmother's nostrils flared)*, a quarter of a cupful of white wine vinegar and one cupful of the soup, and put them aside. To the soup bubbling on the flame in the meantime, add a quarter of a white cabbage sliced very thinly, and continue simmering it for about a quarter of an hour. Finally add the turnip, two carrots and the celeriac, all peeled and sliced into thin strips, and simmer them for another quarter of an hour, add salt and pepper and the grated beet marinated in vinegar, mix and simmer for about another five minutes. The soup can be served with a separate bowl of sour cream, and never forget the black bread.

Steam hissed from the gap between lid and pot and a pleasing, slightly bitter smell, the smell of *borscht*, rose to the kitchen roof. Through the cloud of steam I saw her tormented face as she made the soup, her lower lip bitten in pain and concentration as she poured the vinegar into a bowl, and the phlegm she spat into the big pot of farmers' *borscht*. I poured the soup, rich with vegetables, into a bowl and sat down to eat as she had taught me: I dipped the edge of the spoon into the sour cream and then into the crimson liquid, and sipped the soup that was now pink after being mixed with the white of the cream. Then I tore off a piece of rye bread, dipped it into the soup, and once it had absorbed

421

the liquid, heavy and threatening to sink, I fished it out right into my mouth where I cautiously squashed it with my tongue, as if afraid of dispelling the magic. With each spoonful of the aromatic liquid I poured down my gullet I could feel my grandmother's warmth spreading through my body, and when I sucked the marrow from the bone that lay in the pot like a primeval animal bathing in a pool whose waters had reddened, I suddenly knew the power of her love for me and I, too, loved her with an indescribable love. When I got into bed that night, I whispered a plea for her forgiveness for all the hundreds of bowls of soup she had poured for me and which I sold for a mess of pottage.

A few days later my grandmother died in her sleep. Yosef came to my room on Friday night, told me to come with him and was still reluctant to give me the bad news. Only as we climbed the steps of the house did he tell me that those who go to meet their Maker on the Sabbath eve are considered righteous, and even Simcha, who had lived in sin all her life, for she was a total heretic, was, after all, a righteous woman and who if not him knew that.

The room was shrouded in silence. The only sound to be heard was the quiet buzzing of a few shiny green flies that had fled the adjacent chicken slaughterhouse, and which were now despairingly knocking on the window-pane of the dead woman's room. Every now and again the silence was also broken by the snuffling of Fishke who sat at her side, smoothing her white hair with his broad, scarred hand and weeping silently.

At that moment I knew that she wanted me to console him. I kissed her cold forehead and hurried to her kitchen. The ingredients were waiting for me: Simcha had made sure that they would be ready for me. I washed the beets well, taking care to remove the crumbs of soil sticking to the root beard. I cut the meat and vegetables and sliced the onions into rings. With eyes blinded by tears caused by the pungent onion fumes, I poured the vinegar over the grated beets in the bowl and didn't forget to skim the dirty froth from the surface of the liquid in the pot. And throughout I could feel my grandmother's hands on mine, guiding them, chopping and grating and stirring with them.

With great excitement I put the hot pot of soup on the table, ladled some into Fishke's bowl, and he drew it closer suspiciously, sniffed the steam rising from it, and with a groan declared, 'The smell is exactly the same as the smell of Simchi's soup.' I breathed a sigh of relief as though he had told me that I had passed her test. Fishke fervidly dipped his bread to the red liquid and ate with gusto, as if he hadn't seen food for days. In the silence that hung over the room, that was occasionally broken by the sound of chewing and with groans of what might have been either pain or pleasure, I suddenly heard Yosef clearing his throat and saying in a choked voice, 'Can I have a bowl of soup?'

Fishke was so amazed by this strange request by his son that he stopped eating, and a spoonful of soup stayed suspended in the air between his plate and his mouth.

'The soup, the meat isn't . . . isn't . . . isn't kosher,' I mumbled almost to myself, but before Yosef could change his mind I hurried to bring another bowl, filled it with soup and placed it in front of him, and Fishke and I looked at one another confused as we saw him tear off big pieces from the dark loaf, dip them into the soup, fish them out soft and spongy, and eat the dish with gusto, the dish he had forgone ever since he decided to eat only kosher food. Fishke finally went back to his bowl, finished off the *borscht*, and asked me for what he had always asked of her, the vodka bottle that was kept for him. I brought the bottle and three glasses and poured the transparent liquid into them. With his head thrown back, Fishke drank his off in one gulp. 'To you, Simchi,' he said, banged his glass down onto the table and asked for another. Yosef and I followed suit. For the first time in my life I drank vodka. My tongue was bitten in pain and a cold, searing, merciless fire seeped from my throat, into my stomach, through my bowels and finally reached my feet. My face contorted and my legs trembled until I got up and went to sit down heavily on the bed next to her. At that moment the lump in my throat that was choking me vanished, I got up again and fell into Fishke's arms as he came towards me. For a moment Yosef looked at us in silence, then he, too, came close, embraced me from behind and his arms encompassed Fishke as well.

I could feel his tears wetting the back of my neck.

All through that night, as if ruminating, I told and retold Yosef the last secret she had revealed to me, the telling of which had exhausted her strength and caused her illness and death.

Widow Ziso, too, was sure of this and she was angry with me and grumbled that the terrible secret I had forced from her with my great stubbornness had sent her to her bed from which she never got up. 'She was never ill like that,' she rebuked me, 'all the time you wanted to know secrets, always secrets. You drove her crazy. In the end she told you everything and look what happened,' she said as if blaming me directly for her death.

Then the sentence told me by Avigdor Ben-Ari that I had written in my notebook sprang to mind: 'There are people whose past pursues them all their life, until it catches up with them and kills them.' But as much as I racked my brains I couldn't recall under what circumstances the words had been spoken – had he told me them in answer to one of my innumerable questions, or had he perhaps been trying to hint that I should not force my grandmother to tell me that last secret, that might kill her.

On more than one occasion in the course of her stories about my grandmother, Widow Ziso hinted at the existence of this dark secret but always refused to go into detail. So I fed off rumours and assumptions and made up my mind not to give up until I had heard the whole story from my grandmother Simcha. Then I amalgamated her story with Widow Ziso's version and, as is my wont, added my own embellishments until the final version related here was born.

My grandmother Simcha's mother wanted to kill her over there in Russia when she was still in her womb, which had already given life to ten children before her – nine girls and a boy. I never dared to ask how my grandmother knew this, but I imagined that she sensed the hatred that bubbled like venom in her mother's blood that flowed to her through the umbilical cord, or perhaps she had heard it in her heartbeats that were not soothing and loving, but filled with resentment towards this unwanted foetus which, if it were born alive, would need to be fed too. Unlike her mother's previous ten confinements, this birth was easy. With simple ease the infant slid from between her mother's thighs as she knelt on the hay in the shed, right in the middle of milking the goats, as if she had done her best not to hurt her mother so as not to increase her anger towards her.

Her father decided to give her the joyful name of Simcha, but the infant caused its mother only depression and sorrow and Simcha knew only evil and hardship throughout her infancy. From the moment she was born her mother sank into a deep depression, nursed her only cursorily and reluctantly from her shrivelled breasts, and left her for many hours at a time in her filthy, cold and stinking diapers in the old wooden cradle whose paint had long peeled off. The baby lay there quietly crying, as if to herself, waiting for her father's hands to lift her up and his reproachful voice telling his wife to come and take care of her. When her father was not at home, my grandmother's sisters – Leah'leh, Batya'leh, the twins Sheindaleh and Sarah'leh, Mira'leh, Michaleh, Hanna'leh, Rivka'leh and Racheleh – would take care of her as best they could.

When she grew a little and learned to stagger around on her thin legs, a farmer once found her on the main road sunk into the snow and weeping bitterly, a heavy frozen diaper around her bottom and light felt shoes on her feet. The farmer went from house to house, knocking on every door until he found her house. Widow Ziso told me that Simcha told her that her father, who took her from the farmer almost frozen to death, immersed her without a second thought in the big pot of *borscht* that stood on the stove. For a long time the red liquid heated Simcha's flesh until she thawed out and opened her mouth to cry. It is small wonder, said Widow Ziso, that from that time my grandmother's heart was lovingly bound to the kitchen, and that more than any other dish she loved to make the *borscht* that saved her life. And I could but wonder even more than before why she spat into it as it was cooking.

Following that escapade, her parents decided to lock the door of the house until she grew and learned to collect eggs from the chicken coop, milk the goats and, more particularly, to fend for herself. As she was always hungry, she loved to surreptitiously watch her mother working in the kitchen, patiently observing her as she rolled out dough from which she made noodles, sliced vegetables for soup, baked bread and the Sabbath *challah*, and fried *piroshki* in deep oil. When her mother discovered this, she gradually allowed her to do these jobs for her until she finally retired from the hated cooking and left the kitchen to her youngest daughter.

Krasavitza, pretty one, her father called her; *Urodlivaya*, ugly one, was her mother's name for her, and Simcha never knew whether she was pretty or ugly. She would sometimes look at her reflection in the small sliver of mirror that Leah'leh, the eldest daughter, found in one of the neighbouring city's elegant streets. Leah'leh, the most beautiful of all the sisters, who loved looking at herself in the mirror, agreed to share it with her sisters from time to time, and Simcha would then see a thin face with prominent cheekbones, wide-open blue eyes and thin blonde hair whose locks escaped the rolled, bound plaits on her head. She was especially bothered by her nose that was upturned, '*Kournosaya*' as the teasing gentile boys called her as she passed through the village delivering pails of milk to the houses. The impudence of the bullies among them grew from day to day, especially once her breasts began budding, and she had difficulty in avoiding the hands that grabbed her dress and tried to touch her body, and more than once she returned home crying, her clothes torn and indignation gnawing at her.

Her father, who had been a *yeshiva* student in his youth, gathered his daughters around him every Saturday evening and taught them to read and write in Hebrew and Russian. Simcha's sisters gradually managed to dodge these lessons and only she persevered, so much so that she was actually eager to learn and her father decided to teach her every evening, thus consoling himself for the absence of Motte'leh, his only son, who had been impressed into the Russian army when he was only a youth. When the father discovered that his daughter was attracted only to Russian and not Hebrew, he told her Bible stories in Russian and later even read secular books with her, which he hid under his bed apart from the religious books, which he proudly displayed in his modest bookcase.

Simcha quickly learned to escape her miserable existence through reading. With the heroes and heroines of the novels she obtained from her father she would recline on velvet couches in splendid palaces, dance dizzying waltzes, ride on horseback, chatter in French, sail to far-off countries where she would pass the time with savages with shining ebony skin. When she had finished all the books her father had hidden, she felt as though she had been expelled from the Garden of Eden and sent back to the wretched houses all around her, the rivers of mud and the filth, the bad smells and the boys who bullied her. Then one day she discovered a second-hand bookshop in the neighbouring town, and from then on she took a few *kopeks* from the sales of milk and cheese and visited the shop as often as she was able. The owner, whose yellow face was like transparent parchment, recommended books and lent them to her for a modest fee.

When her father saw her immersed in her reading every evening, he decided that this daughter would do what he himself had been prevented from doing – she would study and become a teacher. So it was agreed that she would enrol at the Jewish teachers' seminary in the district town, but then evil winds began blowing through the surrounding villages and towns and almost each new day brought with it new stories of horror: in one place a Jewish merchant was waylaid and killed as he left his village, his horse, cart and merchandise were taken and his body left on the roadside. In another case several men attacked a Jewish girl and raped her, one after the other, and somewhere else a wealthy corn merchant was accused of overcharging, was asked to reduce his prices, and when he refused his barn was set alight. The gentiles called the Jews blood-suckers, children of the devil and Christ-killers, and the threats and attacks increased steadily.

When my grandmother turned sixteen, the thugs reached her family's home as well. The calamity befell them on the day of Jesus' birth, on the eve of a new year and a new century. Zerach Levin once told me that he was in Moscow at the time and saw the city's inhabitants celebrating this special birthday of their Messiah that was also to herald the birth of a new, better century. It was marked by sumptuous banquets at the city's palaces and restaurants, while in the gaslight-illuminated streets the lacquered carriages glinted, and fir trees decorated with coloured glass balls and artificial snowflakes shone from the gift-laden shop windows, while well-dressed people, acquaintances and complete strangers, wished each other a Happy New Year.

But far from the well-lit happy cities, that night the Jews of my grandmother's village snuffed out the blackened lamps in their poor wooden houses that were planted in the swampy mud like so many floating islands of darkness. In a message passed from house to house, the rabbi told them to prepare for Christmas Eve, the night of the birth of that man, on which the pleasures of the flesh and the spirit are expressly forbidden, and issued a particularly solemn warning that the end of anyone born of a coupling on this birthday of the false prophet would be apostasy, Heaven forbid.

On that Christmas Day, when the rumour spread that drunken hooligans were on the rampage in the villages carrying sticks, pitchforks and burning torches, the Jews closed their wooden shutters, bolted their doors, crouched in their cottages and prayed – but all in vain. The thugs came from all directions, joined forces, moved from cottage to cottage and no bolt could keep them at bay, not even all the furniture piled against the door in my grandmother's cottage. A huge band of them burst in; first they slaughtered her mother and then her father, then one by one they dragged out the five unmarried sisters who still lived with their parents – Mira'leh, Michaleh, Hanna'leh, Rivka'leh and Racheleh – raped them and then killed them. Then they fell upon the quilts piled high on one of the beds. They slashed the covers with their knives sending a cloud of feathers and down into the air, and white clouds of goose feathers floated in the air as if refusing to descend. When they finished amusing themselves inside the house, they smashed the windows and shook the quilts and pillows into the frozen street that was filled with the shouts of the thugs and the screams of their victims. Down from the quilts hung in the air for a moment and then hesitantly joined with the snowflakes in a whirling, frenzied dance in which it was impossible to separate the two, until they finally floated down together to the cold, muddy ground where they were immediately trampled by the hooligans' boots.

Then they turned their attention to the mattresses

and Simcha, who was hiding under a bed, flew out when the mattress above her was stabbed. The inflamed thugs dragged her by her hair, ripped the bodice of her dress revealing her breasts, tore off the dress and mounted her one after another. She lay under them as though dead without a sound, but in her memory she etched the sounds, the sight of the faces above her and the touch of the hands on her body, until she passed out. When they thought she had died, they lit fires in the corners of the house and left. It was the fire that brought Simcha round. Tiny tongues of flame crawled towards her, heated her body and thawed her limbs that had frozen on the earth floor that was so cold that terrible winter. And when the tongues of flame licked at her right foot leaving a deep burn on it, my grandmother Simcha came to and crawled to the door. With empty eyes she looked at the mutilated bodies that had been her family, and she was so calm that she even stopped for a moment, amazed that she was unable to shed even one tear over the death of her parents and sisters. Indifferent to her fate, she collapsed in the doorway of the cottage that was going up in flames, and lay there, alternately fainting and coming round, until she awoke to the touch of a hand that grasped her and shook her lightly. A novice priest was standing over her, looking at her compassionately. He lifted her up with ease, as though she weighed nothing, carried her away from there and sat her down on a stone by the empty goat pen, covered her with a blanket and gave her some melted snow to drink. That night the smell of burning permeated the pores of my grandmother Simcha's skin so deeply that it was absorbed into her body, became her smell and did not leave her until the day she died.

Her four married sisters – Leah'leh, Batya'leh, Sheindaleh and Sarah'leh – who were saved because they lived in the neighbouring town, and Motteleh, her only brother who in the meantime had been discharged from the army, a shell of his former self, and who lived with his eldest sister, decided to send Simcha to Palestine, despite her not wanting to go at all, and promised to follow her to the land of oranges, where the caressing sun shines all day long, and there were good people there who would give her a home and adopt her as their daughter.

Some fifty crushed orphans, pogrom refugees, walked the streets of Odessa, the gay port city, as though in a dream. They smelled the aromas of good food that rose from every corner and fled before the splendid carriages harnessed to noble horses that drove through the streets with bells ringing. Then they were gathered like a flock of lost chicks and taken onto a Russian ship together with a group of pilgrims whose destination was also the Holy Land.

After a long voyage, my grandmother was awakened one morning by a shaft of light coming through the cracks in the children's dormitory door, and on the floor danced an assortment of twirling colours that flashed onto the bunks and the wild-haired heads of the young refugees. With blinking eyes they emerged from the ship's hold and joined the pilgrims who crowded together, excitedly genuflecting and crossing themselves on the narrow deck facing the shore. A small town rising from the shore and climbing up a hill, whose low houses were gathered together in no particular order or system, welcomed the new arrivals with a broad smile of open windows, and all around were yellow sand dunes with blotches of green here and there, and between the town and the ship a strip of shallow water dotted with frightening black rocks.

The ship listed and almost capsized with the weight of the pilgrims and children that almost unbalanced it. The sailors left the pilgrims alone but drove the children away with sticks and curses until they were spread evenly over the deck and the ship resumed an even kneel. Only Simcha went back, leaned on the rail and screwed up her eyes to just a crack, trying to get used to the clear light of the morning sun rising in the east and discovering, against the lightening sky, the dark outline of high mountains. 'Jerusalem is over there,' came a voice from next to her, the voice of Fishke, the boy who had followed her like a shadow throughout the voyage.

A long time later, after they had been checked by a man wearing a tarbush and all their papers arranged, the children went down the gangway, stumbling, hesitant and holding each other's hands, and boarded small boats that took them close to the shore. There, in the shallow water, the porters awaited them, screaming at one another about who would take whom and who what, who would take the children, the pilgrims and the luggage. With a terrible noise they swooped on the children and carried them, kicking and screaming in terror, to dry land. Simcha lay in the strong arms that held her and opened her eyes to the warm sun that was brighter than any she had ever seen, just as her sisters had promised. She tried to draw its warmth into her stiff limbs and absorb its brilliant glare with her eyes. For a long time she gazed at the sun with her clear eyes until the daylight suddenly dimmed, the sky was obscured, and twilight descended on the world, and in place of the vanished light black coins flickered before her eyes, and their number increased until she was enveloped in complete darkness, her sight lost, and even her tears dried in the heat of the sun, and from that time on no tears fell onto her cheeks, and some even thought that her tear ducts had dried up or had even been lost.

When her feet touched dry land, she stretched out her arms and felt her way between the shadows surrounding her in the threatening darkness. Strange hands touched her, patted her shoulders, touched her dress, ran over her hair stiff with salt water, and guided her footsteps. Sweets and oranges fell into her apron pockets, and a soft hand grasped her elbow and led her to a cart, helped her down from it, led her up a staircase, took off her clothes, and laid her down on a bed in a cool room. My grandmother Simcha slept for two whole days and when she opened her eyes, got up and wanted to go outside, she stumbled into the outlines of a cupboard, a chair and a table blocking her way in the dark room. Later, on doctor's orders, drops were vainly put into her eyes every few hours, and in vain Widow Ziso laid cool camomile pads on them – her sight had been taken from her forever, to be replaced by a finely honed sense of hearing built on the ruins of her world that had been burned.

About three weeks after her arrival, they dressed her in a wedding dress and told her that she was to marry Fishke. Seven months after being with Fishke, her husband, in the ritual purification room that served as a private room for the newly-weds, the first infant was born. When they placed it naked in her arms, she gazed at it in wonder straining her extinguished eyes, touched its wrinkled face, and saw, one by one, clearly and precisely, the faces of her torturers. She looked at them one at a time, again touched the face of her baby, and compared, caressing her son's light hair with trembling fingers, running one hand over his body still wet with birth fluid and blood, begged his forgiveness and broke his neck. When she handed him back to the midwife, she tried vainly to support his lolling head.

Then her daughter emerged from her womb only to be immediately taken from her lest she do to her what she had done to her brother, and she was only returned to her three days later. Again Simcha strained her eyes, touched the baby's face and asked Widow Ziso to tell her what she looked like, and she felt that she found a resemblance to the last one of them whose face she had seen through a rip in her dress, and he, too was engraved on her memory before she lost consciousness. And she felt that the boy had reluctantly been pushed into his actions by his friends, because it seemed he was asking her forgiveness, and she recalled a black habit, a novice's hat, and a knot of red hair tied at the back, and she further remembered that she had not felt the weight of his body on hers, apparently because he was propped up on his elbows, and in her blinded eyes danced a multitude of freckles that covered his face. It was his hands that later put out the fire that had taken hold of her clothes and burned her foot, and then carried her outside and given her snow water.

'Call her Nechama,' advised Shoshana the midwife, 'and she'll bring you luck and consolation.'

A long and motley procession of mourners followed my grandmother Simcha's litter to her final resting place in the cemetery where she had been married. It was led by Fishke, supported by Yosef; then came Widow Ziso, who on this day had left her house for the first time since the riots, and she grasped my arm with her twisted, arthritic hand that looked like the talon of a bird of prey, and with her height diminished by the burden of years, and her shining white skin that had not seen the sunlight for many years, she looked like a shrivelled and wrinkled young girl who had prematurely aged; at our side puffed Grandma Abulafia bound up in her corset, with my father Yehuda supporting her back as though she were about to faint, and after us marched many of the citizens of Jaffa – Jews, Moslems and Christians – who had come to pay their last respects. There were pilgrims who had not returned to their famine-stricken country and its edicts, Russian priests with their long hair and habits who loved her rye bread, tall British officers and their wives, who carried white parasols in gloved hands and their delicate noses hidden by lace handkerchiefs lest the stink of the rabble reach them, and a large group of fishermen, butchers, greengrocers and perfume and spice sellers, of all religions, whose customer she had been, and who now had closed their businesses out of respect and come to her funeral. And finally, by the cemetery gate, we were joined by her '*Lumpenproletariat*', the scratching beggars infected with boils and leprosy, who had eaten the leftovers from her pots.

When Yosef said the mourner's *Kaddish*, Fishke, crazy with grief, threw himself onto the mound of earth, begging to be buried with her. He only agreed to come back with me to the room in Jaffa after I bent down to him, embraced him and whispered that his Simchi could see everything from above and he shouldn't make her worry.

When I went to visit her a week later, her grave was raised above ground level, as if something had been placed beneath it to elevate it so she would be able to observe her daughter who had died giving birth to me, and her twin brother who had been born in order to die.

On the thirtieth day after her death, Yosef accepted my proposal of marriage.

We were married ten days later, for a joyous occasion defers mourning said Yosef, thus justifying our hasty marriage. My wedding dress was made by Alla and not Grandma Abulafia, who found the pretext of her eyes not being as good as they were. I know today that she refused because she feared that a dress she made would bring bad luck like the three earlier ones that had been ruined: the one she gave my grandmother, the one she made for my mother and the one she had made for me.

At my request, Alla slightly widened the front of the dress, adding narrow pleats around the waist, which concealed my already swelling belly, and she hid my cropped head with a long tulle veil that fell down my back and flowed behind me.

The wedding was held in the garden of Widow Ziso's house. My father Yehuda welcomed me joyously, his wild hair combed back severely, his long, sparse beard flying in all directions, his eyes shining and a gentle, dreamy smile rested on his face. And Fishke, whose face was beaming as it had on the day he came to us to show Yosef, his baby, to us, grasped his son's elbow with his thick hands as if he feared he would flee from him, and led him under the wedding canopy.

I walked towards my bridegroom carrying a bouquet of white lilies that Fishke had picked for me on the limestone cliffs overlooking the sea. When Yosef broke the glass in commemoration of the destruction of Jerusalem and everybody shouted '*Mazal tov!*' I smiled. I knew that my grandmother was listening to the shouts of happiness up in heaven, and she was very pleased.

Afterwards, as Yosef lifted my veil for the first kiss, all the dead clustered around us: submissive and obedient, a skinny young girl of about thirteen stood at my side, her child's hands red and swollen, her yellow hair like a curtain burned and faded by the sun, and she was wearing the grey dress from the yellowing photograph I had found in the box of old photos. And when she leaned towards me and whispered, '*Mazal tov*, my little girl,' I could see the multitude of freckles that dotted my mother's face. And then, as if he were the best man, Christodolos was standing next to her, his hair loose as I liked it, wet and streaming filthy holy water; 'I knew you loved him more than you loved me,' he grumbled. Zerach Levin and Avigdor Ben-Ari stood modestly at the back like distant relatives, and they waved and even winked

441

at me mischievously: 'Remember that he is a complete Jew,' called Avigdor, 'more than me and more than you!'

Only my grandmother Simcha hadn't yet come. 'She's new with us and doesn't know the way yet,' apologised Zerach on her behalf, and Avigdor, as usual, disagreed with him: 'She first has to make her *borscht* for the angels,' he said. But before he finished speaking my grandmother was standing by my side: 'Grandma. I've married Yosef,' I hastened to inform her and to remove any doubt, I turned to Yosef, and in a flash they all vanished and only the faintest trace of the smell of burning hung in the air. The foetus in my belly gave its first kick.

'Simchi was here,' whispered Fishke, and I nodded.

After the wedding Fishke asked us to go up to her room because he had something to give us. There he took my mother's picture down from its place in the wall, the one painted by Aliza the artist, blew small clouds of dust from it, cleaned it with the sleeve of his best shirt, and asked me to hang it on the wall in my house. I looked at my mother's face in the portrait, that was just like the face of the young girl who had congratulated me under the canopy, and I saw that her hair had faded, her shining eyes were dull, and her dress, that had been painted in gay colours, looked shabbier then ever. I was afraid to look again at the bad changes wrought by time and hurriedly wrapped the painting in my tulle veil. Then Fishke asked us to sit at the table with him and from his shirt pocket he took a worn envelope that he slapped down onto the table. On the envelope were written my name and Yosef's. Fishke told me to open it, took the bottle of vodka that was standing on the table and took a big swig from it. I was afraid of finding yet another secret that might cloud my happiness, but I hesitantly ripped open the envelope. There were a few sheets of paper with writing on them in old green ink, written in dense cursive hand that rose and fell in waves, writing that brought me to tears, Avigdor's hand. In a letter addressed to Yosef and me, my grandmother had enfolded her last secret, translated into Avigdor's florid Hebrew, and in it she asked us to take care of Fishke after her death and allow him to live in her room. She bequeathed the carved bed that Fishke had made for their wedding night to us, Yosef and me, as though she had foreseen our marriage even then, all those years ago.

We sat in her room in our festive clothes and read the letter over and over, despite what she had written being known to all of us, and we mourned her and her life. We were like three orphans, desolate and alone in the world.

Later, after I had taken off my wedding dress and calmed Yosef with my body and whispered words of affection to the baby in my belly, I saw her again, standing on a cloud, stirring her czars' *borscht* in a huge pot, and the chubby cherubs that had vanished from Grandma Abulafia's ceiling were standing around her, golden bowls in their hands and waiting patiently for her to ladle into them the crimson soup of love, which in this world they had never tasted, only smelt, and which this time she had made in honour of my wedding.

We moved from Jaffa a few months later, Yosef because of the memories and me in spite of them.

That year the Arabs declared a general strike that spread throughout the country, and the Arab revolt, supported by the governments of Nazi Germany and fascist Italy, sowed death and destruction. Every day the headlines reported on fresh casualties, death lurked in every corner and did not discriminate between Jews, Arabs and British.

And yet Fishke and Widow Ziso paid scant heed to our pleadings that they come with us; she announced that 'I was born here and I'll die here,' while he said that he would stay with her because he could not abandon an old woman to a life of loneliness. I suspected that he was loath to part from the memories of the love he had known in Simcha's room, and that he still wanted to draw her smell of burning into his lungs, the smell that had stayed there even after her death. So the two old people stayed in Jaffa with the handful of Jews who stubbornly insisted on remaining in their city at that time, when so many others were packing up their belongings and moving elsewhere.

On our last night in Jaffa I couldn't sleep. Before

dawn, when the last pale stars still held onto the sky, refusing to flee in the face of the sun that would soon rise, I left the room barefoot, wearing only my long nightgown and with Christodolos' camera hanging on my chest. As if from force of habit, I peered fearfully down the alley turning pink in the first light, as if Yosef was still lying in wait for me there, seeking to dissuade me from going to the other. I walked slowly to the sea, shivering slightly in the cold air. The closed eyes of the houses behind their shutters accompanied me, shading their dwellers from the sun that was not yet shining and fanatically safeguarding the secrets of families still asleep, and a street dog sniffed at my heels, and like a beggar seeking leftovers of affection, he stuck his cold, wet snout deep into the empty palm of my hand. But I recoiled in fear lest he be a wild dog, and watched him trot away in disappointment, his tail between his legs, to others who might adopt him.

When I reached the beach my feet sank into the wet sand up to my ankles and the hem of my nightgown was dampened by the small waves that touched the shore with their hasty kiss and immediately receded, revealing mounds of seashells that crackled under my feet, and conches that had been swept up and piled on the sand in the night tide. I bent down and picked up a big shiny conch and blew the sand from it. It grinned at me mischievously with its narrow lips, revealing bare gums as in the morning smile of a happy old woman

445

who has not yet put her dentures into her mouth. I brought it to my ear and heard the distant sounds of the sea from its cold, toothless mouth. I raised the camera to my eye and looked around me through its lens, and with the sadness of parting, in the pre-dawn light, I etched the scenes onto a film and especially onto my heart, and knew that from now on they would come back to me in my dreams and memories, and would never leave me.

When the sun shyly revealed its round face, dispelling the night chill and the remnants of the stars, and the shutters on the houses blinked slowly and opened above the eyes of the darkened windows, I went back to our room. I slipped back into our bed, to still-sleeping Yosef, and he awoke for a moment and in surprise rubbed his feet on my cold wet ones that shed grains of sea sand onto the sheet.

Like a couple of traitors we later made our way to Jerusalem. In the small room we rented in the new Talpiot neighbourhood, I put the conch between his holy books, which he no longer needed, and my words of wisdom notebook, and sat down to remove my shoes from my feet that had swelled because of the pregnancy and the long journey through the mountains. I turned the shoes over to shake them and grains of sand made a small mound on the floor. I surreptitiously swept it under the bed so I would be able to touch it whenever the yearning for Jaffa and its shore arose in me.

Some three months later I gave birth to my son in sorrow. For two whole days iron nails pierced me and tortured my body, and my weak heart fluttered with the effort, trying with its last strength to scotch Dr Aberbuch's prophecy of doom. My son was born in a pristine white bed in the Hadassah Har Hatzofim Hospital in Jerusalem, in a room redolent with the smells of the resin of a young pine forest whose needles had been washed by the rain.

And when they put the newborn infant into my arms, I undressed him and examined him thoroughly lest in his flesh, too, stigmata had been imprinted in the womb. Only when I found nothing untoward was I pacified and I gave him my breasts to suckle. And then I saw him, Christodolos, hovering over us with his habit dripping water, a shining halo around his head, and a satisfied smile on his face: '*Ios!*' he shouted, '*Ios, ios, ios!*' he exulted – a boy!

'This baby has an odd smell,' I heard one nurse saying to another as she left the room carrying my son to return him to the nursery.

That night I stole out to the nursery, took my son from his cot, undressed him again and sniffed his body from top to toe: mingled with his baby's scent was a hint of church incense and the smoke of burning.

EPILOGUE

Like a turtle stuck to its home, I will always carry Jaffa on my back, my beloved city that haunts me in memories and dreams.

Even if I wanted to I could not escape it, because its sea seeps into me from everywhere, as if my previous life had equipped me with an inner compass that directs me towards Jaffa alone. The sun setting serenely between Jerusalem's hills reminds me of its fiery plunging into the sea. The flicker of distant lights when twilight descends over the hilltops and slopes are like the twinkling lamps of fishing boats rocking on the waves, their glow adorning the water with glistening gold coins. And when Jerusalem is shrouded in a heavy blanket of snow, I can see the surf on a stormy day. And when my longing becomes unbearable, I listen to the soughing of the waves in the shell I brought with me from the beach, and rub between my fingers the remaining sand I secretly hid under the bed and later placed in a wooden box made by Fishke.

The War of Independence against the Arab armies that raged through the country about twelve years after we left Jaffa brought together a human rabble that crowded into the houses that had been vacated by their Arab residents, mostly Jewish refugees, survivors of the Second World War in Europe. Weary and broken in both body and spirit, these Jews tried to rebuild the ruins of their lives in the torn and devastated city, and with the caution and anxiety of the displaced lived there side by side with the few Arab residents who clung on to it. And all kinds of other indigents, dunghill dwellers, prostitutes and pimps, drunkards and robbers stole into the abandoned homes.

'It is no longer my city,' said Yosef and refused to accompany me on my trips to Jaffa. But I return to it, am compelled to return to it, and perpetuate its scenes with Christodolos' camera that has become a source of income, happiness and sadness.

Every Sunday I forsake the dreariness of Jerusalem and return to Jaffa, like a criminal returning to the scene of his crime, like an exile returning to his homeland.

From a distance I can already smell its smells, see the endless expanse of the sea, take pleasure in the caress of the salt breezes on my face and the burning sun on my skin, and I close my eyes and return to the days of my childhood and youth.

The city gladly extends its impoverished arms towards me and I run towards it and it draws me into its embrace, swallowing me between its alleys, leading me to the limestone ruins that used to be the buildings of my neighbourhood. I climb over them, skirting shattered doors and twisted grilles, skipping over piles of rubbish, fragments of lives that had been lived to the full: dismantled ovens with their entrails spilling out, dented pots and broken plates, an iron railing with a copper ball at its end, a decapitated doll, a squashed ball, an orphaned shoe with gaping mouth sticking out its tongue, slashed mattresses excreting seaweed, and rags of every sort. Among the rags, the blanket covered in faded purple silk and disgorging grey fluff balls will always be conspicuous, and I will always smell the odour of mothballs in it, reminding me of my first kiss in my grandmother's wardrobe. All year round, pale thistles and nettles desperately clutch at the piles of rubbish, extending their sharp thorns as if defending the remains of their possessions, and colourful cockerels peck among them, masters of all they survey. And when summer draws to an end, sparse blossoms of scabwort burst forth, assailing me with their pungent fragrance, a fragrance of memories and forgetting blending together. And the yellow blossoms twinkle at me and the leaves seek to grasp the bottoms of my trousers and their fragrance sticks to me and accompanies me wherever I go.

There, next to one of the rubbish mounds, is the gap that leads me to the house. Every Sunday I return to it and wander through the dim, empty rooms, their windows sealed with concrete, and I am kissed by the slack lips of mildewed air that chokes my lungs, and I listen to the sounds and voices that once were heard behind closed doors. The brittle walls, mute witnesses to my life, custodians of my memories, that over the years absorbed and instilled sounds, smells and images, sing the song of my life to me. Then I once again scrape the plaster on them, revealing the familiar layers of paint, each year and its colour, and put my head to them and hear swearing and cursing, mutterings of the sleeping, the chatter of children, the sighs of lovers, the crying of babies, the shatter of breaking cups and plates, the chanting of prayers and vows, the groaning of bed springs, the sound of creaking furniture, the cries of the slaughtered and the shouts of the slaughterers. And the sounds become clear and mingle with one another and are woven into tales and legends, suffused with sounds, colours and smells, and stealthily creeping over them all is the bubbling of my grandmother's *borscht* on the stove and the redness of its face and the tartness of its aroma.

Gradually, as if waiting for a director's cue, the ghosts of my childhood and youth emerge and rise from the ruins: my mother Nechama, my grandmother Simcha, Fishke, Grandma Abulafia, Widow Ziso, my father Yehuda, Latifa the prostitute, Zerach Levin, Avigdor Ben-Ari, Khaled the greengrocer, my unborn brother, and the infant who was born to my grandmother and buried with his neck broken. And separate and distinct from them and adorned in his purple mantle,

451

Christodolos the monk hovers in mid-air, a crown of green thorns of guilt on his head, a garland he has woven from the nettles he has plucked from the pile of rubbish, which have pricked his hands, drawing tiny droplets of blood.

Every Sunday, rain or shine, I return to Jaffa, because only there, in the ruins and desolation, can I come back and shut myself off together with the people I loved and who loved me, who lived in the houses and palaces that have become heaps of rubble, where they dreamed their dreams, fulfilling some and forsaking most, and their memories and my memories – even if they are no longer alive – preserve this place.

I take Christodolos' camera out of my bag, the camera that I have not parted from since he bequeathed it to me with its photographs, and which has become my third eye, and with its help I coax the ruined houses and discover within them that which is hidden from view, and find beauty within the ugliness. Click after click it clicks at them and they return a dull echo of halls and rooms empty of people and possessions.

When the day draws to an end, I walk down narrow winding alleys to the deserted port, peer into the dark houses that are still standing, searching for new images, to see them and photograph them: an old Arab woman in her window, who might be the only remaining member of her family that has fled, a Jewish family sitting down to eat on the balcony, whose home was possibly

452

destroyed in another country. And I weep with the aged whose children have abandoned them, and I smell the alcohol fumes from the mouths of drunkards standing with bottles clutched in their hands, and breathe the smell of hashish escaping from wasted lips, the eternal cigarette butt still dangling from them. And my camera seeks to capture the distress, injustice, deprivation, the fear and the pain of all those who cannot express them, either because they are dead, or because not a single soul will listen. And the living stare into the Cyclopean eye in sad acceptance of their fate, and the avalanche of the palaces and homes serves as a shattered backdrop of a glorious past that is now a mockery. And the lens clings to the traces of the setting sun which, an instant before it ignites the sea with its fire, dazzles the film and sears its presence onto it, the present estranging itself from the past that once was and is no more.

At night, in my darkroom in Jerusalem, when I develop the photographs, I sometimes discover a hairy thigh pierced with a dirty needle of the syringe of hallucinations, the face of a homeless man sunk deep in sleep, a thin thread of spittle hanging from his open mouth, the wasted face of an Arab woman, scored with furrows of longing, and a pile of junk with the body of a decapitated doll protruding from it. Time after time, I painstakingly examine the photographs and strain in vain to discover within them the back of the monk who was mine as a short-term loan, and the nape of his neck with the gleaming knot of hair fastened to it.

At times of profound sadness, when it seems to me that Jerusalem's cold stone houses are closing in on me, I spread the photographs on the carved bed bequeathed to us by my grandmother Simcha, look at my subjects who stopped breathing for my sake and entrusted themselves to my camera, knowingly or unknowingly, and I take comfort in the power of the photograph to capture the moment and fix it in memory.

In recent years, my photographs are ageing together with me. As my red hair fades and thins, my face creases with wrinkles, my freckles become liver spots and my body thickens, they peacefully and complacently turn gold, as if they know that as the years pass their value increases, just like those artefacts unearthed by Christodolos.

Indeed, when I too pass from this world, and the remains of the houses I have photographed are razed to the ground, they will go on living after me, hanging in museums and galleries and sold in coffee-table books, engraved into the memories of those who see them. Because these photographs grant eternal life to my city, and in them the scabwort, although long since withered and crumbled, will be forever green.

And if you look at them carefully, beyond the ruins you may be able to see the houses that were palaces and the markets that bustled with man and beast and the green stain of the orange and pomegranate groves, and you might even meet Christodolos there, my beloved monk, hiding from me among the ancient walls and the roofless buildings.

And if you find all these, the city that was lost to me will be preserved in your hearts, and you too will be able to touch, even if fleetingly, my stories, my heroes, and my pain.